To John
Thank yo
support a
skills. All

MW01717196

Northwest Passages

A Cascadian Anthology

edited by
Cris DiMarco

hosted by Cascadia Con

Fandom Press
the co-operative division of Windstorm Creative
Port Orchard•Seattle•Tahuya

Northwest Passages: A Cascadian Anthology
copyright 2005 by Fandom Press
published by Fandom Press

ISBN 1-59092-185-2
9 8 7 6 5 4 3 2
First Edition September 2005

The cover artwork by Liz Danforth.
Interior and cover design by Buster Blue of Blue Artisans Design.

All rights reserved, including the right to reproduce this book or portions thereof in any form whatsoever, except in the case of short excerpts for use in reviews of the book. Printed in the United States of America.

For information about film, reprint or other subsidiary rights, please contact Mari Garcia at mgarcia@windstormcreative.com.

Fandom Press is an imprint of Windstorm Creative, a multiple division, international organization involved in publishing books in all genres, including electronic publications; producing games, videos and audio cassettes as well as producing theatre, film and visual arts events. The wind with the trinity circle center was designed by Buster Blue of Blue Artisans Design and is a trademark of Windstorm Creative.

Fandom Press
7419 Ebbert Dr SE
Port Orchard, WA 98367
cascadia@windstormcreative.com
www.windstormcreative.com
360-769-7174 ph.fx

Fandom Press is a member of Orchard Creative Group, Ltd.

"Incident at Agate Beach" was first published in *Argosy Quarterly No. 3*, Spring 2005.

"In the Chief's Name" first appeared in *Historical Hauntings*, edited by Jean Rabe
and Martin H. Greenberg, DAW Books, 2001.

"General Density" appeared in a slightly different form in *Challenging Destiny #16*, 2003.

"Whistling Women" first appeared in *Tesseracts 6*, edited by Robert Sawyer
and Carolyn Clink, 1997.

"Wonderfreaks" was first published in *New Genre 2*, 2001.

Library of Congress Cataloging-in-Publication Data available.

To Jennifer DiMarco
a visionary and an inspiration
to all who know her

Table of Contents

Introduction

It has been an incredible pleasure to edit this anthology. Though it took longer than any of us expected, given the overwhelming response we received from the call for submissions, I feel confident that what you hold in your hands is a body of diverse, well-written science fiction and fantasy from some of today's most talented and thought-provoking writers.

Many anthologies are infused with the editor's own style or preferences. And although I most definitely do have preferences about what I like to read, I've tried as much as possible to set aside my personal opinions and focus on creating a body of work that represented many different points of view about everything from technology to drugs to sex to the fluidity of time, space and the human condition.

The Pacific Northwest has been my home for a decade and I can't imagine ever living anywhere else. Steeped in a rich tradition of culture and myth, it's also home to Nintendo and Microsoft and Boeing, all of whom have had a hand in shaping the ideas and technology that move us inexorably into the future.

Liz Danforth's cover art best illustrates what the folks at Cascadia Con and those of us here at Windstorm have tried to create: A blend of mythos and technology that evokes the experience of living and working here. To achieve that end, I've selected stories that range from the deeply mythic like Rhea Rose's poem "Whistling Women," John Kratman's "Nanuq," Jacques L. Condor's "Them," Marly Youman's "An Incident at Agate Beach" and Ruth Nestvold's "A Debt to Collect" to stories of hard science and theory including Jetse de Vries' "Real Virtuality," Uncle River's "General Density" and Joe Murphy's "A Thin Line."

With these stories at either end of the spectrum, so to speak, I looked for work to flow between the myth and the science. Dr. Philip Edward Kaldon's lovely "The Pulse of the Sea," Derwin Mak's "Transubstantiation," Mary E. Lowd's "Forget Me Not" and Donna McMahon's "Feeding the Eagles" are examples of these "bridge" stories whose ideas incorporate both science and uniquely human experiences such as faith, hope and loss.

No contemporary collection of science fiction and fantasy would be complete without standout examples of the ever-changing virtual world and Jake Bartolone's "Still Life, with Wine Bottle," A. Leigh Jones' "Dance of the Cube Farm Dreamers" and Mercurio D. Rivera's "Rewind, Replay" provide interesting insights into our relationship with personal technology. Related to this group are stories like Edd Vick's "Truer Love," Bruce Taylor's "You Can Hardly Wait" and Jan Wildt's "Wonderfreaks."

Other stories evoked a sense of history and place. Bruce Holland Rogers' "In the Chief's Name," is one such story as are Ken Staley's "Jacob's Tree" and Rhea Rose's "Squatch."

I was also immensely pleased to receive a number of stories that ranged from the laugh out loud hilarious "Free Range" by Suzanne Church, "Slimed" by Louise Herring-Jones and Krista Dietrich's "Sister's Story" to the more subtle, but no less humorous "Mountain Man's Toothpick" by Susan Urbanek Linville.

Eric Choi's "Plot Device" seemed a fitting story with which to close the anthology with its ironic look at what it means to be a "writer"—in more than one sense of the word.

Every author contributed something vital to this collection and I thank each of them for that. Please support them by visiting their webpages and reading their other work. All are talented and I was honored to have had the chance to work with them and their stories. The authors who received requests for editing were generous and forthcoming with answers to my questions, which made my job so much easier!

Finally, I would like to take a moment to thank the behind-the-scenes individuals who made this anthology possible. First and foremost, Bobbie DuFault at Cascadia Con was instrumental in getting the anthology off the ground and into orbit. Always a pleasure to work with, Bobbie truly saw the project through from beginning to end. Additionally, I want to thank Linda Thomas, PhD, J. Ryan DiMassa and Jennifer DiMarco for their input during critical stages—most notably Jennifer who proved to me, and all of Windstorm, the incredible value of an endeavor like this; Liz Danforth for her captivating cover art; Buster Blue and Sarah Gee of Blue Artisans Design for their inspired layout; Mari Garcia for handling the legal details, and my organizational mentor, Carolyn Reed, for creating ways for me and other Windstorm staff members to remain sane during the hectic final push.

Northwest Passages marks Windstorm's first collaborative effort with a convention to produce an anthology, and, despite the steep learning curve, I am tremendously pleased with the results. I think you will be, too.

Cris DiMarco
Senior Editor of Windstorm Creative
Port Orchard, Washington

Northwest Passages

A Cascadian Anthology

edited by
Cris DiMarco

hosted by Cascadia Con

WHISTLING WOMEN

among the quiet cedar trees
a whistling woman gathers pitch,
stroking bark until it bleeds.

sad hemlock sags across the moon
knowing that the morning brings
tears of sap,
its cones, blown in the breeze,
like children chatter

encircled by the moon, whistling woman
stands and with her stick,
stirs the sugar pooled
within her satchel,

into the climax of the woods
through a clearing there
she sees her clandestine gathering—

dsonoqua, her sisters
she-who-speaks-softly,
she-with-clear-eyes,
she-who-is-new,
she-who-smiles,
whistling, they await her.

soon the dsonoqua
in the humus draw
their daylight plans,
and seal them with a touch of hands,
then through the canopy they fly
each one whistles upward.

Dsonoqua, whistling women, sharper than
the devil's club,
in bright of day become

the forest teachers,
taking unsuspecting children deeper,
explaining why their world is green
exposing creatures never seen
in the light of children's lives.

while the forest's teachers wait
and conceal their whistling nature
each one gathers from
her hip
a cooling satchel filled with pitch
and paintbrushes picked
from a mountain's meadow.

When a touring child wanders out of range
pulling at the huckleberry
tearing at the cedar's strings
crushing snail and snake
and snagging flesh on
woodland rakes, then the teachers
make their change

Whistling women seal his eyes with
coniferous glue
and he is left to wander through
deciduous trees,
like the bat he listens
like the coyote he scents
like the slug he tastes the earth
like the millipede with a thousand fingers
he feels the direction of the pointing leaves
as they show him to his place.

the dsonoqua, with their hungry babies,
have stolen from a bolt of light
their cooking fire,
but when one whistles for the boy

the deciduous trees begin to shudder,
their leafy noise prevents
the child from stumbling toward
his end

dsonoqua rush the thicket
spilling out old logs
and stumps,
rolling rocks and rotten mounds
and shuffling the leaves,
seeking under fungal growth
and mushroom cap,
the sugar-coated boy

Deciduous trees have saved the child,
but in so doing
turned him wild
for on his skin he must
feel the sun
nutritious earth upon his tongue,
in his ears lives the wind

because of eyes forever sealed
he prefers the open fields
there he stands
nearly still, the first
green tree upon a hill
in a field of herbs and weeds.

and when the whistling women wander,
scavenging for a meal, taking
school children through the field,
he shudders, trembling he
whispers, *run,*
from the sight and sound of
dsonoqua, whistling women, child-hunters.

Free Range

Cluck bobbed along behind his master, Lois McBride; a cooler slung through his harness. They crossed the street into Genesee Park.

The Independence Day crowds choked every open patch of grass. Fire pits spewed plumes of smoke. The smell of scorched kinflesh surrounded him.

"Keep up, Cluck."

"Yes, Ma'am."

They squeezed between bunches of families, finally settling in a sunny spot near the Lake Washington shore. Lois pulled out a blanket and flared it in the wind. Cluck dropped the cooler and pulled the zipper open. He pecked at the bags of fruits, grains, cheeses, and crackers, fussing to open them and dump their contents on the plastic dishes.

"Why're you so grumpy, Cluck?"

"The barbeques."

She shrugged. "Chicken's popular."

He turned his head away. Over by a bushy pine, a family of ten had pushed several picnic tables together. They dove into a mountain of food. The patriarch, seated at one end of the table, ripped chunks of meat from a leg bone. Cluck wondered who had once used that leg to stand proud.

"Stop moping, Cluck. Show some holiday spirit."

He picked up a paper flag in his beak and waved it.

"That's more like it," she said.

She pulled a library book from her bag. With a chunk of cheese in one hand and the novel in the other, she laid back on the blanket. "Go find a companion to play with."

Cluck dropped the flag and waddled away. He found a cluster of animals behind the restrooms. Two Siamese cats batted paws at each other, their black tails flicking. A poodle and a German Sheppard sat nearby, their tongues hanging out, panting as they soaked up the sun's rays. A little brown hen bocked and batted her wings.

Cluck waddled towards her, pushing his chest forward and propping up his comb.

"Nice day," she said.

"Warm," said Cluck. "But I wouldn't call it *nice.*"

"The barbeques?" she asked.

He bobbed his head in agreement.

"I'm Henni."

He raised his wings and smoothed them down again. "I'm Cluck." He flopped down in the grass and preened his feathers. "I hate this stupid holiday."

"Me too," said Henni.

"They wave their flags and brag about their freedom while they carry us on leashes. I'm bred for intelligence and my master uses me to carry her bags."

"I understand. I'd love to escape."

"So would I. But there's nowhere to go."

The poodle trotted over and sat down. "Hey, you two." She scratched the letters: FRC.COM with her nail in a patch of dirt.

"What—" said Cluck.

"Memorize it." The dog looked left and right.

"What's it for?" said Henni.

"Memorize it!"

Cluck ran the letters through his mind, over and over. The dog rubbed the dirt with her paw until the letters blended away. Then she trotted back to flop down beside the Sheppard.

"I don't know about this," said Cluck. "I don't trust dogs."

"I'm going to check it out," said Henni. "Now I'd better get back to my master."

"Will I see you again?" asked Cluck.

"Maybe." She strutted away, wiggling her tail feathers.

Cluck woke up and checked his watch. Three A.M.. He shook himself awake and bobbed downstairs. Lois kept her computer in the living room. He pecked at the power bar and the system booted.

Every beep and click echoed in the empty house. Cluck waddled over to the bottom of the stairs, listening. The rhythmic snoring continued uninterrupted in her room. He hurried back to the computer.

"Come on," he whispered. "Hurry up." A picture of the sun setting behind a mountain appeared on the screen, and then the desktop filled with icons. Cluck found the web browser and double-clicked the mouse.

He pecked the letters F...R...C...dot...C...O...M and then Enter. A logo appeared, with companion chickens standing proud. Behind them, a banner proclaimed: *California! The Free Range State.*

Upstairs, Lois rustled in her bed, mumbling.

Cluck froze. He counted to twenty, then thirty in his head, waiting for her snores to return. She rolled over, the bed creaked, and she smacked her lips twice. The computer fan seemed louder than a hoverbus. Finally, her snoring resumed.

He answered a series of questions on his breeder and master. A long wait bar slowly filled blue from left to right.

"Welcome companion," appeared on the screen.

Now what? He clicked the mouse a few times. A small white box appeared in the center of the screen.

"Thirty-Eighth and Andover. Noon tomorrow."

The letters started to fade. He shut down the system and flipped the power bar off. With each step he repeated the address in his mind. Lois snored on while Cluck drifted back to sleep.

The next morning, Lois sent Cluck out to buy groceries. The wagon harness chafed at the skin under his black feathers. He had to travel up a steep hill to the grocer. The return trip would be worse though, with a load of dead weight. Cluck would have to reverse the harness, putting the wagon in front of him, so it yanked and dragged him all the way home.

Dogs trotted past, with their shoulder bags and custom cruisers. They always got the good gear. Few people had chickens as companions. Lois was too cheap to pay for chicken-specific gear, so most of Cluck's equipment had been built for pigs or cats then modified for a chicken, making it too small or too awkward for him to manipulate. Lois shook her head, even laughed at him sometimes, as he managed his chores.

He trudged up the hill to the market and parked his wagon in the companion transportation armada. He didn't bother with the lock.

He checked up and down the busy street. No companions in sight. He turned to his left and headed for his destination.

The walk to Thirty-Eighth and Andover would take half an

hour, at least. Lois would nag him for taking too long with the groceries. He hoped to pass a flower shop along the way. She always fell for the flower routine.

At the rendezvous point he checked his watch. Almost noon. He sat down on the curb and preened.

The little brown hen bobbed around the corner.

"Henni?"

Her eyes sparkled in the sunlight. "Cluck! I hoped I'd see you here."

"Hey, beak-heads," sounded a voice behind Cluck.

He turned around. A duroc pig stood beside a hydrant. He wore a baseball hat tied with a string around his neck. Cluck tried not to laugh.

"Saturday morning," said the pig. "Two A.M. at the Safeway on Rainier. Bring the cash."

"Wait a minute," said Cluck, holding up his wing in protest. "The web page didn't mention any cash."

"We don't have money, we're companions," said Henni.

"This ain't a free ride. Five hundred bucks a head or no lift to California. Now beat it."

The pig trotted off down the street. Cluck sat, stunned. *Five hundred dollars?* He shook his head.

"What are you going to do?" said Henni.

"I guess I could steal it from Lois."

"You wouldn't!"

"What else can I do? I'd love to take you away."

She rubbed her beak along his. She slipped and poked him in the nostril.

"Ow!"

"Sorry."

"It's okay." He rubbed his beak along hers. "I'll try to get the money. Make sure you're there."

"I'll be there." She nipped at his neck feathers.

A shiver ran through him.

"I've got to get back."

"Me too." Cluck stood and plodded back towards his chores.

The flowers pleased Lois so much that she didn't notice his extended absence.

Cluck thought about California; the sunshine and living with Henni. But where would he get a thousand dollars? He tried to act calm, but couldn't relax. He was excited and terrified at the same time.

Lois poked her head inside the bathroom. "You're in a good mood today, Cluck. Care to share?"

"No." He swished the toilet brush with his foot. It caught on the lid, he lost his balance, and his rear landed in the water.

Lois giggled. "Come on, Cluck. Who is she? A nice hen from the picnic?"

"It's nothing, Ma'am." He wiggled his rear, shaking the water from his feathers.

She crossed her arms. "I don't like secrets, Cluck. Tell me her name."

"Henni."

"How unoriginal. Who's her master?"

He swallowed hard. "A new family. They just moved in from, uh, California." *Crap. Don't give it away.* "I forget the name."

"Arrange a play date. Have her master bring her here and we'll chat."

"How about Sunday?"

"Or Saturday. Either works for me." Lois walked away.

With any luck, we'll be free by then.

For the rest of the week Cluck prepared the meals and kept the house clean. Lois pestered him for Henni's vid-phone number, but she had only given him her net-address.

Friday evening, Lois stayed up to watch the late news. Cluck pretended to turn in early. He tucked his head under his wing and waited. Every minute took an hour to pass by. The hands on his watch seemed to stand still. *Soon,* he kept telling himself. *She'll sleep soon.*

Lois settled in her bedroom after midnight, but her light stayed on. Cluck counted as each page turned. He glanced at his watch. One-forty-five. The light still blazed from her room.

I'll never make it to Rainier in fifteen minutes.

He jumped out of bed and shuffled to her bedroom door. With a deep breath, he leaned in and looked up at his master. She was asleep, the book fallen beside her.

He snuck downstairs. Lois's purse sat by the front door. He pulled the zipper open and yanked her wallet out onto the floor. Grabbing the corner with his beak, he lifted the wallet up to shake the money free. She might have enough money in there. An image of her catching him with the money in his beak ripped through his mind. He shoved the wallet back in place and zipped up her purse. Without looking back, he slipped out the front door.

His skateboard wheels screeched and scraped on the pavement, loud enough to wake every master on the block. He had less than ten minutes to get to the rendezvous point.

The parking lot stood empty at the Safeway. Cluck rode the skateboard around back. A panel truck idled by the loading dock. The pig stood beside a human, both of them smoking cigars and murmuring to each other. The human caught sight of Cluck.

"You're late," he said.

"I'm sorry. I had some trouble getting away fr—"

"Hand over the cash," said the pig.

"I couldn't get to a bank. I'm good for it."

"This is a cash business, featherhead. No money, no ride."

Cluck leaned forward, trying to see inside the truck. A few chickens huddled in the dark end of the truck. Packsacks and skateboards littered the floor. The smell wafting from the truck reminded Cluck of his breeding coop. Of confinement. Henni wasn't there.

"Please." He jumped up into the truck. "I want to be free. I can work off my debt."

"Hey!" said a chicken from the truck. "If he gets a free ride, I want my money back."

"Me too!" said another chicken.

"No refunds. Now shut your beaks." The man jumped onto the back platform, and shoved Cluck off the truck.

As Cluck hit the pavement, the man slammed the truck door closed.

Cluck hurried away from below the truck. In the shadow of a dumpster, surrounded by the stink of rotten eggs and urine, he cried.

"Psst."

Sniffling, he looked around.

"Chicken. Over here!"

A white rat stood at the base of a streetlight. He wore a gold medallion on a chain around his neck. Cluck hurried over.

"Crying's for sissies," said the rat. His pink eyes seemed to glow in the dark. "Are you a sissy?"

Cluck sniffled. "No."

"You're better off in the garbage than on that truck."

Cluck shook his head. "No way! That was a *freedom* truck."

"Is that what the pig-fink told ya?"

Cluck bobbed his head.

"He's a stinking liar. Those chickens are headed for a processing plant."

"You're wrong. For five hundred dollars they'll drive me to California."

The rat laughed. His gold necklace wiggled and sparkled in the light.

Cluck waited for him to stop, but he kept right on laughing. "What's so funny?"

"You're the stupidest chicken ever. They should have let you on without paying. Would've done the world a favor."

Cluck flopped down and pouted. He wanted to cry, but he wouldn't give the rat another chance to insult him. "You're the first companion rat I've ever seen."

"I ain't no companion. The name's Pinko. Six months ago I was rat number fifty-two in a lab. Now I got a whole sewer full of minions. Them dumb rats would be animals without my guidance." He licked a paw and rubbed it over his face to smooth his fur. "I've watched this operation, kid. Chickens, geese, you name it. They sell them all to a butcher across town. Between the ticket to ride and the take from the shop, they're making a killing."

"But the web site said they're sneaking companions to California."

"Lies, kid. It's a scam. Now go home and clean some toilets. That's what you're bred for."

"I can't go back."

"Suit yourself, kid. I got places to go." Pinko started to scurry along the curb.

"Wait."

The rat turned to look at Cluck. "Yeah?"

"Is California a lie? Are companions free there?"

"Yeah, kid. They got rights down there. But you'll never make it. Go home. The worst you'll get's a lickin'."

The rat scampered off. Cluck sat down on the curb. Bugs hovered around the streetlight. The biting ones flew down and nipped at him. He didn't flinch. Car tires squealed somewhere down the block. A siren wailed in the distance. A dog barked and another one yelled at him to shut up. Cluck wanted to cry, to sob like a chick, but Pinko would probably come back to call him a sissy again. So he sat and stared into the night.

Where was Henni? Did she change her mind? Maybe she couldn't get away. He didn't know where she lived. He pecked at his leg, mad at himself for not getting a vid-phone number. He decided to send her an email as soon as he could access a terminal.

Before the sun lit the sky, a panel truck approached the alley. Cluck didn't want to face the pig, especially if Pinko was right about the butcher scam. So he stood up, found his skateboard, and rode it towards the highway.

Companions don't hitchhike—don't have the thumbs for it. Instead, he rode his skateboard along the shoulder, following the traffic south.

Twice, motorists stopped and asked him if he needed a ride. He shook his head, pretending that he couldn't talk. A dog chased him along the highway for awhile. The skateboard was slower than four legs. When the dog wouldn't stop barking, Cluck turned on him and shouted some choice curses. The dog laughed and tried to bite. He missed and Cluck jabbed him with his beak. The dog stumbled off.

All day, Cluck rode the skateboard. The pavement tore holes in his feet, the sides of his legs rubbed raw against the side of the board, but still he rode south. On foot, Seattle stretched on and on. When a third motorist pulled over, Cluck lied. "I'm lost, sir. Please, take me home. My masters drove in from Olympia. If you could drive me to the outskirts I could find my way home."

The man pulled an old blanket from his trunk and made a bed in the back seat for Cluck. Exhausted, hungry, bleeding, but most of all lonely, Cluck tucked his head in and slept.

When they reached Olympia, the man offered to call Cluck's master. Cluck insisted that he didn't know the number, so the man left Cluck at the side of the road.

The chicken climbed over the barrier and down the embankment to a culvert. The water was brown and smelled of chemicals, but the coolness soothed Cluck's aches. He had hundreds of miles to go and Lois had probably reported his escape by now. The Breeding and Enforcement police would be looking for him.

Cluck needed another ride, but he looked a mess. He might as well be carrying a big sign announcing: "I'm a runaway, call B & E." So he rested in the culvert and planned his next move.

If he could get to Oregon, he might be safer. B & E would be looking for him in Washington. His plan sucked, but it was all he had.

He kept seeing Henni, with her brown feathers and stubby beak. *She needs me. I'll send her money. She'll find her way to me.*

Cluck carried his skateboard in his beak up the embankment. His sore foot twisted over and he fell, smashing his beak into the board. He flipped the board upside down and nudged it with his head up to the paved shoulder.

He started south again. The cuts and blisters on his feet throbbed, but he imagined giant redwoods and warm summer breezes. He daydreamt himself a job and an apartment. The customers at the grocer tipped him for carrying their packages. He won the prize for most sales at the telemarketing office. Henni brooded over their eggs. Respect. Choice. Life.

A woman pulled over to give him a ride. A companion dog rode in the back seat of the car. Cluck sat down beside the dog and introduced himself.

"I'm Angel," said the dog.

"More like Satan," said the woman.

They both snickered. Cluck shrugged.

"Old joke," said Angel. "You look terrible. What're you doing on the highway?"

Cluck edged closer and whispered, "I'm headed to California."

Angel nodded. "Get some rest. You look like you could use it."

Cluck closed his eyes. Angel licked at one of his sore feet. He pulled it back and tucked it under his body.

"Just trying to help," she said.

"I know." He closed his eyes and fell fast asleep.

Cluck woke on a cold cement floor. He opened his eyes. Bars. A cage.

"Hey!" He tried to stand, but his sore feet wouldn't take his weight. He flopped back down to the hard floor. "Hey! Is anyone there?"

A man appeared on the other side of the bars. Cluck's crop tightened and his gizzard twisted. The brown uniform with the blue crest. *Breeding and Enforcement.*

"Keep it down, bird-brain."

Cluck tried to speak, but only managed to bock. He bobbed his head and backed up to the far wall.

"You can't hide. Not when I'm in the mood for a barbeque." He snickered and strolled away.

Shivers racked Cluck's body. From the cold of the room, from the pain in his feet, but mostly from fear. The whole place reeked of it. The B & E man slammed a door closed and an eerie echo lingered along the cell block. Somewhere far off, a dog whined. Another voice, a pig maybe, sang a country ballad.

Bare fluorescents buzzed overhead. Cluck couldn't tell the hour. His watch was gone. The cell didn't have any windows, only cinderblock walls and the raw metal bars. His gizzard growled. He would eat a cockroach if he found one, but the cell was barren.

Cluck felt hot one minute and cold the next. The shivers lingered, either way. The waiting ate at his nerves. One ride from a stranger and he got caught. Any fool of a chicken should have known better.

The B & E man appeared. He unlocked Cluck's cell and shoved him out into the hallway. They passed a bank of empty cells, then one with a little brown hen. She shivered, and looked up as Cluck passed. Her eyes stared through him, vacant.

"Henni!"

She shook her head. "Cluck?"

She stood on wobbly legs.

"Keep moving," said the guard, shoving Cluck ahead.

The pain in his feet roared on. Cluck waddled down the hallway and through a door into a cafeteria.

"Smells like chicken stew," said the guard. "Maybe it was your cousin?" He leaned in closer. "Or your Mama."

Cluck lunged for the man, but missed. The guard grabbed Cluck by the neck and carried him to another door. A woman guard on the other side opened it.

She looked old, like Lois. The thought of his old master stirred his emotions. With her, he'd been safe, comfortable even. He had thrown that life to the wind when he broke the law. She might not take him back. Or worse, she might insist they ship him home gutted and plucked.

The guard dropped Cluck to the ground and shoved him along. They passed door after door along a corridor, until the guard opened a cell and booted Cluck inside. The room was the size of a bathtub, with a low, damp ceiling and no light or window. The door shut with a clang, the food-slot near the floor flapped on its squeaky hinges.

Another cement floor. He could only step four paces before running into the door or the back wall. His feet ached, so he sat down.

Cluck lost track of time, of the day. He stared at the walls. He waited. Each time a guard slipped a metal dish of seeds under the door, he would call Cluck names. "Featherhead. Stew-boy. Buffalo-wing." Thoughts of California were a distant memory now, like worthless tickets on a racetrack floor. He preened his feathers and whispered Henni's name, imagining that she could hear him.

A guard opened the door. "This way, gizzard-head." He led Cluck through one door after another. They stopped outside a glass booth. The woman inside said, "Number?"

"Twenty-three eighty-nine," said the guard.

She studied a clipboard then buzzed open the next door.

The bright light of day streamed through the opening. Cluck lifted a wing to shield his eyes. The guard shoved Cluck so hard he fell to the ground, smacking his beak on the pavement.

"Cluck!" Lois wailed as she ran towards him. "Oh my Cluckie, what have they done to you?" She scooped him in her arms and hugged him. "I missed you. Did they hurt you? Come home with me."

Cluck blinked back his shock. "Lois?"

"Of course," she said. "Who else would post your bail? You weren't cheap. The B & E board doesn't tolerate escapees. But I told them you were depressed because your henfriend left you."

"What?"

"Henni. I knew she was only a fling. I've booked us a hotel for the night. We'll go home tomorrow."

She yanked on Cluck's wing. He limped behind her then stopped. He yanked his limb from her grasp. "No. I can't."

"What?"

"I'm not leaving without Henni."

"She's in there too?"

"Yes. And I won't go unless she comes with us."

"Why should I pay for someone else's chicken?"

"You could keep her."

"I don't need two companions."

"You should see her. She's so sad. Please, help her."

"I'll sleep on it." She grabbed Cluck's wing and dragged him towards the car.

"No!" He pecked at Lois. Not hard enough to draw blood, but enough for her to listen. "I'm not going without her."

She let go of his wing and he hurried back towards the gate. "Guards! Let me back in!"

Lois ran for Cluck and grabbed his beak. "Are you crazy? Stop it." She let go of him and said, "I'll see what I can do."

She spoke to the guards and handed over a fist full of cash. Cluck described Henni, and then waited with Lois in the yard. When the little hen emerged, Cluck ran his beak along her neck in gentle strokes. She staggered to the car.

Back at the hotel, the hen remained silent. Cluck whispered soothing words at her. She snuggled closer to him. Soon after, she collapsed in the corner and fell asleep.

Lois asked, "Why would you run away, Cluck? I gave you a nice home and your own skateboard."

"I wanted to be free."

"Freedom's overrated," she said.

"How would you know?"

She glared at him. "Don't you get beaky with me! I saved you from that horrid place."

"I'll get beaky whenever I please! Send me back. I don't care. I'd rather be a casserole than a slave."

She gasped. "Cluck! You can't *mean* that?"

"I do. I've tasted freedom and I want more. I'll take Henni to California or die trying."

"What'll you do there?"

He raised his wing. "Get a job." He raised the other wing. "Find a place to live."

"People won't hire you. Humans come first in this world."

"Those B & E humans are more animal than me."

Lois crossed her arms and stared at him for a long time. Finally she said, "I've heard stories about the B & E. That's why I paid to get you out of there. And paid for Henni too, I might remind you. I'm your master, but I'm not heartless. I know you don't think much of me, but I love you as much as anyone loves a companion."

"How can you love me and push me around?"

"I don't know." She shrugged. "That's the way it's always been. The breeders have rules."

"Forget their rules. I'm a sentient creature. I think. I feel. I love."

"You're a chicken, for God's sake."

"Does that make me less important?"

"Yes."

"Why?"

"Because."

"That's not an answer."

She grabbed her car keys and headed for the door.

He bobbed over and blocked her path. "I *will* get a job. I worked hard for you, didn't I?"

"That's different. I'm your master."

"Give me...." He pointed at Henni. "Give *us* a chance. Take us to California. You won't regret it."

She sighed and shook her head. "Oh Cluck. The world is

crueler than you realize."

"It can't be any worse than the B & E compound. I'll take my chances."

"It's a long way."

"If you take me, I'll pay you back. The breeder fee, the B & E money, traveling expenses, every cent. I give you my word as a rooster."

He looked up at her, and for the first time he saw her as a person, not his master. She was old and lonely. "Will you help us?"

Lois sighed. "I'm going for a drive." She locked the door behind her.

Lois returned well after midnight.

Cluck sat on the floor by the bed, one wing resting over Henni, waiting for her decision.

"I won't let you go, Cluck. I need your help around the house."

"I'll send money." He stood up and walked closer. "You could get another companion."

"No. I don't believe you. You're coming home with me."

He flapped his wings. "I won't."

"Oh yes, you will."

"What about Henni?" he asked.

"You can do extra chores to make up for the money I paid for her. But I won't take her in."

Henni, awake now, stared at Cluck. Her eyes looked sad again. "You've been more than generous," she said to Lois.

"No she hasn't!" Cluck stormed around the room, flapping his wings. "You have to get to California."

"It's only a dream, Cluck," said Henni.

"Listen to her," said Lois. "She's right."

"No!" Cluck drove his beak into the carpet a few times, pounding his rage into the floor. "I'm not going back. I want to be free. I want Henni to be free."

"Go back with her," said Henni. "I'll manage."

Cluck bobbed over to the hen. He leaned in close so that only she would hear. "Listen to me. The B & E will find you. Second offense is butchery. You'll be hanging in a grocery store window by the end of the week. I won't let that happen."

"Then so be it," said Henni. "But at least I'll know you're safe."

"Is that enough for you?" asked Cluck.

"It has to be," said Henni. "It's all I have."

"But I wanted so much more for you. For *us*."

He flung his wings around her plump body and cried. "I can't."

"Come now, Cluck. Come and sleep beside me tonight."

"Go on," whispered Henni. "It's the only way."

Cluck dragged his feet, one slow step at a time and settled down beside his master.

In the morning, Lois packed their things in the car. After checking out of the room, she opened the car door. "Jump in, Cluck."

"On one condition," he said. "I'll go back with you, work for you, do everything you ask of me. I even promise to never run away again. But only if you drive Henni to California first."

"You're not in a position to negotiate," said Lois.

"Then I'll run away again. Every chance I get. Unless you do this one thing for me. If you take Henni to freedom, I'll cooperate. I'll clean every toilet until it shines. I'll run every errand and perform every chore with gusto, but only if you free her."

Lois looked at Henni, then back at Cluck. "Fine," she said. "But you'll do extra chores to make up for the trip."

"Yes, Ma'am," he said.

Henni hugged Cluck, both her wings straining to wrap around his middle. "Thank you," she whispered in his ear.

"I'll be happy as long as I know you're free," he said.

Lois drove them in silence, all the way to Redding. She stopped in the parking lot of a rest stop.

"Can I have a minute to say goodbye?" asked Cluck.

"Make it quick," said Lois.

Henni turned to Cluck and said, "Thank you. For all you've done."

"I had to get you out of that place."

They nudged beaks. He slipped and poked her in the eye.

"Ow!"

"Sorry, Henni."

"I'll send money," she said. "As much as I can. Maybe I can buy your freedom from Lois."

"Oh, Henni!" They nudged beaks again. She slipped and poked Cluck in the nostril.

He stepped back and looked her in the eyes. Both of them held back tears. "Here." He passed her a slip of paper. "That's my net-address. Send whatever money you can, but stay safe. Stay free."

Then he turned and waddled to the car. He couldn't look back. For if he did, he was afraid he would never stop crying. She was free. And he had a promise to keep.

In the Chief's Name

Rain pattered on the metal roof of the van. Wolf sat on the carpet scraps in back with his eyes closed, listening, waiting for Peach and Raven to finish setting up the antenna. He opened his eyes when the back door of the van jerked open. As Peach and Raven piled in, Wolf could see the lighted second-story windows of the houses on either side of the alley. Inside the van, he could see the jumble of radio gear and tools on the floor, the tangle of wires. The door shut. It was darker than ever.

"All set," Raven said. He dropped something. It sounded like the vice grips. "You ready?"

Wolf clicked on a dim red bulb overhead. He checked his meters and put on his headphones. "Here we go."

Peach put on her own headphones and leaned close to Wolf. She smelled of wet hair and patchouli oil. "Gonna play the loop?"

"Of course, baby." The loop had been her idea. She'd heard something like it while listening to short-wave radio. It was supposed to help listeners find the station they were looking for, although in this case, it was just window dressing. The broadcast signal from the van wouldn't even carry across Lake Washington to Bellevue most nights, and the broadcast schedule was necessarily irregular.

Wolf started the loop. Over his headphones he heard the hoot of an owl, then a howling wolf, and finally his own recorded voice: "This is Radio Free Seattle, FM." After a beat, it repeated. He could also hear the signal of the commercial radio station whose signal they were treading on just enough to pull listeners away from it.

Raven's hands were cupped over his own earphones. "Sounds good, man. This was a good idea, Peach."

Wolf gave Raven a glance that he meant as a warning, but the red light was dim enough that expressions were hard to read. Raven didn't seem to get the message.

"I mean it," Raven said. He put his hand on Peach's shoulder. "It sounds totally professional."

Wolf snorted. "Oh, great. We sound totally professional. We

can all get jobs doing this. We can all have careers."

Peach ignored that and said to Raven, "Thanks."

Wolf grabbed his mic and flipped two switches. Peach said, "Hey, let the loop run for a while. The idea is supposed to be—"

"This is Radio Free Seattle, broadcasting tonight on eighty-nine point seven. Wake up, sleepy heads! It's time to change the world. Radio Free Seattle is here to tell you how. Tonight, we'll be giving the city some of the medicine it needs."

"That's right, we're here to..." Raven started to say. His mic was dead.

"We're here to tell you about direct action," Peach said into her microphone, "the kind of action we're taking ourselves, tonight, to take back the earth from the corporations."

"And what exactly are we going to do?" Wolf said.

"We're going to kill machines," Peach answered. "We're going to monkey-wrench one small corner of the Evil Empire."

"You're so right, honey," Wolf said. "Come Monday morning, when the corporations start up their machines, at least one company is going to be in for a nasty surprise."

Raven had found the end of his mic cord. "This was plugged in when I left the van," he said to Wolf.

"Shit happens," Wolf said over the air. "But it doesn't happen nearly enough yet. It's going to take more than the efforts of Radio Free Seattle to shut down the machineries of enslavement. That's where you come in, citizens. We're on the air to urge you to join us."

Raven plugged himself in. "That's right..." His mic was still dead.

"Now maybe you're saying to yourself, Who are these criminals, and why in the world do they think I'd want to join them. Well, we're just human beings who don't want to be slaves. We're the resistance."

"In case you haven't noticed," said Peach, "our way of life sucks."

"Citizens, wake up! The air is foul. The water is poisoned. Concrete creeps foot by foot over the whole world."

"Cities suck," said Peach.

Raven flipped a switch. "Yeah," he said, but his mic still wasn't working.

"We're on our way to logging the last virgin forest. We're raping the earth with our mines."

"Mining sucks," said Peach.

"Some say it's time to go back to the earth, but before long, there isn't going to be any earth to go back to. We can't see our mother earth any more. We're blinded by money."

"Money sucks," said Peach. "So does farming."

"Citizen, the average hunter-gatherer spends three hours a day getting food and shelter. The rest of his time is his own. How does that sound to you, Mr. Suit-and-Tie? How'd you like to have everything you really need with three hours of work a day, Ms. Cell-Phone?"

Raven reached for a switch in front of Wolf. Wolf swatted his hand away.

"Asshole," Raven said.

"The thing the corporations don't want you to know," Wolf said, "is how vulnerable they are. If technological society falls apart, if it all breaks down, then it can't possibly be started up again. All the easy metals have been mined already. All the easy oil has been pumped. If we stepped back to an earlier time for just a little while, the poisonous technologies and the enslaving corporations would suffer a blow that they could not ever recover from. Are you a happy slave, citizen? You have the power to be free!"

"Every machine that breaks down is a step in the right direction," said Peach.

"A different life is possible," Wolf said. "Break the machines, stop the corporations, and we can start from scratch. How will we do it? We'll do it as free humans have always done. We'll make it up as we go along."

"Don't give in!" Peach said.

"Some people say to me, 'Man, don't you realize that what you're doing is criminal?' Hey, I'll tell you what a crime is. A crime is making people slaves while your advertising convinces them they are free. Most of you don't even see how far it's gone, how powerless you are until you resist."

Peach said, "So resist!"

Wolf opened a book to a page he had marked. He squinted in the dim light to read. "In the words of Chief Seattle, the

Suquamish Indian whose lands were stolen to make this city, 'The dogs of appetite will devour the rich earth and leave only desert.' Chief Seattle saw what we were headed for. Money and technology aren't the answer. Their time is passing. No more machines. Earth and stone, muscle and bone. That's the world we're talking about. That's anarchy. That's freedom. And that's the future. We go out tonight to do battle. We go out in Chief Seattle's name. Long live freedom!"

Raven leaned close enough to Peach's microphone that his voice chimed in with hers when they both said, "Long live freedom!"

"This is Radio Free Seattle. Good night." Wolf shut the transmitter off. "Okay. Take the antenna down and let's get moving."

"You take it down, jerk wad," Raven said.

Wolf looked at him. "What's your problem?"

"You *are* being a jerk," Peach said. "We're all in this together."

"What in the world are you talking about? The microphone? We were in the middle of a broadcast! I can't have Raven fiddling with stuff when we're on the air!"

"You really are unbelievable sometimes," Raven said.

"You're cranky because you didn't get to talk on the radio?" Wolf said. "And I'm the jerk?"

"Yes! You act like...." Raven looked at Peach, then he looked at the floor of the van. "Just forget it," he said.

"No. Say it. I act like what?"

Raven picked his tools up off the floor. "Light."

Wolf just looked at him.

"Peach," said Raven, "kill the light."

Wolf switched off the red light. Raven opened the door and jumped out.

"Remember. You don't own me," Peach said. Then she followed Raven into the rain.

Wolf slapped the side of the pre-amp with his palm.

When they set up again further north, close to Carkeek Park, Wolf made a show of double-checking Raven's microphone before they went on the air. They broadcast pretty much the same message. Raven didn't say much. He was sulking.

This time Wolf read at length from Chief Seattle's famous speech to the white invaders. Wolf invoked Seattle's name at the end of the broadcast. He did this again during their third broadcast from a location way down south, toward Renton. By the time they packed up for the last time and headed for the construction site, Raven seemed to have finished sulking.

"That Indian stuff is good," he told Wolf.

"The dude was righteous," Wolf agreed.

Wolf parked the van two blocks away. Then the three of them made a walking reconnaissance without any gear, just to check things out. The site looked the same as it had on other nights: a pit two stories deep, no security lights. There was a trailer down there with a light on, but they hadn't seen any sign of a night watchman. Two trucks. Four big earth movers. A couple of compressors. Plenty of targets.

Traffic was rare at three in the morning. Maybe half a dozen cars went by during their whole reconnaissance.

Back at the van, they put on the radio headsets, then covered them with hats so that only the little microphones showed, and those were subtle. Wolf put on black gloves. He slung one of the packs onto his shoulder. Raven took the other. At the site, Raven helped Wolf over the fence and dropped the packs down to him.

"Sound check," Wolf said as he walked down the grade into the pit.

"Check," came Raven's voice in his ear. Then Peach: "Check."

At the bottom of the pit, Wolf kept to the shadows and waited until Peach and Raven told him they were in position, that there were no cars or pedestrians that might spot him.

"Okay," Wolf said. "Keep an eye on that trailer, too. Just in case."

He went for the big machines first. Climbing onto the bulldozer, he found and unscrewed the crankcase lid. From one of the packs, he took a caulk gun that was loaded with the mixture they had made at Raven's apartment: oil-based grinding compound and salt. Wolf said, "In Chief Seattle's name," then injected the whole tube into the dozer's crankcase. On Monday, when the workers started the dozer up, the engine would do the work of grinding itself into junk.

The hair stood up on Wolf's neck even before Peach said, "Car." Wolf crouched in the shadows of the bulldozer and watched the lights sweep by on Madison.

"Okay," Peach said.

Wolf still had the creeps. Someone was watching.

"You sure?" he said.

A pause. "Yeah. You're clear."

"Is *everybody* sure?" They didn't use names on the radio, not for their broadcasts, and not for their direct actions.

"You're clear," said Raven.

Wolf still didn't move. "I got a bad feeling."

"Nothing on the street, nothing in the trailer," said Peach.

"Quit being paranoid," Raven said. "You're clear."

Wolf slowly looked over the construction site. Nothing moved. "Okay," he said. He went to the next bit of heavy machinery. "In Seattle's name," he said softly as he monkey-wrenched the crankcase. And he had the same feeling again that he was being watched, that he was being betrayed.

Paranoid, Raven had called him. Well, what if it turned out that he had good reason to be paranoid? Maybe it wasn't some stranger who was creeping him out. Maybe it was Raven. Or Raven and Peach together. If they were messing around behind his back....

Would they turn on him? No, not Peach. Not his Peachy girl. Even if she were going to turn him out, she wouldn't do it this way. Raven, then.

Wolf opened the hood of the first truck. An engine this size only needed half a dose of corundum and salt. Chief Seattle had said that the white man lived like a snake eating its own tail, and the tail was getting shorter and shorter. This was like feeding shards of glass into the maw of the corporate snake. Wolf smiled. "Die, snake!" he said.

"What?" Raven said.

"Car," said Peach.

Wolf hopped down.

"It's a cop car," Peach said. "I don't think he can see you from that lane. Be cool."

Wolf felt his heart beating.

"On my side, now," said Raven. "He's slowing."

"Shit." Peach said. For a moment, that was all. Then, "Two more on my side."

"Tuck your mics under your hats," Wolf said as he grabbed both packs and ran back to the bulldozer. "Walk away. They can stop you. They can talk to you." He tripped, got up. "But they can't make you show ID. They can't arrest you for taking a walk on a public sidewalk." He threw the packs between the dozer treads and crawled in after them. A car door slammed. A moment later, a powerful flashlight beam swept over the ground.

Wolf tried willing them to go away. *There's nothing here,* he thought. *The lock's still on the gate. Nothing's amiss. False alarm.*

Another flashlight beam joined the first. He heard the voices of police radios.

"They're talking to her," said Raven's voice.

"Shut up," Wolf said softly. "What if they're listening?"

"If someone's listening in, then we're screwed anyway, aren't we?" said Raven. "She's cool. I can tell just looking that she's cool."

"Where are you?"

"I'm in an alley. They can't see me."

"They've got lights, asshole."

"Oh, so I'm an asshole for wanting to keep an eye on her?"

"Just keep walking. Get out of here."

"She's waving goodbye and walking away. Told you she's cool. I'll go parallel, make sure she gets back without a hassle. Sit tight, man. Maybe they'll pack up and go away."

"How did they know?"

"Tall buildings. Lots of windows. Maybe some janitor called it in."

"On the weekend? No way, you bastard."

Wolf couldn't see the flashlight beams any longer, but he could still hear the police radios up above.

"What are you saying?" Raven said, but his signal was weak.

"What I'm saying, asshole, is that I'm not so sure you want me around. If my ass is in jail, you've got Peach all to yourself."

"No names," said Peach. "You are totally losing your cool."

"You okay, baby?"

"I'm fine. Don't do anything stupid." Her signal, like Raven's, was thready.

"You neither," he said. He heard another car arrive, something with a rough idle. He ventured a peek. Headlights shone on a section of the fence above. Somebody was unlocking and unchaining the gate. "Shit."

After the police dog had found him, after it was already too late because the cops had their flashlights on him, that's when he thought about his radio. What he should have done, while he still had time, was strip the thing off and feed it into the tread wheels. Or bury it. Anything to get rid of the evidence that he hadn't acted alone. They hauled him out and read him his rights, which he already knew: He didn't have to talk to them. He didn't have to answer any questions. He could even make them stop asking, "Who was on the other end? Who were you talking to?" All he had to do was say he wanted his lawyer present, and they had to shut up.

He'd been over the procedures a hundred times with Peach and Raven. Get caught alone, take the punishment alone. The important thing was the movement. Even if one of them got sentenced to some prison time, the important thing was to keep someone on the outside doing the work that needed to be done, shutting it all down.

Now, however, he couldn't stop thinking about Peach and Raven. Even if Raven were innocent, which Wolf heartily doubted, there they'd be, the two of them. Peach would need comforting. Raven would know just what to do, just how to console her and take her mind off of poor old Wolf, sitting in some cell. There, there, Peachy baby. There, there.

So he gave them up. Legal names. Addresses. The garage where they kept a drum of valve grinding compound. It all went so fast that it was still dark outside when the cops finally moved him to a holding cell.

It must have been a slow night. There was one other guy in the cell, and he was asleep, face to the wall, snoring. Wolf sat down on the opposite side of the cell, on the edge of the shelf that served as a bed.

He put his face in his hands. He was a jerk. He was an asshole. He was every name he could think of. Where was his commitment? After all that planning, he had caved right in and given it all up. Now they were all screwed. One stupid night of jealousy, and he had pissed it all away.

"It's better this way," said a voice from right beside him.

Wolf started. There was someone sitting right next to him. Someone who hadn't been there a moment before. A man wearing a conical hat.

Wolf's heart pounded in his throat. "Who...?" He stood up and backed away.

The man's hat was dripping. Water puddled at his bare feet. Around his shoulders he wore a blanket and a sort of cape made of woven reeds. His face looked weathered, dark.

"When you keep speaking the name of a dead person, you hold him or her to this world. The Bostons didn't understand that. The Bostons didn't understand lots of things." He frowned.

"Bostons?"

"Your people. The white people."

"I don't...." Wolf's head felt light.

"Better sit down."

Wolf sat. "S-Seattle?"

"Close enough." The Indian frowned. "Even if they don't ever say my name right, it's close enough to hold me here." He pulled the cape and blanket closer. "I should be far away by now. But your people had the bad manners to give my name to this place."

"I don't know what to... I'm sorry." Wolf rubbed his forehead. "This can't be happening."

"Life is like that. Death, too. Things that can't be happening happen all the time." He pursed his lips. "It's going to take a long time for me to leave this place now. It's going to take a long time for people to stop speaking my name."

"Seattle. Chief Seattle. I...." Wolf stood up. He sat back down. "Seattle! It's an honor!"

"Mmm." The ghost frowned.

"Oh, your name. I'm sorry. It's just... I admire your words."

"No you don't. Not my words. But all night you were saying my name and sticking it onto words that someone else said.

That was the first thing that made me mad."

"'Continuing to contaminate his own bed, the white man will one night suffocate in his own filth,'" Wolf quoted from memory. "Didn't you say that?"

"No! Some poet said that and mixed my name up in it. Ever since I died, this has been going on. Every time white people change their ideas about what they want Indians to be, someone makes a new speech for me."

Wolf swallowed. "But..." He rubbed his head. Could he really be having this conversation? "But we're trying to take back the land. Maybe the words aren't exactly what you said, but what my friends and I want is a return to the old ways. Your ways."

"My ways? You don't know anything about my ways."

"I mean your people. Living off the land."

"Mmm." Another frown.

"See, the world is going to turn back to simpler ways of doing things. It *has* to. We don't need bulldozers and skyscrapers to be happy!"

"Those digging machines are pretty good for digging."

"We have our hands. We can make stone tools."

Seattle grunted dismissively. "I remember my first iron ax. Now that could cut!"

"Okay, but iron comes out of mines and mines gouge out the earth. Mother Earth, Chief! We need to live in a way that respects Mother Earth!"

"Mmm." The Indian deliberately looked away from Wolf and said very carefully, "Respect."

Wolf felt uncomfortable. Had he said something he shouldn't have? He thought about it. "Ah. Okay. So maybe you're thinking that what I was doing to those machines wasn't respectful. But, see, I respect the people who run the machines. They don't know they have any choice. It's the corporations. It's the system. It's the system that I'm at war with."

"Young men always like to make war. It's the first thing they think of."

"I've got to do *something.*"

"When word came to me that the young men were planning a raid, I would go to the Bostons and warn them."

"Warn them? Against your own people?"

"Mmm. Young men make trouble." He looked at his feet. "This floor is cold."

Wolf had a thought. He didn't like it. "Did you... Chief, you aren't the one who..."

"Called the Boston soldiers. Mmm."

"The Boston soldiers? You mean the police? You called them? *You*?"

"I got inside the wire. There are things you can do when you're dead. Like this."

And he was gone. Vanished. The edge of the bed was still wet, though. Puddles still glistened on the floor.

Wolf sat thinking for a while. His cell mate still snored. The man had slept through the whole conversation. When the puddles dried, there would be no evidence that Wolf had really spoken to the ghost. But he had. What should he do now?

Raven would never believe this. But Peach might. Maybe, just maybe, there was something in what the Chief had said that would help Wolf figure out what to say to her when the time came.

Maybe. Wolf had some hard thinking ahead of him.

But the one clear lesson was this: Ghosts were real. They were bound to the earth by their famous names.

Wolf went to the door of the cell. He gripped the rigid bars. "Houdini," he whispered. "In the name of Harry Houdini."

Feeding the Eagles

Princess Royal Island, Fraser Reach — 2048

When Dezi first saw the eagle she was shivering so hard, arms hugged against her torso in the raw morning drizzle, that she thought she had imagined the movement. She'd just looked back over her shoulder to make sure nobody had seen her sneak away from the barge to take the fish farm path, when she glimpsed dark wings flapping amid the wreckage of a collapsed cannery down at the tide line.

"Oh no!" she whispered to herself. "No, not now, not today! I don't have time!"

She hesitated a long moment on the muddy path beside the terraced potato patches, hoping against hope that she hadn't seen anything, but another convulsive flap banished doubt.

"You stupid bird!" she muttered desperately. "I can't help you!"

But she couldn't just walk away, she couldn't.

Shifting her old shopping bag more securely over her shoulder, she started gingerly across the slimy morass exposed by low tide. The rising sea level had inundated the cannery site, coating twisted metal siding and dead bushes with seaweed and barnacles, reeking of brine. Dezi inched forward, testing each footstep carefully through crack-soled trainers, but she slipped and nearly fell, letting out an inadvertent yelp. The eagle heard. It swiveled its head, fixing her suddenly with black-ringed yellow eyes, and she was instantly captivated by its wild beauty.

It stood almost half Dezi's own five feet, with a wingspan far wider than her arms, but it still had the mottled brown and white markings of a juvenile. A lighter shade around its neck and head showed that it would soon grow its white head feathers. That made it four or five years old—nearly an adult.

"Hey, you're a teenager, just like me," said Dezi softly. "And I think you're a boy." Thankfully. Female eagles were larger than males and this one was more than big enough.

The eagle tried again to take off but only flopped feebly. Its wings seemed intact and Dezi couldn't see an obvious injury, so it must be sick, like the others.

Dezi had helped Steve with eagles before, but she'd never captured one by herself. Gritting her teeth against the raw cold, she stripped off her threadbare sweatshirt, exposing an old t-shirt underneath. She looped her shopping bag securely over her neck and one shoulder, and then approached very slowly, trying to corner the bird amid the wreckage. The eagle glared hostilely and hopped backward, but a rotting plank blocked its path. Dezi tried not to focus on its wickedly curved beak or rapier sharp talons as she moved as close as she dared, then lunged, throwing the sweat shirt over its head.

The eagle shrieked and flapped, but Dezi darted behind it, pinning its wings, then reached under its tail and grabbed its legs. After a few seconds of struggle it held still and Dezi felt a sudden burst of joyful awe. The bird's feathers were soft and warm against her skin and she could feel its rapid heartbeat against her chest. It took her another awkward minute to shift the bird under her left arm, keeping its wings tightly confined and its ankles in a secure grip. Then, whispering reassurances, she picked her way out of the ruins and onto the steep, narrow trail to the lake.

Strangely, carrying the eagle eased her panic. Only a moment ago she'd been terrified as she tried to rehearse speeches in her head, searching for some magic words that might save them all. Now she could only concentrate on trying to hurry uphill with her burden. She'd seen Steve's boat pull in over an hour ago and everything depended on her having time to talk to him, but the eagle weighed more every minute, her legs ached with exertion and her lungs burned. The shopping bag banged against her buttocks. She couldn't go fast; she could only put one foot ahead of the other on the steep trail and plod, panting, smelling the sour scent of starvation on her skin; her body burning muscle tissue because there was no fat left.

The path leveled out near the falls, then branched left along the lake shore. This fluke of geography—a sizable lake spewing a waterfall into the channel—was the reason for Butedale's existence. More than a century before, someone had spotted this remote place as an ideal site for hydroelectric power. There'd been a fish cannery and a town with a thousand people once, but little remained now except for a few crumbling ruins and a lake stocked with trout.

Close to the lake the trail grew muddy and Dezi stepped awkwardly around puddles, brushing against the prickly brown sticks of salmonberry and thimbleberry bushes, just starting to bud. It would be another two months before she could pick here. Rainwater splattered on her from the brush as she thrust her way forward, intruding into the silent landscape with a din of rustling and crackling twigs. When she emerged in the clearing by the lake, Steve stood near the feeding platform watching the trail entrance. He broke into a smile when he saw her.

"Hey, Dezi! Who's that you got with you?"

Dezi smiled back, feeling a familiar wave of gladness. Despite the urgency of her mission, it felt wonderful to be back here, away from the stifling confines of the barge, crammed with exhausted, worried women and children, and out from under the eyes of RJ, their feral supervisor. This quiet, green place was her sanctuary, her sanity. Hardly anybody else came here, especially in winter. RJ had no interest in the fish farm run by the Band. Even the guards, though they were hired from the Band, didn't seem to care. They hung out in the guard shack, making desultory rounds of the barge and checking passing marine traffic on the surveillance net, but mostly watching old action vids or playing cards. Sometimes, when RJ was away, they'd bring in cases of beer and get drunk, and then things got very bad.

"I found him down by the beach," Dezi said, and described what she'd seen. Steve listened without interrupting or lecturing. A dark, quiet man of about forty with long brown hair tied back, he looked like an ordinary white guy to Dezi, not the great grandson of a Tsimshian chief and a member of the Eagle clan, like he'd told her. In old photos, he'd been square built and chunky but even the Natives had run short on food lately, and his clothes hung loosely on him. He'd been managing the trout farm for two years, since he moved back to the village from Vancouver.

"You did a good job catching him," said Steve in his soft voice and Dezi blushed. She wished she were pretty instead of a sallow-skinned runt with lank hair and dark circles under her eyes. Sometimes she dreamed of being beautiful, of living in a city and eating ice cream in restaurants and having a boyfriend, but she couldn't make herself believe it.

She held the bird while Steve bagged its feet with thick cloth and bound its legs, then he took it expertly, wrapping its wings with layers of cloth before removing Dezi's sweatshirt from its head and replacing it with a loose hood. Dezi slipped her sweatshirt back on gratefully, then crouched in a clammy huddle on the feeding platform, watching him take a DNA sample from a broken feather, then unfold his battered notebook and uplink to the Band's ecobase. He looked endearingly awkward pecking at the compact keypad with big, blunt fingers.

"Okay, this here is Olo. He's one of Sitka's offspring from her clutch four years back."

He put the notebook aside and examined the bird. "He's sick and real light, Dezi, must of been starving for a while." He glanced over at her. "Did he shit when you picked him up?"

"Only a little bit."

Steve nodded and probed the eagle's chest gently with his fingers. "I can feel his keel bone sticking way out here." His sympthetic brown eyes met Dezi's. "I'll start him on rehydration and then try to feed him but I think maybe he's a goner."

"Oh."

Dezi knew the eagles were dying—had seen a dozen die the last two years. But it was hard to accept that this beautiful creature she'd held in her arms wouldn't live. She felt tears burn in her eyes and looked away.

As if on cue, an eagle's shriek echoed across the lake, followed by more ululating cries from the huge birds circling overhead. Even after four years here, Dezi still couldn't quite believe the noises. The eagles sounded like ponies whinnying, and the ravens had an even stranger repertoire. Right now there were half a dozen up in the treetops, making popping noises like stoppers pulled out of vials.

To Dezi the tall cedars and firs rising up the fog-shrouded mountain looked like pristine primeval forest, but the lake shore was littered with the rotting and rusting relics of logging. Only the barbed-wired gate guarding the trout farm gleamed with new steel. The trout pens were draped in netting and the floating walkways rigged with smart surveillance, but Dezi and a couple of the kids had figured out how to poach fish by opening a seam in the underwater fencing and swimming through. Dezi suspected Steve knew, but he never said anything.

From a small shed near the trout farm entrance, Steve brought out one of his special eagle carriers—an old sports bag. Dezi held it open while he put Olo in and zipped it up, leaving the bird's hooded head protruding from one end. Steve set the bag aside so the bird could rest and calm down, then he started his feeding session. With the collapse of coastal fish stocks, the eagles were starving, and over a hundred converged from a great distance for Steve's feedings. Last year he'd put out trout scraps and even salmon when he could get it, but this year he'd had to cut back, so he'd been catching rats in the village and bringing them every other trip. He hauled two bulging canvas bags to the feeding platform and emptied squirming rodents into an open-topped bin. As he retreated, raptors swooped down, their wings whumping loudly in the morning stillness, to grab squealing rats in their talons.

It was a weirdly gruesome spectacle, but Dezi loved watching. The older women did not understand her passion for eagles, especially how she could watch the Band feed fish to the birds while the techs and their children went hungry. Some of them hated the Natives and "their" eagles, but somehow Dezi didn't. Steve said that every human being had a responsibility to help save God's creatures from human-caused eco disasters, but she didn't really feel responsible, she just loved the birds and didn't want to imagine a world without them.

But now—she felt a sudden stab of fear as she remembered her mission—now, she had to risk her sanctuary and her friendship with the one person she felt she could talk to.

"Here." Steve pulled a sandwich from the pocket of his plaid workshirt and held it out. "Take it. Please?" He looked very serious. "Pretend it's a birthday present. A really lousy one, okay?"

She couldn't help smiling. She reached for the food, feeling guilty. Well, she could eat half and take the rest back to share.

An eagle swooped, grabbed a rat and flapped up into the trees. Another flew down behind it, but this one moved drunkenly, showing clear symptoms of the neurological disease that afflicted the birds. It was too weak to carry its prey and flapped clumsily to one side of the platform, where it killed the rat and began eating with tiny, fastidious eagle bites. Steve had been researching on the net for months now, teaching himself as much as he could about vet medicine, and even sending blood samples to Vancouver for analysis, but he still had no idea what the problem was.

Dezi took tiny bites of the fried clam sandwich and chewed slowly while she tried to remember the speech that had now deserted her. She desperately wished she was eloquent and clever and self-possessed, because she knew she had to say everything exactly right.

"Um, I brought something for you," she finally started, her voice dismayingly thin and reedy. She handed her shopping bag to Steve. Inside, she knew, were two big canisters of white powder, carefully labeled by hand.

"What is it?"

"Aspirin and vitamin C," said Dezi. Since the Collapse, even common meds were hard to get in this remote part of the north coast. Steve nodded, waiting to hear what she wanted in return for her trade.

Dezi cleared her throat nervously.

"I guess you heard we lost a whole drug batch in February?" Steve shook his head. "Well, we did, and so RJ canceled our food drop. We had some stores saved up but we're running out of everything. And now the new batch is failing, too. Pritam hasn't told RJ yet. She thinks the ingredients are contaminated. That's not our fault, but we're scared of what he'll do."

Steve nodded, then held up his hand.

"I know you're not finished, but I just thought of something you can do for me. Part of a trade, eh? I got half a dozen eagle carcasses wrapped in tarps under that brush pile. They all died of the disease, so I don't want nothing eating them. If I carried them down, you think you could sneak them onto the barge and incinerate them along with that bad batch of yours?"

Dezi, caught off stride, stared for a second, then shook her head.

"Sorry, I can't. The incinerator's broken and we don't have the parts to fix it."

"Broken?" Something in Steve's voice changed. "How long?"

"Umm..." Dezi searched her memory. "I don't know, maybe two years."

"Two YEARS?!"

Abruptly Dezi realized that he was furious. She tensed, suddenly afraid.

"Shit! Two fucking years?! You know what that means?"

She shook her head and then it hit her, just as he said the words.

"It means you're dumping overboard. You are, aren't you?"

Dezi's eyes widened. It had never occurred to her to wonder where the lab waste went. She blanched and huddled in her sweatshirt as Steve stood and started pacing, his face flushed with fury.

"I can't believe we been so stupid! First it was the eagles; now people in village are getting sick just the same way, like they got Parkinson's, but it's kids even. And we're all eating fish! Sure, we test them, but just for a few contaminants. We got no way to know what weird crap you're dumping! Could even be in this lake!"

Dezi felt the familiar sick-cold sweat of fear. She'd blown it, lost the one chance she had to negotiate a way out for all of them. She'd planned to ask Steve to approach his grandmother, who ran the village, and beg her to help the techs on the barge. But now she'd made him angry instead...

Bushes rustled as somebody came along the trail. Dezi jumped up and ran, diving into a low clump of salal and flattening herself among its evergreen leaves.

"Matthews! Matthews, you there? Fuck this rusticating shithole, I got mud all over my pants."

The sound of RJ's voice made Dezi flinch. Salal branches poked her stomach and legs but she lay motionless, enveloped in the rich smell of wet earth and rotting leaves, praying for invisibility. A footstep squelched nearby. She held her breath.

"Where the hell are your buddies?! Shack's empty, and no boat at the dock except yours."

"Don't know," said Steve, his voice strangely flat.

They'd gone back to town, thought Dezi. Lately the night shift had been cutting out early. RJ rarely got up before ten, well after the day shift arrived.

"Well, the deal is you people have three guys here at all times!"

Steve said nothing, but Dezi could guess what he felt like saying, because he'd told her. It wasn't his deal; wasn't even the whole Band's. A small faction had agreed to hide a bootleg pharma op in the Band's large, remote territory, and once the deal was struck the Band couldn't pull out. Nobody wanted to cross organized crime. Besides, money was desperately needed.

"Yeah, well, I've got a message to send and you're here, so you can carry it back. In person. No messaging, no radio, nothing, you got it? There's pharma cops sniffing around and it's getting too hot. Time to pull up stakes. I want half a dozen guys and a fish boat out here tonight to move the barge."

"Move it where?"

"Anywhere real deep. Then sink it."

Sink?! Dezi raised her head slightly, trying to get a glimpse through waxy green leaves.

"That barge is full of chemicals."

"No problem. We'll clean it up today."

"Like you been cleaning up the whole time?" Steve spoke slowly, with eerie calm.

"Yeah, that's right." Dezi didn't have to see RJ to picture his belligerent stance, the thin, dark mustache, or the suit and tie he wore every day in a ghost town in the middle of nowhere. None of the women knew what RJ stood for, but the kids had lots of names for him: Rude Jerkoff, Royal Jackass, Rectal Jam.

"People in the village are coming down sick."

"People everywhere are sick, don't you watch the news? And you're making money off all those people who need meds to keep from turning into drooling morons. But they're just a bunch of Pale Faces so you don't give a damn, right? Well nothing good lasts forever. By this time tomorrow I want the barge vanished. Then you'll get your payoff."

But what about us? Dezi thought desperately. As if echoing her thoughts, she heard Steve.

"And the techs?"

"You heard me already."

Steve sounded angry. "We didn't agree to murder."

"Yeah, well, if the pharmacops find any evidence of that lab, it's your people who will get murdered. Pfaret took out a whole town in the Philippines a few months back to make an example. They'd do it here, too. Nothing to stop them wiping out five hundred Indians in the back of beyond."

And nothing to help twenty-seven defenseless women and children, even more disposable than used lab equipment on a continent with fifty percent unemployment.

Dezi squeezed her eyes shut and begged silently: "Steve, stay behind! I've got to talk to you!" But, to her horror, she heard RJ demanding that he drop everything and leave at once, and the two men walked off down the trail together.

She lay in the brush another agonizing minute, then sat up, wiping tears off her face with icy, shaking hands. She wanted to rush down the trail and warn the women, but she couldn't risk overrunning Steve and RJ. There was another route down by the falls, but it was very overgrown and it came out right by the guard shack. She must wait.

Two days ago the women on the barge had thrown a surprise party for her eighteenth birthday. Maria, who ran the kitchen, had laid out a small feast from caches of food Dezi hadn't known they had left, and she'd even baked a cake with wheat flour and icing, which the children had devoured with noisy delight. Overwhelmed by their kindness, Dezi had burst into tears, and, in that instant, had a revelation. She was an adult now, and she must do anything she could to save all their lives. So she would beg Steve to help them escape. It was such a big plan she didn't dare voice it out loud; instead she said she'd trade with Steve for food, while secretly hoping to negotiate far more.

And now she'd failed.

Tears ran down her face as she stood up and looked for her bag. Steve must have taken it. So much for the precious meds they'd synthesized in secret, she thought bitterly. A thousand times that amount wouldn't be worth the risk of crossing the pharmacops. Then her eyes fell on the eagle. Steve had left Olo behind, and now he might not be back for a week.

She walked over and eased the hood gently off the bird's head. Golden eyes blinked at her; alien intelligence in their fathomless black pupils. It opened its hooked beak and gave a piercing shriek.

"Look, I'm sorry, Olo, I don't have any way to take care of you! I can't save you!" Dezi said, her voice choked with tears. Probably she should kill the bird to save it from suffering, she thought. And then she thought of herself and the other women—of how their lives had been torn apart by disasters they hadn't caused; of how they were being abandoned to die.

"Oh, crap!"

She hooded the eagle again, hefted the heavy sports bag over her shoulder with straps that were much too long, and started awkwardly down the trail.

The old chip barge lay in shallow water next to a rotting wharf that didn't clear the highest tides these days. There were a lot of barges much like it on the coast. Half a meter of dirt had been spread over the old cargo box and planted intensively with food crops. Chicken coops were mounted on the side walls, crudely kludged together from scrap wood and old plastic crates, and a series of tall masts supported spinning wind rotors and solar panels. The rotors were mostly for show—this barge had a hidden power cable running to a hydroelectric generator on shore—but the garden was entirely real. Right now only a few green sprouts showed in the soil and on the vine ropes strung across every meter of space, but in another two months the deck would overflow with greenery. The lab techs fabricated soil enhancers and coaxed extraordinary results from their hardy, gene-tailored strains of fruit and vegetables, even in this gray, sodden climate. Still, an area the size of a suburban house lot couldn't begin to feed twenty-seven mouths, even supplemented by potatoes they'd laboriously dug in ashore amid the old building foundations, and whatever could be scrounged off the beach or stolen from the trout farm.

The women lived underneath, in a seven-foot windowless hold, criss-crossed with bracing. To casual inspection, they looked like common refugees, crammed together in curtained-off spaces with poor ventilation and crude cooking facilities. But a false bulkhead walled off a quarter of the floor space for a pharmaceutical lab.

Since so many pharmas had gone belly up in the global

market meltdown and ensuing political collapses, legitimate meds were in short supply and few people could afford them. Illegal knock-offs filled the gap. The quality was sometimes disastrous, but desperate customers had no choice—and no recourse. One of the most lucrative products was CerebraGen—the only effective symptomatic treatment for Alzheimer Disease. Millions of new cases of early onset dementia had sprung up in the last decade, probably caused by industrial nanopollutants. Using biomass technology to shortcut the approved manufacturing process, the barge lab could produce a batch of concentrated pharmaceutical in six weeks, ready to ship and package elsewhere. RJ boasted that each batch had a street value of two million dollars.

All they had to fear was the private police forces formed by the remaining pharma companies to enforce their patents. The pharma cops had a well-earned reputation for ruthlessness, but with so much money to be made and so many scientists and techs out of work, underground labs abounded.

Dezi's mother, Massoumeh, had been one of those desperate techs, laid off from a company in Vancouver and abandoned by her husband. A job—even a poorly paid and obviously illegal five year contract—had seemed better than starving slowly in a city wracked by epidemics. At fourteen, Dezi had been above the age limit for dependents, but so small and scrawny that she'd passed as a ten year old with her dead sister's ID. It was only after arriving at the barge that she'd realized they were trapped.

And then Dezi's mother died of pneumonia. RJ had been furious and wanted to get rid of Dezi, but the other women intervened and put her to work cleaning the lab. RJ had never officially recanted his eviction, but Dezi stayed, cleaning, gardening, helping with daycare and learning to run simple lab instruments. Four years older than the next oldest child and eight years junior to the youngest lab tech, Dezi had been very lonely until the day she ran into Steve at the lake. Wary from her encounters with their surly, sometimes drunk and violent guards, she'd been afraid of him at first, but he didn't hurt her and he didn't report her to RJ. Instead, he shared the eagles with her. He understood her delight in this vast rainforest and ocean landscape that the other women saw only as a prison.

Throughout the miserable, jarring trip back down the trail and then her dash across the beach to the tottering wharf, the eagle kept very still. Dezi didn't dare take the bird below—she wasn't sure somebody wouldn't kill it for food—so she hid the sports bag in a sheltered corner of the barge garden, whispering "I'll be back, Olo, don't you die." Then she hurried down a makeshift stairway into the hot, pungent hold to find Pritam.

Pritam was a small woman but her regal stride and calm self assurance had made her the de facto leader among the techs. She had lied to the recruiters, omitting her PhD and her history as a senior manager at a biotech that closed down in '41, and she'd even lied about her age, passing her orphaned grandson off as her own child. Dezi found her in their tiny dining area, eating a lunch of cold transcorn mush with Zlata and Maria and bouncing her grandson on her lap—a hollow-cheeked, listless five year old with a constant cough. Behind her, the walls were lined with old chemical canisters, cleaned and converted by Maria to food storage. Most of them were empty.

"Nadezna. Back already?" Pritam always used Dezi's full name, but Dezi hated it. It seemed an especially sick irony to be called "hope."

Dezi rushed over and poured out words in a shrill whisper, hoping to stay below RJ's surveillance threshold. He had bugs all over the barge, though he only monitored the lab closely. But she had to risk it.

"Pritam, they're going to sink the barge! Tonight. With us on it. I heard RJ tell Steve. He sent Steve back to the village to get a boat and more guys."

They'd anticipated it for years—in fact they all had kits packed and ready for instant evacuation—but the women still looked stunned.

"What we gonna do?" whispered Maria. A shy Mexican woman with a crippled leg, she sounded terrified.

Pritam looked grim, but her voice came out soft and calm. "We'll go with our plan."

"We can't!" whispered Dezi. The plan was to overpower the guards, steal their boat and take as many people as possible to the village to beg for help returning to Vancouver, gambling that the villagers wouldn't have the heart to kill women and children in cold blood in their own streets. But now...

"I'm sorry, Pritam, I got Steve mad at us," Dezi stammered, choking back tears. "I told him our incinerator doesn't work, and he said we must be dumping. He thinks our toxins are making his people sick and he's so angry..."

"Shit!" Zlata exploded. "They'll never help us now! They'll call the pharmacops!"

"I'm sorry!" said Dezi, desperately ashamed. "I'm so sorry!"

Pritam patted her arm.

"Nadezna, it's not your fault. And we'll just have to go ahead with our plan. There's no time for anything else." She added more loudly: "Now, can you keep an eye on Sujjan, please? Watch he keeps his thumb out of his mouth."

Dezi nodded automatically. The toddler looked sulkily up at her, tried to stick his thumb in his mouth, and missed, poking his cheek instead. For a second Dezi smiled, then she stared at his feeble grasp and wavering hands with horrified recognition. He has it, too, she thought—the same thing as the eagles and the Natives. Maybe we all have it.

Pritam stood, her thin face very serious as she leaned toward the other women and whispered:

"Ladies, this is it. Tell everybody: Don't hold back. If we have to kill, we kill. We won't get a second chance."

It would never work, thought Dezi miserably. A dozen women, half starved, unused to fighting, and armed only with clubs and a crude sedative gas made in the lab, would try to sneak ashore and overwhelm strong men with rifles. And even if they succeeded, what then? The nearest town with a road link to the outside world was Kitimat, a hundred kilometers north, and Steve said things were so bad there that Band members went armed and in groups when they made supply runs. Prince Rupert wasn't much better. They might try for Vancouver, eight hundred kilometers south. But none of them knew how to run a boat. And where would they get fuel?

In the early afternoon a diesel thrum approached the wharf and Dezi poked her head up in the shadows of the stairwell. A dilapidated fish boat floated in, puffing a faint brown cloud of burned vegetable oil from its stack as the engine revved. Dezi recognized it. The women had tried to steal *Skookumchuck II* last year, but the owner had a hard keyed ignition lock and a guard dog. A man jumped onto the wharf with a rope. Dezi counted the men who followed him; two, three... seven. The last, unexpectedly, was Steve. She waited, hoping to see Steve head for the trail, but he followed the others to the guard shack. Damn!

She was climbing back down the stairs when a thought struck her and she sat abruptly, dizzy with horror. Surely Steve wasn't going to help sink the barge! And if he tried, her own friends would do their best to kill him!

For long seconds Dezi sat frozen with shock and then some deep upwelling of rage took hold. She could not let this happen. She would not.

The pharma lab was a stark contrast to the rest of the barge—a sterile space gleaming with vid screens, steel instruments and laminate counter-tops, and so crammed with equipment and supplies there was barely room for half a dozen green-gowned techs to stand upright. Dezi barged in, ignoring startled looks, pulled open the electrical panel and flipped the main breaker. The room plunged abruptly into blackness. An alarm howled and red emergency lights glowed to life. Someone found the bypass and the siren stopped, replaced by cursing voices.

"...damned idiot..."

"...minute RJ's spy vids go blank he'll be over here screaming at us..."

A hand grabbed Dezi's shoulder.

"Nadezna, what on...."

"PRITAM!" Dezi cut through the babble with a voice she didn't know she had. "You've got to tell me! Are we really dumping poison and making people sick?"

Utter silence fell. As Dezi's eyes adjusted to red gloom she saw all the women staring at her.

"Poison?" asked Lily, a solemn Chinese woman with worry lines etched in her face. Dezi repeated what Steve had told her and all gazes moved to Pritam. In the harsh maroon shadows Pritam looked suddenly very old.

"RJ takes the waste, Nadezna. I don't know what he does with it. I don't even know exactly what's in the waste. We don't test it—we don't even test our product properly. But it could contain toxins or teratogens that don't break down in the natural environment. And if it's not properly contained..."

"It doesn't matter!" The bitter voice belonged to Thu-Lan, the youngest tech, who'd been dragged into the guard shack when the men were drunk. "They're gonna kill us and kill our children!"

"But they've got children, too!" Dezi yelled back. "They're sick, we're sick; they're killing us, we're killing them; this is crazy!"

"Nadezna..." Pritam sounded infinitely weary. "We don't have time for this. Right now we've got to survive."

"Couldn't we at least try to talk? To apologize?"

"What, to those bastards?" Thu-Lan waved furiously toward the guard shack. "They don't fucking care!"

"Not these guys," said Dezi, a sudden idea hitting her. "Look, I'll go to the village and find Steve's grandmother. She's the mayor or the chief or something. I'll offer to trade all the information we've got on the toxins. It's the one thing we have that they need and that they can't get anywhere else."

The women looked at her in surprise, then Thu-Lan shook her head.

"All we've got is batch records, and those are evidence against us. If the pharmacops get them..."

Dezi looked pleadingly at Pritam, trying to read her face in the dimness. Pritam rubbed her forehead, then said quietly: "The cops aren't our first problem right now, saving our lives is. Copy the records fast."

"Samples, too" said Lily. "I'm on it." She moved away with determination.

"We'll have to try the water taxi trick," said Dezi, a little uncertainly, but Pritam nodded. The women had figured out how to duplicate their guards' beer calls to Kitimat; unfortunately they'd long since discarded the ruse as a practical escape route. Water taxis weren't large enough for more than a dozen people, and there was nowhere to go with one tank of fuel except the village or Kitimat.

"I'm not sure how long it'll take..."

Dezi's newfound resolve started to waver, but Pritam gave

her a hug.

"We'll worry about that. You just go. And..." Dezi had started to leave, but she turned back and saw deep sadness in Pritam's eyes. The older woman's voice was rough.

"Take Sujjan with you. It's always harder to refuse a child."

RJ's office/apartment occupied the top floor of the newest building in Butedale—a pre-fab A-frame built and abandoned by an eco-tourism company thirty years before. The guard shack took up the ground floor. Kat, a wiry eleven year old, had perfected a route through the bush behind the A-frame, up a buckling drain pipe and into the back window of RJ's office. She shimmied in, sent the recorded call via his satellite phone, and scrambled out again, grinning, while men's voices rumbled downstairs, oblivious.

For the next few hours everyone tried to keep up a semblance of normalcy. Ominously RJ hadn't responded to the alarm. He and the guards seemed completely preoccupied, but the women still couldn't afford to take chances, so they worked their lab shift as usual. The weather had closed in since morning. A north-westerly wind whipped up waves in the channel and made the barge's wind rotors whine. As the minutes crawled past Dezi started worrying that the taxi might not come.

When a small boat finally appeared travelling from the north, Dezi bundled Sujjan into his warmest clothes and carried him up to the barge deck. Gusting rain slapped her face, and it was then that she finally remembered her eagle. She hesitated a second, then dropped Sujjan's hand and ran over to check. When she approached the sports bag, Olo's hooded head moved and she felt a sudden surge of hope. If an eagle could stay alive against such terrible odds, maybe she could, too. Whispering softly to the bird, she hefted the bag. She'd take Olo to the village and then somehow everything would be okay.

Leaving the eagle and Sujjan waiting by the top of the barge ladder, Dezi climbed down onto the slimy wharf. On the *Skookumchuck II*, a dog barked loudly and she flinched, all too aware of being in line of sight of the guard shack. But nothing happened. Rain beat on her head, running in cold rivulets through her hair onto her face, and soaking into Maria's old winter jacket. In the distance, white spray fountained rhythmically from the taxi's bow. As it neared she caught flashes of orange, then realized she was looking at a small open boat, rather than the old cabin cruiser she'd been expecting. It was a low inflatable with a big outboard engine and two upright seats about half way between bow and stern. For an awful moment she wondered if it was the Pharmacops, but as the boat pulled up to the wharf she saw a tarp-wrapped pile of cargo the right size and shape for two dozen beer cases. A burly, unshaven man in full rain gear sat at the wheel, and another sat beside him with a shotgun tucked under one arm.

Dezi stepped forward, hoping that her olive skin and dark hair looked Tsimshian to a casual glance. The boat's driver left the wheel, walked stiffly to the stern, and tossed her a rope. She caught it and pulled the line taut, then called out, trying to sound confident.

"Hi." She pointed up at the A-Frame. "They want the beer up there. I'll watch the boat."

She felt shaky with terror at this weak ploy, but the men didn't seem to notice.

"Bloody hell. Like we could use some fucking help here," one growled, but incredibly they both reached under the tarp for beer cases, then clambered one-handed up rusted rungs onto the wharf and strode toward the guard shack without a backward glance, leaving the engine idling

Dezi wrapped the rope around a ladder rung and rushed over to the barge for the eagle and Sujjan. She had to carry them one by one onto the wharf and then lower them into the boat. Hands shaking with urgency, she untied the rope, and climbed onto the too-large seat, still warm from the driver's body heat. For a panicked second she couldn't think what to do; then she took a deep breath and focused on the control panel. Steering wheel. Navscreen. Throttle. She eased the throttle forward and turned the wheel. The boat moved ahead, bumping the wharf and grazing an old piling. She pushed the throttle further and they accelerated into an expanse of heaving, wind-whipped chop.

Shouts sounded over the thrum of the motor and Dezi glanced back. Figures stood by the guard shack gesturing, then one swung a rifle toward her. Sujjan was trying to climb into the next seat. She shoved him down, yelling "curl up small!" Hunching her shoulders, she pushed the throttle all the way. The engine growled, propellers bit in and the boat surged ahead in stomach-lurching bounds.

Distant pops. Something buzzed past Dezi's head. Dezi slewed the wheel in panic and the boat careened right, slamming into waves and then surging airborne and falling sideways into a trough. For a terrible moment she thought they would flip over, but the boat righted. Heart pounding with fright, she turned back into the wind.

She heard another bullet thwack the boat and hoped the inflatable wouldn't spring a leak and deflate. She clung to the wheel with a desperate grip until she hadn't heard a bullet for a long time, then risked looking back. Butedale lay far behind, already fading into gray mist, along with the barge that had been her whole world for so long.

"Dezi?"

Sujjan's frightened voice. She eased back on the throttle long enough to lift him into the seat beside her and then accelerated down the middle of the channel, smacking over wavetops at dizzying speed. She didn't dare let go of the wheel to check on the eagle.

The small windscreen provided some shelter from wind and rain, but Dezi soon ached with cold and tried to distract herself by remembering everything Steve had told her about the village. It wasn't much. He had left as a teenager in search of education and a career and returned twenty-five years later with neither, only to find himself a foreigner in his home town. He moved in with his bossy grandmother, whose house was always full of old women micromanaging village affairs. When Dezi once asked, "What about the old men?" Steve's face had gone somber. There weren't many, he said. After the fisheries collapsed in the twenties, a lot of villagers left to find work, and many died Outside in the epidemics of the thirties.

As darkness closed in, Dezi began to feel terrified that she'd lost her way, even though the channel ran as straight as a giant gutter. She seemed to have been travelling for hours and she couldn't turn the navscreen on—it was broken. But when a cluster of lights appeared on her right she realized she could hardly have missed her goal. She aimed for the brightest lights, and when she could see the harbor, a large, empty, well-lit float. Her hands were so numb with cold that she revved the throttle accidentally, rammed the float, and then stalled the engine and found herself drifting away. She was trying to figure out how to restart the motor when a dark-haired young man in a yellow raincoat came running along the dock, carrying a long aluminum pole. He reached out, snared her bow, and pulled the inflatable in. Then he stood staring down.

"Thank you," she croaked, sliding out of the seat and trying to stand. She was stiff with cold, and soaked to the skin under Maria's old jacket. Sujjan sat in a miserable huddle, shivering. She lifted the child down from the seat and the man helped pull him up onto the dock. Then she checked on the eagle. The hood clung wetly to the bird's head and she saw no sign of movement. She felt a stab of foreboding, but picked up the sports bag and stumbled across the rocking boat to grab a proffered hand.

The young man hauled her up, then looked down the pile of wet beer cases, exposed where the tarp had blown loose.

"Uh, this is the float plane dock. And we're a dry town, eh? No beer allowed."

"Then throw it overboard," said Dezi impatiently. "I'm looking for Steve's grandmother. It's an emergency. Steve Matthews," she added, realizing suddenly that she didn't know Steve's grandmother's name.

But the young man nodded.

"Aunty Sam lives just up the road a couple blocks. Hey, are you okay?"

When he reached out and grabbed her, Dezi realized she was swaying.

"Carry Sujjan for me. Please?" she asked and without waiting for an answer, she started unsteadily up the inclined ramp to the main wharf. A few seconds later the young man hurried up by her side, Sujjan in his arms.

Walking through the streets of a real town seemed like a dream. Dezi found herself staring at the street lights and houses, the flicker of vid screens in windows, and a child's red bicycle propped by a porch. Smells swirled past her nose: cookies, paint, laundry soap. A dog barked loudly and she flinched. Sujjan squealed.

"Hey, shut up, mutt!" called her companion. He added anxiously: "It's okay, he's tied up. Um... I'm Jay."

Looking over, Dezi glimpsed his face in a porch light and realized he was about her age, even though he stood more than a head taller. He was the first stranger she'd talked to in years. She'd almost forgotten how.

"Dezi. I'm Dezi. And that's Sujjan." She looked down at the bag in her arms. "And this is Olo."

"So, you know Aunty Sam?"

"No. But I need to talk to somebody in charge."

Jay sounded puzzled.

"Well, I don't know as how she's in charge of anything."

"But..." Dezi stopped in the road, confused. "Isn't she like the chief or the mayor?"

"Umm... no. I guess she used to be on council, though."

Through a haze of exhaustion, Dezi tried to remember what Steve had told her. He'd said his grandmother ran the town, but maybe he hadn't meant it literally. She had misunderstood.

"You want to see somebody else maybe?"

But who? Dezi felt a surge of panic. She knew nothing about the people here, had no idea who might be friends with the guards at Butedale. All she knew was that Steve said his grandmother had opposed the barge deal.

She shook her head and started walking again.

The house Jay led her to was plain and boxy, with a slumping set of wooden steps in front and a carving of an eagle mounted on the weathered front door. Jay knocked and then opened the door without waiting for an answer, calling out as he entered. Dezi followed, stepping into warm air, dizzyingly redolent of chicken soup. Dezi had visualized Steve's grandmother as a wizened ancient lady, but the woman who appeared in the hallway stood tall and straight in faded blue jeans and a gray sweatshirt from "Kitasoo Marine Recyclers—Outboards Better Than New." She had long graying hair, tied back like Steve's, and her face was deeply seamed but she didn't look really old. She stared at the bag cradled in Dezi's arms.

"One of Steve's birds? Well, better put it down."

Dezi just managed to lower the sports bag without dropping it. Steve's grandmother kneeled and took the wet hood off Olo's head. The bird's eyes were closed. She placed gentle fingers against the eagle's neck, then shook her head.

Dead. Olo was dead. Dezi stared down, overwhelmed by a flood of despair. Somehow she'd been sure that as long as the eagle lived then all of them might live, but now.... She'd failed. Her knees started to buckle.

"Oh, Lord! Jay!"

Strong arms grabbed her under the shoulders and she felt Maria's sodden coat being tugged off and a dry towel rubbing against her numb arms. Then she was led into a kitchen, a huge, dazzling place like she hadn't seen since childhood, with green countertops, and yellow painted cupboards. They sat her down and wrapped her icy hands around a mug of steaming coffee that made her fingers sting, but all she could do was sit looking into the brown liquid, feeling tears roll down her face.

Then Sujjan screamed.

Dezi jumped up and ran, following familiar wails down the hall to a bathroom. Sujjan, stripped naked, was pinioned in Jay's arms, struggling. Dezi almost launched herself at the tall man until some part of her brain registered a big white bath full of water and Jay's naked distress, nearly as acute as that on the face of the half starved, shuddering child in his arms. Jay looked up at Dezi, almost in tears.

"I'm just trying to warm him up!"

Dezi grabbed the edge of the tub and kneeled shakily, feeling her heart pound at her throat. She patted Sujjan's back, uttering reassurances. As the pitch of his wails dropped, she said with an edge of hysteria: "It's just a bathtub, Sujjy, see?" She put her hand in the water. Her fingers stung a little, but it didn't seem too hot. Sujjan stopped crying and sniffled.

"Maybe, um..." Jay was blushing. "Maybe you could get in with him."

It seemed like a good suggestion, but....

"No! No, I can't, I don't have time!" With sudden horror, Dezi remembered all the lives depending on her. She pushed Sujjan back at Jay, staggered to her feet and rushed into the kitchen, heedless of renewed wails behind her. This time she noticed that one entire kitchen wall was covered by an interactive map showing several hundred square kilometers of the coast around the village. She'd seen a map like it in school years ago—if you touched the legend it displayed different resource data, constantly updated from an ecobase hub. She tore her gaze away and approached Steve's grandmother, who stood at a white-enameled stove, stirring a pot.

"I'm Dezi from the barge at Butedale. Your grandson Steve says everybody listens to you, so, please, please, you've go to help..."

She poured out her story, tripping over words in her haste. After a few sentences, Aunty Sam waved at her.

"Whoa, whoa! Who you say's gonna do this thing, sink your barge?"

Dezi knew the names of all nine regular guards. As she recited them, she saw the old woman's lips tighten. Encouraged, she kept talking, recklessly offering anything she could think of—vitamins, aspirin, Zlata's nursing credentials, Pritam's Ph. D.—and finally promising: "We'll give you everything we can, do anything we can, if you'll only take the children."

"Children?" Aunty Sam glanced toward the bathroom. "How many children?"

"Fifteen. No, fourteen." Dezi wasn't a child any more, had never felt like one anyway.

"FourTEEN?! " Aunty Sam looked appalled. "You mean it's all women and children working there?"

"Yes."

That made a difference. Dezi could see it in the woman's face. But she only stirred the soup some more. Dezi felt like screaming, "DO something!" but held her tongue. A movement caught her eye and she focused on the hand stirring the soup pot. It twitched, twitched again. Oh God, she thought in horror, Steve's grandmother has it, too.

She forced herself to speak.

"Look, I'm so sorry about the toxins from the barge but we didn't even know! RJ did the dumping. But we've got records and samples. We can find out what the toxins are and what to do. Maybe we could synthesize meds!" She doubted it, but she'd abandoned caution.

Steve's grandmother stayed silent another long moment, then said: "I knew it was a bad omen the eagles were dying."

Dezi didn't know what to say to that. The old woman turned from the stove, took Dezi's shoulder and steered her to the table.

"Here, you sit down and eat. I got to make a phone call."

Dezi stared at the bowl of soup set in front of her. She felt far too upset to eat, but she knew she'd done all she could. And it smelled wonderful. She picked up the spoon. As she ate, people began arriving at the front door. In a few minutes the kitchen filled up with gray-haired women and a few men. One woman with short dark hair and old-fashioned glasses sat down at the table and introduced herself as Chief Councilor Edgar. She studied Dezi's face with solemn brown eyes before speaking in a voice with a faint melodic cadence.

"So, it's your barge has been killing the eagles."

At "your barge" something inside Dezi snapped and she yelled. "OUR barge?! It's not OUR barge, it's YOUR barge. You let them put it here and keep us as prisoners and starve us!"

She stopped, horrified at herself. The Chief pulled back, face turning stony. Dezi held out her hands pleadingly, starting to cry. "I'm sorry, I'm sorry, I didn't mean that. And I'm so sorry about the eagles. I love them, they're beautiful. It's the trout, it's got to be. But we've been eating trout, too! Don't you see?!" She pointed at Sujjan, propped up on the counter being fed spoonfuls of soup by Jay. "He's got it, too! We've all got it."

The crowded kitchen was so silent Dezi could hear a faint hum from the wall map. She knew they were all staring at her, but she kept her eyes on the Chief, who finally gave a slow nod.

"The eagles' welfare is all our welfare."

She turned and spoke softly to the others in a humming, sibilant language while Dezi sat numbly, waiting. All at once the Chief stood and Dezi realized they were leaving. She looked up in alarm.

"Where are you going?"

"Butedale," said the Chief. "You stay here, you'll be okay."

"No, I've got to come!"

The Chief and Aunty Sam exchanged a long look, then Aunty Sam said: "I'll find some dry clothes. But the child stays here."

Dezi remembered abruptly that she was responsible for Sujjan. But he'd be better off here, no matter what, she thought grimly. She nodded.

The villagers took three aging speed boats. Eight people crowded into the cabin of the boat Dezi travelled in, most of them gray-haired, and all of them carrying rifles. Jay sat next to her, but once the boat started moving, the din of engine and water made conversation impossible. There was nothing to see in the dark and Dezi, left alone with her thoughts, found herself growing more and more afraid.

All she could think about was the way the barge had looked when the techs first arrived from Vancouver four years ago, hidden in the reeking hold of an old fish packer. The barge had already been moored at Butedale; its garden carefully tended. In the hold, furnishings had been shoved aside at one end to make room for a newly built false bulkhead and lab equipment, but everything else was intact, as if the owners had just stepped out for a few minutes, leaving dishes, clothes, blankets; even a few toys. RJ told them he'd bought the barge from its owners, but none of the women believed it.

Jay tapped Dezi's shoulder and pointed at an ancient green radar screen on the dashboard of the launch. It took her a minute to recognize the outline of the Butedale wharf. But the barge was missing. Dezi felt the first edges of panic, before Jay yelled in her ear "it's drifting" and she saw a green rectangle out in the channel. The boats passed it in the dark and pulled up at the old wharf. The *Skookumchuck II* was still tied up there.

As the last engine died into silence, muffled gunshots rang out ahead of them. A vivid picture sprang into Dezi's mind—Pritam's blood spattered against a wall and her body sliding to the floor. Dezi bolted from the boat and started for the guard shack at a run, recklessly jumping over holes in rotting wharf planks. She pounded up the old board walk, past the door to RJ's office and, without pausing to think, flung open the door to the guard room.

A flood of light blinded her. Squinting and blinking, she made out a body sprawled face down on the floor in a splatter of blood. Men stood around it, frozen in postures of intense argument. Angry faces and rifles swung to face her and she felt her body tense with terror. She stared down at the body. A hand gun lay beside its limp right hand. The feet wore black dress shoes....

RJ.

She felt a spark of hope and looked up, searching for Steve. He was there, grim-faced, with a swelling bruise on one cheek. He started to speak, then a voice called out behind Dezi, and armed villagers crowded in the door, pushing her to one side. Dezi saw the guards' faces register dismay.

But where were the women? Dezi wondered, then heard a high-pitched scream and raised voices from the wharf. Abruptly she flashed back—she'd run past the *Skookumchuck* and no dog had barked. They must be hiding there! She turned to run to the boat, but Aunty Sam blocked her path.

"Enough!" she said sharply. Then she turned her attention to the room of men and repeated, with more emphasis: "Enough. You all stay here and don't move!"

Aunty Sam went down to the wharf and returned a few minutes later with the techs. Standing next to the villagers the women looked tiny, gaunt, and very afraid, but when Pritam's eyes met Dezi's, Dezi saw a flare of hope and the older woman enfolded Dezi in a tight hug. Jay and three other villagers carried RJ's body down to the wharf while the Chief selected people to meet in the guard shack—half a dozen elders, all the former guards, Steve, Pritam, Zlata and Lily. Other villagers took the fish boat out to retrieve the barge, where Maria and the frightened children were hiding. Dezi and the remaining women crowded upstairs into RJ's apartment, which Dezi had always imagined as luxurious. The reality was strangely disappointing—a shabby room furnished with an old office desk, chairs, a table, a sagging pull-out couch, and a wood stove, recently stoked. The sole luxury was a high end satellite-linked workstation. One wall featured maps and plans for a large fish farm; RJ's cover story for his presence in Butedale.

Exhausted and shaky from her adrenaline-charged day, Dezi told her story to the other women, then sat in a daze while they talked. When the barge tied up at the wharf again, most of the women went back, taking food from RJ's kitchen, but Dezi waited, anxious to know the outcome of the conference in the guard shack. Finally, after what seemed like hours, she heard a door open. She looked out the office window. Below her, the former guards filed out, escorted by a couple of elders. They headed for the wharf. When Dezi saw Steve appear she hurried for the stairs, intending to run after him, but Steve stopped under the overhang of the wood shed and lit a cigarette. She'd never seen him smoke before and paused uncertainly a few feet away, suddenly tongue-tied. He looked up, the flare of his burning cigarette throwing strange, harsh light on his face.

"Hey, Dezi. You okay?"

"I'm okay. Uh... are you?"

"Me, I'm okay," he said. He didn't sound it.

"What's happening?"

Steve leaned heavily against the wall, exhaling smoke.

"Well, we been trying to figure out what to do with the barge. The guys wanted to sink it, hide the evidence, eh? Your Pritam said we got to clean up the toxins first. Then Dave said why not keep the barge so we could make meds and sell them ourselves, but that's crazy. RJ's people would come after us for sure. And my grandmother got mad. She said too much of that money was wasted bringing in rubbish like candy and cigarettes and sim games from outside. She's right, too. We got to be self sufficient. Can't count on outside money any more."

"Then... nobody's going to kill us."

"No!" Steve looked shocked. "No, Dezi. Look, even these guys didn't want to take blood money. They were just afraid. So I helped them figure it out if they had to get rid of anybody, where they should start..." He paused and his face flushed with sudden fury. "That son of a bitch was dumping waste in the lake, right beside the trout pens!"

The glowing cigarette shook in his hand and Dezi suddenly wondered who had killed RJ. She didn't dare ask.

"So... what about us?" she tried.

"Huh? Oh... they're talking. They'll work something out."

Steve sounded very bleak and he still hadn't looked into Dezi's eyes. She mustered her last fragments of courage.

"Steve... are you mad at me?"

He focused on her for the first time, registering surprise.

"Dezi...! No! No, I'm not mad. I'm just... I'm ashamed. I let myself be bullied by this bunch of assholes. But I should of did what you did, go to the elders, not let this go on. Should of done it a long time ago."

An ember of hope kindled.

"Then... we're still friends?"

A ghost of a smile started around Steve's eyes. "Yeah, we're friends." He reached an arm out, and she closed the distance between them, letting him snug her in under his shoulder. Steve's workshirt stank of sweat, but she leaned into it and clung, tears pricking at her eyes again.

"Olo died," she whispered.

"Hey, I'm so sorry, Dezi. He was one beautiful bird."

They stood in silence for a moment, listening to the roar of wind in the channel and rain splattering against the shed.

"Steve, do you think all the eagles are going to die?"

He squeezed her tight.

"We're gonna make it. All of us. Because you and me are gonna make damn sure of it. Right?"

She smiled, felt her heart lift and her whole face crinkle up.

"Right."

Forget Me Not

His confidence drew her to him. The gleam in his eye said, "I can take on the world," and she believed it. Here was a man who could not fail. She was fascinated, and her fascination endeared her to him.

Michael introduced them, but neither Joan nor Leland bestowed a second glance on Michael all night. Their eyes and conversation were reserved for each other.

Five months later, Joan and Leland were living together in a penthouse apartment downtown with a view of Mount Hood, functioning smoothly as a couple. Michael came over for dinner every second or third night. Their home was his second home, and he was best friend and confidant to each of them. Proud of his role, he boasted loudly of having introduced them. He couldn't find a girl of his own, he'd say, but he sure could find them for his friends, couldn't he? Leland would concur, but Joan would just smile and get Michael a second drink.

"When are you doing the parents thing?" Michael asked one night. "I know you're thinking of getting married...."

"So, we better hurry up and get our parents involved? Or else they won't pay for the wedding?" Leland joked.

"That'd be a shame," Michael said. "With our company topping the market, you couldn't possibly pay for a wedding yourself."

Leland grinned. "We're only up there, kid, because I have such a competent engineer."

Michael bowed his head to the compliment, and the men clinked glasses. Though, they all knew it wasn't Michael's engineering that carried Doohan Gadgetry to the top. Perhaps it kept them there, but Leland's uncompromising entrepreneurship was the instrumental ingredient.

"Actually," Joan said, "we already have done the parent thing."

"That's great. How'd it go?"

"Well, Joan's parents loved me."

"Who wouldn't?"

"I mean it. Her dad and I really hit it off, and her mom's got the best, driest sense of humor I've ever heard. Better than yours, Michael."

They both turned to Joan. She hesitated but said only, "Leland's mother was very nice."

"It's just my mom," Leland added, "Dad died when I was a little guy."

"I remember," Michael said. "Was your brother there?"

Leland laughed right out loud. "What a guy! Michael, I don't know what I'd do without you."

The interchange stayed at that, until Leland retired to his home office for the night. He had work to catch up on, a meeting to prepare for in the morning, plenty to keep him busy. Joan saw him to his book-lined cell, kissed him on the cheek, and closed the solid oak door behind him. As she did, she heard him muttering, and she thought she caught the word "brother."

"What was that about?" she asked Michael, back in the living room. "Does Leland have a brother?"

"He likes to deny it. I think they're mad at each other. I met him a long time ago... before Leland's first company crashed. I was an engineer for him back then too."

"Leland had a company crash?"

"He doesn't like to talk about that either. He doesn't like to talk about failing."

"He gives off the impression of a man who couldn't fail... Or, at least, a man who never has." Joan sipped her drink. "You'd think it'd scar him."

"Well, that's probably why he doesn't talk about it. He's keeping it out of his mind."

Joan and Michael chatted on, finishing their drinks. Come two o'clock that morning, Joan finally saw him to the door. She grew quiet, and leaned against the doorframe in such a way that Michael could see something was wrong.

"What is it?" he asked.

"Leland's mother didn't say anything when Leland talked about growing up alone.... How hard it was, just the two of them, after his dad died." Joan played her fingers along the doorframe. Then she stopped and looked Michael square in the face: "Did you ever meet Leland's mother?"

He shook his head.

"She looked sad. But it was a cheerful sad... The kind that

hides its tears."

Michael touched Joan's cheek and wished her goodnight. He was right, though he did not say it: A mother would be sad when her sons did not speak. But Joan wondered if that was all. Why did she play along? If she were Leland's mother, she'd be angry at her sons' childishness. She wouldn't pretend to have one son at a time, even if her sons pretended not to have brothers.

Joan kept hoping to talk with Michael about Leland's past again, but she never got the chance. One week later, Michael was hit by a car crossing Burnside near Powell's Books. Leland was there, browsing the new window displays. He looked up from a magazine about the latest Fortune 500s to see a ratty old Jaguar plow into Michael.

He couldn't have done a thing. Yet, Leland blamed himself, and Joan got to see what happens when the man who can't fail finally does. He breaks.

The daring, fearless, entrepreneurial spirit that carried Leland and his company to the top abandoned him. He claimed that Doohan Gadgetry couldn't get by without Michael, but in truth, there were plenty more engineers. It was the fearless lion who once was Leland that his company couldn't get by without. He questioned his choices, lent credence to his second thoughts and crippled himself with self-doubting indecision.

Joan cried too, and found solace in their shared grief at night. But she was seeing only the half of it: At work, she still functioned, crying only at home. She felt like a hollow shell, but it was just that: *A feeling.* She carried on.

True understanding waited until she came home one night and found Leland sprawled on the floor, leaning against the couch: He was gripping an orange plastic medicine bottle.

"I have to make it go away," he said. He looked like a man bitterly drunk, but he was only drunk on tears.

"What have you taken?" Panic tinged her voice. Joan took the bottle and read the label.

"I haven't taken it yet.... I was waiting for you."

* * *

On her second date with Leland, Joan had asked him, "What was your childhood like?"

"Good. Happy," he laughed.

"Tell me a story from it."

"Okay," he said. "I entered a kite contest once. I spent a week designing and building a kite shaped like a fish. A giant, silvery, scaled fish, flying in the sky. The scales had to be cut out and glued on individually. I remember getting a cramp in my neck, hunched over my work table for hours. I had to get it just right."

"Did you win?"

"I don't remember." He laughed again. "It was beautiful though. On the test run, it positively sparkled... looked like it was swimming in the sky. I'll have to show you sometime. If I can ever find it...."

Joan had smiled at the time, but now the memory took on an ominous tone.

A lot of Leland's childhood had seemed hazy, but Joan's memories from that age weren't so good either. When they got to talking about Leland's career, the stories were of one success after another. Up and up and up. Leland lived in a can-do world, and Joan had loved being swept up into it.

But now she had to face the price.

"You *have* taken it," she said. "You took it after your company crashed, and after you fought with your brother.... When else? How many times?"

"I can't remember."

"Of course not." There was bitterness in her voice.

"I mean, I can't remember the number. Every time. I take it every time."

"So you do have a brother?"

"Yes."

"Do you *remember* him?"

"I remember. I remember! I remember. And I want to forget. The pain reminds me. Brings it all back. And now Michael dying.... I can't take that. I can't suffer through this one with you. If I do, it will bring them *all* back. All the memories.

I'm just starting to taste them again. On the fringes of my mind. My life is riddled with them."

"All our lives are."

"Not like mine. Not like mine. My dad... my senior prom... getting kicked out of Catlin Gable... all the money trouble...." Leland flipped through memories seemingly too painful for him to recount. He latched onto an easier one: "That kite contest... when I was a kid? I *lost* that contest. I dropped my fish-kite in the mud and everyone trampled it. It was *ruined*, and that's why I can't find it. I lost, and it was my own fault too. Clumsiness. I can't remember things like that. I can't *afford* to remember things like that. How would I go on?"

"We all go on. We all fail, and we all go on." She paused, "We'll go on together."

"No." He shook his head. "No, no. But you can take it too. We'll forget together. It'll all be the same as before."

"Except without Michael."

"That can't be helped now."

Joan looked at the label on the bottle: *Amnesia inducing. For medicinal uses only. Keep away from children and those with memory disorders.*

How could she comfort him? He was feeling the pain of every failure, every loss, every bad moment since early childhood. Scrapes and cuts that should have been kissed better years ago bled freshly now. The sting of disinfectant in a million tiny wounds, covering every last inch of your body could kill you, she thought. Joan handed him back the bottle. "What will you forget?" she asked.

"Just the parts that hurt. And the bottle." He shook the orange canister, rattling the pills inside. "I only remember *these* when I need them. Pain makes me remember."

Joan still missed Michael. She was sad, all the time, and Leland could never figure out why. He'd smile at her. Tickle her to make her laugh. Then she'd be cheerful, a thin cheerful stretched across something hidden, horrible inside. When she spoke of Michael, Leland assumed she meant a childhood friend, someone she'd known before he met her. But Leland didn't mind. Her sadness made him think of his mother, the dear creature she was. Dear creatures they both were. Now.

"Where's that old kite I made?" Leland asked his mother when they visited her in her house in Ladd's Addition. "Remember? I made it to look like a fish? A fish-kite?"

"I remember," Mrs. Doohan said through thin lips, with a tender irony Joan found comfort in understanding.

"I want to show it to Joan."

"Try the attic, honey."

Joan stayed downstairs, talking with his mother. The two women let Leland rifle through the attic, reveling in his cherry-glow memories alone.

"Will you tell me about Leland's brother?" Joan asked. The question startled Mrs. Doohan.

"Would you like some tea?" Mrs. Doohan didn't wait for an answer. "I'll get it," she said and busied herself with cups, saucers and heating water.

"Won't you talk about it?" Joan asked, following her to the kitchen.

Mrs. Doohan placed her hands on the rim of the sink and looked out the kitchen window. "What good would it do you to know? He doesn't, and if you tell him.... No. No. Just have some tea."

But Mrs. Doohan reluctantly let Joan draw the story of Leland's past from her. Her other son, Geoffrey, was much older than Leland. After their father died, Geoffrey had tried to be a father figure for Leland. He'd taken his little brother to the park, the zoo and on fishing trips. During one trip to the park, Leland fell from the upper branches of a tree, but instead of falling straight to the ground, he'd gotten caught and had hung there, twisted and hurting, with the wind knocked out of him until Geoffrey was able to find help to get him down.

Geoffrey felt horrible, but his guilt was nothing compared to Leland's lasting trauma. Nightmares woke him and day-mares haunted him. Geoffrey tried to make up for it. He was a researcher at a cutting-edge lab, and their newest project was a memory drug. Geoffrey hoped it could dull the pain, lessen the power of Leland's memory.

A normal course of therapy involved taking the pill many times to fully eradicate the complicated network of memories in an adult brain. Of course, in retrospect, Geoffrey realized a child would only need to take the drug once or twice to fully forget. At first, no one realized Leland was faking it; he didn't need the drug anymore, but only pretended he did. By then, he'd built up a hidden stockpile. A poor test score—a pill; an argument with his brother—a pill; a lost contest—a pill. Leland lived the perfect, happy childhood.

After that, the drug became available on the black market.

Geoffrey begged Leland to give it up. They fought for years. Leland forgot his pains, and Geoffrey reminded him. "Don't fill your life with empty spaces," Geoffrey had said.

Leland retorted, "Stop filling the erased parts of my life back in!" Eventually, Leland forgot Geoffrey, too.

In the end, the pills could never wipe Leland's mother and childhood home away, not like they had his brother. So, Leland would turn up at her door again, ironically, stubbornly, remembering the labyrinthine way through Ladd's Addition. They'd have dinner, and Mrs. Doohan learned not to talk of certain things. Or else, they'd start again. Clean slate.

"He's a responsible, dutiful son," his mother said.

"That's what he'd like to think. That's what he does think. You let him."

"He'll be good to you," Mrs. Doohan said. "He's always kind."

Mrs. Doohan was right, but it was not enough.

In the weeks that followed, Leland worked hard to cheer Joan, and when he failed, he accepted it without complaint. He never yelled, or stormed, or blamed her for her tears. He waited them out. Joan couldn't take that. It made her die inside, to see him watching the clock, patiently counting the minutes until she dried her tears. So, she'd cry in private—in the bathroom, at work, wherever Leland couldn't see. It was hard to miss Michael alone, but she managed.

The day Joan realized that she'd stopped crying entirely—not because she was ready, but because Leland didn't understand—was the day she knew.

"It's over," Joan said.

But in Leland's world nothing good ever ended. He couldn't

understand.

"You need space," he said and helped her pack. "It'll be good for us, to be apart for a while. I'll call you in the evenings, okay?"

His confidence never left when she refused to give him her number. In his mind, they were a couple, and that could never end. Like his mother, she'd always be there for him.

"Then, you'll call me," he said. "When you're ready. I'll wait."

The next time Leland saw Joan, months later, they passed on the street. It was at the intersection by Powell's where Michael had died, and there was not the faintest gleam of recognition in his eye. He tipped his hat, but strode on by.

Joan, however, stumbled and caught her balance, leaning against the bookstore wall. Her heart was still healing, and though she expected he would forget her, she wasn't ready for the reality. Had it all been pain for him? Had every last piece of her been wiped away?

Yet, he looked the same, *was the same*, as the first day they'd met. He didn't remember her. He didn't know he'd loved her. There was nothing of her left in him at all.

But he still lived inside her, and she cherished the time she'd had with him. His fragile perfection endeared him to her even as it renewed her faith in her choice. It had been right to leave him. The fires and floods of emotion that Leland avoided fortified Joan. And she locked her part of him, the part of his life he gave her without even keeping a copy for himself, away in her heart.

Still Life with Wine Bottle

Still picked up another can from the nearly-always-full bin and split it with the nearly-always-whirring diamond saw. He held the two halves open to dump the napkin that had been trapped inside the can into the paper bin, and, after some consideration, discarded the halves into the aluminum bin. He wasn't positive, but it had felt like aluminum.

The discarded halves rattled down a chute, into a larger tube (where it was joined by tributaries from the plastic, glass, fiber, and several other bins in Still's workroom above), and clanked through a sorting machine that never failed to distinguish between the different materials. The machine sent the two pieces roaring down a chute that led directly to an aluminum-processing plant.

If his employers had been keeping track, they'd have noticed how rarely Still's hunches were wrong.

Still cracked two bottles, a jug, and four more cans, using the sprayer to remove gum, butts, and paper, and route them to the appropriate bin. The next item was an old-fashioned wine bottle that had a roll of paper stuck in it.

Wine was not an oddity to Still (he'd sampled a flight of the finest vintages of Chateau Latour just last week), but when legendary wines were recreated they were never trusted to these old vessels with their unreliable corks. This bottle, like all the others, had already been through the label-stripper, so its previous contents were unknowable. All he could do was crack it and pull out the paper that had caused it to be sent to him instead of straight on to the recycler.

As the paper fell into the paper bin, it unfurled just enough that he could see something written in thick strokes on it. Curious, he grabbed the paper before it slid down the tube, and dropped half of the wine bottle carelessly into the plastic bin. He placed the top half, cut-side down, on the floor.

The sorting machine sent the bottom half of the authentic-looking wine bottle down the plastic chute.

Still flattened the paper against the side of the bin, and read the bold print:

"Meet me: March 20th, 4:45 P.M., in Discovery Park by the Iraqi Freedom Memorial."

Still poked his watch, which announced that it was 3:29 P.M. on March 19th, 2043. He looked over at the incoming bin, which was, as usual, full, and started to grind his teeth. He dropped the paper into the bin, and reached for the next object from the pile to quell the itch rising in his bones.

"As you can see, Matt, it's a beautiful day and there are a whole bunch of people out in the park!" Shaun's chipper grin didn't fade, even when the camera panned away from her to capture five or six figures, each blurred by their protective cloudswarm, around a tall slab of featureless concrete.

Shaun blathered through a memorized spiel about the fortieth anniversary of the liberation of Iraq, and the veterans who gathered at memorials like this one even as the rest of the population forgot what had happened. But really, she was looking out the window, hoping she'd recognize who she was looking for, if that person had come, although she was not sure this person even existed.

"Let's take a closer look," she chirped, commanding her heli to dive. She directed it to an individual shrouded by a particularly dense cloudswarm, ignored the telltales that winked to indicate that some of her far-off distractor drones were taking small-arms fire, and ordered her camera to zoom in.

She rattled off the copy prepped for just this shot: this person was likely a veteran of one of the last wars Americans had fought in person, one of the last heroes to put his or her life on the line for others. She droned on about heroism being forgotten in an age of sterile machines of war and soulless longevity. It was similar to yesterday's story about the forced retirement of the city of Seattle's last traffic cop.

While she spoke, she saw, through the thick cloudswarm, a confused-looking middle-aged man, who was not focused on the memorial like the others. She saw that he cradled the top half of a wine bottle in the crook of his elbow. For a moment, there was genuine feeling behind her almost-always-present smile.

She flicked an old-fashioned switch that was hidden from the camera's view, gave the man a dramatic wave that was tied to a patriotic sound-bite in her copy, and ordered the heli up and into the relative safety of a higher altitude.

The camera blinked shut and Shaun's cheery façade faded in seconds. She punched up a flight plan back to the studio tower and listened to the insurance-mandated safety report. Four of her drones were felled by small arms fire over the near North Side, one was slagged by a car-mounted laser on the interstate, and two were hit by rockets launched from a boat somewhere on the lake. She frowned; seven drones would barely put a dent in the station's budget, or in the fleet of eight thousand that gathered footage over various parts of the city. She couldn't rely on the vagaries of random chance.

At 4:41, Still arrived near the Iraqi Freedom Memorial, having temporarily emptied his incoming bin. He had wanted to leave earlier, but had not been able to tear himself away until he'd split and cleaned everything in his queue. Trained to sense his impatience, a valve had eventually cut off the flow.

He looked around, unsure as to why he'd come or what he was expecting, and was shocked to see four other people nearby. His cloudswarm reflexively thickened, and he Googled his newsfeed to find out the reason for the large crowd.

It was forty years to the day since the United States had begun its forced liberation of Iraq. It seemed to Still like much longer than that. He hadn't thought about it in years, burying the memories under a flood of cans and bottles that desperately needed his attentions. He felt as if he'd almost forgotten those sweaty months spent looking for things that, it became apparent later, likely never existed.

He felt the comforting heft of the top half of the wine bottle, cradled between his left arm and chest.

One of the ever-present flock of black helis swooped down, probably to get a better shot of the unusually large crowd for some news program or another. Still was surprised when it veered towards him. It was low enough to be vulnerable to any bored kid's arsenal—but then dozens of these things were shot down every day; it was just part of the cost of getting good footage.

Then he saw something drop out of the bottom of the heli, and a glimpse through a window of a pale arm waving. Still stared at the receding vehicle, sure that he'd seen a living person within—a living person who was exposing him or herself to more danger than any sane person ever would.

Still walked over to where the object had landed and saw an antique wine bottle nestled in the two-inch-high grass. He stuffed it, and the top half of the other bottle, into a deep pocket that materialized in his jacket. He'd seen a tight roll of paper inside the bottle.

That evening, Still had dinner by himself in his bachelor apartment. His one room was set to a dining room configuration, and two greasy paper sacks slouched in front of him. One sack lay on its side, contents disgorged across the simple wooden table. Still had purchased a hack for the copyright restrictions, just so that the bags and the food wrappings could display the appropriate (but now mostly defunct) corporate logo and the slogan "Happy Meal."

On the surface of the table, in between the neatly-cleaned cheeseburger wrapper and the empty french fry sleeve, Still had placed a news channel display. He wiped the last vestiges of grease and salt from his lips and watched a starkly beautiful female face deliver some line about the war anniversary with all the zeal of a commercial pitchperson.

She turned slightly away from the camera, which panned to show a large concrete slab in a sea of green, the soft curve of her shaved head obscuring a corner of the view. The viewpoint dipped down, flitted over a couple of figures, and settled on a middle-aged looking man wearing a heavy cloudswarm. Still recognized himself.

The camera returned to the woman, who finished her story with a verbal flourish, and waved towards the diminishing blurred figure below her.

The camera did not show anything dropping from the reporter's heli, and he ignored the rest of the newscast.

Still stared at the wine bottle, set as if it were part of his dinner, wondering what kind of idiot willingly rode in a heli these days. He had been a pilot once, but hadn't been in one for almost forty years.

He ordered the apartment to reconfigure into his bedroom, which only involved removing the table and paper sacks and materializing his bed in their place.

The next day, Still sat at his bare dining room table for an hour, staring at the elegantly-written string of digits on the paper he'd found in the wine bottle from the park, before he finally asked his apartment to telelink to that number.

Shaun was lounging among wall-to-wall pillows and silky throws, watching a documentary about the American involvement in Vietnam when her telelink rang. She accepted, voice-only, and lolled back into a cushion.

"Hello?"

There was only silence on the other end; she stretched and yawned.

Still stared at the blank video screen on the table, having requested a full connection.

"Hello? I see that you found the second bottle of wine I sent you."

Still inhaled sharply. So she had sent the first bottle, too. He recognized her from the news program, but what did she know about him?

Her link transmitted a quiet gasp through a speaker just behind her right ear.

"Got your attention, did I?"

Still nothing on the other end.

"You don't have to talk if you don't want to. Just listen. Nobody ever really listens anymore, do they?"

Still listened. He was better at that than talking.

"No, I don't suppose they do." Shaun resolved to keep talking until the person on the other end interrupted.

"But you listened to the first message I sent you, and you came to the war memorial." She chuckled softly. "Nobody calls it a war memorial anymore, do they? They call it a freedom memorial because they forgot about the war."

Still had tried, unsuccessfully, to forget. The war had lasted longer than the real freedom, anyhow.

"Listen—I don't know who you are, except that you must work at the sorting plant. I've sent out thousands of messages, but only you responded. I need you."

Instead of responding verbally, he signaled his apartment to transmit his demographics.

She watched his name, address, and telelink number spill across one of her walls.

"Still. I like that name. It fits you, doesn't it?"

"It does," he said. Or meant to say. In actuality he just breathed softly and stared at the blank screen.

"It's only fair, you know. Everybody knows who I am." She pouted and shimmied into a more comfortable position, and two more pillows materialized in response to her discomfort.

I may know your name, but I certainly don't know you.

"Everybody knows who I am," she repeated softly, "but nobody really knows me."

Soft sobbing sounds drifted out from Still's walls. He sat, and listened until she stopped crying and her breathing became soft and regular. He did not close the link, and neither did she. Still didn't go to sleep that night; he amplified the sounds of her sleeping until they filled his senses, and listened until it drowned out all thought.

Shaun prepared to deliver another report from her heli. She'd been asked to do the piece from the studio, but refused. She only felt comfortable enough to wear her charming persona when hovering a thousand feet in the air inside a barely-shielded metal pod. She felt as if the illusion would be broken if there were anyone actually present to see it—but the cameras could be fooled. The computers that ran the network quickly caved, as she knew they would. They needed her.

"Today's economic report brings great news!" She beamed into the camera. "The employment rate is down to four percent nationally, and only thirty-seven percent globally. This is welcome news to everybody pursuing the American Dream."

Her monitor showed footage of men and women of various ethnicities and body types, each alone in his or her own extravagantly-appointed room. Some dined on rich foods, others jammed with simulations of famous rock bands, and no small number engaged in sex acts of some sort.

"Freedom from work, freedom to pursue your whims—this is what we all deserve."

A man on the monitor charged over a simulated hill, rifle in hand, was riddled by simulated bullets and knocked down. After a brief stillness, he looked down at his real but already-closing, wounds, grinned, and got up to continue his charge.

"Even those forced to work for a living are facing smaller workloads, down to an average of fourteen hours a week."

On screen, a woman came out of a white room and closed the door behind her, smiling broadly. The nature of her work in the room was not clear, but she seemed pleased to be free of it.

"Remember: You live in the most wonderful time that has been. We don't have to fear death, or work, or boredom. Everyone has the opportunity to—Fuck this. Does anybody really believe this shit? Who around here is actually happy? Who has any meaning in their life? Who feels like there is any purpose, any reason for us to wake up in the morning and give a shit about what happens to us or to anyone else? Don't you see? We've made ourselves useless, powerless—we've killed ourselves, but we just won't die." Three sharp notes rang out as she slapped the camera, open-handed, along with her last three words.

The camera had been switched off, the monitor showing something totally different, from the instant her mood had changed. She slumped in her seat, and waited, but no tears came.

The next day, Still returned to his subterranean sorting room, not tired from lack of sleep. If his employers had been keeping track, they'd have noticed that his performance was way off. He tossed plastics into the glass bin, forgot to wash gum out of cans, freed napkins from the necks of bottles just to let them drift into the diamond bin—it was the first day he'd ever made serious errors. Even so, the sorting machine (into which all of his output tubes fed) diligently continued to pass the materials on to the appropriate recycling plants. For the first time ever, Still was intentionally doing a bad job. Nobody would ever know the difference.

When the wine bottle appeared in his incoming pile, he grasped it to his chest. The tight roll of paper inside it, like the two others he'd found previously, was the only true communication he could remember receiving. The bottle was cool against his skin as he held it and thought about what it might contain. The message it held could be anything, and in some way was every message ever sent in human history, and would be up until he read it and forced it to condense into one single true message. In its indeterminate state it represented the tears he'd never been able to shed, the sleep he hadn't had, and the loves he'd never chased, all in one outdated package.

He took the bottle to the nearly-always-whirring diamond saw and split it in two, freeing her message. He unrolled it:

"Meet me in the park, right now, where we first met. When you get there, be Still and listen."

If his employers had been keeping track, they'd have noticed him walk off the job without emptying his work bin for the first time in nearly twenty years. Even if so, they wouldn't have stopped him, because he was a volunteer. The valve that controlled flow to his incoming bin registered his departure and closed. If it felt anything like surprise, it had no way of communicating this to anyone.

Still walked to the park, looking straight up the whole time. He'd never really noticed how many hundreds of helis passed overhead during a fifteen-minute walk. He hummed along with their far-off buzz. The streets were empty, and when he arrived he had the park to himself. The sun glinted off something metallic lying in the grass near the concrete memorial.

The long metallic tube felt heavy. He gripped it by the handle and swung it onto

Shaun had been hovering over the Iraqi Freedom Memorial for hours when she saw Still arrive. Nobody else would think to look at a heli passing overhead; it was too common an occurrence to bother with. But Still looked up, and stared at each of the dozen or so in the area collecting routine footage.

She watched him stoop to pick something up from the ground, but was too far away to see it clearly—while the network seemed content to let her control the heli, they his shoulder and then suddenly knew what it was. It was cheaply manufactured, and of a more recent design than the ones he'd trained with more than forty years ago, but the functions of the notch at the end of the barrel and the stud on the inside of the handle were clear.

He heard the heli approaching and ducked, some long-neglected instinct kicking in even as his protective cloudswarm congealed to protect him.

He did not flinch as it bounced off of his cloudswarm and landed nearby. It was an antique champagne bottle, still sealed. The glass was opaque and he could not see what was inside.

He looked up at her heli through the sight, which remained steady even though the rest of him was trembling.

weren't turning on her camera. Even so, she knew what it was, because she had left it for him.

She smiled self-consciously at the camera, which was still off, and pushed the heli into a dive. She waved during the swoop's nadir, twenty feet above him, but doubted that he would be able to see it this time.

She slowed to a hover several hundred feet directly above him and flipped the switch that released the heli's makeshift cargo hold doors. Her gift plummeted earthwards.

She hovered, and waited, unable to see much of what he was doing.

Someone had watched him this way almost forty years ago, he remembered. He did not know, and would never know, who that person was, man or woman (or boy or girl), soldier or civilian. Dead or alive.

He felt something powerful surge inside his chest, and cried out: "Shaun, I love you!"

She could not hear him.

The pressure inside him did not relent, and so, feeling the need to communicate with her, and having failed in every other attempt at communication he could remember, he squeezed the trigger.

She saw a flash, and something small hurtling up towards her. She smiled the first genuine, soul-baring smile she could remember. It felt like her face was her own for the first time, and not a mask she was forced to wear.

Above him, the heli blossomed and fell from the sky. He watched it descend upon him, the black metal like a deep pit inside a fiery bloom, threatening to swallow him.

A foot above his upturned face, the wreck met the edge of his cloudswarm and split down the middle. Remnants fell to either side of him, but he was untouched.

He paused, carefully stepped through the wreckage, and began to walk back to work.

His thoughts turned to the nearly-full bin he had left there, and he itched to empty it.

Behind Still, back in the park, lay the shattered remnants of the champagne bottle. There had been nothing inside.

Truer Love

My lover Dieter came to Duvall last month. I never expected him to drag his chain this far north; but such is love.

Dieter only speaks German. His lover Minette had learned the language to please him, and translated.

"He says his idol has died, Carl. He says he never stopped loving you."

We were sitting on rickety chairs in what had once been a Safeway. It was the largest space in the town, so we'd set it up for daycare and as an indoor playground. I was watching the toddlers that day. I handed Dieter a little girl that had been pulling at his shirt.

"You know I gave up loving," I said.

"He says it's not that easy. He's fixated on you again and wants you to join the circle." She looked me over. "We're a lot longer than when you were with us. After Anne died and you left, we linked with a chain in Colorado."

Anne.

"You're not a circle—if you were, you wouldn't need me. I don't do that any more." I waved my hand around at the kids, from the napping babies in the defunct dairy case through the six-year-olds playing tag, to the five teens near the registers who were pretending to study but were instead sneaking peeks at the chain of people that had come to recruit me. "This is what I do. You know how important it is."

Dieter set the girl on his lap down and spoke for a minute in German, while Minette focused laser-sharp on him. "Dieter says he can't live without you. You are the one he loves, Carl. You've been in the chain. You know what it's like." The jealousy was barely visible below her placid exterior, but it could hardly be gone entirely. It was in her narrowed eyes when she had to turn to speak to me. Dieter was her world, like Anne had been mine.

They were in the chain, thus nearly impervious to logic. I ran my fingers through a little boy's hair over and over until he protested and pulled away. Yes, I knew what it was like.

One of the teens, Manny, rescued me. He was fourteen, and we adult celibates had been expecting him to fixate any day. He got up, put his book on his seat, and walked over. "Hey," he said, looking at Dieter and Minette and the other people behind them stretching away like beads out the broken doors and down the unused highway. Most of them carried food or packs, and some of the other celibates had gathered to barter with them.

"Yes?" said Minette. She knew what he was going to ask. He could barely stay focused on her, so ready was he to be off and seeking his idol. I hoped he wouldn't have to trek too far.

"Do you have any advice about loving?" he said. "Can you tell how far a person usually is from his idol? What if my idol is on the other side of the Atlantic?"

"There are still some small circles and chains maintaining and flying airplanes," she replied. "They can take you across the ocean, if you have to go. Nobody can tell you how far away your idol is. You're going to feel that pull until you find him or her, and then you're never going to want to leave." She reached out a hand to trail across Dieter's shoulder, but he shrugged it off. He only had eyes for me. "Take heart. It's unlikely you'll have to go far. Back when there were scientists they said everyone had hundreds of people in the world they could fixate on. You just have to find one that's not already someone else's idol. When someone fixates on an idol, nobody else can."

"Go away, Dieter," I said wearily. He knew what that meant; he'd heard it from me often enough. "I'm not going to be your idol." I stood and turned him around firmly. He shivered under my touch, and looked over his shoulder at me. I stepped away. "Minette, take him away. Find him another idol. I have work to do."

I told Manny to watch the toddlers, and walked briskly to the back of the store and through the swinging doors. My wife Laura was there; she'd seen what was happening and she embraced me briefly before stepping out to enforce my order to leave. As mayor she had the authority.

Deep down, I knew that wouldn't discourage Dieter or his chain. I just hoped he'd find someone easier to fixate on.

Two days later I was feeding some of the babies while Katherine taught the teens. Her words echoed around the empty space, vying with the racket made by the twins who were follow-the-leadering over the top of the empty frozen food cases.

"Nobody came forward to claim responsibility for the virus," she said. "But before the news media broke down they reported that its origin had been traced back to a research laboratory in Toronto, Ontario. That's up north, in Canada.

"Some people speculated that a geneticist had been trying to make people tamer. Less violent." She held up some old issues of *Newsweek* with photos of terrorists and soldiers. "Not like these people. But some think he, or she, had replicated the genetic basis for stalking."

I could tell that none of her students understood that word.

She must have, too. "Stalking is following someone. Trying to learn everything about them, because you can't live without them."

"Like loving?" asked Manny.

"Yes," said Katherine. "Like loving."

I finished spooning mashed potatoes into the last baby, so I went to the door and picked up a water jug. One of the reasons the celibates picked Duvall was its location next to the Snoqualmie River. We never lack for water. When everybody walked off the job to find their idol, utilities died just as fast as national economies and every other industry.

I walked across the decaying road, after ten years still looking both ways, and picked my way down the slope to the river. Young cedars and douglas firs shaded it on both sides, and cottonwoods grew right up out of it, spread from a pulpwood project started a couple of decades back. It was early summer, and sunny days were still rare enough that I lifted my face to the sun with closed eyes.

Listening to Katherine's speech so soon after seeing Dieter just made the longing stronger to find an idol and love her—or him—with all my might. An article I'd read back when we still had *Time* had said the virus was incredibly sophisticated. It targeted most lobes of the brain in very specific ways: the emotional response governed by the frontal lobe; the sense receptors distributed in several areas of the brain, and especially the sense of religious ecstasy experimenters had found in the parietal lobe. Scientists had focused magnetic fields and made volunteers feel the presence of a greater power. The virus did that for all but a few naturally immune people, but the 'greater power' for us was the idol, the person we loved. The only problem was the idol didn't love the lover back; circles were just giant cluster fucks without the sex.

I wanted to find my new idol, another Anne. I wanted to swim across the snowmelt-cold Snoqualmie and start walking across the fields. Instead, I pushed the jug under the surface of the river and filled it before walking back. Laura met me at the door. One look at my face and she grabbed my hand to pull me along the street. I set the jug down outside the Safeway near the empty newspaper racks and followed her.

Laura led me to the nearest house. We left all the doors in town unlocked. She dragged me upstairs and helped me pull off my clothes. She maneuvered me to the bed—I looking out the window all the while—and pushed me onto it. She rubbed my prick to hardness and mounted me. I didn't want her but my body did.

Afterward, she held me. "We need children," she said, but the corner of my brain still concerned with her knew she needed more. Her gaze was pulled to the window, too.

Manny left the next day. We loaded him down with supplies; our strawberry crop had reaped generous barter from the nearby circles, so we had plenty of food to spare.

With each person that left, Laura got a little more desperate. "You know why we're here, we celibates?" she asked him as the rest of us stood between him and the highway. "Sex. Pure and simple. We're here to make sure that enough babies get born so the human race will continue. We raise and educate kids like you. The lovers don't want babies, it gets in the way of their pure, simple loving circles. They don't want to love and care for children, just like they don't want to have a job or watch television or do anything else. All they want to do is lavish affection on their idol.

"If your idol dies and you can get away, if you can in any way leave a circle, please find the nearest celibates. Join them, please. Help us stay alive."

Manny nodded uncomfortably, his face pulled inexorably away from us. He turned south down the old road, state highway map in hand, headed for the I-90 pass over the Cascades.

I watched him patter away, barely able to keep from breaking into a trot myself. Manny had more hormones, less control, than I did. But not by much. I turned away with an effort, and saw Laura. Unshed tears glistened in her eyes.

"He'll make it," I said. "The pass in summer is going to be a breeze."

She nodded, looking at me, then away.

A small part of Dieter's chain surrounded Duvall the next morning. I suppose they were concerned that someone would hide me far away if they'd been seen coming. I'm glad now we didn't think of it, or if someone did, that they didn't carry the plan through. Celibates had tried to defy chains and circles before by kidnapping an idol, and had been wiped out. Lovers formed chains with tens of thousands of members; our little towns rarely had more than a few dozen citizens.

"I just want Carl," said Dieter through Minette.

Laura looked at the solid mass of lovers surrounding her town. Then she crossed her arms under her breasts and glared at Dieter. "Your chain is no longer welcome here. No one will trade with you. We will tell the other celibates you have stolen one of our own."

Dieter heard her tone of voice, so he looked to Minette, who nodded and translated. He smiled, then laughed with childlike joy. Reaching into his pack, he found a pair of handcuffs. One cuff went around my right wrist, the other on his left. Laura's threats meant nothing next to his love.

"Let me say goodbye," I said. Laura brought me the baby and the twins. I kissed them all. Our hugs were awkward, constrained by the chain.

"You won't be cuffed for long. Just until we get you an idol," said Minette. "We have a few possible ones in Seattle. Then you'll be free."

"Carl. This is Natalya, she's from Minsk."

I stared at her. Natalya was short and stout and middle-aged and gray, by far the most beautiful woman I had ever seen. I would never want to look anywhere but at her, ever again. I reached out to touch her, but she backed up a step. "I love you,"

I whispered hopelessly.

"She was in a small circle," continued Minette. "Forty people. They operated a fishing trawler, but it sank off the San Juans. She made it to shore and the LaConner Circle helped her out before sending her our way."

That was how it went. Any chain got passed all the single people that weren't celibates, in case one of them was the one that could extend the chain. Maybe be the special one to turn it into a circle. Chains met tail to head all the time for the same reason.

She was something like the fortieth person they'd hauled in front of me. Dieter was staring at her with the same expression of distaste that Minette had for me. Everybody disliked their idol's idol. It would be funny if it weren't so goddamned sad.

"Do you speak English?" I asked.

"A little," said Natalya. The sound of her voice sent a shiver through me. My penis was heavy and hard.

"I just want to touch you."

"No. You will not." She waved a finger. "No touch. Just give me all."

"All," I said. "Of course. Everything."

The walk from Duvall and across the floating bridge had taken two days. Our chain was doubling on itself; we'd passed hundreds, thousands of people. They greeted us in passing as they sat on streets, yards, and highways. When night fell they each set up their tiny shelter and slept next to the ones they loved and the ones who loved them.

Dieter unlocked the handcuffs, sure that I wouldn't leave him now.

We started south the next morning. The tail of our chain was in Santa Barbara, far to the south. When we got there Natalya would be introduced to whoever was at the tail. If we were very lucky, that person would be Natalya's idol, and our chain would become a circle, every lover an idol, every idol a lover.

Circles were much more stable than chains, but lovers died, breaking them. When a chain came apart, it unraveled from the front since the first idol didn't have an idol of their own. What the head of a chain did get was a sense of near-completion in the hope they'd find an idol, and all the best stuff. I say 'stuff' because they got everything. Lovers passed the newest clothes, the tastiest food, the best toys to the head of a chain, idol to idol to idol. Most chains didn't unravel very far. Such is greed.

Evening found us just south of Boeing Field. An earthquake several years back had damaged the runway, but near the north end. None of Seattle's skyscrapers had yet fallen but it likely wouldn't be much longer. Everybody was still waiting for the Big Quake.

We built a fire on the median and forty or so of us sat around it while a heavily bearded man in a wheelchair stirred a stew. His lover cut carrots and potatoes with arms that looked like Popeye's from pushing him everywhere. Similar fires stretched down the dark highway.

"Natalya is a doctor," said Jo, Minette's lover.

"That's lucky," I said. Chains and circles were happy to have anyone with medical experience, or woodsmanship, or just about any craft.

Jo was a talker. "Yeah, she worked in a hospital in Minsk before the virus."

"Maybe she could have saved Anne," Minette said. When I glared at her, she smiled sweetly.

"Anne? Your original idol?" asked Natalya. "How did she die?"

"He killed her."

Natalya sucked in her breath and put both hands to her mouth.

Everyone looked at me. All of them knew the story. Everyone but my love.

"Anne was a lesbian," I said. "She was also into S&M. You know what that is, Natalya? She liked—loved—women, but in a certain way. She wanted her lover to hurt her; it made her feel loved and protected to be hurt in ways she controlled. I don't pretend to understand. It's not easy to put this simply for you. She would have her lover tie her to the bed. She loved the blindfold." I saw Natalya didn't know the word. "A strip of cloth across her eyes, so she couldn't see. She wanted to feel pain or pleasure at the will of her partner. Her lover might tickle her with a feather, she might cut her or strike her or caress her clit or pinch her nipple. She might—" My voice broke.

"Anne was forced by the virus to leave her partner," said Jo. She laid a hand briefly on my knee. "The first idol of her affection was a man, which scared her even despite the attraction. She did not like men, but was forced to love one. Then Carl fixated on her."

Ten years ago, when the virus struck and the implications had been aired on CNN, all anybody wanted to do was to find their idol. Word was: the President had walked out of the Oval Office and fixated on a visiting school teacher from Kenya. The world organized itself around vast dating circles. All transportation was co-opted for use in shuttling hordes of singles around until they could find their idol, no matter where that person was. I'd been handling cargo at O'Hare, my first job. Then it was rush rush around the country by bus and plane and train. Finally, in San Francisco's Golden Gate Park I'd been found by Dieter, then I found Anne and her idol, all in one week. So lucky, I'd thought.

Tears spilled out of my eyes. "Anne was in love, but unhappy. She couldn't stand being near me, but she saw how to get away. She taught me how to love her, her way. She made me cut her, tie her, blindfold her. She m-made me choke her."

Jo saw I was all out of words. I leaned far forward, hands over my head as if to ward off a blow, as she continued the story. "We took over a hotel in Sacramento. We'd completed our circle, just under three hundred people, and were so proud of ourselves. We drank wine from Napa Valley and ate the best steaks we could find. Everybody got drunk, but of course no idols let their lovers have sex with them, because it would interrupt their fixation on their own idol. No idol except one. Anne. She let Carl make love to her."

"He choked her to death," said Minette.

"At her command," finished Jo.

"Before we leave Seattle," I said, "could we visit the mall?" We trudged south on Interstate 5. Around the next hill we'd be in sight of Southcenter Mall and the huge shopping complex that had grown up around it.

Minette shook her head. "Natalya is the leader," she said. "It's for her to say. But any mall will have long ago been looted."

"A house then. Can we look in some houses? I just want to get Natalya something nice." I heard the whine in my voice.

Minette did too, and smirked.

Natalya looked around from her place ahead of me. "He may find things for me. A dress, perhaps. More."

That was that. The leader had spoken. Different chains had different ways of making decisions, but most deferred to the head idol. It kept them happy and everyone knew they were the one with the biggest drive, the drive to find an idol of their own. Soon enough we would continue south.

Tukwila was the suburb nearest us. It hadn't burned like most of West Seattle and some of the towns on the other side of Lake Washington. We walked down the off-ramp at Interurban Avenue, and wandered west into a neighborhood heavy with apartment houses and smaller residences. The houses on the major roads around here were picked over, so we wandered up a side street, leading our chain of lovers. The blackberries had taken over the neighborhood, even cracking the pavement in many places. We squeezed past them when we could, hacked at them when we had to. Avoiding homes that looked too difficult to break into, we eventually found a street with older, larger houses. I picked one that had a jungle gym in the yard, figuring I was more likely to find women's clothes there, something nice for Natalya. We broke through a picture window and several of us scouted through the house. Jo waited anxiously at the window.

I ran up the stairs after Natalya, Dieter after me, and found the master bedroom. "Up here," I called.

The light was fading, so we grabbed armloads of clothes from the closet and dresser. Dieter stepped into the bathroom and came up with a razor, some soap, and other sundries.

Back in the yard, we built a fire and looked through our spoils. Natalya picked three dresses, several pairs of nylons, and a cashmere sweater. No doubt she'd make me carry them. I looked forward to doing that for her.

* * *

I woke up well before dawn, chilled. We had dragged a mattress out of the musty house and Natalya slept on it. I lay nearby, fully clothed, but hadn't yet started carrying enough covers to be comfortable on cooler nights. I crawled to our pile of castoff clothes, pulling along my ground-cloth, and looked through it. We hadn't thought to bring any men's clothes down, but I figured I could pull most of the pile over myself and get warm that way.

The fire had burned down but the moon was near full. I pulled at the clothes, and then I saw them. Scarves. I picked one up, then another, drawing their smooth silk through my hands. They were beautiful, some patterned with bold flowers and birds, some pastel solids. I shivered in the cold.

I walked to Dieter. He slept nude. He always had, but he had silvery sheets to protect him from the weather. I shook him, and he came awake under my hand. He looked up at me, abject love in his eyes. He made a motion to offer me his sheets, but I shook my head. I put a finger to my lips and beckoned him to follow.

He came after me to the jungle gym. I turned my back to it and he was so close to me that our breath intermingled. I reached out and touched his stubbled chin, his cheek. He trembled; I had never touched him before except to push him away. I put a finger on his lips, then on mine.

I held out the scarves to Dieter. "Hurt me."

He shook his head. Those were words he knew. I used more.

"You love me." I touched his hand, enjoying the quiver that ran through it. "I know you do."

And he did. He tied one hand high up on the steel structure, then the other. He knelt to secure my feet, and I said, "Don't." I was ready.

"My neck, now."

He couldn't pretend not to know what I was talking about. Shaking his head, tears streaming down his cheek, he whispered 'nein' and backed away from me. But not far.

"Come here... My neck. You saw what I did to Anne. You love me."

And he did. I could see his cock up and straining toward me. The depth and power of his love was horrific. I didn't want it to be the last thing I saw. I didn't.

"My neck. Now."

He passed a light-colored scarf around my neck and put the ends together.

"Tighten it."

He did. He took the two ends of the scarf that had been passed around each other and pulled. He twisted them. Did it again.

"Tighter."

His hands moved. He sobbed aloud. The scarf grew tighter and I could hear a humming rush in my ears.

I forced air past the block, whispering, "More." The band around my neck constricted. I realized I couldn't see the moon any more, then I realized the world was going away.

I woke to birdsong. I opened my eyes. Natalya leaned over me, clinical concern evident on her face.

I choked, bile rising into my throat, and rolled over on my side to vomit into the grass. One wrist was still circled by a scarf, but the one around my neck was gone.

Sitting up, I accepted the cup of water Natalya offered. Surrounding us was a circle of lovers, watching in the early dawn light. I looked around, finally rising to peer over the first rank of people. People stepped apart, and I saw him under the jungle gym, the blade from his razor in his hand. His neck was open from one side to the other.

"Dieter destroyed himself," said Natalya. "He thought he had killed you."

As soon as she began speaking, I whirled to focus on her. My love for her was as complete as ever.

"Sit down," she said, so of course I did. Hands nearby handed us bread, cheese, and jam; I didn't look away from her. We fixed our breakfast together. I gave my half to her; it would have hurt too much to swallow, anyway. After the first bite, Natalya looked around.

"We are a chain of two now, not connected to you."

A sigh went up around us. They knew it, but didn't want to know they knew. With Dieter gone we were no longer a part of their chain. Minette was now their head. "You took him away from me," she said. Her eyes were dull and she held the almost physical pain in with both hands across her belly. It wouldn't last, I knew; soon she would feel the kind of anger I'd feel if anyone tried to take Natalya away from me.

"I free you, Carl," said Natalya.

I knew what she meant. But I couldn't accept it. She just couldn't have said what I thought she'd said.

"You are celibate now, Carl. I will find another chain, one that can give me more than you can. I will go south with Minette's chain for now. You will go north, back to your town." She stood and so I did. She motioned for me to turn away, then gathered up her few possessions and walked off.

If I looked around, I was lost. I'd follow her anywhere. I stared straight ahead, then took one step. One became two, and soon I was walking back to Laura.

I hear that there are three circles of two people in the entire world. I think it's an urban legend, but if it's true then those are the luckiest people. Imagine perfect feedback. Imagine loving your lover.

I'll take Laura. I ache to turn around, but I'll take her.

Wonderfreaks

...Life piled on life
Were all too little.
—*Tennyson*

Seattle, 2007

Bookstores were the pickup joints.

I sipped a macchiato—caffeine wasn't my thing, but it's part of the game. My notepad was up, and I peeked over it. She peeked back—for the dozenth time. Some guy was at her table, trying to talk to her.

The propped-up pad was the sign. A non-freak propping a pad in an Amazon Café was like a young, slender straight male bopping past a gay bar with keys on his right belt loop—he'd learn real fast.

The guy went to the restroom. I flung pad in pack, went over, and took his chair, her face open, accepting, smiling.

—Whaddaya know? we both said, and laughed.

She'd've been a fun date.

—All right, I said. Your place or mine?

—Here, she said, impish.

—Animal. Let's go.

We could have. But it's best horizontal and in private. Some say it's the earth's magnetic field or some shit, but to me it's just wiring: We've taken our pleasure that way since time immemorial.

Her place was closer. On the way, making nervous chitchat, she asked what I had.

—That's a newbie question, I said.

—Ooh. I'll just have to find out the hard way.

—I'm gonna give you all I got, baby. I'm gonna slam my luuv inta yew hard as I know how.

Routine freak patter, but she was thrilled enough to try to hide it.

She was green—you think I cared?

We got to her apartment, just off-campus, and went into the bedroom.

—My roomie's in class, she said. We have all day.

I searched her eyes. There it was: vertical nystagmus, the tiny up-down oscillations that mark the wonderfreak in lust. She was ready, bigtime.

—All day? I said. Who do you think I am, McD?

She smiled: —Be gentle, okay? You're only my fifth.

Her up-for-anything approach put me briefly in mind of the first girl I ever loved, ten long years ago—nine before the plague—when we were both fifteen and all bodily wonder, and maybe that's the connection.

Eros is an *affinity* of things: bodies, facts, Leibnizian monads. It all comes together in your head.

I threw my jacket down. My hand went to her shoulder—archaic gesture of kinship. I managed to suppress my tremor while we tumbled to the bed, where we held each other, locking gazes as desire crackled and surged.

Then we did the thing.

We osculated.

It's uncool to wake your partner up prematurely, so I arose, put my jacket back on, and paced a bit, at peace with the empurpled world.

The mantelpiece had a couple of Fabergé eggs on it. Replicas. The real Fabergé eggs were made for the Russian imperial family—the first in 1885. *The most ever paid for a Fabergé egg was $5,587,308 in Switzerland in 1994.*

—Hey, she said behind me.

I turned around. —Hey. So I'm Steve.

—Hi, Steve. I'm Lisa.

—You were very nice, Lisa. Very giving.

—Thanks, she said. You too. I... really wanted to give you everything. I think you're sweet.

It's something you say. All of us always give everything.

—You're not embarrassed?

She looked down. —No. And smiled. —You?

—Past that, babe.

Her hand went to her mouth; she bent to a wastebasket and retched.

—First time for that?

She nodded.

—I was too much. It'll pass.

She took a minute to collect herself: —So, get anything good?

—You never know right away, I said. But the five-million-dollar egg? That was you.

—Yep. That one right over there. She pointed to one of the replicas.

—You didn't share that part, I teased.

—Did too.

I squeezed her soft hand. —Look. I'll see you around.

Part of me, an old and useless part, wanted this to be more than a one-shot deal.

—It'd be nice if we got together sometime, I said. For like a movie and stuff.

—Not how it works, Steve.

Very good, Lisa.

—I just said it'd be nice, I told her. And walked.

2

Later that day I was at the main university library, the Suzzallo—but I'd dropped out of grad school months ago.

Some lady from *Time* was cruising it, looking to do a story here in little old Seattle, ground zero of the wonderfreak phenomenon and still the only place with a population. The disease requires a reservoir of people in one community for transmission—and recipients are pretty much obliged to stick around. It takes a village to raise a freak.

Her name was Joan, and while she was not one of us, she homed right in. May have had something to do with my rather pathetic pawing through *J Appl Econ Research* after being stood up by this beautiful babe I'd met earlier in the day. I'd had visions of a knee-trembler in the archaeology stacks. Instead I had this bitch with a clipboard in front of me, asking about my first time.

—Who've you found already? I countered.

—Two others, she said. Both on the fourth floor. Both males: sorry, guy. Unless that works for you.

It figured. Guys outnumber girls about two to one.

—It doesn't, I said. Set me up with a female and we'll talk.

—You'll run off with her, she said. Which was true. —Come on; tell me about your first time. I'll make it worth your while.

—I doubt that, I said. But I told her.

Six months ago, when I was still in school, I was knocking back brewskis in this bar just off-campus with some guys who used to be my friends. We weren't hittin' on women, but we were doing a lot of talking about it. I wound up dancing with this bodacious item—she asked me. Some old ZZ Top tune was blasting and we boogie-oogie-oogied. I went off with her to her table and we exchanged names and that. There was mutual attraction. And suddenly we were in each other's arms and full-on soul-kissing right there, lost to the world.

Sure, I was up for that.

We tonsillectomized for a minute or an hour until I disengaged, bewildered, with the weirdest notion that I'd just awakened from a dream. It had slipped past me almost completely, but I distinctly remembered about the last two seconds: it was like I was a pad or a desktop, and while we were kissing I had downloaded a huge file from her, ripping like the chatter of runaway tape.

I only caught the very tail end—but I felt surreptitiously and expertly violated, and for much longer than a couple of seconds.

As I puzzled over this, she watched with knowing amusement.

—What.

—*By George, I think he's got it,* she said—a line which, more or less, occurs in *My Fair Lady* (1964) but not its source *Pygmalion* (1916). —See ya around, she said. You'll have questions.

But I never saw her around.

A tad dazed, I went back to rejoin my buddies. On the way over, it hit me: *the* Sakutei-ki *of Toshitsuna (ca. 1050) lists seventeen taboos for the placement of stones in gardens, one of which prohibits a horizontal stone in a northwest orientation.*

—It hit you, said the journalist. Like you'd been wondering about ancient Japanese gardens for years?

—Never.

—But 'it *hit* you.' As in seeing it for the first time? Or not exactly?

—Not exactly, I said. And then I knew this gal knew her shit. —It didn't feel like a new fact. It felt like I must have been... born knowing it. Because I couldn't recall ever *learning* it, what TV show, whose book, what year.

—But you'd never integrated it with other stuff you knew.

—*Right.* Which immediately started happening. It integrated *itself*, burrowing in there. I mean, *why* would northwest be bad? Something to do with wealth. Because I already had some fragments of old Japanese cosmology in there somewhere... you know?...

She waved away the impending discourse: —And how did that feel?

—Wonderful beyond description, I said slowly. Like little pieces of the universe coming together, and I was helping them do it.

She shook her head and smiled: —You guys all talk the same.

A ***thin-film resonant cavity filter*** *is a Fabry-Perot interferometer, or etalon, in which the mirrors surrounding the cavity are realized as multiple reflective dielectric thin-film layers.* It'd been surfacing all afternoon: Lisa had apparently thrown me, among much else, the better part of an entire text on optical networking, and I'd caught damn near all of it. This was good. A solid graduate-level textbook is just about ideal: a self-cohering chunk of specialized knowledge, well in accord with the larger body of accepted truths.

I'd be buzzed for three or four hours, easy.

A library security guard passed by and glared at us. I waved.

—Scum, stay the hell out of here, he said. Skankin' around in the stairwell with yer goddam girlfriends. This place is for *learning.*

—Let's go someplace where we can talk, I told Joan.

Not everybody can be a wonderfreak. There's a genetic susceptibility. One in twenty. The other 19 are mortals—'mere mortals,' some wag's pejorative for normal people, coined in happier days. The term has stuck. But we're the ones dying like flies.

And the disease is so new—a year, tops—that only a small fraction of Seattle's five percent have been exposed. Yet.

But we know who we are.

While you're munching your morning cereal, will you read the ingredients list if nothing else is around? Do you leaf through the *World Almanac* on the can? Can you never leave a bookstore without impulse-buying a bunch of books—each from a different section of the store?

Is the accumulation of useless random knowledge an end in itself?

Then hang with us. Or better: stay away.

A decent predictive test: read someone Tennyson's "Ulysses" (1842) out loud. *Yearning in desire/To follow knowledge like a sinking star.* A blank stare is a mortal. The knowing nod's a freak.

Or soon will be.

3

The next morning I was hanging out in the apartment with Rafe. Rooming with a fellow freak can be a pain in the ass. It's not like druggies, where the two of you can go out and score, divvy, shoot up together. There's always a competition.

—Had a weird thing, Rafe said. Dude picks me up a few days ago. Takes me to his house. Wants to do the whole thing in the dark, start to finish. We go in his friggin' *basement.*

Rafe is bi: best deal a freak can get. Twice the playing field. That's why they're so well-represented in our ranks: it's a survival advantage.

I've been cursed with a straight orientation, and believe me, if I could muster it for a guy, I would. But my limbic map is what it is. You don't control what turns you on: it's passion, not action.

—I'm like, wo, is this like John Wayne Gacy here? He really got into it. *Drooled* all over me, man. But, dude, it was the biggest wad I've ever known. It was righteous. I woke up early from pure excitement.

—Asshole, I said. I'm almost jealous.

—Heh heh.

—Biggest wad ever. Where's *he* been hiding?

—I turn the light on? He's laying there waking up. I'm like, dude, what was *that*?

—I need in on that, Rafe.

—Man, you are not worthy to receive that thing. I didn't catch one percent.

—Fix with a chick next time, okay? Then line her up with me.

—Fixed with a chick last night. Dee-licious! I love 'em skinny.

—You love 'em fat, Rafe.

—I was gonna get her number for ya. Slipped my mind.

—Asshole.

But I'm the same way. We can't be bothered for anything as abstract as mutual benefit. Expecting freaks to set each other up is like expecting a bunch of smackheads to retain a Congressional lobby for the legalization of heroin.

And the few times somebody's passed me a number, she was either out of the house, not in the mood—

Or dead when I got there.

The doorbell rang.

—Remember me? Joan said.

Shit. I'd forgotten I invited her over. I made a perfunctory introduction. I was hoping to hit the streets real soon.

—Pleased to meet you, said Rafe. Hey, I hate to run. I've got some *errands*?

—Maybe we can get together soon and chit-chat, said Joan. I'm trying to solve the mystery.

—We're dying by the boatload, Rafe said. Solve that.

—Anything you can tell me would help.

—It's happening too fast. Faster than two weeks ago, even. Used to be, a freak got in a really bad way? Okay, he might off himself. But not like this. Last week I went to my buddy's place? He's there. Ritually disem*boweled*.

—That's horrible!

—Big long carving knife. He was *not* that far along.

—These days we all have stories like that, I said.

—And I don't think it was because he'd just got a bunch of Japanese feudal history. Know what I'm saying? Are we dying, or are we being killed?

That goosed her right in the reportorial instincts.

—Really. What gives you that idea?

He reflected a bit and concluded: —I dunno.

—Rafe, I said. Too many *X-Files*, man.

—You check it out. I'll see ya.

—Oh, definitely, said Joan. Wow.

—Rafe's full of shit, I said.

—Hey, I won't rule anything out right now. It's early in the process. Which brings me to my pitch, Steve.

—Yeah, what.

—Me Dante, you Virgil.

—I beg your pardon?

—The *Divine Comedy.* Virgil was a classical poet who—

—Yeah, I know. *Dear child of gods, great progeny of Jove!*—the *Fourth Eclogue.* Honey, I've got most of the classics, all of the fourteenth century, the collected Faulkner, and even some Linear B in here, which I admit I don't quite get.

—You get the Faulkner? she quipped.

But don't go thinking my wad is just some cross-section of a musty academic library. The totality of human knowledge is biased toward the mundane. 'Knowledge' is whatever's publicly codified—pulp novels, pop tunes, and movies, not to mention ads, bumperstickers, email, and Web porn. In my head the agricultural treatises of Tull (ca. 1701) bump up against the retrohedonistic lyrics of Beck (2000).

The growing, aching wad of a wonderfreak waves flagellae in *n*-space, trolling for data that fit and connect. If you already have some Sanskrit, it might glom the *Narada Bhakti Sutra* in the original; if you're solid on materials science, it'll snag a passing admonition to *temper cold chisels at 540 F (until the cutting tip glows purple).*

—So, Steve, I want you as my guide and protector through...

—I know. The wonderworld.

I didn't mention that my own *Commedia Divina* was

looking seriously abridged: just the descent into hell.

—I see a Pulitzer in this, she said. We could share it.

—Babe, don't say 'share'. It gets me excited. And what care I for worldly honors? I've blown off school, job, family, love life—my *dog* left, okay? What's in it for me?

—I'm trying to learn how it all started. Looking for the cure.

—Join the club.

—And who and where is McD?

I snorted. —McD's what you call urban folklore. Like 'Kilroy was here'. If he ever did exist, he's dead.

—You sure about that?

I gave her a look. —Babe. We'd *know*. Don't you think?

—Freaks think you know it all, she said. McD is real. And alive.

I greeted this nutty assertion with the same skeptical aplomb that *Simba showed Rafiki* (The Lion King*, 1994) upon hearing that Mufasa might still be around.* But my heart quickened.

No one dared hope that McD was alive. If he were *alive*—

—there might be a way out.

To stop fixing, we needed a cure. To find a cure, we had to stay alive and functioning; that is, we had to keep fixing.

Which was certain death.

Each fix enlarges the wad, ramifies it in *n*-space. Leaving that much more (*n*-1)-dimensional surface aching for completion. The need for new stuff thus grows almost hyperbolically. It takes a while to get going. But once you're near the knee of the curve, it comes suddenly, faster than any drug addiction, even crack. Demand outstrips all possible supply, and things get just nasty over a couple of days.

We don't know much about it. Those who've preceded us weren't terribly forthcoming... in their brief time left.

—I have a few leads, she said. And I have all the resources of an international news organization to bring to bear. I *will* find McD.

—You're ridiculous, but you're my kind of ridiculous. Sure, I'll help.

—That's the spirit.

—Look, I've got a commitment for the next few hours.

—I'm sure you do.

—Meet me at Bobo's at three. By the elliptical exercise machines.

—A gym?

I laughed. —Thought it was all cappuccino and libraries, huh? You *do* need me. You can shadow me through the whole insular and hermetic subculture of freakdom if I get face time with McD.

—Beautiful, she said.

I called my mom in Bellevue and told her I'd be too busy to come out for dinner this Sunday. Again. She was disappointed, but understood: what with all my 'studies' and my 'new job', I just didn't have time. She couldn't really complain—the way I'd turned my life around these past several months, from scruffy professional student to clean-cut, muscled 'high-tech entrepreneur'—why, I just *looked* healthier!

My eighteen-year-old sister lives with her—sharp kid; I'm sure she carries the gene. Last time I was out there, she felt compelled to ask me what I was looking at... twice.

You can't go home again.

4

I'd found Bobo's a couple months back. Excellent female-to-male ratio. Cruising time was during the soaps—phalanxes of aerobicizing young housewives dropped the kids at preschool and moved in. Sure, they could be thirtyish. But if you're that old and a freak and still alive, you're *extremely* buff and hot.

See, you can't just freak with any other freak. You need to find your partner genuinely attractive. The data transmission system is limbic. Before you can share, those limbics have to be lit up.

And so we've adapted: we look like a race of supermodels. Olympian outside, ruins inside. That outrageous mouth look now seeping into the New York fashion mags—high-albedo, layered, fluorescent—evolved in our eco-niche. I've entered those bruisy extravagances, plundered their nectars.

An unusually diverse range of effects—including impaired emotional responsiveness, reduced susceptibility to addiction, and decreased capacity for appropriate social interaction—results when a single brain nucleus, the amygdala, is ablated bilaterally in macaque monkeys.

My freak flag was a T-shirt with UNIVERSITY OF MASSACHUSETTS emblazoned on the front. I was working random weight stations, scoping each exercise class as it let out, a sheen of lust and fear on my glowing physique.

Then I saw her: young, svelte, unleashing an ungodly thick brunette mane, then pulling a maroon UMASS sweatshirt over a bod no sports bra could tame.

Ten seconds ago I was in control. Now the pre-shakes were starting.

I walked right over and busted a move:

—Looks like we went to the same school.

—Uh, yeah, she said. We did.

Something wasn't quite right. But I went on.

—All done pumping iron, I said. Time for pumping *ions*.

—Awww, I get it. I've *known* you, Steve, remember?

Oh, man. That terrible, awful feeling.

—Huh? I said weakly. Am I losing it that bad?

—Sorry, Steve. It's me. Josie.

You can only really freak with someone once. Second time's a letdown; third's a total waste. We don't know why. Even if they've incorporated the whole damn Library of Congress since you've last known them, it won't transfer. Something to do with novelty, a new brain, a fresh perspective.

—Gee, Josie. You're different.

—Well, you too.

—Breast implants, I said. You permed your hair. God, it's great. And what else?

—Well, lost the glasses.

—Lost the glasses. Jesus. Good old stringy-haired, flat-chested Josie. How long ago—three months?

—Very early in both our careers.

—Too early. We should try it again.

—No, Steve.

—It was so long ago. I have so much to give you now. Josie, my wad is huge.

—Steve. That's from hunger.

—Last I checked, hunger's what it's all about.

—I'll take your number. Okay?

—We're looking smug. Aren't we. Ready to lock and load.

—None of your business.

But her smirk spoke louder. —Goddammit, Josie. Your *teeth* are whiter.

—Go check the exercycles, she said.

—You're trying to get rid of me.

Up sauntered a red-haired babe with total-body freckles. Breasts of the perky sort poked at her tank-top. She paled next to Josie—but I could conjure some excitement.

—Hi! Josie said. Steve, this is Candy.

—Oh, man, I said. *She's* your fix?

—These days, why not? said Josie. *There are more things in heaven and earth, Horatio, than are dreamt of in your philosophy.*

—O Wad, I'd like to bind you in a nutshell, said Candy, *and count myself a thing of infinite space.*

Which cracked them up. Me, I was getting less jocular by the second.

Hey, *wait—*

—Forget it, pal, said Candy, reading my face. Three's a crowd.

—Candy, said Josie. Steve knows. He's not a newbie, take my word.

—Oh. You're thinking *me,* Stevie boy? Then two's a crowd.

—Come on, I said. You're hot. I'm hot. Your number, at least.

—I don't do guys, she said, and turned to Josie. —We need a shower.

There is nothing worse in the world, ever, than tasting your fix and having it yanked away.

Freakin' in the girls' room. I shook. Why was it getting this bad so soon? I didn't want to know. I knew.

Jonesing for heroin, I'm told, involves pain, irritability, insomnia, crawling flesh, sweats—bad things that are somehow the very opposites of the neat features that got you hooked.

Jonesing for wonder is the same way.

If you have to ask what's so great about wonder, you'll never know: that deep satisfaction of facts falling into lacunae. The disease, that diabolical contrivance, first invests you with the benign impulse to give. You're full to bursting with good news; you were born to share it. You've got all this luv to give and you go on the prowl.

It's hip to say *lu-uv*, all hot buttered asphalt, like Barry White.

But soon you're aching on your own behalf. You're a convoluted (n-1)-manifold of burning pain. The world turns to shit. What once lovingly connected now won't fit together: the hostile mutual repulsion of facts.

The inverse of wonder is apathy. You don't care about eating, urinary continence, breathing. In the end, the universe is no more than a nightmarish collocation of atoms, congealing at random into things just solid enough to dash hopes. The opposite of eros is death.

Without heroin, a junkie might not feel so good, but without wonder he'll kill himself. Every time.

There was no one. Bobo's was drying up.

As the fifth aerobics class got out, I leaned against the leg press and cursed fate.

—You don't look so hot, said a female voice.

I turned. It was only Joan.

—What we call jonesing, I said.

—What's that like?

—What's that like. I'm roadkill here and she wants to know my feelings. You're early.

—Two o'clock, right?

—I said three. You spying on me?

She looked hurt. —Easy. You said two.

—Okay, I said two. Sorry.

—A momentary lapse of memory, Joan said.

—What are you saying, bitch. You think I'm that far gone?

Because the more you've downloaded, the bigger it gets: your database, your wad. 'The stone.' As in that old Pink Floyd tune (1977): *Dragged down by the stone.* You become like every other *idiot savant* in human history. The growing wad remodels your brain, pushes stuff out your ears.

Stuff like remembering your appointments.

Have a good drown as you go down, all alone.

What does a wad 'look' like? What is its fine structure? Think of a tree, or the tree's root system, or better the mycelial network of a fungus, sprawling and densely interconnected. Best of all would be that mythical fungus supposed by certain crackpots to permeate the Earth's soil, a vast all-penetrating organism threatening to develop its own intelligence, so that if you dissolved away every trace of rock and dirt from its hyphae you'd have a planet-sized shell of filamentous branching life. I sometimes glimpse its overarching shape—the contours, perhaps, of a face, or of its hyperlinked analogue, the soul.

Carrying it around is no joy. The wad is a trash-heap, an accretion of highs gone by. We wanted that fugitive pleasure, nothing more—the galvanic zap, the serene integration—but never the wad, that dead tangle of tracks in the mind's cloud-chamber, spoor of the flown unknown.

The rush is in not content, but coherence. Not integration but *rate* thereof. The wad is pleasure's mere third derivative: the slimy undies heaped on love's chamber's throw-rug.

—*Okay*, Steve, take it easy. Joan laid a steadying hand on my shoulder. —I may have shown early, but you guys are undependable. I was afraid you'd hook up with somebody and go zone out.

—Who, me? I lifted the hand off and gave it back. —As you can see, I have obligingly refrained. At great personal cost.

—Not even her?

She pointed to the exercycles.

An angular black lass, anorexic-trim, pedaled away in mid-Tour-de-France over there. Many of the spinners had books or pads, but only hers was propped vertically on the readout panel. Her hair was up in a bun, and she'd stuck a pencil in it.

Nice touch, that. Stylin' with a stylus.

—Joan, you just saved my sorry ass.

—Well, don't kiss me in gratitude, she said. I like to watch. And what's this U-Mass stuff?

It's an allusion to Nicholson Baker's phone-sex novel *Vox* (1994). Two people making love via oral data exchange. There's a funny but completely unfathomable post-'coital' line on the final page—we like to think it was presciently placed there for us, a decade early:

That was—that was—man, *she said. I saw the great seal of the Commonwealth of Massachusetts when I came.*

5

Funny how it plays with your mind—you've got her in your car, driving to your place, and your limbus is perfectly willing to equivocate on the plan—maybe a fix, maybe just good old-fashioned sex. That vestigial urge. You half-believe you're gonna fuck her brains out.

Nice choice of words.

—Steve.

—Shanté.

—When did you last?

—Lass night, she said offhandedly.

—Jesus. Everybody's gettin' some. It's been twenty-seven hours for me.

—How bad is that?

—A couple weeks ago, no big deal. Now it's bad.

She averted her eyes. Being closer to the end was impolite to mention.

I changed the topic. —You don't know how happy I am, lookin' at you.

—Not as happy as I'm gonna be when you hit me with all that hot monkey lu-uv, she said. You gonna juice me up, baby. I *know* you got a lot.

—Baby oh baby. You got me dizzy. We're doin' it at the red light.

I was thankful Joan wasn't hearing this happy horseshit—she'd gone on ahead. But nothing we do is unselfish. We each had an interest in getting the other worked up, facilitating transmission.

I saw Joan's car parked on the street a couple of buildings away from mine; she was already deployed in my bedroom closet.

Hey, right then I'd've done it at home plate in Yankee

Stadium, okay?

My arm was around Shanté's waist as we walked into the apartment. She was waif-skinny, recalling the slenderness of my long-lost first love: a girl named Heather.

Shanté turned to face me: —Hey. I *been* here.

—With my roomie? I said. Rafe?

I got a you-idiot look. —I din't ketch his *name*.

—Cool. Um, not here, okay? The bedroom.

Where the closet door was slightly ajar. We sat on the bed. Mutual close-range optical inspection. On her face was that earnest look generally given only to yourself, popping your zits in the mirror, deathly solemn.

Damn. She was a goddess; I, a trembling god. This'd be good.

—The bet-room, she said. Ain't *we* romannic.

—Oh but we are.

—Lass night he jes' zap me out there.

—Shut up.

Our lips approximate.

Tongues slide. Heads push maximally close. The brain-cores, the limbics, sense each other through bone and tissue, mutually primed and kindled. Mine, the needier, whips out a scanning field; hers unfurls in response. Two clouds overlap and interpenetrate.

Resonation. Release.

The two-way burst: the mutual transfer of everything, optimally compressed. The white-hot fire of creation, blown faster than light through all channels in massively parallel fashion.

They say it lasts several seconds. It lasts forever. A full-on firehose blast to the head. In it, I discern her every datum in microfractal detail, fine-grained as ground glass.

And she has readied me too, the sweet warm scan seizing and snugging with a whore's concision, and I yield up my precious store, gushing into her as though my will commanded it.

And the big zap segues into the dreamy afterglow.

Going under, I noted that over a certain 400-nanosecond interval I'd received, in alphabetical order, all fifty official state seals cribbed out of some almanac: someone's idea of a joke.

—You should have seen yourself, said Joan, coming out of the closet.

—Get back. She could wake up any minute.

My watch said an hour had passed.

The seven-nucleotide sequence CUUAGGC is usually recognized by Leu-tRNA at CUU, followed by Arg-tRNA at AGG. However, the Arg-tRNA is scarce...

Joan closed the door on herself.

—What did I look like? I whispered.

—Heh, heh. You tried to chew each other's faces off. Then you both just stopped. Slack. Eyes closed, lips locked. Then a string of drool dropped down from somebody. Then you crashed out. All in all, not an activity that lends itself to voyeurism. Do you dream?

—Yes and no.

The loss sets in immediately—nostalgia for what you'll never integrate. You've just had fifty or fifty thousand times more data blasted at you than you can possibly grab. For a fleeting moment you have everything. But it *is* just like retrieving a dream: in saving some, you sacrifice the rest.

Like sperms at an ovum, the data swamp your puny mind, competing for purchase. What sticks? The easy stuff. The stuff with 'hooks.' 'Velcro.' Whatever best connects to what you already have.

At first it overwhelms you, and you sleep. But it goes on past awakening, integrating at deep levels, reaching consciousness only as a mellow satiety, erotic in some root sense. Clarifying every minute. Things take on a friendly electric cast, a sort of imaginary hot-lavender. The very strength of the hydrogen bond is attuned to your own well-being.

It used to last several hours.

You'd think that after consummating our relationship I'd at least have had the decency to take Shanté to dinner. But you're not a freak. What's there to say over a burger and fries after you've given each other the entire contents of your heads?

I couldn't afford it anyway.

It was Joan who took *me* out, on her big expense account. A nice Italian place over towards Ravenna—a mile or so away, and light-years from the Chef Boy-Ar-Dee in my kitchen.

—I could get used to this, I told her, decimating a pile of steamed mussels. —'*This could be the beginning of a beautiful relationship*'.

—Humphrey Bogart.

—I got a million of 'em.

I was riding high now. Subconscious integration was well underway, the new stuff snuggling in, salving the furious wad. The salt and pepper shakers seemed to smile. For a while I'd be fine.

She took the opportunity to get nosy.

—So, she said. What about sex?

—Gosh, Joan. I hardly know you.

—Ha ha. Don't any of these encounters of yours have a conventional climax? You're a red-blooded American boy.

—Oh, this is better than sex. Better than chocolate, even.

—This head-zapping is superior to the deepest intimacy you have ever experienced with another human being?

—Put it that way, I said, and it's too close to call.

Unstoppable, she was. Every guy in ninth grade wanted her.

I didn't stand a chance. Me, a devotee of the disgusting solitary vice: reading. But I saw Heather Greenfield on a beach towel in the park, doing a crossword puzzle, and we connected.

Most guys bored her. I didn't. We shared a restlessness of mind.

We were each other's first.

—*Heather?* said Joan with something like derision—mindful, no doubt, of certain stereotypes *promulgated by the movie* Heathers *(1989). Christian Slater, Winona Ryder.*

—I know, I said. And she was from California, *and* giggled like an airhead. But she was sharp, Joan. The main thing to know about Heather was that she ruined me for every woman after.

—That's about Heather? That's about *you.*

—Hey. For one time in my life it was just pure giving on both sides. I was happier giving than taking.

—You mean pleasure?

—I mean Hostess Sno-Balls, whatever. I'd wake up and ask myself how I was going to make her happy today. Steve did not exist.

—That's nice when you're fifteen, chum.

—Everything since has been contaminated by some—some *motive.* Me trying to get laid, her trying to latch onto somebody—you know.

—How's this for a motive, said Joan: trying to get back what you thought you had with *Heather.*

—But their attempts at love / Were only imitations of / My old flame.

—I don't know that one.

—*Belle of the Nineties.* Mae West, 1934.

—Belle of the nineties. Cute.

The waiter poured us some 2001 Santa Margherita Pinot Grigio—*a richer-than-average exemplar from the Alto Adige, falling short, however, of classic Alsatian crispness and acidity.* I took a sniff: Thunderbird minus sugar.

—Is your libido decreased?

—I'm as libidinous as ever. I do different things with it.

—When was your last actual sex?

—Maybe two weeks ago. But only because it was the first time I had trouble finding a fix. Withdrawal does that. I mean, sex is better than nothing. If a junkie doesn't have smack, he'll fend off the demons with Valium, Dristan, whatever.

—Was she hot, Steve?

—I found myself wishing she'd been better versed in the microshear properties of buckminsterfullerene nanotubes.

Joan shook her head.

—You're a cute guy. Nice, too. What a waste.

—I'm probably too young for you but thanks, I think.

—Oh, I'm *old* now. How'd we get on this?

—I'm guessing thirty-nine.

—Thirty-eight. What's Shanté's full name and address?

—I didn't ask her, but it's probably in here somewhere.

—Steve. *Start.* Somebody out there knows McD. If we get a

lead, we'll need to trace it.

—Why do you think McD's alive?

—I'm not at liberty to say. All my sources get the same protection.

If McD was such a prolific fixer, you'd think traces of him would be stamped all over people's wads. But Inner Thoughts don't transfer. Inner Thoughts are unexpressed personal beliefs and perceptions—the things that make you you. They never stick.

It's easy to see why. You catch the stuff with 'hooks'—intersubjectively verifiable content. Inner Thoughts are slippery.

If you think the President's a pompous ass, I won't catch that. If you've published a letter to the editor expressing that view, I might: now it's a matter of record. It can be seen.

I've got a bunch of driver's licenses and credit card numbers in here, most of them without a context. For all I know, one could be McD.

—Here's what I've heard, Joan. McD has a whopping 9% of all human knowledge: an order of magnitude more than any other freak.

—Really.

—Oh, there's more. McD had 100% of human knowledge and killed himself because there was nothing more to know. And ascended into heaven. And freed himself of his affliction and lives as a normal happy person with a size-1 wad. McD brought this plague onto humanity in fulfillment of Scriptural prophecy. McD lives, but sleeps 24 hours a day; moreover, he died of an exploded head. And oh, yeah: If McD did not exist, it would be necessary to invent him.

I tried the marinated octopus. It got larger in my mouth as I chewed it.

—Let's maybe try the other Big Question, Steve. Any *useful* thoughts on how this all got started?

—Sure. Okay. Look at the time course of this thing. I first got zapped a half a year ago. A year ago, there was hardly anybody. We've put that together—we've shared and figured it out. But it just peters out after we get back to eight or ten people, and no one knows what or who they had in common. Course, now they're all dead.

—Do you know their names?

I gave her a look. —Does the Pope wear a funny hat? Hey, don't *you* have anything on this?

—You're my guide to the underworld, remember?

Yet she had 'sources' on McD. I wondered what else she might be holding back.

—My theory, I said, is that those eight or ten were probably *not* the originals. In fact, the originals may have been way earlier.

—Oh?

—Well, look. My first zap didn't hook me, right? It just activated me. I only started *needing* it after four or five exposures. Which came fairly fast, given the vibrant community of fellow freaks around me. But these eight or ten people a year ago—each of them was operating in a vacuum. In fact, freakdom only took off after they found each other and developed their nascent addictions.

I scarfed another couple forkfuls of *scalloppine alla Milanese* and went on:

—Who knows how long *they'd* been activated? Without knowing it? Remember, my first zap was near-subliminal. And I even had help recognizing it.

—Swallow your food, Steve.

—These eight or ten—the first time they found weird new stuff in their heads, they didn't even know how it got there. *That's* why our history stops with them. *They couldn't share what they didn't know.*

—Brilliant, Holmes. But how'd it *start*?

—A genetic mutation, maybe.

—Then how did it spread? A mutation's only one person.

I scratched my unshaven chin.

—I don't know. This person was somehow endowed with the ability to stir up something dormant in five percent of us. But it took quite a while to get going. Your first freak or freaks were merely activated, *not* hooked—for a long time. So they weren't on the cruise, looking to fix. They were just going about their lives, occasionally smooching in the quaint way of mortals, and only one in twenty smoochees ever got activated in turn.

I watched her face. Was this old news to her?

—That whole scenario is going to take quite a while to get going, Joan. Maybe years.

She was giving me that rapt, first-date, hanging-on-every-word look: you're so fascinating, Steve. It was phony as hell.

—You've thought a lot about this, Steve.

—I haven't, I said, truthfully. But it's there.

6

The next morning Rafe still wasn't back. All-nighters weren't his style. Midmorning was his time, like—

Like mine used to be. But a 24-hour rhythm wasn't cutting it anymore.

Joan was supposed to meet me at ten for a cruise-a-thon. She was smart enough to show at nine-thirty.

—Do you ever change that green shirt?

—You're not my mom. You're not my girlfriend. What do you care?

—It's your third day, Steve. And I do care. I've been thinking.

—Cool. Think in the car.

—No. Listen. Where's your roommate?

—Out fixing. Like all good freaks.

—No, Steve. You don't have to do that anymore.

Jesus—now what.

—I've heard… stories. You can quit cold turkey. You can pull through this.

—That's for druggies, dear. Every freak who's failed to fix has died. Your brain goes sour. Suicide becomes reasonable. Then persuasive.

—But the more you fix, the sooner you start to believe that! Smash through it, Steve. It's been done.

—Where'd you hear this?

—I'm not at liberty to say.

—Then forget it.

—You freaks tend to isolate yourselves. You get all alone and *then* you drive yourselves crazy. Show me a freak who hasn't died alone.

She had a point there.

—The ones who've kicked it have all had a support person. I want to be yours, Steve.

She stood before me, frontally unguarded. Frank gaze, parted lips. Take me. The ghost of Steve, chained and silenced inside, would have been all over her.

Me, I couldn't have cared less.

—Kind of beyond the call of duty, aren't we?

—Steve. This isn't about my job. I... don't want to see you hurt. I don't know.

—Let's hit the streets. Talk later.

—Steve, no.

—This is going faster than I thought, Joan. I need it every day. More than every day.

—Would you rather fix or live?

She wasn't coming on. Who was I kidding? My brain was just doing what it does around now: hankering for connections. Making them where they weren't.

—I know what this is about, Joan. You want to watch me lose it. A nice purple passage in your article. Fuck that shit.

I headed for the car. She followed—tearful? Who cared.

—I'm coming with you, Steve.

—Do what you want.

Normally I'd have stayed in the neighborhood. The Amazon Café, Bobo's, the Darkwood—they'd all been easy pickings before. But the difficulty at the gym yesterday bothered me.

Maybe we'd reached ZWG. Zero wonderfreak growth—dying now as fast as we were being born. Maybe faster.

It was time to go to Mecca: the Unreliable Narrator, an indie-bookstore-cum-coffeehouse up on Capitol Hill. Better known as the U.N. The world crossroads of freakdom. Mainly mortals, like anywhere, but for us it's holy ground: the original freaks hung out there, and ever since it's been one scene you can count on.

And today I wasn't dicking around. Joan found a table and I went to get the coffee.

No sooner had I taken a barstool than I found myself face-to-face with a smiling, bleach-blonde wet-dream. A hot-pink leopard-print microdress clung to her frame by a couple of spaghetti straps, stopping high above knee-length leather boots. A button over her left breast said SEATTLE WEB GRRRLS.

—You're in my seat, she said.

—Sorry. Here.

—Relax, studmuffin. Maybe your seat and my seat should meet.

She beamed at her own witticism.

—Really, I said. Well, whaddaya know.

—More than you've ever dreamed.

—You a freak, then?

—Oh yeah.

—A wonderfreak?

—A what?

I gave her cheek a friendly pinch. —Forget it.

Back at the table, mochas in hand, Joan and I scanned the room.

Three hours later: still scanning.

The lunch crowd, a gaggle of mortals, was tapering off. Things had taken on the faintest orange-y cast, the hue of an electric stove burner on high: the ominous *VISUAL DISTURBANCES. The tetrad of (1) 'infrared'-tinted visual field, (2) tunnel vision, (3) vertical nystagmus, and, in advanced stages, (4) lexical slips ('typos') is pathognomonic of the withdrawal syndrome, the first an apparent correlate of the faint ultraviolet cast reported during integration phase.*

I knew that.

But I might not have put it that way.

And as far as I was concerned there was nothing *CONFIDENTIAL* about it.

This was written up somewhere. Some freak out there was carrying around the Real Story.

At the moment, I didn't give a shit.

—This sucks, I said. I've got to find somebody.

—It's a sign, Steve. You have to quit. Come back with me.

Sir Mix-a-Lot recorded "I Want a Freak" for Nastymix Records in 1988, but the lyrics are not germane.

I found myself saying: —Yeah, maybe.

It was happening twice as fast as yesterday.

On the way back we pulled up behind a car festooned with streamers. In cursive shaving cream on the rear windshield, under a blue-orange sky, was the legend *Just Maimed.*

I'd never been this far before.

—What do you suppose McD stands for? Joan asked idly.

—Got me.

McDuck, Scrooge. McDivitt, James A. McDonald's.

OVER 100 BILLION SERVED.

—Who fucking cares, I said.

—We're just going to stay here and get you through this, Steve. I'm not going to let you hurt yourself.

—Try and stop me.

—Think about a happier time.

—I won't dignify that silly-ass idea with a response of any kind.

—Think about *Heather.*

—Fuck you.

But what the hell—I wasn't going anywhere.

I treasured her every last stupid Heather-ism: I'm like, *as if.* Famous last *words.* I don't *think* so. Leavened with the odd French loan-phrase: she'd call us 'our *folie à deux.*'

Well, after the *folie* subsides there's always one of the *deux* who wants to keep going, and that was me. We'd melded, obliterated the mucosal boundaries, and when of course she had to move on, to new and different fun, I tore and bled raw. My missing puzzle-piece.

One night not long before the end, we lay under the stars. A providentially clear Indian-summer night in the mountains. My folks thought I was at an all-night cram session for the high-school Academic Decathlon.

—What's it like when you come?

—Gee, Steve. Weren't you paying attention?

—Tell me how it feels. A girl orgasm.

— Sorry! I'll need, like, a reminder, *nudge nudge wink wink.*

—Come on, Heather.

—You are weird. *It's like, you know. Like* yours, *silly.*

I adduced various anatomical reasons why this could not possibly be the case.

—Deep inside we're all the same, she said.

—We're not. Here you are right next to me, Heather. And I'll never know.

—Some people might say so what.

The crickets chirped a thousand times. Eventually I said:

—Interstellar space.

—Huh?

—That's us. Stars. Burning brightly. And out there all around us are other stars. We think we get it. We think we can go there someday. But in the end there'll always be huge gulfs of space. Cutting us off. All I can do is... admire you.

I flashed, now, as I couldn't then, on Dante's sequel to Homer at *Inferno,* Canto XXVI (Pinsky translation, 1995). Ulysses' soul, a voice enclosed in flame, tells how he urged his men, now *old and slow,* to sail one final voyage clear *behind the Sun: So little is the vigil we see remain / Still for our senses, that you should not choose / To deny it the experience...*

And thereby met his end, *as pleased an Other.*

—Geez, said Heather. She yawned. If you go to a star, you'll just get burned up, you know.

—We're not going to last, Heather. Are we.

—Shhh. Steve.

—All I see is your old light.

Later I'd catch glimpses: Heather in a deep groove at some frat party, shroomed out of her mind; Heather and some guy cracking up at the Slurpee machine in the Seven-Eleven. Always in mid-vignette, waving 'hi.' Always a snip from the trailer for 'The Heather Greenfield Story.' Soon to be a major biopic; Al Tennyson, screenplay.

She tried all the drugs, tried everything, jetted off to this or that exotic locale with the guy-of-the-month. On him. *I cannot rest from travel; I will drink / Life to the lees.* Because she could.

—I got news for you, Steve. You never loved Heather. You loved her hunger, her never being done. And looky here. You got what you wanted.

—It worked for a minute, Joan. I felt better. Then you

started talking.

—She dumped you, pal.

—She said we were too young to get married.

—Weren't you?

—She preferred to remember it as wonderful, which it was, rather than let it slide into some routine. The end of that road was to wind up like her mom and dad, and did we want that? Sleeping in separate beds? Cheating? Throwing chairs at each other? You married, Joan?

—Married to my job.

—The girl understood me, Joan. A basic human need.

—A selfish little shit.

I tried arranging my arms different ways. Shaking again. —I think she wound up in Maui, or Bali, or something. Some paradise I know I'll never see.

—You're a melancholy sort, Steve. I'm not surprised you sought solace in addictive behavior.

—You're my *support* person? I'm going out.

I had a plan. At this depth, what you did was hit some club full of largely hideous mortals and speed-hustle any of the few pretty, intelligent-looking women to the point of kissability, one after another, ducking punches from the inevitable boyfriends, until *maybe* you lucked onto a protofreak, a one-in-twenty, which got you a half-assed zap from her size-1 wad and maybe an hour's reprieve, or maybe a night in jail.

—Steve, you'll do nothing of the sort.

—What are you, my dorm boss? *I'm reaching critical mass.*

Her eyes narrowed: —You're what?

Bewildered, I repeated: —Reaching... critical... mass?

My wad! It's approaching critical mass!

Like hell. My fucking wad was disintegrating before my eyes.

Yet I'd just thought the opposite, with the utmost conviction.

—I'm cracking up now, I said. This is what happens.

Or *the thought was someone else's.*

If so, it would be the first wad-fragment in history with an implicit personal pronoun.

An *Inner* Thought.

HIGHLY CONFIDENTIAL. To: PHC-9037 Distribution

List. (Crisis Response)

Joan in my face: —What's got critical mass, Steve? Your *wad*?

—I don't know, Joan. I don't know what that means. But you seem to.

Critical mass. Meaning: big enough for something. But what?

Think. Think. Clearly, something that can send across an Inner Thought and make it stick.

But no wad's *ever* big enough. No freak thinks like that. Unless it's uniquely humongous.

Legendary.

There's an easy way out. You're looking for it. 7734 Pilkington Ave N.

Holy shit! I didn't know the address, but the map in my head put 7734 Pilkington Ave N square over in Green Lake.

—Don't play games, Steve. You're in a bad way.

—Okay, Joan. I'll tell you. I'm getting little pieces of what look like memos. Now help me.

—Memos.

—These little memo fragments. Top secret. Some freak has seen them. They describe my visual symptoms to a T. This whole deal is on file with the CIA or something. Right?

—The CIA? Not that I've heard.

—Oh, it definitely is.

—Talk about that.

—You talk. Why so tense, Joan?

—What about *you*? You keep looking at my hand.

—Your wrist, actually.

—Slender, attractive? What.

—Your pulse. Way up.

—New leads excite me, Steve. Among other things.

—We flirting now, Joan?

The function of courtship is to provide releaser stimuli for the mating instinct, which at the same time block hunger drives.

—We're fucking, Steve.

She was on me, smothering in a way that would do a freak proud. *Copulation is a hazardous and frequently fatal undertaking for the male. The female's predatory instincts are inhibited only briefly, as she* trickled energy at me in the pathetic manner of normal humans. *The inner face of the tarsus contains a syringe-like structure into which spermatic fluid must be transferred, prior to copulation, over as long as three to four hours.* All accompanied by no-doubt-well-rehearsed blandishments: 'Pure giving? Take this.' 'I'll show you a freak.' *Copulation, which consists of inserting the highly modified terminal joint of the first pair of legs ('pedipalps,' unique to this order) into the female genital orifice,* was easier than I thought; *the chelicerae may be held in special postures which may involve the spreading apart of the paturons and/or extending the fangs downward from the paturons.* Like a strung-out smackhead I was closer to mechanical readiness than I realized, my sick brain doing what it could to connect. *The male performs various tapping, scraping, and stroking movements with legs and palps on the female's abdomen,* but I can't say my heart was in it. *She opens her fangs and the male catches them with the hooks on his front legs. He then forcibly pushes back the cephalothorax of the female, at the same time drumming on her sternum with the patellas of his pedipalps.*

During copulation the palps are inserted simultaneously and the two spiders stroke and caress each other with their forelegs.

It bought me a half-hour. But the whole time I'd felt my limbics trying and failing to engage, up against a mortal's brute wall. Like a woodpecker, bashing out its brains on downtown concrete—and jonesing for a tree, full of treasured grubby life.

7

Joan seemed to think I was having trouble putting my clothes on. So she helped.

I still felt like shit. What I needed was at 7734 Pilkington Ave N.

—*Now* I'm going out.

—Steve. Didn't that help?

—A little.

—Stay here and tough it out.

—I'm going.

She got in front of me.

—You can't drive, she said. It's not safe.

—*Out of my way,* Joan.

—No.

Her stance was balanced, relaxed but alert; feet the least bit pigeon-toed; knees slightly bent. An aikido readiness stance.

My brain knew all the moves. My muscles didn't know shit.

—You're not going anywhere, Steve.

Now this was intimacy: Joan revealing herself as the enemy.

—House arrest. Is that it?

—It's for your own good. Don't you want this over?

—Okay, Joan, check this out. I have McD's address. We'll go there.

—Bullshit.

—It surfaced in a wad-fragment. Shanté's, probably.

—Then what's McD's name? she said warily.

—I didn't get a name. But it had to be him: I got an Inner Thought. You know about Inner Thoughts, Joan?

If she understood the momentousness, she didn't show it. All she said was:

—What's the address?

—Oh no. You'll see when we get there.

—You don't seem to trust me all of a sudden, Steve. After what we've shared?

—We didn't share. We screwed.

She didn't like that very much.

—Sorry, Okay? I'm not myself. Go ahead. You can drive me.

She helped me on with my jacket and said: —See, chivalry is not dead.

Carnage House. SPIROCHETES. The secret truths of the street, its hotels and haircut emporia, flashed through the darkening world as we rolled through town. Over 100 Billion Severed.

Green Lake wasn't a freak part of town, nor was 7734 Pilkington N a freakish-looking place. Freaks lived in apartments on down. This was a small, well-kept detached home.

It was about 10 P.M. I rang the doorbell. Joan stood behind me off to the side.

—Trick or treat, I muttered.

Peeking out the window was an average-looking geek—a mortal, by all odds. Possible Microserf. The porch light came on.

He opened the door and I said:

—McD?

He glanced briefly at me, but he only had eyes for Joan. Joan was equally googly. And not in a pleasant way.

—Why, *Norm*, she said.

—Joan. What are you doing here?

—Steve, you sure this is the place?

—This is it, I said.

—Well, that's very interesting, Norm. Because wonderboy here seems to've sniffed you out as a fellow *freak* and in fact the fabled *McD*. Steve, if you'll excuse us? Norm and I need to talk alone.

The consternation on Norm's face passed, and he smiled.

—No, Joan. I *am* McD. Come on in, both of you.

—Praise Jesus, I said.

Joan shot him a look: fool, what are you doing.

—It's all *right*, Joan. Everything's going to be all right. I mean *everything*. Come in, sit down, let me take your coats! I'll explain.

I said that was an excellent idea.

The three of us sat around a coffee table amid the Ikean stylings of Norm's living room: a surreal kaffeeklatsch.

—Steve, I'm a scientist at a company that does drug development and marketing. Pharmcorp. We make glyglitazone, the new antidiabetic? *Cool it*, Joan; as of tonight the problem is solved. He gestured at her: —My boss.

Norm's boss was over there looking very tense.

—See, Steve, six years ago Pharmcorp developed a new compound that showed some promise as a 'study aid'. It tested effective in rats and monkeys—with no side effects. So we started human trials in a small group of volunteers.

—Norm?

—Joan. Would I be doing this if *everything weren't all right*? I have the answer! I'm working directly with the Board on this.

—The Board would have informed me, Norm.

—I think the Board is content right now to have you continue what you are doing, *without* distractions. *Precisely* because you're doing it so well.

Whatever that meant, it shut her up.

—Anyway, Steve. The human trials didn't go so smoothly. The stuff wasn't as effective, and the FDA rejected our next-phase application. Which was just as well. Because about five percent of our subjects—four of them—eventually developed a side effect with which I see you are very familiar. At Pharmcorp we call them the 'Freak Brothers.'

Phineas, Franklin, Fat Freddy: there were only three Fabulous Furry Freak Brothers.

—I'm gonna puke, I said.

He considerately passed me a spread-open newspaper. —We know now that the stuff unexpectedly lysed cells in a certain very specific subsystem of the brain.

I ralphed, or tried to. I hadn't eaten much. Dry heaves and a lot of drool.

—Remember those kids who ate some bad Esctasy in the '80's and then came down with Parkinsonism? Highly selective neuronal destruction. Same sort of thing.

1-methyl-4-phenyl-1,2,3,6-tetrahydropyridine, but I was in no mood to say so. I wiped my mouth on my sleeve: —You said it didn't hurt rats and monkeys.

—Good *point,* Steve. Gosh, you want a job? Heh heh. Rats and monkeys don't happen to possess this particular brain subsystem.

—The cure, Norm? said Joan. And it better be good.

Norm fiddled with his pencil.

—First, my embarrassing confession. I was a freak, Joan.

At length Joan noticed herself bugging out and closed her mouth. —Gee, Norm. Do go on.

—Ever since we tested the first subjects. Yeah—I sampled some.

I said: —You... *were...* a freak?

—Yes, Steve. I'm cured. I can't tell you what I had, but I hear it was... pretty big.

He turned to Joan.

—You know, our company really missed an opportunity. To

this day, we're the only ones on Earth who know the deal. And what do we do? Circle the wagons! We don't give a rat's ass for them. Oh, we're real big on *identifying* them—

—We *are* working with them, Joan said tightly.

—Not in a terribly sympathetic manner.

—*Shut up*, Norm.

—Excuse me, I said. I know I haven't been keeping up my end of the conversation: Norm, you're *not hooked* now?

—Come and look.

I understood. I labored to my feet and went to him, close enough to inspect the portals to his soul. Anyone who's freaked even once has irises that micro-twitch constantly, a characteristic sub-millimeter flutter.

His were rock-steady.

—Help me, I said, falling to my knees. Help me, McD.

—Take it easy, Norm said. You're gonna be all right. We owe these people, Joan. We fucked them up.

—Norm, you're preaching to the choir.

—Bullshit.

—I get it now, she said. Your on-the-job performance was dipping. Irregular hours, absences... I figured you had a new squeeze.

—That's all over now, Joan. It's *all* all over. As of tomorrow, no more innocent victims. The Board will meet with the entire project team and announce my discovery. The antidote.

—Got some on ya? I said.

—It's in a vault at the lab, Steve. I have to reconstitute it. You know, Joan, our friend here's not looking so good. You'd better let him do what he has to do tonight. Then bring him to the lab tomorrow—say eight. We can dose him right there in front of the team. It'll be a regular dog-and-pony show. And we can all wake up from this nightmare.

—Count me in, I said. I started to fold Norm's messed-up newspaper. It was today's *Seattle Times*, the newly-revived evening edition. *The recent rash of deaths in and around the University of Washington community is drawing added police scrutiny in the wake of two more apparent suicides last night.* A female, 22, OD'd on antidepressants. A male, 23, blew his brains out in an alleyway. Their names were Josie and Rafe.

8

The world falling apart: a jittering, closed-in place glowing like embers. I never should have tried in this ridiculous universe.

—Well, said Joan grimly, that's good news.

—Drop me off anyplace.

—I have to get my *car*, she said.

—Oh. Right.

I was not thinking clearly at that point. Or else Norm's peculiar way of saying goodbye had made me a little nervous.

He'd brought me my jacket, which felt suddenly heavy—a perceptual distortion, no doubt. He'd taken my hand in both of his and looked into my eyes and said meaningfully: —Take care of yourself.

Something new and hard and lumpy was in the pocket: a webphone.

—Shhhh, he'd whispered.

In the car, I'd stuck hand in pocket and appreciated that the phone possessed a grip, a barrel and a trigger.

Around it was curled a piece of paper, which I now extracted and perused in the passing streetlights.

Hastily-scrawled. —*WANTS TO KILL YOU.*

Wait a sec. *KISS YOU.*

No.

SHE'S EVIL. SHE WANTS TO KILL YOU. I can Help!! *Be back here in ONE HOUR. Be ALONE. Whatever you do DON'T FIX!!*

Hey, no prob, Norm.

P.S.: It's a Glock 42. Just aim and fire.

—What's that? Joan said.

I folded the note. —Freak club. Where the creatures meet.

—*She lives on Love Street...* The Doors, right?

—Jim Morrison is Mr. Mojo Risin', scrambled.

—I didn't know that.

I'd never fondled a firearm in my life, but I knew there was a lot to it. Hammers to cock, little safety levers, *their gear and tackle and trim.* If you didn't know that shit, you had no business playing with guns. I didn't even know where the fucking safety was.

On the other hand, *with the exception of the fully-automatic Glock 18, Glock, Inc. (Smyrna, GA), manufactures exclusively 'safe-action' semiautomatic handguns.* Which, by definition, *have no frame-mounted external safety—nor a manually-operated hammer,* if I wasn't mistaken... and I knew I wasn't.

Just aim and fire. Surely it wouldn't come to that.

We rode in silence, Joan tapping on the wheel.

—I haven't been completely honest with you, she said finally.

—Nope.

—Can I come in? I need to talk about it.

—Some other time, Joan.

—I won't take long. I feel terrible about this.

—I need to fix.

—And I think I left my pager in there.

Of course. I took my time getting my key in the door. She guided my hand.

—I won't have you driving, Steve.

—You're right. We'll order out.

—I didn't think you'd help me if I presented it as an internal company matter.

—Not so internal.

—Norm's a bit high-handed about this, don't you think? It wasn't our fault. We test a compound. It's ineffective and the subjects are lost to follow-up. Years later, other people get sick—who could make the connection?

—He seems to think you could have prevented some deaths.

—When we realized there was a problem, we focused on a cure. So we needed to understand exactly how the drug was acting. We embarked on a crash research program.

—None of which you bothered to mention.

—Steve, you're entitled to a full explanation.

She took a pad out of her purse, snapped it open, and punched something up.

—I think this says it best.

Executive Summary. HIGHLY CONFIDENTIAL. To: PHC-9037 Distribution List. (Crisis Response)

Re: Proxipathic Dependency Syndrome (PDS): Background and Context #3.

—I'm blanking. Can't read this shit.
—'Proxipathy'? Close-up telepathy. From—
—No. You read.
—Poor baby.
She began:

The crucial role of social development in the evolution of primate intelligence was first noted by Darwin in The Descent of Man…

—Cut to the chase, I said.

... Recent studies (reviewed in Patton and Spruance, 2007) provide decisive support for the hypothesis that certain higher-primate behaviors classically categorized as either instinctual or observationally learned are in fact acquired proxipathically. Capuchin monkeys raised in a communal enclosure but denied < 1 m proximity to other group members compared poorly to controls in a variety of cognitive- and performance-based tasks (Ossman et al., 2005); information relevant to such skills is now known to be transferred by a process requiring cranial proximity (Drayton and Ridenhour, 2006) of 'source' and 'destination' subjects.

While thought to be both common and necessary for normal development in the great apes and certain other primates, proxipathic transmission in man was limited to anecdotal reports in the paranormal literature until very recently (Pharmcorp, internal); however, remnants of the relevant neural circuitry are indeed present in man (Pharmcorp, internal).

In addition, neuroanatomical studies (Pharmcorp, internal) indicate the existence of an inhibitory subsystem—unique to Homo sapiens*—whose purpose appears to be* suppression *of the proxipathic faculty.*

—'Neuroanatomical studies'?
—Quiet:

The adaptive significance of this inhibitory subsystem is highly speculative, but it is suggested that proxipathy became maladaptive with the advent of representational speech and language ability in hominids; the vast amount of information newly available via symbolic representation would have poured through the proxipathic floodgates in such volume and with such intensity that affected individuals, for various reasons, would not have survived to reproduce—just as is currently the case with PDS-susceptible individuals. The inhibitory subsystem, then, probably evolved pari passu *with language skills.*

As with any trait deprived of adaptive value, the proxipathic faculty has fallen victim to random spontaneous mutations and is now probably non-functional in the majority of the human population. However, it appears to remain anatomically intact, beneath its inhibitory overlay, in roughly five percent of a sample of the population of Seattle (Pharmcorp, internal).

The mechanism of PHC-9037-induced destruction of inhibitory neurons is well-characterized....

—Gee, I said. You guys have really done a great job on this.

—I can't believe Norm thought I'd fall for it. There's no way he's McD.

—He isn't?

—He's much too high-functioning. He's kept his *job*, didn't he? You and your sub-McD-size wad haven't even done that.

—But you didn't call him on it.

—I'm playing along. He's up to something. This was a desperation move. He must have thought it up on the spot when he saw me and you at his door. I'm beginning to get it.

—You know who McD is anyway, I ventured. You've known all along.

—All right, Steve, I've had a pretty good idea. Because a wad that size must have been active from the very beginning. But the first several generations of wonderfreaks are all dead—with one possible exception. One of the four original Freak Brothers has never been located. And now we have your 'evidence' that McD *is* alive and... transmitting.

—You just needed me to find him for you.

—Gosh, Steve, I hope that's not what keeps us together. Because *you* can't seem to find her either.

—Her?

I've got so much to give you...

—We've learned a lot more about these brain subsystems now. If we don't find McD some real bad juju could happen. Think about it, Steve. You yourself are starting to receive McD's Inner Thoughts.

Steve... sweetie...

—Her name's Heather, okay? Heather Greenfield. Now do you or do you not know where she is?

I want only you.

—I don't, I moaned. I haven't seen her in years. What are you gonna do to her? How'd you learn so much about our 'brain subsystems', anyway? From operating on dead wonderfreaks? Or live ones! Heather!

—I believe you, Steve. I truly believe you don't know where McD is. You're of no further help.

—You're killing us!

—Steve, that's not true. By and large you people are perfectly happy to do that all by yourselves. Not that we're above nudging.

She took a blue object from her purse. It was a Playtex dishwashing glove. She put one on, then another.

—Corporate damage control, huh? You chickenshits!

—Oh, it's not just a PR problem, she said. She dug into the purse and came out with a pistol of her own. —Unless we exterminate every active wonderfreak on earth, there *will be* a catastrophe of Biblical proportions.

She dandled the gun in her hand, not aiming.

—It's been a lot of legwork. But we're finally gaining on you.

—You're crazy! Wh-why not just let it spread? We'll kill ourselves if you let us!

—Because we can't have any more McD's. *One* is unthinkable.

—What the hell is a McD?

—I don't have time for this, Steve. You just offered to kill yourself; I'm taking you up on it.

She still wasn't aiming.

—You can do it by your own hand—or it can look that way. Either way, you were just another freak who couldn't cut the mustard.

My hand slithered into my jacket pocket.

—Cute, Steve. I dressed you myself—remember? Your pocket's empty.

Just aim and fire.

I failed to account for this silly little thing called recoil. The gun damn near kicked out of my hand. Ears ringing, I fumbled for a second shot, panicked that I'd missed altogether—but fortunately Joan was inspecting her left shoulder with more than casual interest.

I'd gone for a gut shot, but I could work with that.

By the time she looked back up at me—betrayed and deeply hurt, it appeared—I'd clambered to my feet like some old geezer and used my firearm in a more responsible manner—I coldcocked her with the gun-butt.

I was much more considerate than she would have been. After I'd tied her up I wrapped a compression dressing around the wound in her shoulder. I relieved her of her pistol and lit out for Norm's place.

9

On the way there, a building with particularly bad *feng shui* interposed itself between my destination and my car, almost totaling the latter. The thing still ran, fitfully, and I pressed on.

I swear to God, I'd've stopped and smooched the first functioning female vertebrate I saw—but I wasn't seeing so good.

Joan's memo: it figured. Animals that mentally masturbated tended to get eaten. But language changed that. Language opened up a huge conceptual space.

The physical realization of this space was the human neocortical apparatus for symbolizing, prioritizing, reasoning: the gray convolutions, the white slabs thick with connections. The *mental* realization was a gigantic vacuum, in which something needed to happen.

Animals don't need laughter, or love, or awe at the starry sky. But humans live and die by these inventions. Which are not just inventions: they're *us.*

Language begat wonder.

And wonder had turned against us. Proxipathy had emerged full-blown in a talking, thinking species. The synergistic fix was in, potent and forbidden.

Starry-eyed awe was destroying us.

Norm opened the door: —Did you fix?

Then he got a good look.

—Outstanding, he said.

—She tried to kill me. I tied her up.

—I couldn't tell you the truth with her around.

—If the truth is that you're not McD, she's guessed.

—Come in.

I followed him down a hall.

—I'm guessing you were never a freak either.

—Nope.

Down some stairs.

—But the cure.

He turned around. —Depends on you, Steve.

We walked through a basement hallway.

—Joan thinks McD is somebody else, I said. This girl named Heather.

—No shit.

—I used to know her. Long time ago.

Norm opened a door. —Well, you should see her now.

A *sanctum sanctorum.* A soft-glowing bank of monitors, flickering like candles. Punctuating the quiet, the periodic *hisssss* of a respirator. Its corrugated plastic tubing trailed over to a hospital bed, on whose inflatable mattress, radiant in repose, lay Heather.

—McD lives, said Norm.

The world went ultraviolet with hope.

Her eyes were closed. Beatific. The unperturbed beating of her heart sepatinated the fabric of her gown there.

Sepatinate is not a word.

—The last thing to go is the respiratory centers, Norm said. That was three days ago. She's maxed out.

He was a distant yammering. The white-hot girl in front of

me was the center of my collapsing universe.

—She... she hasn't fixed in three days? She's in agony! She needs it right away!

—So do you, Steve.

Her lips were full, glossy, parted: he'd done a fine job on her makeup. Flooding through me was that oh-so-special, this-better-be-irrevocable relief: a sure fix in my sights.

—I—I'm trying to quit, I mumbled.

Norm laughed.

—I still adore her, Steve. Six years ago she answered our ad in the student paper and volunteered for the study. It was love at first sight. We had a wonderful year together.

—That must be a record.

—So vibrant, so positive... the world needs more of that. She broke my heart, of course.

—She does that.

—I couldn't get her out of my head, said Norm. Yeah, I was a mess for a while. Then early this year I ran into her again—now *she* was in a bad way. Freaking and jonesing. I took her under my wing. She was incapable of love at that point, just like you are now, Steve. But she needed me. For a change *she* needed *me*. Pathetic and sick and I loved her no matter what.

—Did you even know? About freaks?

—That was how we found out. Heather educated me. I had to get us working on a cure. I kept her name out of it—wisely, as it turned out. Sure enough—do I know these assholes?—they started chasing freaks down. Interrogating them, experimenting, sometimes leaving them in the street to die of withdrawal. And sometimes doing post-mortems. I took Heather completely out of circulation. I'd stash her in some motel and pick up freaks and bring them in. When she started losing motor control, I'd bring 'em here. Blindfolded if I had to—you guys don't care. By then her wad was attracting attention. I'd turn the lights off, let 'em think it was me...

He went on. He saw that the best tool for solving Heather's dilemma was Heather herself, her tumid organ of synthesis. To the library of scientific journals in her head he added Pharmcorp's clandestine research, everything they had. She wanted to live; he refused to let her die.

Her eclipsing brain came up with this: the fixing wasn't coming fast *enough*. What looked like a downward addictive spiral was more a fetal craving for nutrients, not to be denied even at Mom's expense. This was a growth process, with a defined ripening and end. *The force that through the green fuse drives the flower.* Holding it *back* was lethal.

Repeated doses of PHC-9037, courtesy of Norm, stripped away that inhibitory circuit completely, vastly improving her reception. She far outdistanced every other freak.

—Then what's the endpoint, Norm? All human knowledge?

—No. There's too much of that now for any one brain. The endpoint is cerebral capacity. It's done when the brain is completely occupied. And now it's ready to cut loose—which is where you come in, Steve.

—I don't think so, man.

—It's whole now: the world's only full-grown wad. It's no longer tethered to the particulars of Heather. We hope and expect it will leave her completely and pass... to you, probably all at once, with perfect fidelity. And I'll have my Heather back.

—That'll kill me.

He chuckled. —Not necessarily. It might just leave you a vegetable. I messed her up, and now I'm gonna set things right. Making me the only socially responsible employee at Pharmcorp.

—You never did have a cure, did you. No stuff in your lab.

—Sorry, bud. That was just to placate Joan. Till I got you here alone.

Shouting down at me from the alpine fastnesses of my highest neocortical centers, the faintest voice of self-preservation was doing its best to reach me down there in Death Valley.

It was all I could do not to fall on her.

—No fucking way, I said, trying out the words.

Norm laughed again. —Just trigger her. Kiss her for one second and then move out of the way, heh heh.

—Right, Norm. Pull out between the second and third squirts.

—For God's sake, *I'll* pull you off her. Steve, you're going to do it!

I moved to the wreckage of Heather, laid shaking hands on her cool shoulders—first touch in ten years. An ancient Eden blazed and died.

—There's a tube in the way, I said lamely. It was the last excuse I could think of.

—Oh, God, *no.*

Come on, Norm, I thought, not even I buy that one. But it was something else: he was scanning the ceiling, alert.

—Somebody's here, he said.

Abstractedly, I caressed Heather's cheek.

—I didn't hear anything, I said.

—You left your car out front, didn't you? Idiot? You said you tied her up!

—I'm kind of a fuckup lately, I explained.

Whispering floorboards now: footfalls from above.

—She saw the light, said Norm, pointing to the wall opposite the door. There was a small, grimy transom at ceiling level, the only glass in the room, with a fateful half-inch gap in the curtain. —Looked in the fucking window already. *Damn.*

He crossed to the door, closed it, threw the deadbolts.

Ten seconds later Joan rattled the knob.

—Steve! I know you're there! What's going on?

—Male bonding, I said. You wouldn't understand.

The door shook on its locks, hard.

—Go away, Norm said.

—Steve! Listen to me! Don't do anything. *Don't touch her,* for God's sake!

—Do it, man, said Norm. She asked for *you.*

—Steve, goddammit! The fate of the human race depends on this!

Christ, Joan. You really will tell anybody anything.

A loud BAM at the door. I jumped about a foot.

—Kiss her and you're a dead man! she screamed.

Another BAM, and another. She was trying to kick the door in: considered, well-launched blows, three or four seconds apart, aimed right at the doorknob.

—Can she do that? I said.

—It's pretty solid. I think.

—Would she have another gun?

—She'd have used it... Hey, *wait.*

He came over, fished his own piece out of my blown-out pocket, and examined it: the gun looked different, extended.

—The slide hung up on your jacket lining, he said. You fired from inside your *pocket*? How the hell did you aim?

He worked the slide back into place, aimed the gun at the door, and pulled the trigger. Nothing. He cursed, popped the clip out and back in.

—Plug your ears.

This time he put a couple of bullets through the door, right at heart level.

No scream, no thud, nothing.

Deathly quiet. *Hisssssssss.* Quiet.

—Steve, Norm said softly. You and I. We both loved her. Please.

The arm. It stirred; it rose, zombie-like, from the bed. Its hand clapped me on the bicep, held a second, slid off.

Heather's eyes tried to open.

Then they stopped.

Suddenly there came a tapping—at the transom.

We looked and it shattered in, showering glass on the consoles and floor. A squarish bottle of—apple juice?—nuzzled partway through the curtain and just hung there, absurdly, as though proffered by an anonymous sommelier. Tunnel vision notwithstanding, I saw a happy red cow head printed on the glass: a common milk bottle. From outside Joan said:

—Special delivery, assholes.

She flipped the thing into the room. It trailed a small bright orange arc and popped on the floor, whereupon Norm, the monitors, and one entire wall simply vanished in rolling billowing flames.

I moved away, my whole left side about to burst reciprocally ablaze. But Heather, so far, was unscathed. Luminous, luscious. The light at the end of the tunnel.

Kiss her and you're a dead man.

Goddammit, I was dead already.

—Fuck you all! I yelled, a wordless moan.

I pulled the tube. Ropy spit dangled, refracting firelight. Alarms blared and shrieked. The word DISCONTENT flashed, urgent, red.

DISCONNECT, rather.

A humanoid wad of fire broke from the mass of flame and tumbled, slamming the opposite wall. So much for pulling me off, Norm.

I pitched the tube aside and fed.

From infinite distance at infinite speed, the lambent edge of the new hurtled at me, different in degree and kind—the feathery rushing precursor of something brilliant, massive, dappled.

Yet all experience is an arch wherethro' / Gleams that untravell'd world.

My one second was up.

Teeth cut my lips. I wondered what was the harm in staying for one second more—I couldn't come up with an answer, not for the life of me.

THE END

So we're both just standing *there in the living room. Which is like* really warm?

I giggle. She giggles back.

"Made it. Wow."

"Sure did," Heather says.

"Your lipstick's a mess. *I am so totally not kidding."*

"You should see you,*" she smiles.*

I mean *that. Her mouth doesn't form the words or anything. She just...* smiles.

I raise fingers to my lips. They come away smeared with the same colors.

"Well, Steve always wanted to be like—"

"Us," Heather says.

"Hee hee."

In the mirror I am *Steve. I mean, rugby shirt, brown slacks, et cetera et cetera. I wave at the guy.*

Steve waves back, grinning. Just like I remember him.

"Well," I go, "I'm up for anything."

And we look at each other, me and my first love.

"Let's get married," I say.

"That's kind of de trop, *isn't it?"*

And I'm, like, giggling again. Everything is so funny!

But then we get serious. Cuz we have an idea?

"Après vous," *Heather says. "You're the guy."*

"Avec plaisir, mon chèrie."

I walk outside and just stand in the front yard. Behind me, the whole rear of the house is blazing. The warmth is nice.

Aha. Sure enough. There's that evil gal running to her car, all lit up orange. The little sneak was watching behind a bush. Had to make sure.

I clear my throat: —He wasn't kidding, Joan. Norm found the cure.

Tee hee. And the first time I use my voice it's kind of hoarse.?

Joan keeps the car between us, wary. —No, she says.

I do a little boxer shuffle. —Hey, do I look sick to you? Feelin' good, feelin' strong. Wanna mix it up? Huh? Huh?

My best Steve-isms. I'm sorry, but you don't wrap a guy around your finger without learning him inside and out!

—You want proof, come check the eyes. Come on, Joan.

She walks about halfway, then stops. I coax her with both hands. She takes a step backward.

Sirens wail in the distance, and people are gathering on the street, drawn by the midnight flames. Sparks and smoke fall up into the black.

—You're gonna fry for this, Joan.

—On the contrary, Steve. I think I just saved the planet.

—You killed Norm, I tell her. Then I add, with a perfectly straight face: —You killed Heather.

—No jury would convict me.

—Nope, probly not, says Heather from behind her, looping the rope over and cinching it tight.

I step up. Joan's arms are pinned, so what can she do? Knee me in the balls? I'm sure I want to experience that. *So I twist, grab under her upcoming knee, and flip her down on her back.*

—Oof, goes Joan.

And before she even knows it? My buffed-out bod's on top of her. Heather's got the legs.

I take Joan's head in my hands and get nice and close.

—What are you doing, you moron! Joan screams into my mouth, struggling.

—I'm not one of you!

—Famous last words, I giggle.

And give her all we have.

THE BEGINNING

We lived happily ever after.

And we *did* get married. And our wedding night in Bali was like *so dynamic*? I mean, the two of us together, for the first time once again, beneath the stars? It's like, we know each other *so well*, you know?

You don't?

You will...

Dance of the Cube Farm Dreamers

Cirri faced her view screen, headset hooked around her left ear, the gray half-walls of her cubicle pressing closer. She plugged the extension into the node at the base of her neck, adjusting her microphone until it hovered just below her mouth. Fully linked to the Company Communication System, her implants made the external hardware obsolete. The headset was nothing more than window dressing, Unity Standard, like her tunic and her shoes.

Cirri pressed cold fingers against her temples and glared at the dark coffee cooling in the foam cup on her desk. The caffeine beckoned, but her stomach burned in protest.

Two quick beeps in her left ear gave her fair warning of the incoming call.

"This is Unity," she said, leaving the slightest pause between each word. "My name is Cirri Bijou and it's my pleasure to assist you today."

The warmth in her voice was well practiced; a mask, it formed an easy barrier between work and self. She listened to the caller's requirements, carefully sorting through the lines of color as they rolled across her screen. She used both her fingers and her thoughts to create the image which would represent the requested Virtual Projection.

The stiffness creeping through her joints was an unwelcome reminder of time spent with Dek, and Cirri shook her head to clear away the memories. Reaching across her desk for a half-finished bottle of water, she refocused her attention on the view screen.

The software she used to build the interactive personalities played shape and color against each other, the final product looking more like abstract art than anything else until it was plugged in to the system. Primary colors were physical traits; combinations, shades, hues, all developed different characteristics; curves and angles and their inverses were personality components. A builder with skills could combine form and color with function until the mask was essentially undetectable.

And Cirri had skills.

She didn't take them out of their painted boxes and let them run wild in the streets, not like she used to, not anymore. She didn't listen to them laugh out loud, playing in the wind and whispering about chance and chaos and games. She couldn't.

She was Unity now.

Unity's clientele required VPs for a variety of reasons, from business representations to pornovid romps. It made little difference to her. She preferred creating the personalities from scratch, coding the new character into whichever program the client requested. But most clients just wanted the simple enhancements to their personal VP that made it possible for them to project into the Net as younger, stronger, better looking versions of themselves.

How anyone could be too lazy to construct their own cyber presence was something Cirri could barely comprehend. She'd learned to do it as a teenager, minutes after her first implant went live. Of course, most of Unity's clientele didn't have the sophisticated hardware she had now, but it didn't take much tech to alter your Netself. Just imagination and desire, and Cirri had more of both than she knew what to do with.

Like everyone else, she'd projected her own image the first time she jacked in, complete with every flaw she had or thought she had. It hadn't been long before she was able to manipulate her projection at will, and these days she was making a damn good living building VPs for businessmen and housewives, perverts and playmakers.

But her favorites were the gamers—they were the most demanding, the most challenging of all the Unity clients. Sometimes they requested Cirri by name, projecting into the Company Communications System with just enough credits to work the bugs out or start the hardcode of whatever they were flying at the moment. If the lines weren't busy she would work on their projects despite the credit-flash advising her to terminate the CCS session in progress. She shouldn't have, but she did it anyway. She did it because it was against Company policy, because it made her pulse race with remembered freedom. And because she was a sucker for the gamers. Always had been.

The games were a forbidden pleasure for Unity Employees. According to Company policy, long term exposure to gaming environments was incompatible with their implants, and Cirri, like all Unity Employees, was subject to random blood sampling to verify her system was clean. As a builder, she was expected to have a certain amount of exposure, since she routinely tested her work before releasing it, but it was too minimal to have any lasting effects. Besides, the lab techs noted her current projects at the time of each sampling, rendering any work-related exposure irrelevant.

Cirri sighed as the snack-bot rolled past her cubicle, hovering in the center of the aisle. She motioned it over and requested an apple, sliced thin, and water, chilled and unopened. Two beeps in her ear warned her of another incoming call, and she mouthed *Coffee, hot and black* to the bot before turning her attention to her screen.

"This is Unity." Her rich voice was perfect for the CCS. "My name is Cirri Bijou and it's my pleasure to assist you."

As she worked, moving the colors in long thin curves, blending and shading, the tension drained from her shoulders. Cirri ate the apple slices slowly, each bite crisp and sweet, a stark contrast to the strong coffee she looked at but couldn't bring herself to drink. The bottled water was long gone, and she motioned to a passing bot for another one.

Before she was recruited by Unity she'd worked as a freelancer, picking and choosing projects for the challenges they presented or the credits they paid. Freelancing was a tough gig, but at least she could jack in to the games whenever she had time to spare and credits to burn, which wasn't all that often. Despite Unity's policy, she knew the gaming environments in and of themselves weren't truly dangerous, but she also knew she was better off without them. Gaming had brought her nothing but trouble.

Gaming had brought her Dek, and now that he was back in her life, trouble couldn't be far behind. When he'd re-appeared at her door a few days ago, with his bright eyes and chapped lips, she knew she should have turned him away. She should have reported an intruder in the building, eaten her supper and made an early night of it. She knew it, but she let him in anyway.

Cirri focused on her time display, bringing the visual to the forefront of her screen. She couldn't jack out for at least ninety minutes, not without losing credits. She swallowed hard and tried to leverage thirst against urgency. It was impossible; she couldn't focus on her work with her throat ragged and her skin itchy, nor could she concentrate if she had to pee so badly her foot shook and her thighs clenched.

Even so, she accepted another bottled water from the bot and drank. She didn't have to go quite yet.

A flat tone in her ear indicated an internal call coming through. It didn't make much of a difference to Cirri if the calls coming through were Company or not, but sometimes these were more interesting.

"We are Unity." She switched to the internal greeting; professional but inclusive. "My name is Cirri Bijou and it's my pleasure to assist the Company today."

The exec projecting through the CCS wore her short blonde hair in a sharp pixie cut, eyebrows a darker arch over pale eyes that were every bit as manufactured as the navy tunic she wore, its swirling insignia hovering just above her right breast. Her appearance marked her as Unity Corporate as surely as the flat tone marked her call. The tag floating at the base of Cirri's visuals identified the woman as Officer Erika Söder.

Officer Söder needed to alter her projection for the next seventy-two hours. Negotiations with a promising North American client were opening, and she required a male persona in the mid-Kennedy range: blue eyes, sandy hair, not too tall.

"Do you wish to alter the standard, Officer?"

"Explain," Erika Söder requested, snapping her eyes from her hand screen to the larger desktop visual.

"It is my pleasure to alter the voice print, appearance or personality of the standard if you would prefer a custom interface."

"I see." The officer's expression was steady, piercing. "Are you making a recommendation Representative Bijou?"

Cirri's foot began to bounce and she wished she hadn't asked the question. She held her own disinterested smile in place, deciding the Officer's question was not one that required an answer. Instead, she offered a timeline. "With standard modifications your virtual projection will be available for download in seventy-five minutes. Customization of the VP will require additional resources."

Officer Söder shifted her gaze, and Cirri guessed she was accessing her schedule.

"Alter the voice print. Refine the accent until it's so subtle it's barely there. And deepen the standard tone. Download the finished product to this location as soon as it's available." A mapping string for the download flashed into Cirri's view. "Create background files for Officer Erik Söder using my credentials." The pathway to the stored information appeared beneath the other data in Cirri's view. "Erik Söder's information should be accessible through all Unity ports and integrated into my projection as well."

"Certainly, Officer Söder."

"Your efficiency has been noted, Representative Bijou."

"Thank you, Officer Söder. It will be my pleasure to serve you again."

Cirri finished her water, tossing the empty bottle into the recycling bin, and flicked her eyes to the right to access the time once again. Already her bouncing foot was gaining momentum. If she could keep her focus on developing the Söder projection, she could lose herself in the CCS until she could jack out safely and dash to the lounge.

Cirri blamed Dek. *Damn gamers and their damn drugs,* she thought, knowing it was the Juice that Unity tested really for, not exposure to the gaming environments themselves. Gamers were jacked in for hours at a time, sometimes days, altering the balance of the biogenic amines in their systems. To beat the blues they swallowed chemi-Zac, which in itself hardly mattered; even Unity didn't care about Zac. It was the Juice they were looking for, the Juice that made the games come alive and let the gamers fly. Everybody knew somebody who knew somebody who stayed inside too long, mainlining Juice, leaving their body to waste away in some dank corner of reality.

But it wasn't exposure to the games that had Cirri parched and itchy today, she hadn't been gaming in ages. It was exposure to Dek. With an effort of will she wasn't sure she possessed, she forced Dek from her thoughts and immersed herself in her work until the screen dulled, indicating her scheduled break.

Internal housing was for ranking Executives only, which was fine by Cirri. She loved riding the Underground, loved the feeling of fleeing at the end of her shift, loved the press of traffic in the trains. She imagined the other riders, each with their separate lives, moving just for the moment in the same direction. So she'd chosen a flat that was a comfortable commuting distance from Unity, but still near enough to the old City that Cirri felt connected to the world she'd left behind, skater boys and two-wheelers, flying in shadows of Mount Hood.

High quality projections like the one she built for Officer Söder today were the usual way Representatives climbed through Company ranks, and Cirri had a growing list of recommendations in her file. The problem was, she wasn't sure this was what she wanted. Unity was stability, constant credits, bleeding-edge hardware with all the upgrades, tech she could never afford on her own.

Working on the outside had its benefits, though. She didn't miss the credit fluctuations of the freelance life, or the pervasive sense of uncertainty that came with it, but her heart sank whenever she peered over the edge of the fuzzy half-walls at work and watched the vast cube-farm of the Communications Core buzzing around her. She missed the street level view of the old City, the smell of dawn rising as she fell asleep, warm rain and burnt coffee, the feel of the Juice in her veins, jacked in and gaming like there was no tomorrow.

Unity is the best thing that ever happened to you, she reminded herself. She repeated it over and over, like a mantra, riding the Underground to the third stop, trying to keep from telling Charlotte about Dek. Charlotte and Cirri lived in the same building, and they spent more than a few of their off hours together. Charlotte came from the old City, too, although she'd been with Unity for several years now. She had an easy laugh and collection of graphic novels that could draw Cirri up to her tenth floor flat even when the lift in their building was out.

When the train flashed away from the second stop,

Charlotte scanned the remaining passengers and finally let her eyes rest on Cirri. Her hard stare made Cirri clear her throat and stop scratching the back of her leg.

"Spill it, Cirri," Charlotte demanded, causing Cirri to whip her head around, checking for other Unity workers in their car.

"We're alone," Charlotte stated, raising an eyebrow in silent admonition. As if she would have said anything had that not been the case. Strictly speaking, they were hardly alone, but no one else within earshot was Unity. "Spill!"

Cirri answered with a shake of her head. She couldn't, it was too risky. She would say goodbye to Dek tonight, if he was still around, and then she would focus on getting her system back to Company standard.

"I think I know the signs, Cirri," Charlotte said, giving her a meaningful look. "And they all point to a man."

Under that penetrating gaze, Cirri finally admitted that her ex was back in the picture.

"He isn't Unity," she said, allowing herself the thrill of disclosure in the disguise of half-truth.

"I knew it!" Charlotte whispered, reaching out and gripping Cirri's hand. "This is so exciting. You know I wouldn't say anything, right? But you have to be more careful, Cirri. If I figured it out, someone else might, too."

Her flat was empty. A mixture of relief and disappointment snaked its way through her system. She discarded the bulk of her clothing in the bin beside her bed, hanging her Unity tunic in front of the open window. With a little luck, it would air out enough to wear again.

Cirri closed the door and turned on the shower, not bothering to let the water run hot before she stepped in. Traces of Dek littered the bathroom. His black curls in the drain, a dab of tissue spotted with blood, a damp towel heaped in the corner. He'd even left the seat up.

What was she going to do? Dek walking back into her life had never been part of the plan. When Unity recruited her last year, she told herself she would take the job, take the tech, and split as soon as she had stored enough credits to get out clean. Now she found herself reluctant to follow through, not because she liked the Company, not especially, and not because she didn't want to go back to the streets she'd come from, but because it was simple, easier to stay where she was and just keep doing what she was doing. Before Unity, she'd managed to carve out a decent existence, but it had taken years of scraping by, squatting in rundown corridors and living hand to mouth before she'd found any comfort at all.

Now Dek was back, with his dreams and his freedom, flaunting them both and then disappearing again.

Cirri dressed quickly and escaped the press of her flat, spinning into the twilight like a dancer in an old-time ballet. She walked slowly, savoring the feel of the city, cool against her freshly scrubbed skin. It was a good night for noodles—comfort food from way back, when she could afford nothing else. These days the vendors were clean and the corners well lit, but street food was still street food, and the tangy broth warmed her from the inside tonight as it had so many nights before.

She could feel him in the dark even before she opened her eyes. Dek's voice was whisper smooth, soothing her nerves, reminding her how much she had missed him. The scratch in her throat and the goosebumps racing over her skin reminded her why that was. She watched him strip, a solid shadow shedding its skin, and for three and a half minutes she considered kicking him out of her bed and out of her life once and for all.

His breath against her throat weakened her resolve, his warm hands on her body banished all thoughts of asking him to leave. Cirri could smell the games on him, taste the sweetness of the Juice in his sweat. Her body craved it, craved him, and she knew she had to stop this.

Now, before his mouth moved any lower. Stop, before she got any closer to the Juice that was already bleeding off his body and into hers.

His mouth closed over her, hot and wet. His tongue tracing lazy whirls, chasing the chill from her body, filling her with heat. Her fingers wrapped into his hair, Cirri bit her lip and let the orgasm take her.

Dek growled, his skin sliding over hers, mouth closing over

one stiff pink nipple. "Again," he demanded, burying his fingers inside her, biting her lips before he kissed.

Cirri knew it was the Juice her body was reacting to, pushing toward. She needed it, needed him to give it to her.

It's only been a few days, she reasoned, forcing her mind to pull away. *Just a few days.*

How long before the dehydration exposed her to her colleagues? How long before Unity's lab techs flushed her system and found the contamination? How long before she was jacked in and gaming, the decision to leave Unity or stay taken away from her by the Juice?

It wasn't too late. Not yet. She could still detox over the weekend and never look back.

"Come back to me, Cirri. You're oceans away." Dek drew his finger across her lips, letting her taste herself, salty and sharp. He held her face, looking into her eyes. "Stay."

Her body betrayed her, pressing itself against him.

"Stay with me, Cirri."

She started to shake. It started inside her thighs and spread in a pulsing wave, taking her with it. She couldn't think, she didn't know where words came from anymore.

Juice. It was just a whisper, a rush of her breath pressed into his bony shoulder, not meant to be heard.

"I know," he breathed, eyes dark. For just a second she heard something else in his voice, something besides desire. Regret? And then it disappeared in the need.

Cirri wrapped her legs around his hips, pulling him closer, pulling him in. She needed him inside her now as much as she needed the Juice. She needed to feel him, thrusting, defining her, marking where his body ended and hers began.

He lifted her easily, reversing their positions.

"No," Cirri whispered. "The Juice..."

"I know," he breathed, his mouth around her small breast, teeth searing her skin. "Don't worry."

His fingers against her as she rode him, his tongue darting against tortured nipples, sucking and biting until she fell against him, boneless.

Cirri felt him move slowly inside of her, felt the first slow bleed of the Juice tingling her muscles and flashing colors behind her eyelids.

"Please," she whispered.

And then he was on top again, pounding into her, his head back and face twisted until he exploded, pouring into her, seed and Juice and everything else he had to give.

They lay, a tangle of limbs and sheets, breathing heavily, lost in the haze that they made.

Dek reached for the water by her bedside, careful not to pull out yet. "Is this all you want from me?" he asked, balanced just above her, his face dark and unreadable.

Myriad images moved behind her eyes, some of them memory some of them not, all of them fully formed and flying. What *did* she want from him? Just a good fuck and the Juice that came with it?

Was that all?

When she'd opened the door to her flat and seen him there, the slow smile spreading across his face, had she known then? Known how easy it would be, known how quickly the Juice would take her? Maybe, maybe not. She couldn't tell.

"Cirri?"

"Yes?"

"What about it?" He lifted himself from her now. She had the Juice; there was nothing left that either of them cared about losing to the sheets.

"Is it all you're offering?"

"No, but it's the only thing I have at the moment."

She snuggled closer to him. She could last another month or two at Unity, if the lab techs didn't get her first. Long enough to have her system upgraded again, long enough to stash away the credits they would need. Longer than that maybe, if they were careful.

"Tell me," she whispered. "Tell me again and again."

She listened to his gamers dreams, ideas dancing around them both, the node at the base of her neck tingling with the promise of freedom.

"We can do it, Cirri, I know we can," he breathed, brushing her ear with his fingers.

She believed him for no other reason than because she

wanted to believe him. Because the Juice made everything seem more real than it was, because his fingers were soft against her skin. She believed him because she hated the blue tunic hanging in front of her window, its swirling emblem flashing against the night; because she spent her days leashed to a desk; because she had sold out once already and it had cost too damn much.

Cirri faced her view screen, headset hooked around her ear, gray half-walls pressing closer, fully jacked in to the CCS. Two beeps in her left ear signaled fair warning. Cirri moistened chapped lips with her tongue, savoring the swell of tenderness she found there.

"This is Unity," she said. "My name is Cirri Bijou and it's my pleasure to assist you today."

Her foot bounced its own rhythm against her calf. She swallowed hard, letting her fingers fly through the projection without giving it much thought. She shifted slightly, feeling sore and a little sticky. She smiled a secret smile, accessed the time, and verified her credit balance once again.

Soon, very soon, she would jack out of the CCS, follow the corridor past the lab where the techs waited in their starchy coats, and take the Company lift all the way down to the Underground. She would board the third train on the far track, Dek by her side, his black curls flying free and dreams on fire.

She would never look back.

Mountain Man's Toothpick

Preston Blackburn paused, though he wasn't normally a man of hesitation, and glanced up the steep grade, following the path with his eyes instead of his feet. Thirteen marble steps glistening with morning rain. They wound up the gorge adjacent to a gurgling stream, ending at redwood bridge that opened into the shadowy fir and cedar forest. Thirteen steps to damnation. Some folks said they had been here more than four hundred years, long before the warming or the creeps, back when Everett, Sultan, and even Skykomish were overrun with people. Right now, he didn't much care. His only concern was putting one foot in front of the other and keeping Jenny. That was why he'd come. No bishop was going to annul their marriage, even if he had to become a sinner to make it so.

He wiped sweat from his brow, threw his shoulders back and put boot to stone. The weathered marble grated beneath his weight, a sound like bones grinding. He wondered how many men had preceded him. Surely more than would admit to it, and there was Bill Harmond, of course. He had not only admitted his sin, he had flaunted it before God and Church.

Preston remembered that day in front of the church; the Bishop's gray robe flapping in warm spring winds, sky dark and ominous. Harmond's penis stood so erect Preston couldn't help but be envious. He had prayed all the next day for God to deliver him from covetous thoughts. "This man is an abomination," Bishop Gore had repeated three times. "Defiled in the eyes of God and man by the *old science.* Excommunicated from the church. Banned from the community."

The bridge took Preston across the rocky crevasse, ending at a narrow path that wound between thick-leaved underbrush to a conifer grove where trees grew in neat lines, a remnant of old planted forests. As he set foot on that brown-needled floor, the sounds of the natural forest dropped away: no crickets playing tunes or mice gnawing seeds, no birds flitting through leaves or cones dropping with a soft thud.

Dead spot. He had spent enough time down near the coast to recognize one.

He studied the ground, looking for telltale signs of *creeps.* They were there all right, flickering like miniature stars amid brown needles and mosses, never very noticeable but never quite absent either. The hair on his nape bristled. He smelled their faint acrid scent mixed with damp clay and fragrant fir. How could he go through with this?

He thought of Jenny's eyes when she was happy, a different kind of sparkle that warmed his face instead of chilling the back of his neck. How could he *not* go through with this? He would be safe enough if he washed his boots and was careful where he touched.

At the far end of the grove, dangling over the path, a man-face mask with yellow skin, flaring red nostrils, and green cheek stripes glared downward with wide eyes and grimacing mouth. *Pagan idols. Sins against the true God.* Preston breathed deep but did not stop, fearing he would never get going again. Keep the faith, he thought. He stooped to pass under the mask without touching it.

Hope and faith is what we have, Jenny always said.

When their first cabin burned in the mountain fire, she'd told him that their things could be replaced. They had each other and that was what mattered. When a mudslide destroyed town and washed out most of the farms, she insisted God would deliver what they needed. On their second-year anniversary when the elders stopped for their annual visit, she told them she was young and had faith God would give them a child. The elders hadn't contradicted her, but Preston knew by the way they looked at him that they suspected Jenny's childlessness had nothing to do with God and everything to do with him.

And then, on the way out the door, with Jenny out of earshot, old Theo Martin had smiled apologetically and made it blunt: "If we don't have no more babies there's not going to be nobody. We got to think of the community, right? Three fertile years, Preston, is all we can spare. Walker Fuller can take Jenny on as a concubine if you two don't get a gift from God soon." Preston remembered the hair bristling on the back of his neck and his fists tightening. He had never in his whole life wanted to strike a man more than at that moment.

Air coursing up the Cascades from the ocean cooled his arms and back. He reached a gate constructed of woven cedar branches that stood ajar between white limestone pillars that looked like they belonged in Seattle, not here in the mountains. He slid through without touching it.

A flower garden stretched before him as if someone had taken a paintbrush loaded with red and orange and yellow and splashed it across the forest floor. But there was something odd about this place: too many blooms he didn't recognize, smells that were too sweet by half, plants too large to be true-grown. *Old science.* He turned away from the thought as quickly as it came, hoping that would somehow make his visit a lesser sin. Surely God saw a difference between *knowing* and not wanting to know.

More marble steps, these ones level and less eroded, continued onward. Orange day lilies bowed toward the path. *They only stay open for one day.* Jenny had told him that. He touched the smooth edge of a bloom and thought of her soft skin, the feel of her in his arms. Making love. Not that they *really* made love, not the way a man and woman should.

The garden gave way to a clearing where a totem pole towered over everything, including a whitewashed cottage. Carved faces peered at him from the pole: ebony ravens, crimson bears, turquoise beaked birds, three miniature green men with tall hats at the very top. The cottage, huddled behind the pole, wasn't a log cabin like most people built, but more like cement molded into a dome shape, smooth curves and shimmering textures that made you want to touch. Preston wouldn't let himself think about it. "I'm here to see the Doc," he said, trying the words out, tasting them on his tongue. The Doc, he thought. The Doc who can make me whole.

The overlarge redwood door to the cottage was centered deep with in the totem pole. High on the door was a carving, a red mouth with hands attached at the top and feet below.

"Shit or get off the pot." A woman's deep voice from behind him, as jagged as granite and twice as hard.

Preston turned.

The Doc was no taller than his armpit and not much thicker

than his leg. Her white hair was pulled back so that only the tail stuck out from beneath a wide-brimmed straw hat decorated with black, blue and brown feathers of varying shapes and sizes. Her face was smooth and pale, accentuating dark brown eyes. Instead of a dress, she wore men's denim work pants and knee-high rubber boots.

"Sorry."

"Just arrived and already you're apologizing." She pushed past him and opened the door. Cool air tinged with cinnamon and oats brushed his face. "Flocker," she muttered.

His cheeks warmed. *The Doc.*

"You live in a barn or what, hang dong?"

"No," he managed. Close the door and leave, he thought. No proper man would put up with this treatment. But then he remembered Jenny's sweet voice. *The elders do God's work,* she'd said after that last visit. He'd seen a hint of fear in her eyes then, soft brown eyes as deep as a quarry pool. *We have to keep trying, Preston. Don't give up. We will be fruitful and multiply. You'll see.*

But Preston *did* see. That was the problem. A childless marriage was a sin in the eyes of God. It wasn't just some cruel edict meant to punish them, but a practical matter. Last year, he'd skipped the salmon run because of talk there was something in the meat, another creep they couldn't see or maybe an old poison. After a few months and no difference, he'd tried a sling bag until he got such a rash between his legs he could barely walk, let alone do carpentry. Next came the tonic, a green concoction that tasted like swamp water. That didn't last long. Nothing worked. Nothing natural, at least.

"You're the Blackburn boy. The woodworker."

"Preston," he said. She nodded like she knew him, but they'd never met.

He'd seen her in town over the years, sometimes at his dad's hardware picking up screws and things. Some people called her Ingun Witch, others Old Squaw or Mountain Devil. People only called her Doc when they needed her medicine. Even the Bishops put up with her presence in town, partly because Cascadia was a free country, but mostly because the Doc could often cure things that God could not.

It is the old science *God objects to, people said, not her natural herbs.*

"Well?" the Doc said. "If you're coming in shut the door."

Jenny still clung to her hope. Preston suspected that God more often helped those who helped themselves. Maybe if he was a better Christian he'd be more patient, but with only a year to go and Jenny's belly still flat, it seemed to him the Doc was his last chance, probably his only chance. He stepped across the doorsill like a dog following its master, a sinner following the devil into hell.

The interior, even the wooden floor, was as white as the outside. A wool blanket with geometric blue, black and tan faces hung on one wall to his left. A disk-shaped crimson mask guarded the next doorway. Dried flowers and herbs hung from ceiling beams and baskets filled with leaves and twigs dotted the floor. Maybe I'm wrong, he thought. Maybe the Doc *was* just an herbalist, mixing potions and brews to cure ills. Rumors about the *old science* were probably just that, stories to tell around the evening fire. That's how teenage boys dealt with the fear that they'd be half-men like him. They could look at all the naked women pictures they could find, but when it came to *doing it?* Thirteen. Limp as a dead catfish. Fourteen. Wilted as an old cucumber. Fifteen. Floppy as a dogs' ears. They didn't dare talk about it with their friends, so they told tales about the *old science* turning boys into tree-men with bark covered peters or rooster-men with peckers for peckers.

"What brings you here?" She tossed her hat on a table and wiped sweat from her face with a red-checked handkerchief. "Damn heat."

"I'm here to see... I need a Doc," he forced himself to say.

She chuckled. "Well, you're seeing her."

He looked at his feet. "I got a problem." He wasn't sure he could get the rest past his lips. He didn't even talk about it with Jenny. She must have suspected that first time out in the Phillip's barn, but she hadn't run out in a panic like most girls would, just hugged him tight. *Just because the torch doesn't burn with the first flint strike doesn't mean it won't ever burn,* she'd said.

He looked up, mouth opening, but the Doc's impatient stare

stopped him short. She already knew.

"Do you have a potion or something I can try?" he said.

"No potion's going to help your problem." The Doc laughed. "Weak wong. Droopy dong. Perkless peter."

Preston chewed his lower lip. The Doc strolled around him hands on hips like she was buying a horse. "Healthy otherwise?"

"Yes," he said.

"What you need is a toothpick." She motioned for him to follow and walked into the next room, a shining maze of stainless steel tables, needles, tubes and knives. A refrigeration unit buzzed like a beehive, out of synchrony with the florescent lights fixed overhead. His stomach knotted and his hands grew clammy. He remembered falling asleep in church one Sunday, his dad switching his butt with a willow stick and screaming that sinners pay for their sins.

Dead spot, he thought at once. He didn't see creeps flickering like he had in the forest, but *felt* them all the same.

Grandpap used to tell stories. *Their science blinded them from the start. They said that God didn't exist, then tried to become God themselves. And where are they now, huh children? Dead by their own hands, by their creeps and poisons and general disregard for natural ways. Now only we God-fearing are left to rebuild His world.*

The Doc slid a pair of plastic gloves from a box and pulled them over her hands with a snap. "How are you at building bridges?"

"What?"

She patted a steel table. "Hop up here."

"Mainly build chairs and tables and such," he said, following her instructions. The table was hard beneath his backside. A chill crept through his pants.

She pointed to a glass case hanging on the far wall where finger-sized and smaller curved bones were mounted neatly in three rows and labeled with animal names: *mink. coon. wolf.*

"Mountain Man's Toothpicks, some used to call them," she said. "Love bones. Pecker bones."

Preston pressed his legs together.

She lifted a bony club easily as long as her forearm from a counter beneath the display. "The Inuit called this one an oosik.

It's from a walrus." She smiled. "Don't think you want one this size do you?"

"You're going to give me a bone?" How many nightmares had he awakened from, sweating and sick, wishing he were a whole man, a man with a penis he could use?

The woman raised a smaller bone. "Coon," she said. "Much smaller, but don't you worry. I've modified the coon genes just enough to give a man the right size."

"I don't need no bone. I just need... something."

She shook her head, expression softening. "There aren't any miracles Blackburn. No magic pills or potions, just straightforward biomechanics and genetic manipulation. Some body modification creep has mutated to affect the vascular system—"

"Old science." Sweat rolled down Preston's face. His blood felt ready to boil over. Grandpap had told them about it: *Creeps to kill insects, creeps to eat garbage, creeps to keep the skin young. Creeps that turn animals into men and men into sinners.*

"Call it what you will." She opened a drawer hidden on the underside of the table and pulled out a stainless steel pan with a lid. She lifted the lid and exposed an instrument that looked like scissors, only the blades were curved as if they were meant to cut something round. It didn't take a Bishop to figure out what they were for. She lifted the device high like a pagan worshiping a masked god. Preston felt the blood rush from his face. His ears rang. Everything went white.

"Wake up, flocker," the Doc's voice echoed. Preston felt the hard table against his back. He opened his eyes. His hand went to his crotch.

"Your thing's still hanging there," she said. "I don't take anything that isn't offered me."

"I didn't—"

"You didn't what? You didn't think I was going to cut your pecker off?" She chuckled. "Well, the one you have isn't working and it's never going to work. In the old days they had drugs that would do a half-assed job, but those days are long gone. This is the choice you've got. You can stand up and walk out the door you came in, or you can let me grow you a dong that's going to come when you whistle."

"No," he said. "Put some creeps in me. Stick a bone into what I've got, but not this." His eyes settled on the silver shears.

"Takes fifteen seconds," she said. "I put a tourniquet at the base to stop the blood flow temporarily. The cut takes about a second. Then I cap it with a regenerator, complete with gene regulators, growth hormones, antibiotics, coon bone genes, and what you will be most interested in, neural blockers. No pain."

Preston's heart drummed. Was he man enough to let her hack off what little manhood he had? Sinners pay for their sins. He hadn't expected to pay this much.

"Won't be pissing standing up for a while, but the regenerator has a urethral opening and you won't have any trouble there if everything goes right. And you should have a fully functioning pecker in about sixty days."

"To get Jenny with child?" he stammered.

"Don't know that. Sterility is a problem these days too, but at least it'll give you a better chance than whatever you're trying now."

Part coon, Preston thought, remembering Harold Halley, two years older than the other boys who used to swim in the creek. Harold had told a story about a guy who fell asleep in the woods after gathering up the coons on his trap line. Never mind that you trap coon in the winter and that no one would fall asleep in the cold. As the story went, before the guy knew it the creeps had crawled off the coons and up his pant legs. When he woke up the next morning, he had a big hard dick, but no girl would take a second look at him because he also had black hairy circles around his eyes and long whiskers.

"I don't have all day," the Doc said.

Preston thought of Jenny's soft gaze as she watched him struggle with a saw too far gone to sharpen. She'd just stand there as serene as sunshine in a blue sky and the world would suddenly be okay again.

The woman replaced the coon bone in her display. "I take trade for my work and could use a bridge over a ravine out back."

Preston imagined himself standing before the elders with a striped tail and whiskers, or worse, standing before Jenny with no penis at all.

"Is it a deal?"

"There's no other way?" Preston's words came out a hoarse whisper.

The woman shook her head. "Your elders are a bunch of damned fools, you know. Things weren't so dreadful in the old days and science wasn't the monster they'd like you to believe. There were good people and bad, but most didn't give a damn. *They* were the ones who put us in this mess, not the warming or the brain fevers or the creeps."

Preston pictured Jenny's stomach swelling with child, her face lighting up. It's a miracle, she'd say. He imagined placing his ear to her belly and hearing a muffled heartbeat. A miracle, he thought. Sixty days. Surely he could hide this from Jenny that long; he'd take a hunting trip up north. Only the Doc and the devil would know about the sin he'd taken to himself to make it so.

"Well?" the Doc said, her tone regaining its gruffness.

"Yes," he said. "I'll do it." He'd pray every morning and thank God every night. Maybe that would be enough.

The Pulse of the Sea

Dim.

Wherever Cari was, the lighting was dim. The sound of machines sighing in the background dominated, while the rest of the room felt cool, quiet... controlled. Not that she could really see. More like she had just awoken and, thick with crusts around her eyes, couldn't open them completely or focus.

"Miss Ohtagawa."

The calm, pleasant voice hung in the air. She knew he would speak again to get her attention, if she did not respond.

"Do not try to move or speak. You are in a hospital and have been gravely injured."

The train crash.

The train had crashed. It began to come back to her. With a start, Cari felt a sense of panic and tried to open her eyes, but she couldn't. Something felt very wrong with her face, and she was unable to move her hands to find out.

"My name is Doctor Takeshi, Miss Ohtagawa. You are in a hospital," the doctor repeated. "Please do not panic. You are being take care of. You will be made whole again. You are safe now."

She wanted to know about her family, about her brother. She couldn't feel her toes.

A clicking sound diverted her racing thoughts.

"I have made a slight adjustment in your medication, Miss Ohtagawa," the doctor said. "You should feel calmer in a moment. An artifice, I am afraid. But I need you to focus."

Cari didn't understand his meaning, but the room began to envelope her in a warm embrace from his medicine.

"There. I can see in your readings you are more at ease. I am sorry to do this so soon. But you have been very badly injured and are at the present hooked into several machines. We cannot keep you on these machines forever. I have installed a new heart for you. It is running in tandem with the machines. We must cut the cord, so to speak. Separate you from the machines so that you might begin to live on your own again."

A new heart? This sounded serious to Cari, who almost laughed. Of course it was serious—she was in a hospital!

"Try to open your eyes. You will not be able to see well, there is considerable swelling."

Easier said than done, she thought, unable to feel whether her left eye was open or closed. A blurry image came through on her right, though she couldn't open it all the way.

A figure in a thin, white lab coat emerged out of the fog in front of her.

"Hello, Miss Ohtagawa. I am Doctor Takeshi," he said, bowing slightly.

"Mmm...," she murmured.

He leaned forward with a damp cloth and wiped around her mouth. She became aware of the bandages swathed around her head. "There, you might be able to speak. But do not overdo it."

That was a laugh—as if she could overdo anything right now.

"When... when do you turn off the machines?" she said.

Cari could just make out a smile on the face of the Japanese doctor.

"It is already done, Miss Ohtagawa."

She closed her eye and listened. It was true—the sounds of the machines were gone. She felt... odd.

"Your new heart administers a continuous flow of blood," he said. "It will take some time to be adjusted to it. From time to time, you may feel light in the chest. Do not worry. We are continuously monitoring its operation and your vital parameters. Needless to say, you should refrain from any heavy lifting in the near future."

A joke. Doctor Takeshi had made a joke.

She closed her eye and let herself fade away on the medications.

"You're going to make us late."

Cari Ohtagawa smiled as she checked her hair one more time in the mirror. Her mother always made it seemed so much more desperate, as if her father wasn't going to get them to the station on time.

"Hey, Sport," a cheerful voice came from the open doorway and now Cari's smile turned into a big grin—she worshipped her older brother Brian. "You're going to make us late."

"Yeah, right."

"Wow—you look like a doll."

"An *expensive* doll, I hope," she said, putting one more long gold comb into her upswept hair.

"Oh yeah."

"My bag's there," she said, pointing with her free hand. "Make yourself useful."

"Yes, my princess."

"And have the slaves whipped—Mother is *such* a wimp about that."

She trotted down the stairs and on the next to bottom step, she held up her arms as if to announce *I have arrived.* Her mother managed an approving smile. Her father applauded. It was hard not to appreciate the overly dramatic in a fourteen-year-old teenager. Cari had already made off with Brian's tech jacket, as she did whenever he came home. It was far too big for her, but fully charged up it adjusted itself to fit as well as it could and would warm her in the cool outside breeze.

"And now it is time for the cab to arrive," her father announced.

"You mean it's not here yet?" Cari asked.

"I allowed for you to make yourself presentable to your grandparents."

"Hmph," she sniffed. He knew her habits too well, it seemed.

At the downtown Portland station, Ken Ohtagawa held up their passage document in front of Gate 2. Somewhere a scanner read it—the plastix said that they had Club seats on the eleven o'clock and they were passed on through. Cari liked traveling this way. It wasn't as if her family was rich, because they weren't. But as seventeenth generation Japanese-Americans, her father was big on traditions and he considered going to Vancouver to see her grandfather and grandmother one of those family traditions. So they "dressed in their best and rode above the rest," in his words. The train tickets for four were expensive, but they paid for speed. With two stops, they would be in Vancouver an hour after they left Portland.

The station glowed airy and light in the May morning, while inside their Club car seemed soothing, cool and pleasantly dim. Half the car was large single swivel seats, the other half set in facing pairs. The Ohtagawa's sat together in one of the latter groupings, the last in their car—the train already beginning to move silently even before they were seated. Cari didn't mind sitting backwards, and slid along to the window to watch where they had been. Her brother joined her. He was content to close his eyes and sleep most of the way. No doubt, she figured, he had been out late with his friends, as he did whenever he came back from the Moon.

She glanced down at the sleeve of her brother's tech jacket, watching the display cycle through its many modes. The physiological data fascinated her and she watched as it recorded her breathing, temperature and the little beating heart icon which gave her pulse. Someday she wanted to go to space, maybe to work on the Moon like her brother. It wasn't that living in PacNorWest was bad, but there was adventure out there as Man made its early forays into deeper space.

From some distance away Cari could hear some sort of a rumble and felt the train car sway slightly. It was disconcerting, because you never felt anything once the PORT-SEA-VAN Rail trains got up to speed. Her father always described the trip as *silk sliding across glass.*

And then it all went wrong... horribly wrong.

It was 11 May 2396 and safety was one of those issues which no one in Cari's family would have spent any time thinking about, because so much thinking had gone into the development of the high speed PORT-SEA-VAN Rail line before a single section of track had been laid. Had an accident simply occurred, there were numerous systems in place to ensure their survivability.

But this wasn't an accident, rather a deliberate act involving people dedicated to the No Growth movement along with a metric ton of thermaplex strategically arrayed along a half kilometer of track. The resulting combination of the extremely fast train and the dissolving track line rendered complete and utter chaos.

Cari only remembered feeling a heavy pressure from the back of her seat and the horror of seeing her parents flying diagonally into the aisle, as the train car slowed and turned—her parents' motion unchecked—before the car began to buckle and crumple. Vaguely she was aware of Brian trying to reach for them. Then a very hard noise and blackness.

"Hey, somebody secure that medtel!"

Somewhere in the mangled remains of Club Car 3, a medical telemetry unit screeched for attention. The first responders had gone through and tagged as many victims as they could with the portable transponders. And it was good they made such a racket, but it was hard to think while they were screeching. And anyway, their telemetry and coordinates were already in the rescuers' database, so the alarms should have shut down until needed for location. But this medtel kept sounding.

"All Net—I said to secure that loose medtel."

"All our medtel's are registered on the net, captain."

The Thurston County Fire/Rescue captain swore. "Shit—someone's wearing one."

Another helo-lifter arrived on the scene, this one from the Sony Medical Center in Seattle. The captain was grateful for any help, but he was aware that the Japanese team would be looking for their people in the wreck.

Cari's awareness faded in and out. She wondered briefly where her parents were, and once she wondered where her brother was, but mostly she felt tired. So it was only with semi-detached interest that she saw the light change.

"There!" The voices were stronger now.

"I need a saw!"

"What is that thing?"

"Don't take the silver jacket off," a new voice said, young but with firm authority. There was something annoyingly familiar about it. "It is what has kept her alive."

She heard two strange thumps and then the sound of metal

being hit with a cutoff wheel began again, only a lot closer.

"Okay, someone get a bag—this'll be a slice-n-dice. Billy! I need transport to General."

"No," the firm voice said. "This girl is American Japanese and I am taking her to Sony. We can do a skin job on this one."

"Whatever you say, Doc."

The firm voice seemed to come from a serious looking Asian face which now peered at Cari from a strange angle. That was what she had noticed. The careful inflection of excellent English spoken by a Japanese doctor. "Miss Ohtagawa, I am Doctor Hiredo. We are going to cut you out in a minute, but first I am going to give you some very good drugs. This is called Marzipan-2 and I am going to inject this in your cheek because I can see it most clearly."

Something moved towards her and she wanted to flinch because it seemed too close to her eye. But she couldn't move and then she felt something like a pin prick. After that, she really couldn't keep her eyes open any longer.

The last thing she was aware of was a voice which said something like, "She's out. Go in."

They wouldn't let Cari see a mirror, so she knew it had to look bad. The hospital room was impressively neat and clean, and as she couldn't really move, even Cari had been perfectly set in her place. If she looked down she could see the dressings on her mangled left arm. She could neither see nor feel her right. Nor her legs.

Cari had finally learned the rest of her family had been killed. By some accident of fate, she had survived. Or at least they told her she had. Her two doctors, both conscientious and dedicated young men, seemed certain of her survival.

But they didn't let her dwell on it very much, keeping her sedated most of the time while healing and operations progressed.

"Why did you do this to me?"

Doctor Hiredo sat down on the side of the hospital bed and checked the readouts from the assist pump, before allowing himself a sly smile. "Do you mean save your life, Miss

Ohtagawa?"

"Save my life, all this," Cari said, indicating with her good eye all that surrounded her. "Cutting me off."

"Or do you mean why did I select you to save?"

It wasn't the question she thought she wanted to ask. But when his question resonated within her, Cari realized she really did desire an answer. "Yeah," she said, barely croaking out the word.

"It is very simple, Miss Ohtagawa. I saved you because I could."

"There were other Japanese—some even from Japan. And others..." Her voice faded.

"Yes. Many others. And many who could not be saved. But I think the best reason why I selected you was to honor your brother."

"My... brother?" Even now it was hard to talk about him.

"His jacket kept you alive. Whether intended or not, I choose to believe that he is honored to have saved you."

"But if he was wearing it..." Suddenly she felt terribly selfish and her good eye began to tear up.

"Had your brother been wearing his jacket, then both of you would have died, Miss Ohtagawa. Your brother's injuries were too great to overcome. The medical safety capabilities of a spaceman's jacket are not magic, they are limited. And therefore you are the beneficiary."

"Oh."

He reached out and smoothed some of the long hair framing her face. What Cari had not yet seen was how they had had to remove most of her hair—her elaborate metal combs did considerable damage when they were ripped from her head. But Hiredo knew if he could give her the illusion of having a head of natural hair, it would make her feel more alive, more feminine, until it was time to re-implant her own hair. At this fragile state, even such a deception was important.

"You have more questions. Much you must confront and come to terms with, Miss Ohtagawa. But you should rest now."

"Yes, rest," she said, leaning her head back and closing her eye. She did not see him touching the control on his belt, instructing the meds to put her gently under again.

Her new room had a window, but in the early morning Seattle fog there was nothing to see outside. Inside it was rounds and Doctor Takeshi, the internal specialist. Hiredo dealt more with limbs. Or so the nurses had said. In practice she tended to see both nearly every day and felt they overlapped enough to be interchangeable. But she wanted to see Takeshi today.

"I remember the crash—and right after," she said.

"Oh?" Doctor Takeshi looked up from his medboard. "And what do you remember of the aftermath?"

"A phrase. I heard Doctor Hiredo telling someone that he could do a *skin job* on me. What did he mean?"

"Human skin is itself a complex organ. Doctor Hiredo has been able to save large sections of your own skin from your arm and legs.

"I see."

"Something else is troubling you?"

"He wants to take my left arm, too," Cari said.

"It is badly damaged, Miss Ohtagawa. You will never recover full functionality or use of it. After you have been fitted with your new right arm and it has been integrated into your nervous system, you will see that we are right on this matter."

"But I can wait."

"Yes, of course. You are not ready for your new limbs. There is no need to process your left arm at this time."

It all sounded so reasonable. So clinical. So machine-like. But she didn't have to decide today. That was good. Perhaps she would feel better about it later.

"I feel strange sometimes," Cari said, sometime after her new heart was functioning on its own. "Listless. You said I would."

"Your new heart is a continuous flow pump—it doesn't have a beat."

"I thought you had to have a pulse to be alive."

"It's symptomatic of a conventional heart, but not required."

Cari wasn't so sure. "Yeah, but aren't there valves and things in the leg veins?"

"You no longer have your legs. We are giving you new ones."

"And no arm veins?"

"Because we shall give you new arms."

Cari sat still for a moment. "What do I have left?" she asked in a quiet voice.

"All which is most important," Doctor Takeshi said.

"Two arms, two legs," Cari said. "An eye, an ear, an ear implant. A new face."

"The face is still yours. The damage is primarily superficial. Your nose and some of the facial bones were broken, but that has been corrected. We are letting your face heal, before we return it to its proper state." Doctor Takeshi didn't mention the bioreactor they had integrated into her gut to allow her artificial limbs to be powered by the food she ate. That was internal—this conversation concerned her outward appearance and how she would address the world.

"There's not a lot left of me, is there?"

"I will not deceive you, Miss Ohtagawa. Your injuries were most severe. But your health is stable at present. And when you leave this facility, you will do so under your own power, on your own two legs."

"They'll be artificial legs."

"You will be whole again. Is that not enough?"

Cari didn't know.

Portland was the City of Roses, a fact the designers of the Sony Medical Center in that city hadn't forgotten when they built an extensive hothouse to supply fresh cut flowers to the rooms all through the year. Eight months after she had been rescued, Sony had moved her from Seattle back to Portland in the middle of the night. One morning she awoke in a different hospital, a different room, at home of sorts. At first it didn't matter. One hospital seemed the same as the other. Eventually, however, bits of Portland life began to leak into Cari's new existence. When one of the nurses dropped off a Nihonmachi Pizza from Old Town and she could eat it with her new right hand, Cari began to open up.

She liked working with the hothouse plants. It gave her something to do and they didn't care what her face looked like or what stage of treatment she was in the middle of. Not that anyone here ever seemed to look. It seemed funny now to realize she had always known how many Japanese and other Asians had settled in the PacNorWest territories. It was only so much more apparent here at Sony Medical.

The other funny thing—she found she craved rainy days. Bright sunshine could flood through the many glass windows throughout the hospital. But it only seemed to emphasize that she was in a hospital. Rain, on the other hand, rattling on the glass panes of the hothouse—she could lose herself in the noise.

It didn't rain enough in Portland to suit her.

Grandmother arrived alone to visit. She seemed not to notice or to fuss over Cari's appearance either. And for what Cari had always thought of as a frail old woman, Grandmother was quite willing to stroll along the wide corridors and cross the wide glass covered walkways connecting the buildings. So Cari had brought her here, to the hothouse, to show Grandmother the flowers.

The old woman stopped when they stepped through the airlock and breathed deep. "Ah... it is a good, clean earth smell."

"Yeah," Cari said, self-consciously pushing her long bangs back behind her good ear. The great diagonal gash across her face was more of a faint line now. Had she wanted to go out, a good layer of makeup might have hidden it completely. Then there was the eye patch covering the new socket for the Sony RE-512 with the Carl Zeiss optics they had promised. It would be installed next week. So this week, Cari walked carefully, without proper depth perception.

"You must always remember to come to places like this."

"Why?"

"Because otherwise you'll begin to think you are a machine." The comment was so blunt it took Cari aback. But then Grandmother said something which astonished her. "I know."

"You... you know?"

Grandmother stopped, held tightly to the railing around a raised bed of yellow daffodils and then seemingly without effort raised her right leg straight out to the side.

"They did it to me, too. Twenty years ago. Cancer took my

leg. They replaced it."

"Grandmother! I didn't know."

"No one knew," Grandmother said, standing again as straight as her age and her other leg would allow. "Your grandfather insisted on that."

"Was he shamed by it?"

"No, of course not," Grandmother said. "The doctors assured me they had caught it in time and it was only a leg. But we didn't need the sympathy and needless concern. I was not going to die from this. And he was right, too."

Her mother's sister Celia took Cari in after eighteen months in the hospitals. There would be more finishing treatments over the next six months, but she was whole again, learning to use her new limbs. The new eye was not perfect, but it had a built-in zoom lens which she found useful from time to time. And once it was properly adjusted, she forgot all about her new ear and hearing on the left side.

They had kept at her studies the last year and she resumed her classes with her friends. Everyone was nice to her—hardly any of the boys tried to tease her about anything. But it wasn't quite what it all was before. And they had closed her old house and boxed up the contents. She hadn't looked at any of it.

On top of that, she often still felt spiritless. Cari floated without feeling from day to day. It was never enough to drive her to despair, but each day still had to be endured and on to the next day.

She felt like a fraud here at the New Heart Recovery Group. Most of the people were older men and women who were simply candidates for replacement hearts. At sixteen, Cari was by far the youngest person here. So she sipped at half a cup of coffee—more gave her too much of a caffeine hit and kept her awake all night—and stood off by the side, waiting for the meeting to convene.

"We have a new member here this week," Miss French said, when she came in, smoothed her smock and took a seat at the head of the circle, clipboard computer at the ready in her lap. "This is Cari. Cari, everyone. Everyone, Cari."

"Hello, Cari," a chorus of voices said.

"Hi," was all Cari could manage. The group was the largest number of new people she had had to interact with since... since... since getting on the train.

She didn't remember much of the discussion.

Afterwards there was more coffee, as well as some cookies and other snacks on the sideboard. A woman who looked to Cari as if she were in her mid-thirties, wandered in and seemed to know most of the heart patients. She glad handed them, made chirpy, cheerful small talk and seemed to be handing out party favors.

"Hi—howya doing?" the woman said when she had made it over to Cari.

That was when Cari noticed the enameled brass nameplate on the woman's blazer. She worked for NuuHealth Medtronics, a factory rep for one of the brands of artificial hearts.

"Fine," Cari said.

"I'm not sure we've met, dear."

"We haven't."

"Well, I'm with NuuHealth. Whose heart do you have? Ours? The EverBeat? Best-selling heart on the market."

"No."

"PlasLink? Bo-Pump?"

"No," Cari said finally. "No. It's a Sony. M-1164r."

"A Sony?" The woman's face said it all. "You mean you got a Japanese heart?"

"Well, I am Japanese after all."

"I'm sorry. That came out wrong," the woman said, trying to backpedal.

"And it's not like I had a choice."

The light went on in the sales rep's eyes. "You're the girl from the PORT-SEA-VAN crash."

"Yeah. Guess you know your business then."

"Well, yes, I..."

But Cari wandered away. She didn't need to have this conversation.

"We call it Robofish," the guide at the Salmon Fish Ladder and Research Complex said, pointing out the one adult salmon swimming slowly in the holding tank which had a camera coming out of its head. "Besides the datalink to the video camera, we can override its central nervous system and direct the Robofish to look at what we want to look at."

"Do you have to control it all the time?" one of the boys asked.

"No. The rest of the time the Robofish is just another salmon, doing what salmon do."

That brought out a snicker from the back of the group of high schoolers. Cari, who hadn't really wanted to come on this field trip up along the Columbia River, found herself staring at the Robofish.

"We've learned a great deal about the lives of PacNorWest salmon populations," the guide said, then went on describing some of the science.

But the boys near Cari were still acting like high school boys with a good joke to overuse.

"Is that a *fish* or a *machine*?"

"I thought a fish *was* a machine. An eating machine."

"That's a shark. A salmon is more of a sex machine."

"Yeah, is that a boy Robofish or a girl Robofish?"

"I suppose you want a Robogirl for Christmas."

"Oh yeah! That'd be great. *Ow!*"

The last boy rubbed his upper arm where Cari had used her artificial right arm to punch him.

"You couldn't handle a Robogirl any more than you could a real girl," she said and stormed out of the center.

"What'd I do?" the boy asked in an injured tone.

One of the girls found Cari standing in amongst the trees.

"Cari? Cari?" She reached forward and touched her.

"What?"

"You were just standing there... so still."

"I was listening."

"To what?" The girl was confused.

Cari turned back towards the trees and closed her eyes. "The wind," she said. And as the quiet descended around her, she could hear the tree branches move and sway and creak in the wind. It was a random sort of noise, but somewhere she could sense some pattern of repetition in it.

It made her feel peaceful.

Doctor Hiredo finished looking in her eyes. The rest of her vitals he could get directly on his telemetry pad.

"So... am I still alive?" Cari asked.

"Of course," he said. "But then you knew that."

"Why is it so hard?"

Hiredo put down his pad, so he could give her his undivided attention. "It is easy to repair physical damage."

"Easy—ha."

"You still have a long journey ahead of you. We have given you back the gift of time to make that journey."

"I didn't sign up for this trip."

"No," he said wryly. "No one ever does."

Cari stood on the damp sand, unable to pull herself away. There was that rhythm again. The sound of the surf coming in, the watery rumble of the waves splashing feebly a few meters from her feet. The tide was going out now, if she stayed here transfixed for another hour, the water would be much further.

It was only as she turned, chilled in the cold wind, that Cari saw the other person standing fifty or sixty meters away. He, too, stared at the sea. She almost walked on, before she realized she had seen the man before. But where?

She had given herself this holiday, first to see the puffins on the rocks. Then to walk on the beach. Cari had intended to wiggle her toes in the Pacific Ocean, but decided against it once she got here. It was still her skin, but the toes weren't real. What would be the point?

The man was still there. Still staring at the surf. Then he turned and saw her.

Where had she seen him?

To her consternation, the man seemed to recognize her and was walking this way. Dumbly she stood, brushing back her hair each time the wind blew it back in her face.

"You're from that new heart group," Cari said in a sudden rush of recognition. "I'm Cari. Cari Ohtagawa."

The last name meant nothing, but *Cari* seemed to jog the

man's memory. "Oh. Uh, yeah. Yeah... I remember you," he said nodding. "You looked scared at your first meeting. I only saw you twice."

"Right. You were the only other one there who didn't have an Everbeat."

Now the man smiled. "PlasLink Plus."

"That means we have something else in common," Cari said. "No true pulse, as the doctors say."

"Right. I've got a condition with platelets—they didn't want the pumping action to accidentally start a clot and stroke me out."

"Gee—that's a nice thing to worry about," Cari said. "Man, the stuff the doctors make you learn."

"No kidding," the man said. He finally extended a hand. "Name's Bill. Bill Wright."

"Yeah, Bill," Cari said, nodding as they shook hands. "I remember."

They talked for a little while longer in the cold, but finally Cari had to go.

"See you sometime," she said waving.

"Oh, I'll be here," he said.

She puzzled at the cryptic little smile on his face after he said that.

The storm had raced in from the sea and pummeled the coast. People used to doing as they pleased seemed surprised at news reports that some of the coastal roads were either flooded or blocked with broken and fallen trees. Cari saw the indignation in the faces of these people and wanted to laugh at them. They had no clue about the power of nature or the fallibility of Man.

She had wanted to go out to the beach, or at least the rock breakers, and witness the storm, but couldn't. So as soon as she had free time from her job and could borrow a bubble car, she sped out to the sea.

There her beach was transformed, littered with driftwood and seaweed and other more unlikely trash.

But none of that mattered. There was still the surf, still the beat of the waves.

Bill was there, too, and Cari understood why.

"It's the pulse of the sea," she said as soon as he was within hearing.

"Yes." His smile was still sad. "The law of unintended consequences."

"We were born in the rhythm of our mothers' hearts," Cari said.

"And always our own pulse in the background. Day in, day out."

"Until the day we die."

They stood looking, not at each other, but at the sea.

"It's what I've been missing in my life," she said. Neither moved for several more minutes.

"I've a place along the beach—two kilometers up the line," he said finally. "Would you like some coffee?"

"Do you have decaf?" she said. "A lot of me is machine now."

"I understand," he said. "I think we can arrange something."

Slowly they walked along.

"Can you hear the surf where you live now?"

"Every day when I get up and every night when I go to bed," he said.

"That's nice," Cari said. "I think I'd like something like that."

Without really thinking about it, they linked arms as they walked. Cari was lost in her own thoughts—about the wind, the sea—and found within herself a new awareness about life. Later, she would probably look back at this moment, the moment when she began to live again. But that would come later. Right now, all she cared about was the sound of her new pulse crashing around her. They could replace much of her body with machines, but they couldn't take that away ever again.

Overhead a seagull began its raucous cry for attention. Life did go on, after all.

An Incident at Agate Beach

"Where did you come from?"

Marsha had jumped when the child materialized at her side, peering over her arm to see what it was she was doing, and she glanced about to look for his parents. But no one leaned from the cliff or climbed slowly down the path; no one was in sight along the beach in either direction, neither strolling along the rock pools nor bent to see what agates and jasper the tide had uncovered.

"What is it?" he asked, not bothering to answer. His eyes moved from the linen in her lap to the sewing basket, the lid thrown open to reveal a tumble of crewel embroidery thread mixed with silk and cotton floss. The circus gaiety of the contents must have drawn him, for he put his hand out and fingered a hank of purple thread, then ran his fingertips over the cloth tomato, studded with hundreds of pins, many of them a plain stainless steel but others topped with bright, transparent heads.

"It's—"

"Sea urchin?"

"A pincushion," she told him, pulling a redheaded pin from the sawdust to show him.

He took the pin from her and studied it, whispering *ushion, ushion.* Curious, he tapped the point against his arm.

"Ow!"

"Yes, it's sharp. The pins are to hold the fabric when I hem or appliqué." She saw that the words meant nothing to him. "Look. You see?" She took another sampler from the basket, turning it over to show where she had hemmed half of a side, leaving a picket of pins in place.

He seemed fascinated, touching the heads as if he were counting.

"How old are you? You look about seven, I'd say."

"Yes." Though he spoke, all his attention was on the sampler with its motto and vases of flowers and birds. His home-cut hair hung low on his forehead and covered his ears, though he somehow managed to look refined despite its carelessness—it must have been the delicate features and the sharp straight nose. The hair was a pale gold, shifting all together, like a cap. The boy seemed compounded of quickness and light, his fingers darting eagerly across the stitched scene.

"Do you like it?"

"Yes. But there are no fish. There should be fish."

Marsha laughed, folding the cloth and tucking it under the thread.

"It's sad, but very few samplers have fish," she told him. "Now and then you might see a bit of waves and a fish or two. Not often." She wasn't surprised that he wanted fish. Why, seaweed was tied at his waist like a kilt. The pale bladders shone among the dark leaves.

Reaching under the basket, she took out her laptop and showed him some other samplers she had recently completed, along with a project that was still in the planning stage. She had not quite finished copying the stitches onto a grid and making a key as to their colors and types. Her husband had formatted a program for her, so that she could type in the number of threads in warp and woof and the dimensions of the piece and immediately begin work.

"I don't know what it is." The boy patted the unfinished sampler in her lap and added, "I like this one better. It's soft and pretty."

"These are just pictures, you see? You've never seen one of these at school? This is a computer. I store the images of my samplers on it. That's what I do you see—I make museum reproduction kits, and people buy them and make copies of samplers that some little girl stitched a hundred years ago."

"Why?"

"Oh, I don't know. Because they like them, I suppose. For the fun of making."

"Why would you want to *store*?" He appeared to be struggling to follow her words. "That's not how *we* save things."

"What do you mean, *not how we save things*? What do you do with them?"

"Oh, the stones, you know."

"The stones."

"You know, the stones. The ones with the letters on them. We call them *ogil* stones."

"What an imagination you have!"

"You should throw this away." The boy tapped at the metal rim of the computer. "It doesn't belong. But don't toss it in the waves!"

She was amused. "Why not?"

"Because it's not for the sea."

"Well," she said; "I'm not so much on computers. That's my husband's domain. He's a real wizard with programming." And she thought of Jim, somewhere by the shore, searching for agates, as he had done years ago as a child growing up along the coast. She liked seeing him this way, barefoot and away from his desk. Only three months had passed since the day they'd met, and now they were married. His job remained mostly a mystery to her. She had barely seen him at work—two or three times she had watched him rotate figures or objects of white mesh on a blue background. They had appeared rather like the result of a cross between a wire dressmaker's dummy and a 3-dimensional drawing of the Earth, showing latitude and longitude like a stiff net holding in an endless sea. Then the next time they had substance and color, and she was disappointed. She had liked them better as enigmatic and blue, glimpses from another world.

"I'm sorry," she said; "I wasn't listening."

"My brother is in love with you." The boy smiled, showing bright nubs of teeth and tiny canines.

"But I'm married," she protested. "He can't be in love with me."

"Well, he is. He told me so. He has been watching you every afternoon, and he loves you."

"I'm on my honeymoon. He can't be in love," Marsha said severely. "And what's your name?"

"Bramble?" He looked hopeful. "You could call me Bramble. Or Ramble. Or Scramble."

She laughed. "All right, Bramble it is, at least for now."

"Good." He gave her a smile of intense sweetness. "And my father is in love with you, no matter what you say."

"Now you're confusing me! You said your *brother* was in

love with me. Are they *both* in love?"

"Oh. Well, it's not that. We just don't count us that way—we're just all close and we don't think about those sorts of things. Brother, father, all that. Though he's really my *half* brother." He seemed a little confused about how to explain his meaning. "We're born out of nowhere, right? And so we're all the same."

She lifted her eyebrows. "Okay," she said. "We're the same."

"No, not exactly. Some people are just born knowing. Other people are like you."

"Were you born knowing?"

"Of course."

Every afternoon for three weeks Marsha sewed while Jim poked about the tidal pools or went searching for agates and jasper. Afterward they would wander hand in hand along the shore or swim, and sometimes they would go up to the big bedroom with the plate glass window that framed the sea and the cavernous rock formation (wild when the tide was high) and the beach with its rocks and its animal flowers. They had a keen sense of how rare and precious their time together was, and that it wouldn't come around again—the two of them free to spend the day any way they liked. Both meant to sleep late but neither ever did, as the window had no curtain. Marsha could never get over her feeling of surprise that the sun didn't come up over the edge of the ocean, though the increasing light still managed to wake them at dawn, when they would stir and make love and go back to sleep.

They always intended to do nothing one day, just to stay in bed, but the big swashbuckling sky flung down its swords of light onto the sand and the sea, and they could not stay inside. Jim still had a child's excitement about what he would find and came home from his beachcombing with sacks of treasure—a curve of fossilized dolphin bone, a fossil clam, a bloodstone, opaque jasper in shades of butterscotch, red, brown, and green. He brought black agates, pink ones, occasionally pale blue. The owners of the house had a notebook in which they had recorded the best places to look or dig on or near the beach, and he pored over this homegrown guide, scouring it for clues.

Occasionally Marsha went with him, but she had deadlines to reach on new kits, so usually she sat under an umbrella, detailing the pattern of a sampler on her laptop, or else sewing a reproduction. The few hours apart made them eager to be together again, though it wasn't as if Jim were entirely absent; often she caught sight of him wading in the surf or clambering on the rocks.

Because their access to the beach was a private stairs—the house belonged to Jim's boss and was seldom used by any but his wife and daughters—she didn't see many other people. It wasn't much different from plenty of other nooks along the coast, and the owners called it simply *the agate beach*, though that was the name of a dozen or more near-nameless spots.

Now and then a group of runners would skim by and vanish into mist, and once Marsha had seen a line of karate students punching and blocking their way across the sand, not looking toward her as they moved in unison, each step—right leg, the left, the right—inscribing a crescent on the air. She wondered idly what the name of the move was. A man in a black gi moved swiftly alongside, correcting a stance or the position of an arm. Only he glanced her way and smiled.

The boy came to see her almost every afternoon. Some hours after the karate class had passed, he came and stood before her like a wading bird, one leg up. She kept sewing and didn't look, and he began pivoting, kicking at the air with his raised foot.

"Did you see the teenagers run by? Did you see the yellow belts and the green belts and the brown belts?"

"I don't know what you mean," he said, stopping with his leg still up, the knee bent.

"I thought you must know karate."

"What is *karate*? You mean those people who do this?" He dashed about the sands, kneeing imaginary opponents, striking them with elbow and fist, and ending in the horse stance with a great shout of *Hoah!*

"So you do know karate." She took the fabric she had been working on out of the hoop and tucked the needle with its gold thread into the pincushion. "Bramble, isn't it? I couldn't remember what you wanted to be called."

"Today I would rather be *Eetsch!"* he declared. "But I don't know karate. I just followed them because they were interesting, and I watched when they fought the mist." He came close and leaned against the rock where she was sitting. The faded old tomato caught his attention. Picked up, it sagged against his fingers. "This is so hard and bumpy on top. Soft underneath. But something could grab underneath and tear its guts—"

"What do you mean, *fought the mist?"* Marsha took the cushion from him. It had been her grandmother Josephia's, and she felt a mild attachment to the idea that their hands had touched the same thing, performed the same work.

"They went down by the water, and they did this—" here he flashed about the sand again— "inside a cloud. It was torn to pieces but came back together and won, so they had to go home."

"You have quite an imagination," Marsha observed.

"No," he said, looking puzzled; "I just have eyes that see things."

"So some people have eyes that don't see?"

He didn't appear to think this question worth the answering. Perhaps it was too obvious; perhaps he thought it merely rhetorical.

"The black man asked me to come with them. He chased me, but he couldn't catch me."

"The black man? Do you mean the devil? Oh, I know—the black belt. I thought he looked friendly. What did he say to you?" Marsha tugged at the sampler, straightening the cloth. It had puckered around a large urn from which fantastic flowers sprouted.

"He wanted me for himself. To do his magic. He said I took to it like nobody's business. What did he mean by that?"

She looked at the lithe frame and the feet that seemed never to be still but danced and pattered on the sand.

"He meant that you could be good at karate, that you looked like a natural—somebody who can do it easily by imitation. At least, that's what I suppose he meant. What did you tell him?"

The boy jumped in the air and sank into the horse stance, rocking and grinning at her. "I said *Hoah!* in the deepest voice in the world, deeper than his, so deep that it scared some of the hairs out of his head. Then I shouted *Yah! Yah! Yah!* and *Catch me!* He raced after me, but I lost him in the stones. They were all running after me," he said with satisfaction, "but nobody could catch me. I looked out at them and laughed."

"How? Did you hide?"

"I swam into a rock pool and stirred up the sand so they couldn't see, and I hid in a crack." The silk of his hair swung, as if nodding in agreement with the words.

Marsha wondered if any of his tale was true. Just then he gave a snap punch and another, and began scuttling about comically, still crouched in horse stance.

"Well, you are limber and quick. I don't doubt that he would have wanted to teach you. But you shouldn't hide in the water like that. What if you drowned?"

"You're not calling me *Eetsch*, you know. You should call me *Eetsch*. I'd never drown. I can swim better than you. Better than any of those punch-punch boys. If they had come close, I could've jumped into the sea and swum away from them all, till they gave up and drowned." He put out his chest like a body builder, grinning at her.

"What a little Puck you are," she said, rather charmed by his boastfulness.

"What's that?" He frowned, wrinkling the smooth area between the two gold bows of his eyebrows. Martha felt like touching them, they were so fine and glistening.

"A sort of sprite. A fairy."

"You mean with wings? Oh, I like them."

"Do you know any?" She laughed in sheer pleasure.

"Well, I've *seen* them. You'd have to talk to my brother about those. He knows them—he's met them far out in the ocean, riding on a whale's back."

"Birds, I suppose," she said softly. "So today you are *Eetsch*, and he's your brother again."

"Yes. But I'm really always the same, and he's really all the same." He reached for the pincushion, catching his fingernails on the steel heads.

"Careful with that—"

"And he still loves you. He'll always love you."

"Why?"

"Why love you? I think maybe it's your hair." He crept close and combed his fingers through its ripples. "Looks like gold."

"That's a silly reason."

"Why? Maybe it's not that. You have sea eyes." The boy peered into her face, coming so close that she drew back. "And you sit on the rocks and sew. He likes the songs that you sing..."

"Well, he shouldn't. I'm married, and I love my husband, and we'll live a long and happy life together. If all goes well," she added, crossing herself. It seemed bad luck to have said it outloud.

Eetsch's nimble fingers were working with the pins, making a pattern of jags and triangles out of the colored ones, with the steel heads outlining them.

"What's that?"

"A rune, a rune," he caroled.

"What for? How do you know about runes?"

"I don't think there's a word for it." He paused, staring at his handiwork, before squatting to start another shape.

Idly leaning with chin on hand, elbow to knee, she watched him turn the pincushion, stabbing the cloth surely and swiftly.

"You're a strange little boy," she said.

This made him laugh. Already the cushion looked like some beaded monstrosity from the Victorians, though perhaps it was too geometrical for that—more like a native product from the Cherokee in the mountains where she had lived until she met Jim.

"It's not like a voodoo doll or something like that, is it? You're not trying to do me some harm? Or what about Jim? Maybe your brother would like Jim to go away?" She slipped down beside him on the sand, in the shadow of the boulder.

Although she had been teasing, he took the question quite seriously.

"No, it's joyful. I just don't know how to say it. You keep the pins the way they are, and everything will turn out all right in the end. The way it should." He didn't look at her; his fingers were too busy. "You see?"

Marsha touched the top of his head; the sunny hair felt hot against her palm. For an instant, he froze. Then he relaxed and went on with his patterns.

"So he wouldn't hurt Jim," she murmured.

"No; why do that if you love him? Besides, he likes Jim." He inspected the pincushion as it caught the blaze of afternoon and seemed to ignite in his hands.

"Likes Jim? Have they ever met?"

"No, of course not. But my brother watches out for me, and he sees Jim, too. He helps him with his—his works."

"His works?"

"Yes, my brother puts the pebbles and the big ones, the cobbles, in his path so he can't help but find them. It's a game. He hunts for lovely ones under the water."

"You mean agates and jasper?"

"Yesterday he put out pink agates, and the day before it was blue ones, the kind that you don't see so often. He said that Jim was very pleased."

Marsha gave a little twitch of unrest. It was true; she remembered that he had found blue agates two days back, and he had left pink ones on her pillow only the afternoon before. The coincidence of the thing was queer.

"Did you talk to Jim? How did you know?"

"I told you. My brother told me. I don't talk to Jim. Like I don't talk to the black man."

"Jim wouldn't chase you. He's seen you in the distance."

"I know. I let him see me. Here." He held out the tomato, wrapped in runes. *If they were runes,* Marsha thought, *and not just his play.*

"And what shall I use when I need pins?"

"Oh, there's some left over. I put them on the bottom." So he had, but he couldn't resist the flourish of putting the silver pins into the shape of a star.

Eetsch leaned close to her and made a clicking sound with his tongue.

"What's that for?"

"It's my kiss. I invented it."

Once again she was struck by his smile, which seemed a thing of great purity and sweetness, and on impulse she put her arm around him and pressed him close. Perhaps children were a good idea, she reflected, if they were as bright and nice as this one.

He wriggled out of her grasp and jumped to his feet, laughing at her and showing the sharp little chips of canines—baby teeth, still unshed.

"Should I thank your brother, I wonder?"

The boy shrugged. "It doesn't matter. He did it because of love. Your Jim, what kind of stones does he like best?"

Marsha stared at him, feeling certain that this was a very odd sort of conversation. He drew her gaze and kept it. She would miss him, and the aesthete in her would miss looking at him. Though not conventionally beautiful, the dark eyes and fair hair and the slender, almost sharp features gave her a good deal of satisfaction—the sort of pleasure she might have gotten out of examining a valuable and fascinating sampler, say.

"He likes all the jaspers and agates. But he hasn't found any sagenite, the type with the threads shot through the stone, and I know he would like a good enhydrite. Do you know what that is? The kind with water trapped inside?"

"Sure, I know."

His eyes were no longer on her but on the waves.

"You should go up to your house," he said. "The sea's turning."

At once he sprang away, his shirt ruffling in the wind, and raced into the water. Marsha stood, calling, and witnessed the boy throwing himself into the ocean, under the shadowy lee of a massive rock. Then he was gone, though she raced after him and searched until the tide was waist deep and pouring toward land.

"Marsha!" There was Jim on the cliff steps, with her basket in his hand. "Over here—it's coming in fast."

She knew it was too dangerous to stay. Spars and timbers near the rock pools were floating on the low water. The owners of the house had warned against swimming anywhere but the public beach down the road because a log, riding on a glaze of water, had sometimes killed. Even grown men had been struck and crushed. It wasn't like the beach at Kill Devil Hills where her parents had rented a cottage each summer, where the flags had told them what to watch for—the fluttering red cloth marking rip tides and strong currents.

"This way!" He pointed to a narrow defile between stones where the water was rushing and foaming, and she splashed up from the sea, casting a glance over her shoulder now and then but seeing nothing.

To her relief, the next afternoon the boy was back with a shirtful of sagenites "from my brother," lovely clear and golden stones shot through with needles of air. Marsha and Startle—he had named himself *Startle* for the day—left one on each step of the twisting staircase up to the house, and Jim had been well surprised.

"He'll be stunned," she had told the boy. "Happy."

The newlyweds made love on the boss's king-size bed with the stones all around them on the sheets and pillows. Jim had set them on her naked body and, when she closed her eyes, balanced two ovals on her eyelids.

"I feel like a queen laid out in a Neolithic barrow."

"I'll be a greedy cave man, sacking and pillaging the dead and coming home with treasure."

She arched against him, feeling the stones slide from her skin. The sagenites struck one another with a noise like the clicking of dice.

"My lady of the agates," Jim whispered, reaching for her. He looked exposed and vulnerable without his glasses, like a sea creature out of its shell. His skin was pale, his eyes dark.

The sagenites slipped, momentarily sticking to one and then the other as he pressed against her. When the tide of their lovemaking had broken on the stones and begun to ebb, the smooth shapes lay against her torso, outlining the curve of her side, her waist, the flare of her hip.

"My beauty." Jim took others and outlined her nakedness, then curled beside her with his arm across her breasts and his face nestled in the curve of her neck. She smiled at the strangeness of his fancy and at his delight in the polished forms, which was different but no less than his eagerness for her breasts and thighs. Wasn't it like a boy to pick up stones or sticks?

"Like a man's genitals," she whispered, drawing her hand along the ridgeline of his spine. Was he asleep now, a cobble clasped in one hand like a toy in the hand of a child? "Nothing but a stick and two stones."

As she drifted after him toward sleep, she thought for the

first time of how the brother—if there was a brother—had collected the air-needled stones and held them in his hands, so that, if he existed, he had in some sense touched her intimately; or, at least he had reached from one moment in time to another as surely as grandmother Josephia with her much-handled pincushion.

Jim was swimming; she could just detect him, far out, where they had seen the black and white orcas turning leisurely in the sun. Then she glimpsed something in the circle of rocks that the owners had said was named *the devil's porridge bowl* because its contents churned to white at high tide, and she was frightened and called for him to come back, though of course he couldn't hear.

"It was someone—I saw an arm reaching out of the water. But nobody ever surfaced."

She had stayed at the edge of the waves until Jim swam to shore and rose, dripping, from the shallows.

"You saw something. Probably just a trick of the light."

"No, I'm sure. It was a man's arm, and there was something odd... bluish, maybe, I'm not sure."

Jim was scrubbing himself with the towel she had brought, his skin becoming rosier by the instant. She hadn't been able to make him understand how afraid she had felt, seeing the arm and hand, knowing that he was out of reach. Perhaps she wasn't even clear on its importance—that instant of seeing the hand.

"Well, if it were a man, he'd probably be blue with cold. It's chilly out there."

"If it *was*," she corrected. *Because it was, it really was,* she thought. "You're not taking me seriously." She dug her bare toes through the sand grains, dredging crystal from below the surface.

"What am I supposed to do? You tell me that you saw an arm in the ocean, and I'm supposed to do something? We could call the Coast Guard, but they'd think we were crazy."

His hair stood up in spikes, and Marsha reached to flatten it with her hand.

"No, not that. You look like a pincushion." She remembered the boy, holding the tomato in his hand. "A sea urchin."

"An urchin that needs a long hot shower," he said. "Brr, I'm going in. You could come along, you know."

"All right. I'll be there in a minute." She had caught sight of a white shirt, fluttering from behind a boulder.

When Jim had climbed halfway up the stairs, the boy came running out to see her. He had a slender spear in one hand, tipped with an arrowhead; he wore a look that she had seen before on his face: excitement, tamped down. Marsha realized that she would miss him when she went away, and that she no longer worried about his parents or where his house might be. He seemed to be well able to take care of himself, and to think that everything that called to his attention was interesting. She liked that about him.

"I saw an arm. In the devil's porridge bowl." She nodded toward the low, jagged walls of the cauldron.

The boy pursed his lips. Perhaps he was busy thinking, perhaps listening. His profile seemed to rest against the light, as if leaning on it for support.

"Where? I mean, exactly."

"You see where there's a jag? Where the rock goes up and there's a curve, with a sort of hole?"

He unbuttoned the shirt, tucking it into a crevice in an upright stone. Then he was naked, all but a necklace she had noticed before—pierced with a hole and ringed by runic shapes—and the long fringe of seaweed hanging from his waist. Skipping into the waves, he quickly waded out, and in an instant he was standing inside the walls of the devil's bowl and reaching up to feel inside the opening she had seen. He waved at her; he was clutching something as he leaped from the cauldron. At other times the hemmed-in surf foamed and was wild, but now the water sloshed gently against the sides.

"From my brother." He put the cobble into her hands. It was a large sagenite, pierced by many shafts.

"It's lovely." She wasn't looking the stone which was, indeed, remarkable, with traces of blue like clouds, so that its whole aspect bore the air of a picture in a bottle—a cloudy scene with sunlit rain coming down. Instead, she was staring at the spot where she had seen the arm.

"Here." He held up the pendant around his neck, and she grasped the stone's edge, unsure what he wanted of her.

But before he could say another word, she caught a glimpse of something, right through the opening in the center. She made out a man's face rising from the sea. She blinked once, found the head again; then a third time she saw him, looking straight toward them, but when she drew away and stared, she detected nothing, nothing at all. The boy's features were impassive, and he let the necklace fall back to its place. Hardly enough time had elapsed to register the features in memory, but she thought that there was a resemblance and felt—how? The waves could play tricks on a person, she told herself: no reason to be anxious or afraid. And hadn't Jim been swimming out that far, half an hour ago? Perhaps it was a snorkeler who had been floating on the waves and was only occasionally seen.

"What do you call yourself today?"

"I call me *King-of-Fishes.*" He smiled as he stared at the Pacific, peaceful now and dark blue, sparkling in the sun. "That means I'm in charge of all the fishes. But my brother is king over the sea and even the deep gulfs and the creatures of old fire, so he is better than me. Though I am quite good enough," he said proudly.

"And what did you show me just now?" She wasn't sure that he had done so; she wasn't positive of anything except that Jim would be waiting for her at the top of the cliff, and that he would forgive her for not coming to him in the shower when he saw the big sagenite that the boy had put in her hands.

"Did you see something." He spoke softly, walking away from her.

"What is that device around your neck?" She followed, touching him briefly on the hair, where a dazzle of sun rested like a crown.

"Oh that. That's my toy. It's a thing that binds me and heals me and brings me back when I go away. It's my blessing."

He fingered and gave the cord a tug, checking to see if it held secure; his hand reached for the knot at his nape. Afterward he gave the stone a swipe, as if to polish it.

"Sometimes you don't sound a bit like a boy, you little King-of-Fishes."

"But what does that matter? Even when you're an old, old woman, you won't feel any older inside. You won't feel any older than you do today, except for the weight on your breast." He tapped the pendant. "Not this. The dead, I mean, and the things that didn't happen. And mistakes you made."

"Now I know you're not a boy. You're a wise weird thing that's thousands of years old." She drew away from him, teasing him and turning to look back at the ocean and scan the waves for something—a little interruption that was neither whale nor bird nor buoy.

"No, I'm just me. King-of-Fishes." He took her by the hand, and his fingers were cold and a little tacky, as if he had been playing in brine and mud. "Remember what I said at the start. Some are just born knowing. It's easier that way."

At the start of what, she wondered.

"I'll be going home soon." It was surprising how sad saying the words made her feel.

King-of-Fishes leaned against her, his arms chilly against hers, and he made his clicking noise that meant a kiss, and she clicked back at him, pressing her cheek against his. She marveled at how she had become so fond of this boy, when she'd never met his parents and knew almost none of the usual things about him—where he lived or went to school, his favorite movies and games and books. They looked at the water together, and far out a whale breached and showed a flash of black and white, tidy as a domino. *An orca.*

"You'll come back," the boy told her, his voice dreamy. "I promise."

Then he jerked his head up, as if in response to a shrill note—someone close by had whistled.

"Wait, I've got a present for you—"

He darted away between stones, the seaweed flying, and Marsha kept still, her gaze traveling slowly across the surface of the sea but finding nothing to arrest its motion. In only a few minutes he was back again, flushed and smiling.

"This is for him—"

He handed her an enhydrite, cobble-sized. She exclaimed in surprise, holding it up to see the water trapped inside. It had been erratically worn and was smoother on one side than the other.

"My brother told me to give it to your man. Said that he

shouldn't go home without one. But I've forgotten his name—"

"Jim. His name is Jim."

"It's hard to remember when the names never change. It's so dull. Don't you ever want to be something besides a *Marsha*?"

"You liked my name because it sounded like marsh, and you like the wet places."

"Yes, but sometimes you could be *Bog* or *Pool*." He was serious, pressing against her, tilting his head. Its silk clung to her arm.

"A *Puddle*."

"*Rivulet* is nice. I like the sound of it. Or you could be Queen of the Ocean. You *ought* to be Queen of something."

He was absently rubbing the stone that hung from his neck, and when he looked up at her, she thought that his nervous, delicate features were beautiful. Yet she didn't remember finding him so at first. The idea occurred to her that she could take the boy home and adopt him. But it was too soon; she had known Jim for such a short time.

"Maybe Queen of the Sea Slugs."

"Yes."

She was amused to see that his face was serious. He was turning a small bundle in his hands and hardly seemed to notice her words.

"Would you like to live where I do, in a city?"

He pulled away from her, shaking his head.

"I would be crazy," he said; "I would be like that man who fought the sea. *Hoah!*" He scampered toward the waves and jumped in, kicking and whirling and slashing with an imaginary sword. She saw the package fall, striking his leg and tumbling into the shallows. He spun around, feeling the loss, and knelt, groping with his hands. She could hear him crying out, "No, no no, no..." and then with a great upward leap he shot from the water, punching the air with his fist.

"I almost lost it," he panted; "My brother would have been very angry. I would have been angry too."

The package was bunched in his hand, its gold cloth poking out in puckers between his fingers.

She knew to wait, that he would show her if he chose. And if she asked and he didn't want to share, King-of-Fishes would be off, the drops flying from his heels.

"It's for you. Open your hands, and I'll give it to you."

She did as he said, seating herself cross-legged on a heap of pebbly crystals and offering her cupped hands. The enhydrite lay before her.

"Now," he told her. "You must keep these for yourself and not give them to the—to Jim. It's very important, because they're meant only for you."

He stared at her. "Well?"

"All right," she agreed. "I won't give them to him or anybody else. I'll keep them for myself, because they're from you, and I'm fond of you and will miss you."

The boy frowned, kicking at the sand.

"It's not exactly from me—that is, my brother gave them to me. For you. And there's one for each of us."

"Your family?"

"That's what you would say, I guess. The ones who are together."

"I suppose that's a family," she told him.

He stood on one foot, thinking. "It's like a school of fish. How they all turn to and fro. We just know the same way—where we are and what's happening and who's going to do something next."

"But you're here with me. You're not with anybody else." She combed her fingers through the fine threads of his hair.

"That's because I'm a boy. The children always have adventures on the beach. That's how it's done. Because they're in between, not a baby and not grown like the sea and the land are when they're together at the shore. Not sea and not earth."

Marsha had entirely forgotten about Jim and the shower. "What stories you tell! I really am going to miss you."

He stamped hard against the sand with his foot, then lifted it up to see the imprint. "You're not holding out your hands anymore."

"Sorry. I forgot."

She cupped them again; obediently she shut her eyes when told to do so. He laid one after another—something smooth and cool—on the shadowlines that separated her fingers. The last he placed on her right palm. Opening her eyes, she looked at the seven enhydrites. In coloring they didn't appear like any she had seen in shops or in Jim's collection, and they were all of similar size and shape, about as long as two of her finger joints. When she held them to the light, they glistened, blue or turquoise with occasional glints of rose and green. No, she had never encountered anything like them.

"Sweet," she said.

He ignored her; perhaps that wasn't enough praise, or perhaps it was just wrong. "This one is me." He pointed with his pinkie finger, indicating the smallest stone. "And this one is my brother." Here he tapped the one that lay on her palm.

"And there are others."

"Of course there are," he said, sounding puzzled that she needed to say so.

"Is one of them your mother?"

"My mother died when I was a baby. I don't remember."

Ah, now we're finding something out, she thought. *So his mother is dead, and maybe the brother acts like a parent. Because his father may be gone or dead as well?*

"If you ever want me and my brother and the rest of us," he said, staring intently and drawing his face so close to hers that his features went out of focus, "you just sow the stones in the ground near the sea."

"You could come and live with us," she suggested, hardly listening, but he gave a jerk of the head in dismissal.

"I would be crazy. I just *told* you, remember? I'd be like that man who tried to kill the sea, remember? And look what happened when I pretended—I lost the stones! I can't live without the sea."

The boy drew back. "You sow them in the earth if you want us. But it has to be by the ocean, or else we'll die. Are you listening to me?" He grasped the thin cloth of her cover-up, gathering it in his hand.

"Yes, but—"

He ran away from her, not even stopping for his shirt, and was lost among the crowd of rocks near the devil's bowl.

"King-of-Fishes," she shouted. "Come back! I'm sorry." But she had to go up the stairs without saying goodbye that afternoon, carrying the cobble and the seven enhydrites, which she wrapped in the strip of gold.

On the last three days she hardly saw him, only spying his figure in the distance. She had finished her projects and now accompanied Jim on his forays in the rocks. Once she saw the boy bounding from steppingstone to steppingstone, and once she saw him perched on the lip of the devil's bowl, staring into the water. Another time she thought that she could make out the shapes of two pale-haired swimmers, far from shore.

Feeling a little disloyal, she had hidden the seven stones in a jewelry case. Jim had been pleased with the enhydrite and wanted to find another. Once when he was asleep she carried the box to the window and scrutinized them closely, noticing lines like the shapes on Josephia's pincushion incised on the surface. A flake of something bright inside the largest one caught her eye. When she held that one up, she detected a thin shard suspended inside the stone's pocket of liquid. It glinted, fluttering in the water like a leaf falling through air.

When Jim was loading the car, she hurried to the beach, hoping to see the boy once more. She looked for him near the stairs and in the hollowed-out boulder where she had once found him sleeping. He must have been watching, but he let her search and call his names and didn't answer until she wandered into the grove of upright stones. He laughed, jumping up to rush at her and throw his arms around her waist.

"Who are you this time?" She leaned and pressed her cheek against his hair.

"I am *Sad*," he told her. "I am sad."

Back in the apartment in the city, the whole episode seemed far away. She put the case on the wardrobe with some other jewelry boxes, and immediately she forgot. The image of the boy in his seaweed skirt and a spear in his hand, the face she had glimpsed as through a keyhole, the hand in the devil's bowl: they appeared like nothing but dreams.

Even her life with her husband became illusory, beginning with the third day of their return. On that date, a truck failed to stop at an intersection and ploughed into the driver's side door of her car. His car in the shop for an overdue inspection, Jim had borrowed hers. He was killed only a few blocks from the apartment. Just like that. Simple. *Dead on arrival.* Her car totaled. The death seemed like something that hadn't happened, it came so quickly. Its very abruptness seemed to mitigate against tragedy and to suggest an unreality. Only at the funeral did the loss begin to sink in, though she had an intense desire to get up from the pew and leave the church, to abandon this—this *undertaking,* which was nothing she had ever wanted. His body was cremated, and the ashes placed in a metal tube with a stopper. The cylinder possessed the heft of a costly kaleidoscope, and its sound was a mix of rattles and shifting sands. But there had been nothing to see, neither light nor color: only dark. She hid the blind thing inside a lidded vase.

Strange how Jim's exit from time seemed to distort time. The evenings were long and cavernous and held a multitude of thoughts. Grief seeped in little by little. She bought a television—a device she had always disliked—and let it eat the hours. Marsha sat on the floor in front of the screen, rocking back and forth as she cried, the volume turned up so that no one in the nearby apartments would know.

"I met you three months before we married, and we were at the coast for three weeks, and then we returned and you died on the third day." She gave the vase a shake, as if she could get his attention. "So there were just three months, three weeks, and three days."

At the beginning of her period, she slumped in front of the television with the urn in her arms, crying without making any attempt to stint her tears. She was weeping for their children, who were not and would never come to be, and she was mourning for the body that wanted a baby when it was too late. The image of an enhydrite with a flake of mineral trapped inside came to her mind.

The loss might have been easier if she had not been an only child, born to a mother almost fifty and a father of sixty. Both her parents were now dead. And it might have been better if she had moved to the Carolinas again, but she couldn't make herself do so. She couldn't bear the idea of explaining to everyone she knew what had happened, and hearing how, yes, it was tragic and terrible but that time would heal. For that matter, she didn't want to pack up or get rid of Jim's clothes and the objects in his study. She wore his shirts and bathrobe; a faint fragrance of him lingered in their closet.

Jim's boss always brought her flowers on the seventh day of the month. The two had been best friends since boyhood, and they had gone to Cal Tech together. When small, the pair of them had been called *JimJase,* they were so close. Jason suggested that she go back to the house by the beach of agates and jasper to sprinkle her husband's ashes on the waves. She thanked him but said that she was not ready.

At night she lay in bed, aching for Jim to reach for her or to curl at her back, his breath warm on her neck. Sterile limb, the hand that gripped the tissue was useless, merely her own. No other touch would arrive in the dark, secret and surprising. She often dreamed of seeing him at the shore. He would be wading at the edge of the ocean, picking up jasper and agates, his head down as he examined his finds. She saw that they were nothing like the stones of day; they glowed, and burning needles pierced the sagenites. He would turn but not see her, and the weight of the cobbles looked heavy in his hands. When she pursued him through a labyrinth of upright stones, he only receded into the background until she could not tell him apart from the gray, bent rocks.

She would awake, tears on her face and a terrible pain in her chest, and she would turn on the lamp and stare at the dark windows and at the pale arc lamps in the street.

In time, she had to set his pictures around the house because she began losing his face. She matched the exact shade of his shaggy hair to a hank of Theolian's *bloodroot* floss. His eyes were less easy, and she settled on *wood umber.* Studying his images, she found him slippery and hard to keep. The fashionably ugly glasses got in the way. She wanted to see the exact shape of the line moving from brow to orbit to cheekbone, but it remained elusive. After all, they had had only the three months, three weeks, and three days. *In time. After all.* She hated the words; sometimes she thought that she hated language. When she no longer needed it at night, she donated the television to the nearest Goodwill store. A dullness set in, and she found herself still uninterested in needlework projects, though she forced herself to continue.

The worst was when spring came and brought fresh forgetting. Shouldn't April have brought a renewal of desire? But it was impossible to remember a man every minute, every hour. She sat under the fruit trees, sewing a new sampler. The original had been purchased by a private collector, who let her study and measure and take notes in return for a document—an accurate description and an assessment of value. The naked man and naked woman were crude but charming. The faded apples on the tree had turned to salmon, as had many of the birds. Petals drifted onto the cloth, and she brushed them away. When she tucked the linen into the basket, her hand grazed the pinheads on Josephia's cushion. Drawing it from the bottom of the basket, she felt surprised all over again by the designs made by the colored and silver pins. She had forgotten—it had been so long since she had needed more than a hoop and a paper of needles.

That night she called Jason and his wife, thanking them for the latest delivery of flowers, left on the mat outside her apartment door. They urged her to use the house again if it wouldn't make her unhappy to be there. Perhaps it would be a help, a resolution, an ending: a something. She would think about it, said that she was not "getting over" Jim but that she seemed to be putting his memory at a little distance, as if their days together had been collected and given a museum space down the hall. That evening she went into his study for the first time in months. Cobbles and pebbles were spread across the library table, dusted with silt. A magnifying glass lay on the blotter of his desk. She took it in her hand, feeling for his grip around the handle. A memory of rolling across sheets littered with sagenites drifted into her mind, and she tried to fix the moment so that it would grow. But the images slid into the shadows and would not stay.

Copies of Jason's sketches for a new game lay scattered in loose sheaves on bookshelves. She inspected one, noticing for the first time that the hero bore a vague resemblance to her husband.

Then, remembering the seven stones, she went to her bedroom and scoured the dresser and chest and wardrobe but found nothing. Only when she looked under and behind the furniture did she find the jewelry case, wedged between the wall and the paneled back of the wardrobe. Unknotting the bundle of gold cloth, she strewed the contents across a pool of lamplight. The fingerlings of stone were lovely. She had forgotten how unusual the color was, almost turquoise in places, with blues and flecks of other colors. Again Marsha felt sure that she had seen nothing like them in Jim's books. The runes were scratched onto the surface and might have been made yesterday, they looked so fresh. Rocks were among the eldest things, but they remained mysteriously youthful. A thousand years from now someone might hold an enhydrous agate in her hand and wonder who had incised it, who had held it, what had become of them—and was the treasure lost only last year or a hundred or more?

They might as well have been elf bolts, flung at her, because they woke a sleeping curiosity and desire. How had she forgotten the boy for so long? She remembered his sharp-cut nose and the darkness of his eyes. How comical he was, wearing a seaweed kilt and a too-big oxford shirt, probably left behind by a tourist. She had seen him bathing naked, diving off the outermost rocks of the devil's bowl. Never had she spied him in mundane dress or looking like an ordinary child in company with his playmates or parents. Once recalled to mind, he became the focus of her thoughts, and she felt eager to see him.

She and Jim's mother, along with Jason and his wife, met at the beach house in June, and they waded out to an island of rock and each tossed a handful of the grit and ash from the cylinder onto the water. Afterward the others lingered for an hour to collect stones, because that seemed right. Roaming along the spits of rock and over black bands of sand and heaps of clear crystal, Marsha had a pleasant sensation that the boy was close by, but after the others departed the feeling drained away. It must have been seeing them at a distance, bending to examine a pebble or toss one into a bag, that made her feel that the day had become familiar—like those lost days when she could spy her husband hunting for treasure, beyond the next pile of shillets or the next curve of the beach.

Although she called for him and looked, she saw no evidence of the child except for his homemade spear, wedged in a crack in the rocks. The shaft was broken, but the stone was still good, bound to its stake with a strip of dried grass.

She felt disappointed and a little worried. He had always been so quick to appear!

When it was time to turn out the lights, she felt afraid and left a lamp burning. She didn't know why or what she feared. The bare-faced moon shone through the glass wall overlooking the sea and lit her empty bed. The evening made so many homely or pleasant figures wear a different aspect. If she were to spy her husband by starlight: what horror. Even seeing the boy tapping on the glass—impossible, as the house jutted from the cliff—would scare her, she felt sure. And if she walked down to the beach at night and saw a pale arm in the surf, or two faces, she would be too trembly and weak to climb the stairs.

"You said that I'd come back," she told the handful of enhydrites, "but you didn't say that you wouldn't be here."

Seated close to the edge of the cliff, she surveyed the coast and sea, the pale sands and the black sands, the forest of upright stones, and the devil's bowl. For three days she had searched for the boy, even going so far as to ask at a another house whether they had seen such a figure, dressed in seaweed. Nothing. A heavy silver spoon lay in her lap next to the smooth finger joints of stone. After a while she got up and dug into the soil, prying up low windblown plants she didn't recognize; their roots held crystal, clear or amber, with here and there a jot of red or green jasper. The narrow trench, a few inches long, looked like a model of the grave of some ancient king, heaped with precious jewels. She laid the largest enhydrite in the pit and pressed the plant roots and sand into place. Immediately she felt the impulse to dig it up again but did not. Levering up another clod of sand and roots, she slipped the smallest stone under it. She remembered the year that she had planted tulips upside down and wondered whether there was a right way and wrong way to do this. How close together? She settled on two feet apart—about the width she had used when planting perennials.

"I must be mad to do it," she murmured, patting the last piece of turf.

Looking around, she saw that the soil looked undisturbed, as if she had done nothing, and wished that she had marked the sites. It would be hard to dig up the stones again. Perhaps she would never find them all. But what did it matter? She didn't believe anything would happen—and if not, why were they important? No, it was fine, whether she found them again or not.

The next day she stayed indoors, only once venturing to the beach to watch a rainstorm pelt the standing stones until they were black and glossy. Then she returned to the house and took a shower, the hot water sluicing her back until she was relaxed and sleepy.

She thought of reading a book, but words had lost the meaning for her that they once had held. What was the use of a story? She had been in a story of happily-ever-after; then she had fallen out of it, as if the writer had excised her with a flood of ink.

The next day she saw a morning rainbow, and she took the fading vision as a lucky sign. Wind blew away the clouds and rubbed the ocean against its nap, tossing foam. Going to the cliff's edge, she saw that the ground was still saturated, so wet that water had collected in a shallow depression. Although on waking she had decided to dig up the stones, not wanting to lose them, she now planned to wait a day until the ground had dried. That afternoon she walked for miles up the coast, stopping to visit pools of stars and anemones. She came across the black belt, watching his class perform calisthenics, and she paused to examine the faces of the younger boys.

"Excuse me, do you remember—"

He swung around, a wiry, slightly bowlegged man with his hair in a ponytail.

"Do you remember a boy with seaweed—around his waist, I mean—he was very quick and light. He followed you one day and imitated your class."

The man gave a lopsided grin, shaking his head.

"I tried two or three times to catch that one! He used to tease us, but I thought he would have been champion material, with a little training."

"Have you seen him? Recently, I mean."

The class was doing push-ups now, while the surf frolicked to and fro, undermining their grip on land.

"No. I don't think I've seen him since last fall. You know him?"

"He used to come and play and talk to me, when my husband was out of sight. I just hoped nothing had happened to him."

The instructor turned back to his class, perhaps disappointed to hear about her husband. "If you find him, tell him to join my group and be a winner. There's a real spark to that one."

"Perhaps he was afraid of you. He called you *the black man*."

Amused, his eyes flicked to her face.

"Like the devil, you mean? I've got a reputation as a taskmaster, but that's quite a distinction." His hand went to his throat. She noticed a small Celtic cross and chain between his fingers. "*The black man*. What was the kid's name, anyway?"

"He never had the same one twice. I don't think he ever told me a real name, or certainly not an ordinary one."

"I wouldn't worry about him. He had the look of a kid who can take care of himself. Say, about that husband of yours... Are you happy with him?"

This seemed a difficult question, and Marsha puzzled it over in her mind for a second longer than confidence warranted. The ramifications of it seemed more and larger than she would have guessed. Was she content now, with what was left of him—that is, memories of three months, three weeks, three days? Was she capable of living with the Jim that was absence and being at ease, perhaps not now but later? Was he in any way still hers, or still a husband, though separated from her by time? She wondered whether she seemed bereft and abandoned, to make this stranger ask such a question.

"Whenever I have been with Jim," she said at last, "I have been happy." That much she was sure of. The answer was no doubt clouded, but she felt it was the best she could do.

"I guess that's—somehow I thought he might have run off—well, you know where to find me," he said cheerily, jogging away from her and calling for the class to follow.

When she returned to the stairs in the late afternoon, she noticed that the cliff face was marked with long tearstains. Drops plummeted from the lip, and, as she cocked her head to look, one splashed onto her forehead. Checking the top, she noticed that the pool had not shrunk but rather had grown larger. The vegetation was soaked and a brilliant green. Moisture seeped, collecting in rivulets that inched toward the brink.

She supposed that it had rained more than she knew. Inside the house, she curled by the big window overlooking the ocean and stared out. She was hungry but didn't feel like eating. It was restful by the cool glass, with the waves wrinkling the sea's surface and the shadows of the rocks growing long. She took a sampler from the basket but pulled the needle through the fabric only once before letting it drop. The long walk in the sea air had tired her. Like a gradual tide, the night edged in, blurring the line between wakefulness and sleep. In the morning she woke on the floor with her head pillowed on her arm.

Stumbling to the pantry, she took out a sack of coffee. From the kitchen window she could see the moon to the southeast, hanging over North America in a tissue of clouds. As if by magic, the veil turned red, and the crescent glowed a pale, bright sage. She stared, drinking her coffee, until dawn yielded to the daylight. Only then did she rummage in the freezer and find some waffles, eating them fresh out of the toaster with neither butter nor syrup. Without Jim, she no longer had an interest in cooking, so it didn't matter. Nothing inside the house really held her notice; all she wanted was to go outside and wade in the surf and climb the rocks until she became weary.

Barefoot, she stood on the stone doorstep—blue and shaped like a child's drawing of a cloud—and listened to a pattering. The sound, so pleasurable and erratic in its notes, startled her. When she went to look, Marsha found that the water could no longer be thought of as a large puddle. Streamers of liquid splattered against the rock face, blown by the breeze. Peering over, she saw that a stain of considerable size had spread over the sand. All day the pool grew, until it was some yards wide and constantly spilling over the edge of the cliff.

"I wonder," she said aloud, but left the thought unfinished. Although cautious, she ventured close and finally stepped into the shallow circle. The water felt as cold as a mountain spring. "Maybe a coincidence. Could you be coincidence," she muttered, bending low and combing her hand through the low coastal plants to see if anything had surfaced from the ground. Nothing: nor were there cracks or perforations of any kind. "If you're not a coincidence, what then? Should I feel worried, alarmed? I've done something—what?"

By nightfall, a miasma tinged faintly blue hung over the pool, which was deeper and faster-flowing than before. When she picked her way through its current, Marsha felt streams of bubbles flying against her ankles. Kneeling and then crawling on the drowned plants, she felt her way across the cliff-top.

"Seven. There are seven. Like sand creatures buried by a wave and sending up bubbles." Her voice was muted by the fog that swirled slowly around her. When she moved away, it seemed to settle in columns above the water.

And still she was not afraid. She had no desire to drive off in Jim's little blue sports car with his prescription sunglasses still stuck in the pocket of the visor. Only when the moon rose and the stars came out did she begin to feel uneasy, alone under the zodiac with no one to see or to care what happened to her. Her old friends were three thousand miles away, and only Jason and his wife and perhaps some of Jim's other colleagues knew that she was staying in the beach house—those plus her mother-in-law, who hadn't cared for the daughter so abruptly foisted on her. She didn't go inside, all the same, even when the mist over the pool thickened with dew and streams rushed from the ground and became a torrent, wallowing and then eddying at the base of the cliff until a finger of liquid trickled across the sand and vanished between stones, heading toward the sea. In less than an hour, the waterfall had made a rutted course and now flung itself pell-mell from height to sand to stones, losing itself in the tide. At once, with a *whoosh!* the cliff emptied itself of liquid, the creek twisting in the air like a silver otter with a tail of mist, vanishing between the standing rocks.

Marsha, who had been kneeling on the damp ground, exhilarated by the strangeness and increasing force of the falls, got to her feet. Her gaze was on the silvery track, winding across the sand. The water was gone, diving into the sea and hiding itself. The end was as mysterious as the beginning. Going to the site where the pool had formed, she bent and looked closely at the surface in the moonlight. Though the expanse appeared quite undisturbed and felt no more than ordinarily damp to her palm, the seven enhydritic stones were lying close together on top, as if she had never buried them.

She retrieved one after another, tucking them into the pocket of her cover-up, a clingy garment that had been a favorite of Jim's. It recalled the colors of the ocean, an aquamarine with streaks of darker blue and green. The wind tousled her hair and cooled her flushed cheeks. What to do? In the house, she looked at herself in the mirror and turned away, momentarily frightened by the intensity of her own stare—a glittering in the eyes. Out again, she left the door unlocked and slipped slowly down the cliff stairs, her hand on the rail. It wouldn't hurt to go halfway down and see what remained of the waterfall, the stain of its passage glistening by starlight.

The wind toyed with her hair, tickled her skin. The night seemed heartbreakingly lovely, with an edge to its beauty that didn't come from her memory of Jim's loss or from her grief afterward. Just now she seemed to have gone beyond that private sorrow. Motionless in the sky or rocking on the mirror of the sea, the stars drew her thoughts away from self—a mote in the oceans of time and space. Also infinite was the flux of waters that went on forever, wrapping round the globe, and the sadness that was in her like blood and bone seemed for once to be parceled out and shared with the tide and pulse of the sea and the outward-going stars, sailing toward the ever-retreating end of the universe.

A bat-like flittering caught at the corner of her vision. She looked toward the upright stones, stabbed onto their flimsy shadows.

"Marsha!"

The boy leaped into a patch of light.

"Come down," he called to her, and she ran down the steps to meet him.

"Thank God! I was afraid you were drowned—"

"Not me! I'm a fish! You remember; I'm a king of the fish. The dolphins love me. They'd never let me drown." He laughed, the pearls of his teeth flashing. Shyly, he put his arm around her waist and smiled up at her.

"You're taller—and where's your seaweed?"

He glanced at the cloth knotted around his waist. The fabric didn't cover much more of him than the seaweed kilt had done, but lacked the impromptu air of his former guise. "I'm older. My brother said that I was too big to dash about the world naked."

"Where have you been?" Marsha touched his cap of hair, silky as ever, and her hand brushed against his jaw. In the moonlight she could see the veins twining blue under his skin.

"Oh, around." He jigged in place, full of the irrepressible joy she remembered.

"I'm glad you came back," she told him.

"Of course. Why wouldn't I? And I knew you wished for me." Here he turned a cartwheel out of sheer excess of spirits. "Besides, my brother wanted to see you again. It's still the same for him as last time. Once we love, we love for keeps."

Marsha watched as he fled through the standing stones, weaving in and out of the light. In a few minutes he returned, skittering across the sands, and took her hand in his own. The fingers had the same slight tackiness that she remembered from before.

"Jim—you know that he died last year, after we went home. Did you know?"

The boy looked at her warily, without smiling. "You know my mother died, didn't you?"

"Yes, you told me. I didn't forget." She wanted to put her arms around him but was shy about it. They felt useless, hanging at her sides.

"Well, that's how I know about your husband. You just told me. I'm sorry, though. He liked the stones. We would have given him better ones this year. My brother said that we should give him some from our—from where we live."

"That would have been nice. He would have liked them." This time she reached for his hand, and he let her take it.

"I wish nobody ever had to die," he said in a low voice. "My mother is the only one that I know who died. And I don't remember her. Why did he?"

"A traffic accident—a truck hit him on the road and killed him."

"I've seen those... I knew he hadn't drowned, or the fishes would have told me."

He looked so matter-of-fact in this declaration that she laughed, lacing her fingers with his and letting him tug her across the sand, nearer to the waves that were steadily pouncing closer and closer to shore. She had forgotten how peculiar a little being he was, with his stories about the sea and stones and his ignorance—fancy a child never having held a pincushion! Or perhaps that was twenty-first century life, with clothes readymade in China and Mexico and Thailand. That must be where all the pincushions had gone. She wondered if the boy knew that China existed, and if he would let her teach him the things that he should have learned. She believed he must never have gone to school... What she saw after burying the enhydrites was pushed aside now, as if it hadn't occurred at all. The reality of the boy's quick, dancing self overshadowed the past days and made them appear as insubstantial as dreams. Even Jim was merely a shadow, and speaking of him hardly grazed her with sadness.

"You don't believe me! You'll find out—" The boy smiled but not at her, glancing toward the sea.

If she hadn't felt the stones pressing against her hip, she might never have thought of them. But she took out the fingerlings one by one and then spilled the fistful into his hands. He gave another secret smile and tucked them into the waistband of his garment—a short sarong, she thought it might be, if such a thing was worn by boys. The stubby figures were pressed against his skin. No, not figures, she remembered: just stones.

"And I have something for you. Close your eyes." He grasped her hands, pushing them into the shape he wanted. Something hard skimmed her palm, then flopped onto its side.

"Oh—"

It was a cord and pendant, the latter like the one around the boy's neck: that is, transparent, circular, perforated in the center, incised with what he had called runes. Chambers of water were trapped inside, several of them holding minute flakes.

Marsha held the necklace at arm's length, staring at the ocean through the hole. It seemed that she could make out four or five figures in the water, unless they were merely rocks, jutting up from the sea floor. As she moved the stone slowly across her field of vision, she saw something else: the figure of a man, leaning from a jagged perch. She could tell no more from that starlit distance except that he appeared muscular, with fair hair.

"Here, bend down and I'll put it on you."

She didn't give up the pendant for several more moments, staring until she knew that she could learn nothing more.

"Did you see my brother?" He tugged at the string to make sure it was tied well, afterward lifting the pendant to look at the runes.

"I suppose so." She felt a blankness, the sort of bewilderment one feels at the top of a stairs, realizing that the reason for ascending has been left entirely behind. Marsha shivered; a breeze had sprung up. She looked back at the steps and the cliff, with its stain that still marked where the waterfall had flung drops against earth. In a few minutes she would go to the house and sleep, and in the morning she would find the boy and ask him to go away with her. She could adopt him; she might even name him after Jim.

The crisp incisions on the hoop of stone pressed their messages against her skin.

"What do these signs mean?"

"It's hard to say. It's like a song. See, here's the sign for *air*, just under the one for *water*. See? *Air* under *water*." He touched each with his fingertip, rubbing lightly. "This one is a binding or a blessing, see, right next to *heart*. Here's *fish*; here's *woman*. There's healing in it, and reviving, and protection in childbirth. And long life, too."

"That's a lot." She twisted the cord nervously in her fingers. *In the morning.*

She would go away with the boy in the morning. "You seem older this year," she said, a little sadly.

"My brother made me learn things. Not just the runes. But I skip off where he can't find me whenever I want. I'm a king too. He can't make me."

"And what do you call yourself? Today, I mean." She remembered the jumble of names, ending in *Sad*. Perhaps he would be happy now.

"Tonight I'm *Merlin*. *Mer*, that's the sea."

"And a merlin is a bird—"

"A falcon who stoops to catch a silver fish!" The boy whirled, his arms lifted into wings and his hands gripping the air like claws.

"Yes, and a wizard who was a seer—"

"I'm a seer too. I see and see and see," he declared, ending with a somersault.

"What do you see? Do you see my future?" She asked but he wouldn't or couldn't tell, so she lifted the pendant to her eye like a monocle. The swimmers bobbing in the waves were gone, but the man was still musing on his rock. Wind lifted his long hair. The skin at his throat and on his chest looked bluish. Maybe that was a trick of the moonlight, though.

"Did I tell you that the black man asked about you? He wanted you to learn karate..."

The boy let out a peal of merriment. "He'll never catch me! Not so long as I have legs to run. I would swipe off his head with my sword arm. You hear him talking? *Draw arm, sword arm,* all that, and there's not a blade or scabbard in sight. He's a fool who fights the mist."

Back in the city there would be things that he could learn. Perhaps he could take lessons—he was quick and bright, he would be good in fencing or any of the martial arts. At first he would need a tutor for school.

"I must go inside now," she told him. "But you'll come see me tomorrow, won't you? We can sit and talk all day, and maybe you could come back to the city with me in Jim's car?"

What a rubber face! She suppressed her laugh. He had contracted his brow, squinting at her, and now said only, "Traffic accidents," as if that settled the issue.

"Tomorrow, we'll talk about it then," she insisted; "I need to rest."

"But I wanted you to meet my brother," he said. "Look, we're already at the ocean, and he's just right there. Come on." His grasp had a surprising firmness, and she exclaimed as he tugged on her arm.

She stumbled at the edge of the water, going down on one knee. He stopped and waited as she stood up but didn't offer to help.

"A little ways—can't he come here?" She was breathing fast, nervous and—she now admitted it to herself—afraid. A chill flashed over her as she remembered strewing Jim's ashes. His atoms were now the sea's, his death swallowed and spread on the currents.

"What's the matter?" The boy looked at her, frowning.

"I want to go home." She was trembling, not just from the cold. When she lifted the pendant and glanced through it, she saw that the figure had moved from the rock and was chest-high in ocean, moving gently up and down with the rhythm of the waves.

The boy was determined, pulling her in the water, teasing and laughing at her fear, vowing that she would soon see his brother face to face.

She had the sensation that they weren't alone, that others were close around them, urging them on, taking her by the hand, pushing against the force of the waves. Along this portion of the coast, the floor dropped away quickly, and soon she felt helpless, riding on the swells, her legs dangling.

When she lifted the necklace again, she saw with a shiver that the boy's elder brother was swimming swiftly in their direction. As he came closer, she glimpsed his face, strong-jawed and bold in its contours. In a few more moments, he was close beside her, so that she could only catch glimpses of him through the lens of the stone.

These quick angular snapshots frightened her more than ever, because something about him was not right—not just the blue and turquoise flush to the skin but the whole muscularity of him, the too-handsome, chiseled face, and the irises of the eyes that were cool but radiant like two pieces of sagenite set in sockets of stone.

The boy was laughing at his own success. Marsha gripped his shoulder, pinching him tight, as the brother drew her toward him. They each had her by a hand, and for an instant she was drawn against the man and felt the muscular hardness of him along the length of her body. She cried out, and water filled up her mouth with its murmuring.

A jogger in a black gi was leaping through the surf. He heard the sharp note of distress and stopped, staring at the sea.

From the shore, all that could be seen was a slight disturbance in the water, over in an instant. The swells became smooth. Waves kept pushing their freight of sand and weed to the shore, reflecting the upraised sickle of the moon and a harvest of starlight.

A Debt to Collect

"The haul-out is just over that rise," Elisabeth said, indicating a rocky outcrop ahead that formed the northern edge of a small cove. The moisture in the air was somewhere between a heavy fog and a light mist, obscuring the coast with wisps of gray and leaving only the edge of the water visible to the eye. Clouds moved in the breeze, transforming the landscape from moment to moment, hiding one feature and revealing another. She pulled her parka tighter. Beside her, Mrs. Kvanbeck had her odd, old-fashioned leather jacket buttoned up to her double chin. Perhaps Elisabeth should have waited another day to visit the haul-out, but she wanted to see her seals, needed something she could rely on. The seals would be there. They came to this location every December, were always there when she and Russel arrived after turning in their grades for Fall term. She twisted the ring around her finger. This time, it wasn't her husband trudging next to her through the sand, but her landlady.

"We call this *havbryn*." Mrs. Kvanbeck spoke with a faint Scandinavian accent, although she was born and raised in the Puget Sound area. "The place where sea and land meet and nothing stays the same."

"No kidding." Maybe Norwegians had as many words for the sea as Eskimos had for snow. A fog horn boomed somewhere out to sea, and the gulls screeched in answer.

She took Mrs. Kvanbeck's elbow as they began to climb the rocks, but the eighty-year-old disengaged herself with a gentle shake. "I may be old, but I can still walk, you know." The smile she gave Elisabeth was forgiving and not the least bit impatient. "It has been a long time since I visited the seals. Since my husband died."

"I'm sorry."

"No need. Forty years we had together. He loved the selkie folk, as he called them." The rounded vowels and lilting emphasis of Mrs. Kvanbeck's speech were soothing, reminding Elisabeth of her maternal grandmother and making her feel at home. Which was probably why she came back to the same bed and breakfast every winter.

"Why 'selkie'?"

"Selkies are different, you know. They are only found on western coastlines, where the past is drowned in each sunset."

Elisabeth shook her head. "Seals are found on coasts everywhere in the world."

"Seals, yes, but not selkies."

"Ah. Magic seals. No, I don't presume they're found everywhere."

"Just because it is not in your books does not mean it isn't true," Mrs. Kvanbeck told her, the regular emphasis in her voice compelling. "What do you call them in your books?"

"Pinnipeds," Elisabeth said with a smile.

Mrs. Kvanbeck took Elisabeth's elbow this time and faced her, peering up through thick glasses. "Good. A smile again. You must smile more."

A shot cut through the fog, clean and pure, followed by sounds of yelping, snarling, and splashing, and then another shot.

"No!" Elisabeth scrambled the rest of the way up the rocks. Three men stood on the beach, two with rifles aimed at the seals slipping and diving into the water.

"Stop right now!" Elisabeth yelled, jumping from rock to rock to the beach and running in front of the men with the rifles; they had no choice but to lower them. "What do you think you're doing?"

"Taking out seals," one man said.

"They've been stealing fish from the nets," the second man added.

"You can't kill seals without federal authorization," Elisabeth panted.

"There's our authorization." The first man nodded in the direction of the man without a rifle.

Slowly, she turned to face the third man. He was standing back, obviously reluctant to claim responsibility. When her gaze caught his, he shrugged and stepped forward.

"The salmonid stocks in the area are running dangerously low and we've authorized taking out some non-depleted pinnipeds here." The man actually scuffed the sand with the toe of one shoe.

She stared at him. "Who's 'we'?"

"Name's Adam Gunnarson." He stuck out one hand and she stared at it too. He shoved it back in his pocket. "From the Washington State Department of Fish and Wildlife."

"That's not federal."

"We have federal authorization for lethal removal."

He was eye to eye with her, even slouching in embarrassment, which probably put him at just over six feet. Taller than he looked.

Elisabeth shook her head. "But these seals are part of a research project!"

"There was a public hearing. And we consulted with the University on the removal," Adam said apologetically.

"Which campus?"

"Tacoma."

Elisabeth took a deep breath. If she hadn't been so caught up in the divorce, she probably would have heard of it. "I'm with the University of Washington. Elisabeth Hoffmann. With an 's.'"

"Excuse me?"

"Elisabeth with an 's.'" But her attention was no longer on the embarrassed government official. She was craning around to get a look at the rocks, the haul-out site of the seals, the seals who trusted her and Russel, trusted humans. One remained on the rock formation, still and brown. A pregnant female, with mottled markings of lighter brown around her neck like a ring.

A sob escaped her. "Jane!" She ran across the sand and into the surf, clambering onto the rocky haul-out wet to her thighs. She dropped to her knees next to the dead seal, and her tears mingled on her lips with the tang of salt in the air, dripped and fell into the surf filling the tide pools. These seals were so accustomed to humans, they no longer fled when one came near. And now, Jane was dead. The uneven surface of the rocks dug into Elisabeth's knees and her jeans were soaked, but none of that mattered. She looked up, scanning the waters for any of the other seals. There had been two shots—perhaps one had been injured. Even now, even after a human had killed one of their own, they weren't careful enough. She saw one head and then another, Ovid with his spots and silver-gray Virgil. But not

Dante. Then another seal bobbed up, dangerously near the rocks where she knelt. Dark and sleek, he stared at her with deep brown eyes.

"Dante," she whispered, tears still threading down her cheeks. The seal gave a very human-sounding grunt and dove below the surface again.

She dropped her head to her palms and sobbed.

Mrs. Kvanbeck's wet, thick-stockinged ankles appeared in her line of vision, followed by a pair of bony male feet, pants rolled up to the tops of his calves. Her landlady wore skirts to her knees and heavy tights all the time. Another thing Elisabeth could rely on. She concentrated on thick tights, banishing thoughts of death and divorce, the seal in front of her and a half-empty house in Seattle—the remnants of five years together.

"This young man has offered to drive us home," Mrs. Kvanbeck announced in her soothing sing-song. "Are you ready to go?"

Elisabeth looked up at the older woman. "Soon." Her gaze slanted over to the government official, his hands in his pockets and his gaze barely meeting hers. "You see the tag on the hind web of this seal?" she asked. He nodded. "I want you to promise me that no more seals with this tag will be 'taken out.'"

He nodded again. "I'll see what I can do."

Elisabeth allowed herself to be hauled up and dragged back through the surf. She hardly noticed that she was shivering with cold. Shivering and couldn't stop. Behind her, she heard the yelping of one of her seals as they helped her to the car.

"It's good you're feeling better today," Mrs. Kvanbeck said, bustling around the kitchen behind her. "I was worried about you. The young man too."

Elisabeth snorted. "Well, let's hope he remembers how worried he was that when he's explaining to his boss." She looked at the letter addressed to the National Marine Fisheries Services propped up next to the salt shaker on the kitchen table and helped herself to more *lefse*—thin pancakes rolled up with generous servings of butter and brown sugar. Comfort food. Mrs. Kvanbeck was spoiling her rotten. She didn't have any other guests at the moment and was grandmothering Elisabeth to her heart's content.

"He was only doing his job."

"Don't worry," Elisabeth said through a mouth full of *lefse*. She took a sip of the weak coffee. "I'm complaining more about the decision than the carrying out." She thought of Jane, lying still on the haul-out, and Dante staring at her with his mournful dark eyes.

She got up and started to put her plate in the dishwasher. Mrs. Kvanbeck waved her away. "No, no! I'll take care of all that."

"Thanks. That was a wonderful breakfast." She picked up her pack from a chair near the back door and put the letter in the front pocket.

"Will you be back for lunch?"

Elisabeth shook her head and smiled. "I don't think I'll *need* any lunch."

She closed the door on the comforting smells of flour and butter and sugar and made her way through the mist to the small downtown area and the nearest mailbox. In the last decade, the town had transformed from fishing village to tourist trap, and now the main street was useless for most practical purposes, as it was lined with souvenir shops and fish restaurants and Scandinavian heritage knick-knack stores. But it did have a Starbucks, which hadn't been there five years before when she and Russel had started coming to observe their seals. After dropping her letter in the mailbox, Elisabeth headed over for some real coffee. Mrs. Kvanbeck might have a Norwegian accent, but the coffee she made was traditional American.

"Elisabeth!"

Elisabeth turned and wished she hadn't. Adam Gunnarson was bearing down on her, head forward and glasses askew. He stopped next to her and pushed them back up his nose. "I wanted to apologize again about the misunderstanding yesterday. That haul-out is now off-limits for the thinning operation."

What an awful vocabulary these bureaucrats had with their "thinning operation" and "taking out" and "lethal removal."

"Good. But that's not the only haul-out of tagged seals in the area."

Adam nodded. "That's why we need to get together. You have to show me the other haul-outs the seals in your study use. How about dinner tonight?"

"Dinner?" She stared at him and turned the ring on her ring finger.

"Okay, so that wasn't such a good idea." He looked down at the sidewalk and shrugged. "I know we met under really inauspicious circumstances, but I was hoping...." He noticed her gesture and stopped. "Oh. Are you married?"

"Divorced. But I'm still not interested in dinner."

He smiled, a surprisingly charming, diffident sort of smile. She suddenly noticed that he was actually quite attractive, if you liked intellectual-looking types.

"No, of course you wouldn't be," he said. "I'm the enemy. I need the information on the haul-outs from you, though. When would be a good time?"

"I still want to visit the seals today. Why don't we meet at the Starbucks around two?"

"That's actually better than dinner, since we were planning on going out again this afternoon. I'll bring my maps."

Elisabeth nodded, her gut tightening at the "going out." Another lovely euphemism. "Good. Bye." She turned to continue on her way down the street for her morning caffeine fix, the prickle between her shoulder blades telling her he was staring after her. Which was unusual enough to have the charm of novelty. Probably all some men needed was blond hair and long legs, and they were willing to overlook a long face and pallor.

She ordered a tall cappuccino, sat down at a table next to the window and pulled the latest issues of *Animal Behavior* and *Marine Mammal Science* out of her backpack. Both had some interesting articles on pinnipeds she was looking forward to reading.

"Is this seat free?"

Elisabeth lifted her eyes reluctantly from her magazine to gaze upon one of the most beautiful men she had ever seen. He was tall and dark, with drowned brown eyes and shining brown, almost black, hair curling around his temples and at the neck of his jacket.

She looked pointedly at an empty table just behind him

before replying. "Sure."

He draped his jacket over the back of the chair opposite her and flowed into it with a grace that seemed wasted on such a simple, everyday movement. Elisabeth returned her attention to her magazine with nearly as much reluctance as she had felt at the interruption. The difference between an ugly and a beautiful stranger, she thought to herself and smiled.

"What you're reading doesn't look that amusing," he said. His voice was low and rough, a bit hesitant, as if he didn't speak much.

She shrugged. "I think it's fascinating. But of course it wouldn't be if you're not interested in marine mammals."

"Oh, I wouldn't say that." He smiled at her and she nearly choked on her coffee. This man was danger incarnate. His smile captured and connected, persuading the rapidly firing synapses in her brain that she knew him from somewhere, knew him well—the sudden feeling of intimacy signaling the onset of infatuation. She vaguely remembered the feeling, but it hadn't happened to her for a very, very long time. It seemed this was a day for novel experiences.

Elisabeth shook her head and lifted her magazine from the table. "'The copulatory behavior of *Zalophus* has been studied extensively and the polygamy and extreme sexual dimorphism linked by a number of researchers,'" she read.

The stranger laughed out loud. "Fascinating, yes. I might have chosen different words, but the subject matter is very promising." He gave her an intimate smile, and she blushed to her hairline.

"Excuse me," she mumbled, shoving her magazines into her pack and starting to get up.

He stopped her with a touch on her forearm that she felt to the soles of her feet. "Don't go. Please. I'm sorry if I offended you."

Elisabeth sank slowly back into her chair, staring into his pleading brown eyes. She was overreacting. But he had thrown her off-balance completely.

"I've been looking for you," he said.

"But you don't even know me."

"I've seen you often."

"I only got here yesterday."

"You come here every year."

Elisabeth stared at him. "How do you know?"

He smiled again, and her stomach did something that had to be a flutter. Fluttered, her stomach actually fluttered. She couldn't believe it.

"I'm always here this time of year too," he said.

"But I've never seen you before."

He shrugged. "You've never come alone before."

She sat back in her chair and crossed her arms in front of her chest. "Is that why you were looking for me?"

"That's part of it."

"What's the other part?"

He was silent so long she wasn't sure he would answer. "I have a debt to pay and a debt to collect," he finally said.

"I don't get it."

"You will understand eventually."

"Look, I don't have any patience for riddles, okay?"

He smiled again and nodded towards the blue pack holding her magazines. "No. You like facts, don't you?"

"Yes. And I don't like strangers."

"But we aren't strangers. My name's Dan." He held his hand out to her across the table, long, graceful fingers, tanned and smooth.

She took the proffered hand. "Elisabeth. With an 's.'"

"Nice to meet you, Elisabeth-with-an-s."

Elisabeth laughed; she couldn't help it. The joke was lame, but he was holding her hand in his, the pad of his thumb caressing the skin between her thumb and forefinger. His fingers moved to her ring and touched it, a question in his eyes.

She took a deep breath, drew her fingers away and stood up. "It was nice meeting you too, but now I want to go visit my seals."

"'Your' seals?"

"The seals my husband and I tagged for a long-term study five years ago. We concluded the study in May, but I've been coming here every winter for five years. I couldn't imagine a December without them."

"Even without him," Dan murmured.

Elisabeth nodded.

"Do you mind if I join you?" he asked.

She didn't. She didn't mind at all. She had never been very sociable, and since the divorce she'd started actively avoiding people, even ducking into empty classrooms when someone she knew was coming down the hall who might try to strike up a conversation. But Dan was easy to talk to and easy to be silent with. He touched her often, leaned into her casually with his flowing grace, and she didn't pull away. She knew it was an illusion, knew sexual attraction was playing havoc with her rational mind, but by the time they reached the cove, she felt like she'd known him for years.

And he knew a lot about seals. He didn't have the technical vocabulary, but he knew their habits and their habitats and seemed to understand her passion for them.

Despite the shooting, several seals had returned to the haul-out, but none of Elisabeth's particular favorites were among them.

"What are you looking for?" Dan asked as they stood at the edge of the beach. The mist was thicker than the day before and she had problems recognizing the seals on the rocks just offshore.

"Not what, who," Elisabeth said with a smile. "Ovid or Lucretia or Dante or Romeo or any number of others. They don't seem to be here today."

"Interesting names you have for 'your' seals. How did you come up with them?"

She felt a blush staining her cheeks and turned her face away. "Russel and I were in Italy for our honeymoon."

"The man who is not here."

She nodded, pulling the ring half off her finger and pushing it back up again. He seemed to sense that she didn't want to talk about it and fell silent. They ambled over to the shelter of some protected rocks and sat down, watching the surf and the seals and the mist moving in and out between the rocks and the shore. When Dan leaned into her and put his hand on her knee, she didn't draw away, just sat enjoying the warmth of the contact.

"Ah, there," she said, pointing at the surf just to the south of the haul-out. "I think some old friends are arriving. Those are the ones we named Ovid and Romeo."

He nodded.

The two tagged seals didn't stop at the haul-out, however; instead, they swam in close to the rocks where Elisabeth sat with Dan and began diving in front of them and slapping the water.

"They're acting so excited," she said. "I wonder if it has to do with the shooting yesterday."

The shooting yesterday. Adam. She looked at her watch.

"Oh, damn." Elisabeth scrambled up, brushing the sand off her jeans. "I was supposed to meet someone at two. I have to run, I'm sorry."

By the time Elisabeth got to the Starbucks, it was almost three and there was no sign of Adam. She wasn't too pleased with herself. It wasn't like her to forget an appointment for a pair of brown eyes.

At the bed and breakfast, she found Mrs. Kvanbeck in the kitchen, as usual, baking cinnamon roles. Elisabeth often wondered what her landlady did with all the food she made. Her figure was certainly substantial, but no healthy person could consume the amount of food that came out of this kitchen.

"Did the man who brought us home yesterday mention to you where he was staying?" Elisabeth asked.

"Ah, you mean that nice Mr. Gunnarson?" Elisabeth grimaced and nodded. "I think he said he would be in the Seaview Motel."

"Thanks."

Elisabeth went to the alcove next to the living room where the public phone was located and called the hotel, but he wasn't there.

He'd said he was "going out."

She continued to sit in the alcove next to the phone until the sun went down, curled in a big, overstuffed chair. The hearty scents wafting out of the kitchen told her that Mrs. Kvanbeck was making dinner for her again—which was not in the contract. Normally Elisabeth would have at least gotten up and asked if she could help, even though her offer would have been turned down, but this time she just sat there, unseeing, as the room got darker and darker.

Finally the phone rang. Elisabeth snatched it up.

"Hello?"

"Elisabeth?"

"Yes."

"Adam Gunnarson. I'm sorry to inform you but we took out another tagged seal today."

The next day, she drove out to the beach where the seal had been killed. She and Adam had gotten together with their maps last night, and he had given her the tag. The number was Virgil's.

She trudged up the dunes between the grass, head down and hands deep in the pockets of her parka. When she reached the rise overlooking the beach, she saw Dan sitting on a driftwood log staring out to sea. She sat down on the log next to him, pulling her parka tighter around her, and he glanced over, his dark eyes almost black.

"Did you hear about the seal getting killed too?" she asked.

He nodded, his gaze once again fixed on the gray ocean. "It's my fault."

"Your fault? How could it be your fault?"

"I kept you from your meeting."

"I forgot my meeting."

He shook his head. "If I hadn't gone with you to the haul-out, Virgil would be alive today."

She stared at him. "How did you know it was Virgil?"

"You told me."

"I did?" Elisabeth propped her hands on the log and leaned forward, training her gaze on the gray ocean with him. The wood of the log was smooth and cold beneath her hands, worn to a fine finish by water and wind. She hadn't told him about Virgil, she knew she hadn't. Maybe Adam had. She couldn't remember if she'd told Adam the seal's name when he'd given her the tag. Probably.

But why would Dan know Adam?

"Are you a fisher?" she asked.

Dan smiled at her, just a hint of a smile that pulled up one corner of his mouth and touched his dark eyes with melancholy amusement. "You could say so," he said slowly. "Yes."

"Do you want the seals taken out too?"

"No. There aren't enough fish for everyone. But, I don't want the seals taken out."

She sighed in relief. "I'm glad."

Dan took her hand and she let him. "I haven't yet thanked you for saving those seals the other day." His low, rough voice made his thanks sound like a promise.

"I didn't save all of them."

"No." He gazed back out to sea, quiet and sad. His warm fingers held hers lightly, the pad of his thumb moving over the back of her hand. He grieved with her. She was content to have it so.

They sat that way for a while, ignoring the mist and the cold, comforting each other with silence. When he rose and pulled her up, she slid into his arms easily, taking his kiss without a word.

But that night, she took the rest of him with both more and less than words. He moved over her like a magic touch, his movements as flowing and graceful in bed as out. She buckled and wept and held him tight, slid up to him and around him while he slid into her, skin smooth and cool then sweaty and hot, sliding and slapping against each other.

"What's that?" Elisabeth asked the next morning, pointing to a clean, round wound on his ankle. She was sitting on the edge of the bed, still naked, while he pulled his shorts on over his dark-skinned, muscular thighs. So perfect, at the same time rounded and hard. He had to be one of the most singularly beautiful things she had ever seen.

Dan shrugged and shook his dark curls back from his bare shoulders. "Occupational hazard."

They dressed and went down to a fine breakfast of homemade cinnamon rolls and weak coffee which Mrs. Kvanbeck served to both of them without batting an eye, although she did look at Dan long and hard.

"Dinner tonight?" Elisabeth asked when he got up to go.

Dan looked down at her with his drowned brown eyes and nodded. He had the kind of long eyelashes some women would have said were wasted on a man, but Elisabeth didn't find them wasted at all—they were decadent and exotic and she loved to look at them.

"Shall I pick you up here at six?" he asked.

Elisabeth was sure she must be smiling like an infatuated schoolgirl. "Sure," she said.

The screen door banging shut behind him echoed for a while in the near-silence of the kitchen while Mrs. Kvanbeck cleared away the breakfast dishes. "That one won't stay, you know," the old woman finally said.

"How can you be so sure?"

"He's a selkie. They never stay."

"Selkie?" Elisabeth laughed out loud. She had long known that Mrs. Kvanbeck was mildly crazy—in a good way—but this beat everything. A selkie!

Mrs. Kvanbeck paused in her busy rounds between table, sink and dishwasher. "It is good to hear you laugh again. You should laugh more often."

Elisabeth shook her head, still chuckling. "A selkie."

Her landlady sat down in the chair vacated by Dan and stared at her intently through her practical, round glasses. "You called him to you when your tears mixed with the ocean. My neighbor Maureen, bless her soul, says that if a woman is dissatisfied with her man, she can call a selkie to her by shedding seven tears into the ocean at high tide."

Obviously, Maureen was the ultimate authority on selkies to Mrs. Kvanbeck's way of thinking. Elisabeth tried to couch her own arguments in the same terms. "It wasn't quite high tide. And I wasn't the one who was dissatisfied; it was Russel." She pulled the wedding ring down to her first joint and pushed it back up again, pulled and pushed.

"But you aren't happy with him now."

"Not exactly, no."

"You see! So you called a selkie to you."

It was hopeless. Laughing, she got up and gave her landlady a big hug. "You are such a dear."

A glint of what might have been tears shimmered in the old woman's eyes. "He makes you laugh. That is good."

Elisabeth shook her head. "No, Mrs. Kvanbeck, it's you who

makes me laugh."

Her hostess looked skeptical. "Perhaps."

"Mrs. Kvanbeck, have you seen my parka? Dan will be here any minute and I can't find it."

"No," the old woman said slowly, drawing out the "o."

Elisabeth stopped in the middle of the living room full of knick-knacks, her hands on her hips, and surveyed the vicinity critically. "I can't think what I could have done with it."

Mrs. Kvanbeck went to the coat closet and pulled out her odd, stiff leather jacket. "Here, take this, dear."

"I can't take your jacket," she said, chuckling. "It would be much too short."

"And wide," her landlady added, a twinkle in her eyes. "This isn't mine. I had it made especially. It belongs to another. For you."

Elisabeth didn't particularly care for the style, but she was moved anyway. "You shouldn't have."

"Please, take it." Mrs. Kvanbeck pushed the jacket toward Elisabeth almost violently.

"What did I do to deserve this?"

"You are a good customer," the other woman said roughly. "You come back every year."

The doorbell rang and Elisabeth rushed for the door, feeling like a teenager. "Bye!" she threw over her shoulder.

"You have a good time, now!"

Elisabeth opened the door, still slipping into the jacket, and immediately gave Dan a quick kiss on his full lips. He started. "Still shy?" Elisabeth asked playfully.

"No," he said, staring at her. She found the intense attention a bit unnerving, but she smiled and took his arm.

Encased in the dark and the mist, they walked down to one of the fish restaurants on Main Street. In the restaurant, a young woman on a small platform in the corner of the room was singing a mournful ballad, Joan Baez style. The decor was dark, the tablecloths pink, and the food expensive but good. The atmosphere didn't quite live up to the prices, but it was Elisabeth's favorite place to eat in town.

Dan ordered anchovy canapés and blackened salmon

medallions, and Elisabeth had scampi in garlic-wine sauce with a crab salad. He told her a little about the area, his favorite beaches and retreats, and she watched him, his dark brown eyes, smiling but with a touch of sadness; she savored the fine flavor of the shellfish, listened to the melancholy voice of the singer, and let happiness wash over her slowly like the incoming tide.

The singer launched into a rendition of the old Scottish ballad "The Selkie of Sule Skerry," and Elisabeth chuckled.

"This song reminds me," she said. "Mrs. Kvanbeck told me this morning in all seriousness that you're a selkie. Can you believe that?"

Dan paused and returned his fork to his plate slowly, staring at her.

Elisabeth shrugged. "She's a little crazy, but she means well."

He shook his head, still staring at her. "I thought you knew."

"What do you mean?"

"I *am* a selkie."

She swallowed her wine quickly and put down her glass. "Not funny, Dan."

"You really did not know?"

Elisabeth felt her ears start to grow warm like they always did when she was mad. "Sure I knew. I always assume the strangers I meet are actually seals in disguise."

"But the jacket. When I saw it, I was sure you knew."

"Jacket?"

"The one you were wearing tonight."

"It's from Mrs. Kvanbeck."

"Ah."

"What does that mean, 'ah'?"

"It's seal skin."

"It is?" He nodded and Elisabeth shuddered. "I can't wear seal skin."

He smiled his melancholy smile. "But as long as you keep it, you keep me. I can't go back unless you return it to the sea."

"This is not a nice joke."

"No, it isn't."

Elisabeth sat back and stared at him, her heart going double-time. The woman in the corner sang in a clear, true vibrato:

For I am a man upon the land,
And I am a selkie on the sea,
And when I'm far frae ev'ry strand
My home it is in Sule Skerry.

Dan took her hand across the table. "I would prefer to return home, but I will stay with you as long as you have the seal skin. There are worse fates."

He looked completely serious. She glanced down at her hand in his, motionless on the pink tablecloth. What did she know about this man, after all? Nothing, absolutely nothing.

A shadow fell across the table and she looked up to see Adam Gunnarson at her elbow. She found herself actually relieved at his presence. Introducing him and Dan to each other was an easier task than getting her mind around what Dan was trying to make her believe.

But he and Adam didn't know each other. So how had Dan known about Virgil?

"Would you like to join us?" Dan asked.

Adam looked down at their hands linked across the table. "I don't want to disturb a romantic evening."

Elisabeth withdrew her hand. "You're not disturbing us."

"Maybe just for a moment then." Adam pulled a chair over and sat down. "Are you an animal rights activist too?" he asked Dan.

Dan shook his head. "A fisher."

Adam looked at her with one eyebrow raised. "One of the bad guys?"

Dan chuckled. "I may catch fish, but I don't agree with taking out the seals. I can understand it, though. We all compete for our meal." He indicated the remnants of the seafood delicacies spread out before them.

"Not me," Adam said, shaking his head. "I'm a vegetarian."

Elisabeth looked at him in surprise. He smiled wryly and pushed his glasses up his nose. "What? Doesn't fit with your image of the seal-killer?"

She had to agree. "No."

"I've been wanting to talk with you."

She waited.

"I spoke with the head of your department at the University of Washington. He said the study you were working on had been completed."

Elisabeth glared at him. "I intend to begin a new study with those seals. The tagging has already been done, which makes it much easier."

"Don't worry," Adam said. "I still intend to avoid the haul-outs you told me about. I'm sure we'll fill our quota anyway," he added with a grimace, pushing the chair back and getting up to leave.

"It was nice to meet you," Dan said, extending one hand.

Adam's smile was lopsided as he took Dan's hand. "Nice to meet you too." He turned to Elisabeth. "I probably won't see you again. I've ordered the operations moved north and we're leaving tomorrow."

She swallowed. Without a doubt, she had not been fair to him. "Thanks. Look me up when you're in Seattle and we can go out for coffee."

He nodded and moved to a free table on the far side of the room. Alone.

"Even though he authorized my being shot at, I have to admit I like him."

She looked back at Dan across the table from her. She had almost forgotten the outrageous claim he'd just made.

He smiled, slow and wry, and caught her gaze with his, caught and connected. "You still think I'm joking."

"How can I not?"

"What if I tell you, you tagged me at a haul-out site south of here in May four years ago?"

She stared at him, not answering.

"You and Russel snuck away from the others during the lunch break and made love on a blanket at the mouth of a small cave. I think it was blue."

Elisabeth blushed. "I don't want to know how you found out about that."

"We thought if you were watching us, we had a right to watch you too."

"Ha."

"It's only fair."

She looked over at the folk singer in the corner, her joy at the magic of the evening gone, her hands clenched tight in her lap, a tear slipping slowly out of one eye.

Dan leaned over and wiped it off her cheek. "Elisabeth. You always were my favorite of the watchers, you know."

She gave a choked laugh, picked up her fork again and began to shove the last scampi around in a circle on her plate. "Okay, so let's assume you really are a selkie. Why did you come here?"

"I told you, I had a debt to pay."

"You came to thank me for saving your skin," she said and winced at the stupid choice of words.

He nodded. "You called me to you when you spilled your tears into the ocean."

"You also told me you had a debt to collect."

"I lost a mate."

And had he come to collect one? Elisabeth drew a deep breath. "Jane."

He nodded, his gaze going past her, beyond the dark-grained wood of the walls of the restaurant. "The only one you gave a name that had nothing to do with Italy."

"Jane Austen is one of my favorite authors," she replied mechanically. The singer in the corner was now warbling about trees growing high and leaves growing green, but all Elisabeth could think of was gray mist and gray sea and the man sitting across from her, a man she had slept with and knew nothing about. But he had known about Virgil, and he had never met Adam. He knew she came here every winter, knew she came with Russel, yet she was positive she had never seen him before. He wasn't a man a woman could ignore or forget easily, not even a married woman—as if marital status made a difference in whom you noticed. He had a clean, round wound on his ankle, the kind of wound you might find on a seal which had once been tagged.

"Dante," she said.

He nodded again. "That's the name you gave me, yes."

She looked into his brown, brown eyes, looked and saw the seal gazing at her across the short expanse of gray winter ocean.

Looked and saw why she had been so sure she had already met him when he sat down across from her at Starbucks a few short days ago.

"You were always my favorite too, alpha male or not," she said.

Dante gave her a wide smile which finally chased the melancholy out of his eyes. "That's why you called me to you and not Romeo or some other."

"Romeo would have been too young for me."

He laughed out loud and found her hand under the table. "Yes, if I must leave the sea, there are worse fates."

"But you would rather go back."

"I won't deny that I didn't intend to stay."

"You wanted to pay and collect your debts and then leave again." She looked down at their clasped hands. A mate, he had said. Jane had been pregnant when she was shot.

She wondered how far his magic really went.

It was like Mrs. Kvanbeck had said: Selkies didn't stay—unless they were forced to.

Elisabeth wouldn't have thought it possible, but sex that night was even better than it had been the night before. Afterwards, Dan curled up behind her, fitting his body around hers, her ass nestled snugly in his crotch, his arm draped under her breasts, comfortable and unfamiliar. For once, the ever-present cloud cover had broken, and she watched the persistent remnants chase the moon. He fit her so well. She could keep him. With a little magic courtesy of a well-meaning old lady, she could bind him to her for as long as they both should live. He would stay. He hadn't intended to, but now he was in her power.

She slipped out from under his smooth, warm arm and turned over, wiping the tears out of the corners of her eyes and propping her head on one hand. His breathing was rhythmic, but his face held the trace of frown.

Just as the sun was sneaking above the horizon, masking its arrival behind the once again victorious winter clouds, she slipped out of bed and into her clothes. Dan slept peacefully, the covers bunched just above his waist, his hairless torso dark against the sheets and his decadent eyelashes dark against his cheeks. She gazed at him for a long moment and then let herself out.

Downstairs, she found Mrs. Kvanbeck in the kitchen, as usual.

"I'd like to have my parka back," she announced gently.

The old woman took off her glasses and began to polish them vigorously. "Why do you think I know where it is?"

"You needed an excuse to give me the other jacket."

Mrs. Kvanbeck continued to polish without looking up.

"I can't keep him here if he doesn't want to stay."

Finally her landlady looked up, her pale blue eyes shimmering with tears. "But he makes you so happy."

Elisabeth smiled. "Yes. Like your husband made you."

"What do you mean?"

"He was a selkie, wasn't he? And you kept him."

Mrs. Kvanbeck stared at her, not answering.

"Did he ever return to the sea?" Elisabeth asked quietly.

"We *were* happy together," the old woman said, tears slipping out of her eyes. "Happy."

She chose a very dramatic section of coast near one of the haul-out sites, the cliffs jutting up straight out of the water. She parked in the viewpoint turnout, got out of the car and walked to the railing. The shifting mist shrouded her and everything around her, transforming the landscape from moment to moment. *Havbryn*, the place of transition.

Elisabeth pulled the seal skin jacket out of her backpack and flung it as far out into the ocean as she could.

She watched the jacket float for a while on the gray surface until a wave caught it and pulled it under. Then, impulsively, she pulled the wedding band off her finger and threw it after the jacket. Two seconds later she knew it had been supremely stupid—a very expensive—gesture. But her ring finger felt much lighter.

Elisabeth sat down on a rock next to the pathway leading to the beach. She had no idea how long she sat there, nearly motionless, staring at the sand and stones and sea below her, staring at nothing. The shades of gray in the rocks and the mist and the ocean weaving in and out of each other made a pleasant pattern, undemanding, and the cries of the gulls were as soothing as a lullaby.

After what could have been either mere minutes or hours, she saw a graceful brown form emerge from the waves and dive back into the water, swimming for shore. She watched the seal's progress until he reached the beach and waddled onto the sand, as ungainly on land as he was graceful at sea. Dante looked up at her and barked, waddling closer to the pathway leading up to the parking lot.

Elisabeth got up and made her way down to where the seal was waiting for her.

"I see you are home again, my friend," she said quietly. "Happy?"

Dante stared at her, his brown eyes huge in his smooth, mottled-brown face.

Despite the cold, she sat down in the sand to be on a level with him. "Mixed feelings, too?"

He bobbed his head, nodding.

"Well, whether it's true or not, it's kind of you to say so."

The seal nodded again, this time toward where her feet were stretched out in the sand. There, next to her left boot was the wedding band she had carelessly flung into the ocean. Elisabeth laughed and picked it up. "Mrs. Kvanbeck said you made me laugh. I guess she's right."

Dante seemed to smile at her, then turned and waddled back into the surf. Once he was in the water again, free and out to sea where he belonged, his movements became fluid and smooth, part of the landscape of waves and sand, of the gulls diving and soaring.

Elisabeth gazed after him as his sleek, brown head disappeared from sight, hugging her parka tight against the wind. When the brown speck on the water had vanished completely, she smiled, dropped the wedding ring into her pocket, and hiked back up to the parking lot.

Jacob's Tree

"You sure it's okay with your doctor for you to be climin' my trees?" Ben Carlson asked.

"I just entered in my second trimester," I responded, smoothing the material of my *Baby On Board* tee shirt across my barely swelling stomach.

"How many pounds you lookin' for?"

I pointed to my empty boxes. "About forty pounds."

He nodded with a shrewd estimation of my containers. "Faller me," he said as he turned up the row of trees and I followed the old farmer into his orchard.

Tall and slender, Ben Carlson wore faded bib overalls, had gray hair that stuck up like last winter's straw, and looked to be somewhere between sixty and the age of dirt. He even had a calico handkerchief flagging from his rear pocket. Mr. Carlson's much stained baseball cap said John Deere across the top of the bill.

"I've never seen so many cherries," I said. The trees sagged under the weight of the fruit. I was certain that, given time, I would hear branches groan under their burden. "You don't usually have to brace cherry trees, do you, Mr. Carlson?" I smiled at the old man as he raised one of those rickety, A-frame ladders popular with orchardists. I wanted to show that I had some basic understanding of orchards, and cherries specifically.

"No, ma'am," he said with a smile. "Have to during good crop year, though, 'specially with young trees. Happens about one year in ten, fifteen mebee. This tree'll do just fine."

"How do you manage to keep the birds out of them?" I wondered aloud. "The birds always eat mine at home before they have a chance to ripen. When I picked at Edward's Orchards last year, they seemed to have a real problem with birds."

"Cat stands," Mr. Carlson nodded and looked across the valley, towards Edward's Orchards. "Yep. Edward's got the frost late and lost most his crop this year. I'm a bit lower in the valley than he is."

"I beg your pardon," I said. "But did you say 'cat scans'?"

"Nothin' so fancy, ma'am," Mr. Carlson smiled widely, his

white teeth gleaming in his much tanned, completely wrinkled face. "Cat stands. You'll see 'em in the trees, about every three, four feet. I used to shoot them birds, but they passed new laws and now the county gives me tickets for killin' song birds. Kinda hard to write a cat a ticket, I suppose."

"You must have lots of cats," I said as I looked through the orchard, trying to spot one.

"You'd be surprised," Mr. Carlson said. "It don't take so many. This here is Old Jake's tree, and that one, and the three over there. He kinda rotates among them."

He sat a picking bucket down on the ground for me and turned to leave. The last part of his conversation was more for his benefit than mine. "A'course, he's gettin old now and not as frisky as he was. Then, so am I." He turned back at the end of the path leading into my row in his orchard with one last warning. "You watch out for Old Jake. Don' let him give you a bad time."

I worked steadily for half an hour, lost in a suspended lassitude, that almost idyllic daydream repetitive manual labor sometimes offers when the physical demands aren't excessive.

"What are you doing in my tree?"

I'd been concentrating so on cherries that the voice startled me. Varying shades of red filled my vision.

"Did you say something, Mr. Carlson?" I called. I looked down the ladder, towards the path, but thick, green and red branches blocked my vision.

"What are you doing in my tree?"

"I'm sorry, Mr. Carlson," I said as I climbed down. "But I thought this was the tree you said..."

Mr. Carlson was nowhere to be seen.

"Hello?" I walked to the foot of the row of trees, to the edge of the orchard, absently wiping my hands on my pants. "Hello?"

Mr. Carlson was dozing in a lawn chair near the U-Pick shed where I'd first met him. He came awake with a start.

"Was just napping," he said as he slowly stood. "Did you need something ma'am?"

"No... I... I thought you called to me," I said.

"Not unless it was in a dream," he said with a smile.

* * *

A shower of feathers greeted me as I climbed back up the ladder. On one of Mr. Carlson's cat stands, three feet from the top step of the ladder, sat the largest gray tabby I've ever seen. He'd just finished dining on a robin and flicked the carcass aside like he would ashes from a cigar. He yawned grandly, his pink tongue flashing out beneath his fangs, and began cleaning himself slowly.

"You naughty thing!" I scolded. "That was a robin!"

The cat paused his bath, stared at me like I was stupid, then said, "So it was."

I almost fell off the ladder climbing down. I ran down the foot of the path, stumbling and glancing back to make sure the cat didn't follow me. Mr. Carlson must have heard me coming.

"Lady, you look like you seen death," he said. "Are you all right?"

"I... the cat... he..."

How could I tell a total stranger that his cat talked?

"He killed a robin," I finally managed to stammer.

"An' brought it down to show you, did he?" Mr. Carlson nodded. "That's Old Jake. Always got to show off his treasures. Can't tell you the number of snakes and birds and mice I chased outta my house when he was in his prime. Now he just eats them. Sometimes he likes to scare strangers, though."

"He talked," I stammered, knowing how foolish and crazy it sounded, but I hurried on, unable to stop. "He asked me what I was doing in his tree."

A look of concern crossed Mr. Carlson's face. "You better sit down, lady," he was solicitous as he steered me to his lawn chair in the shade. "You been in the sun too long. You rest a few minutes while I fetch you a glass of water."

"Perhaps if I changed trees," I suggested after I rested for awhile. I felt embarrassed. Mr. Carlson was right; I'd just had too much sun, over-did things. "I really don't have to pick that many more. Maybe a tree nearer the shed?" I asked hopefully.

I worked haphazardly for the next half an hour, stopping now and then to check my surroundings, making sure that I was in the shade and well away from the top of the ladder. Although it was impossible to stay away from all of Mr. Carlson's cat stands, I tried to work as much as possible between two of them.

I checked constantly to see that they stayed empty.

"Changing trees doesn't really matter," Old Jake said. I don't know when he arrived or how he got to the stand without my seeing him, but there he sat, another robin twitching its final death throes beneath his claws.

"You talked... can talk," I stammered, grabbing onto the ladder.

"Most cats can," Jake said as he eyed the bird carefully. "But very few do. So few humans are really worthy of the effort, especially when all it takes is a simple meow."

Jake let out the most pitiful meow I'd ever heard, enough to make me want to cuddle him. I smiled. My pity for him ended as he tore into the breast of the robin.

"Lunch," he said as he tore a section away.

"But it's scarcely ten o'clock in the morning," I stammered, not knowing what else to say to a cat about to eviscerate a bird.

"Luncheon, still," Jake said. "Breakfast was an hour before dawn. Nap time comes earlier and earlier these days." He scarcely ate any of the bird at all before flicking it aside and beginning his cleansing ritual.

"Seems a terrible waste," I said.

"No waste at all, dear lady," Jake said. "You see, I only sup on the hearts, the liver and the gizzard of local birds. Those who have migrated from the south are barely edible. Too many pesticides concentrated in their organs."

"It doesn't seem natural," I mumbled.

"Ah, a naturalist. I see," Jake curled around himself on his perch and seemed ready for a nap. His twitching tail, however, showed interest in our conversation. "Tell me, what happens to those cherries you're picking. Pie? Jam perhaps?"

"Christmas cobbler," I replied. "It's my specialty."

"Do you suppose Christmas cobbler is natural for a cherry?" Jake asked.

"What do you mean?" I asked.

"What is natural to a cherry?" Jake didn't wait for my response. "To ripen, grow fat, fall at full fruit from the vine, hopefully onto fertile soil, and sprout into a tree. Perpetuation of the species. Like cats, few cherries left in their natural state, ever really die."

"What do you mean, 'like cats'?" I asked.

"What constitutes a generation, in human terms?" He sighed, evidently bored.

"About twenty years," I replied.

"And how long do most cats 'live'?"

"About seventeen to twenty..." I stopped. Jake looked pleased with himself.

"You think it mere coincidence, I see. Cats never die, not really. Surely you've heard of our nine lives."

"But that's just..."

"A myth," Jake smiled broadly, most pleased with himself. "I've lived so many lives, I've forgotten most of them. The times I can remember... could remember. Not now... it's all so.... Now it's almost time to shed this body for a new one."

"A new one? A lion or a tiger I suppose," I said.

"Barbarians," Jake scoffed. "Hardly feline anymore. Such a waste of good fur. Lion, indeed. Do you know how difficult zebra is to digest? Those tough, gamy stringy things? Still, there is something in being that magnificently brutal. When you're a lion, the whole world is your sand box and no one dares rub your nose in it."

"You'll come back as another house cat?" I asked.

"That is the usual course," Jake said. "Why do you think there are so few true cat fights? We know each other, have known each other for centuries. Oh, there are individuals that I don't like... none here, thankfully. We grouse and howl at each other, but rarely fight. Only when a truly new cat at arrives..."

"What do you mean? If you don't die, how can you... this is all so confusing." The sun had passed noon and I was no longer in the shade. The weight of the picking bucket called me towards reality. I shook my head to clear my eyes and mind.

"So few humans are really worth talking to," Jake said with another long yawn and stretch. "They have so little patience and their understanding is so limited. I've used my nine lives, you see, and now I must drop a bit lower on the food chain and start again. It's so rare one has a chance to choose at this stage." He arose and smiled... and vanished.

"Thirty-one pounds, ma'am," Mr. Carlson said. "If you want, I can help you get another nine pounds real quick."

"No, it's all right, Mr. Carlson," I said.

I filled out my check, ready to hand it to him almost before he finished weighing my fruit, hurrying the process along. Mr. Carlson helped me load the cherries into the trunk of my car.

"Thank you," I said as he opened the car door. I was more than ready to leave everything behind. Mr. Carlson tipped his hat and returned to his chair. I'd calmed down enough to convince myself that what I'd seen was merely a sun-induced hallucination when I felt a cat twining itself between my legs. I looked down to see Old Jake.

"Of course, we don't always come back as cats," Jake said. He smiled and purred... and vanished.

"What?" I stammered.

Inside my belly, the baby kicked for the first time.

A Thin Line

"Not *Folk* music," Director Hays was shouting when I entered the dome. "It's *Filk*, you fool. Filk!" Hays stood nose-to-nose, or as close as his five foot, three inch frame would allow, with Thibs. At six two, Thibs (short for Thibodaux) stared back at the director, clenching and unclenching bony fists.

"It's a different kind of music," Director Hays raked a hand through thin blond hair. "From a different time, a different place in history. Don't you know anything about music?"

"I'm a combat engineer." Thibs' ears reddened, blue eyes gleaming with too much moisture. He glanced uncertainly at the rest of us. "We're all combat engineers. Long as it sounds good with a cold Happiness bulb, I don't care."

"Hey, Thibs." I blinked warm Cambrian rain from my eyes and squeegeed it from my scalp with a hand. "I really need your help outside."

"Sure, Lowdeal, sure!" Thibs turned my way, a thin appreciative smile forming on his long face. He glanced once more down at Director Hays and started towards me. Over in the corner, I saw Patchgirl relax and turn to her console.

There. Got my buddy out of trouble, I dared think. But Hays grabbed Thibs by the elbow and spun him around. Thibs' arm came up, his lanky frame instantly in defensive stance.

"Before there was engineering," Hays folded his arms smugly. "Before there was mathematics, before civilization, humanity had music. One day, we'll have a chance to move beyond it all. Beyond even life as we know it, and do you know why?"

Thibs cocked his head, scraggly brown curls and beard making him look like a puzzled terrier. "Uh, music?"

"Rhythm!" Director Hays lifted his hands to the heavens. "It's hard-wired into us. The basis of music, even thought itself!"

Hays backed toward the dome exit. Deep grey eyes, filled with a haunting anguish gazed at us before his mouth thinned and his jaw clenched. Abruptly, his small hands slapped his thighs. His feet stomped the clear vexine floor until mud pulsed beneath it.

A dance? Seizure? I couldn't tell but I'd never heard anything like it in all my life. The rhythm drilled into my brain, far more complex and subtle than anything I could imitate. With a final percussive cadence, Hays vanished through the exit, the door's pneumatics wheezing it shut.

No one moved. We all stared at the exit, holding our breath. Finally, Patchgirl dropped her headset and it clattered over her console. Her warm brown eyes blinked and glanced our way. Her thin lips curved into a worried frown.

Over by their table, our three so-called comrades from the Martian Republic gazed back at us. The heavyset one in the middle, Han-Yon stood and opened his mouth. Ruth Ayn, the woman beside him, frowned and pulled on his arm. Han-Yon shrugged and sat down. Ahmed, the thin guy on his other side, began whispering in Han-Yon's ear.

"What did you want, Lowdeal?" Thibs touched my shoulder.

I jerked, arms and limbs tingling as the director's strangely compelling rhythm vanished from my mind. A queasy shiver ran through me that had nothing to do with the blood-temperature rain trickling down my spine.

"The Waldoids," I managed. "They're stuck again." Adjusting my headset and pulling up my hood, I followed Thibs out the other door.

The low rolling hills of North West Laurentia, second largest continent of the Cambrian period, surrounded us. The hills, covered in a dull, washed out green of simple algae and lichens, oozed a soured laundry stench. Low grey clouds with a greasy sheen blanketed the sky and shrouded the pale disc of sun. Just past the domes, a shallow inlet filled with flat, grey water extended toward the horizon.

It was hard to believe that 540 million years from now, the mud we slogged through would become mountains in British Columbia. The far side of the inlet would hold a vast treasure trove of fossils known as The Burgess Shale.

"I don't get it, Lowdeal." Thibs hunched deeper into his rain poncho. "I'm minding my own business, helping Patchgirl fix the com. So maybe I was humming. Hays asked me what the song was. Then he gets crazy."

"What was it?"

Thibs shrugged and stared back at the dome, eyes all big like a newly spanked puppy. "Just a tune, I guess."

"Well, was it Folk or Filk?"

"How should I know?" Thibs picked up a shovel and started off. "What the hell is Filk anyway?" He snorted, and then wiped his nose. "All I know is Hays must be filked up."

"This mission's been like that from the get go," I muttered as we trudged along.

Thibs, Patchgirl, and I were veterans of the Peace Quests. As combat engineers of the Autonomy we had fought the Martian Republic from Saturn's moons to Honduran jungles. We'd fought until both governments collapsed; a new progress-oriented coalition The Bureatomy seized control.

Now, along with our Marsie counterparts, we were stuck in the Time Quests—learning to get along. The Bureatomy maintained this was a healing process. But the Cambrian seemed a good place to stick people you wanted out of the way for a while.

The Bureatomy had ordered us to build a base here so their SciTech division could come in and compare Cambrian population density with recorded fossil density. What kind of crazy government needed data like that? Still, it was better than fighting, I guess—maybe.

I tuned my com to our secret private frequency. "Patchgirl, any idea what Hays was on about?"

"That dance thing at the end was way past weird." Patchgirl's static-filled voice crackled through our headsets. "Might be temporal shock."

"Maybe. But he didn't have the shakes," Thibs responded. Temporal shock was the term applied to a collection of symptoms sometimes caused by time travel. Paranoia, hallucinations, schizophrenic reactions, they'd all been covered in our briefings—a condition easily treatable by the medbot.

Of course, we'd also been briefed on Cambrian geology, topography, and climate. And on minor malfunctions that occurred when electronic gear was subjected to the magnetic jolts and neutrino flux of time travel. Like our temporal shock briefing, and perhaps all briefings I pondered, inaccuracies existed.

Which left our group abandoned some nineteen kilometers from the targeted zone, with equipment that barely functioned, up to our asses in mud SciTech had assured us was rocky slate and a splendid site for a base. Did I mention rain? Forty-five straight days.

"See what's in his med file," I suggested to Patchgirl.

"You'll get me in trouble," she crackled. "Besides, the medbot's on the fritz."

"One problem at a time," Thibs sighed. He turned to me, fists on his hips. "You coulda told me it was a slide."

I shook my head, staring at what remained of the waldoids. "It... It wasn't this bad when I left."

I'd been guiding six waldoids through a shallow valley when their segmented feet had become mired in mud. Heavy, with 700 kilograms of vexine slabs apiece, I'd had them drop their loads and try to lever out. No go.

Communications down again, in the half hour it had taken to get back to camp, a hillside had come loose, sluicing down upon the hapless machines. Wasn't anything left above mud but their antenna.

"Any end to this rain?" I growled at Patchgirl.

"Scans show clouds all the way to Gondwana," Patchgirl sighed. "We're on our own, boys." A time transmitter can punch through 540 million years like butter—but rain stops it like a vexine wall.

"Send out the remaining waldoids with their digger attachments." I waded in close, wrinkling my nose at the mud's rancid odor. "Send the Marsies too. We got a big mess here."

"Like the Marsies are ever any help." Patchgirl's scorn vanished in a static howl, the rest of her message lost.

"I don't want to be healed." I unslung my shovel, turned it on, and waited for its repeller field to shimmer. "Why can't they just let me retire? I've only got two years left."

"Two years." Thibs readied his shovel and dug in. "Plus five hundred and forty million."

"Careful," the thin Marsie, Ahmed Li needlessly advised. He perched above water on another stanchion. A slender hand wiped the rain from his bristly black hair before shielding dark eyes in a gaunt face. The other hand stuffed a meat bar into his mouth.

I stood up to my chest in warm Cambrian sea, the water remarkably clear yet reflecting the gray clouds of another rainy day.

Bobbing in the shallows, two waldoids, still in leg-mode maneuvered a 500 kilogram vexine stanchion onto its base. A third waldoid in swim mode, its three directional propellers churning, wove between them with the programmer.

Vexine, the very thought of it would put a warm cozy smile on any engineer's face. Hard enough to stand a nuke or soft enough to make a mattress, programmable for any quality your heart desired.

Sadly, Arthur Vexine the inventor, when denied patents by our government, had dissolved his own dome, killing himself, about a thousand others, and setting back lunar expansion some five years. There's a thin line between genius and madness.

Still, vexine remained the perfect building material for the Cambrian, even the waldoids were made of the stuff. Turn off the power and it would dissolve before any chance of fossilization. Possibility of future contamination remained a big sweet zero.

"To the left a little, I think," Ahmed Li directed.

"Just do your job," I growled, one hand deep into the waldoids' control box. "And let me do mine."

"What's that?" Ahmed Li called, a sharp edge to his words. "What you say?"

I had an answer coming; the guy had been on my butt all day. Then the stanchion settled into place and I eased the swimming waldoid closer. While the other two stabilized the stanchion, the swimmer programmed the pieces to adhere. Job done. I backed the waldoids off, then sent them to shore for the last stanchion.

Around me in the water, plants that Ahmed had assured me weren't plants, but animals called sea pens, fluttered wavy green fronds. Cup things, that looked like sponges but weren't, swayed with the sluggish current. Worms that were not worms, but pre-worms, pseudo-worms, or some such garbage, covered our work like jeweled lumps of snot.

A small yellow one with five eyes, what Ahmed had called an opabinia, studied me from the top of the stanchion. It waved a proboscis half as long as its body as if to say, "When you're dead you're mine."

"You'll probably evolve into somebody's tapeworm," I muttered.

"Got news, Lowdeal." Patchgirl's transmission came on our secret frequency. "Finally found Hays' data while I was working on the medbot."

"The medbot? Thought it was broken." I whispered, turning away from Ahmed, pretending to study the waldoids as they picked up the stanchion on the muddy shore.

"Which is why I was working on it," Patchgirl said with some exasperation.

"Oh yeah."

"Now get this," Patchgirl replied. "Hays used to run a whole SciTech division but the Bureatomy demoted him. They dumped him here and he only had three years to retirement."

"Man, I know just how that feels." I took control of the waldoids as they lumbered closer, the stanchion half out of the water above them. "No wonder the poor guy's acting funny."

"Hey, deaf boy!" Ahmed shouted. I turned just as he jumped up, standing on the stanchion waving a slender vexine bar. "Heads up!"

A cross between a giant water bug and a toxgas hallucination swept alongside Ahmed. Numerous legs undulated like oars, moving it over the surface. Multiple brown segments stretched and contracted as it turned. Beneath two bulging red eyes, twin spiked tentacles as long as a man's forearm twisted and churned.

SciTech's briefing had claimed there were no dangerous predators. The Marsie girl, Ruth Ayn had disproved that one, so Ahmed was (ha ha) protecting me. Ruth Ayn's leg was doing well, considering the medbot's unworkable condition.

"Got a big one incoming." Ahmed whacked at the creature with the vexine bar, our only weapon since there were no predators and this was a healing process.

"A gatorbug all right." I pushed the waldoid controller around my back, letting it rest on the neck strap, freeing my hands.

"Anomalocaric." Ahmed swatted at the thing again, somehow missing its two-meter long body. "A good engineer would naturally use appropriate terminology."

I stepped back as the creature oozed past Ahmed and came towards me. Thibs had made up his own name when one chased him out of the water. It sounded right to me, but no point arguing. All I'd ever gotten from a Marsie was a hard time. "Just throw me the bar, man."

Never mind this was Ahmed's job. The Marsie wasn't about to put his butt on the line for mine. He tossed the vexine bar my way. It splashed in front of me, filling my eyes with seawater. My hand brushed it but the bar sank before I could get a grip. I had to go under, the gatorbug already around the stanchion, those wicked spiked tentacles writhing eagerly. A school of inch-long trilobites fled past my face as I sank to my knees and picked up the bar.

Gasping, I came up just in time to ram the vexine right into the gatorbug. Its feeder tentacles instantly wrapped around the bar but then thrust it aside when it discovered vexine wasn't good to eat.

"Head towards shore!" Ahmed called.

My glare should have boiled the water around him. It had no effect on the gatorbug either. Cambrian carnivores didn't have the brains to circle; it just kept coming. I whacked it between the eyes then rammed the bar into the head. The bluish ichor that suddenly clouded the water only seemed to excite it more. It thrashed and lunged at me again. I backed steadily, putting myself behind the motionless waldoids.

For a moment, I thought it might go after the machines. The waldoids, however, jerked into avoidance mode and helpfully cleared out of its way. I slammed the bar down between us again, making a big splash.

"Damn it! Get to hell away from me." I banged the bar across its back this time. The creature doubled up and surged forward. Waist deep now, I was just considering making a run for shore when something big splashed behind me. I whirled, bringing the bar up.

"Not me, idiot." Director Hays raised a hand to shield himself. "Look out now."

He ducked past, a look of concentration hardening his pudgy features as he studied the gatorbug. The creature paused; perhaps confused by this sudden choice of meals. Hays used the moment to his advantage—I guess. He cupped his hands, and then brought them down smacking the water.

"Hu neh hu neh new hoom!" Hays played the water like a drum, voice bellowing the strangely accented syllables. I could just make out his feet beneath the surface as they rhythmically stomped some hapless coral that probably wasn't coral.

The gatorbug grew still, its many legs limp as it rode the ripples caused by the director's hands. Apparently even Cambrian Age predators were disturbed by insanity. I gaped at Hays who continued this water drumming, weaving a rhythm I couldn't copy, yet couldn't get out of my head.

Hays' left hand finally hit the surface too hard and splashed water in his face. He paused, coughing. The gatorbug shook itself, and then surged at him. Having caught my breath, I slammed the bar down hard. It hit the thing between its knobby head and first segment. The gatorbug stiffened then curled up. I raised the bar again, but the creature slowly began to drift.

"Why did you interfere?" Hays wiped the water from his eyes and scowled at me. "It was almost under control."

"Control?" I stepped back and scratched my head. "Sir, it's a gatorbug, not a waldoid in a monster suit."

"Don't be facetious." Hays turned to watch the gatorbug floating away. A swarm of tiny trilobites had found the body and were playing Find the Tasty Bits.

"You both need to learn how to protect yourselves." Hays rubbed his jaw. "I can't afford another injury on top of everything else." He looked towards the stanchions where Ahmed still perched. "Mr. Li. Join us please."

Ahmed stared at the water uncertainly, then finally eased into it and waded our way.

"This creature has a nervous system," Hays said to us. "That should be apparent even to you."

Ahmed shrugged. I nodded.

"Nervous systems function according to electrical impulses. Okay?" Hays asked.

Ahmed nodded. I shrugged.

"Impulses, even electrical, produce a rhythm," Hays went on. "Such rhythms can be copied. Projecting the precise rhythm back at the targeted nervous system cancels its own rhythm. A temporary paralysis occurs." Hays spread his hands and studied us. "The effect is especially pronounced in Cambrian life forms."

"I was unaware of this phenomenon," Ahmed said cautiously.

"Yeah, me too." Hands on my hips, I stared down at the smaller man.

Hays' hand lashed out in the direction of the now partially consumed gatorbug. "Well, you just saw the Anomalocaric stop."

"See?" Ahmed folded his arms. "Our director speaks precisely."

"The gatorbug paused," I admitted with some irritation, "But then it came on again."

"Anomalocaric Canadensis." Hays shrugged. "So I missed a beat." A warm cozy smile spread over his face. "Still, my theory works."

"But how did you know this rhythm?" Ahmed asked. "It would have to be specific to the creature. Wouldn't it?"

"Specific to the species." Hays beamed at him. "Methods exist now for determining an organism's primary rhythm. My methods. Rhythmonics is *my* theory."

I wasn't sure how to respond. Neither was Ahmed. We both shrugged, and when Hays' frown deepened, we both nodded.

Hays sighed. He rubbed the bridge of his nose. "You're just like those SciTech fools. I couldn't make them listen either." He cupped his hands. "Just try it."

Ahmed and I looked at each other. We cupped our hands and copied Hays' stance.

"Hu...neh... hu... neh... new... hoom..." Hays slowly accented each syllable with a slap to the water.

"Hu...neh... hu... neh... new... hoom," we tried.

"Good, but not so good." Hays shook his head, positioned his hands over the water once more. "Quicker now. Hu neh hu neh new hoom."

"Huneh huneh hoom."

"It's hardwired into the simplest creatures." Hays shook his finger in my face. "Why can't you get it?" He repeated the drill.

Still unsatisfied, he made us do it again. Then again.

We kept at it. My fingers puckered and my eyes stung. The sky turned from light grey to dark. A cloud-filtered full moon appeared. The sea grew murky, except for the luminous froth our drumming churned up. The waldoids waited silently, getting nothing done.

"This is just the tip of the iceberg," Hays muttered. His hands clawed his wet hair as he whirled and sloshed through the water. "I can't even teach you the basics. There's so much more..." He staggered up on the bank, glaring at us, arms spread wide. "Rhythmonics will revolutionize... everything!"

"Yes sir," Ahmed and I answered, hands stuffed beneath our armpits.

"Everything!" Hays stormed up the beach, into the darkness towards the domes.

We stood there until he vanished. After awhile, the waldoids automatically switched on their lights. As we trudged back to the stanchions, Ahmed looked at me.

"I'm afraid our director is a crazy person," he whispered.

"There's a thin line between genius and madness."

"He's standing on the wrong side of it." Ahmed paused to stare back at the now softly glowing domes.

"Oh, I don't know." Strange rhythms still haunted me as I reached for the waldoid control box. "He could be onto something."

Later that night, I told my buddies about the gatorbug. Thibs, Patchgirl, and I huddled on our side of the dome, a half dismantled waldoid between us. On the far side of the dome, the three Marsies had their own huddle around a camp table. I didn't know what they were doing; I was too tired to care.

"That's the stupidest thing I ever heard," Thibs said.

"Still," Patchgirl's brown eyes twinkled. She brushed at one of the dark curls framing her face. "Rhythm is the basis for all music."

"And music has powers to soothe the savage beast," Thibs chuckled. "Ever get a song stuck in your head? You can't get it out no matter what you do."

"Been known to drive people crazy." Patchgirl's smile

turned wicked.

Thibs reached over, picked up a waldoid servomotor, and wiped at the mud with a self-cleaning towel. "You been a little crazy lately, Lowdeal."

"This mission is making me crazy," I snapped. "You're not looking so good yourself."

We got quiet for a while, perhaps hypnotized by the steady rhythms of rain on vexine. Abruptly the Marsies stirred, rising from their places. We looked up to find them looking at us. They moved around their table and came over. We didn't make room but they squeezed in anyway.

"Let's talk." Ahmed squatted down. Ruth Ayn, still favoring her leg, settled stiffly. The heavy-set Han-Yon eased into an awkward cross-legged position, his fleshy face creasing into a broad smile. The dome's fluorescents highlighted the greasy sheen of his hairless head.

"About Director Hays," Han-Yon said softly. As one we all glanced at the door. "We know you know more than you tell."

"He deserves our support." I shrugged. "He's the director."

"But he does not direct." Han-Yon spread his hands, again glancing toward the door. "Supplies run short. Project way behind. Injuries. Breakdowns. Where is he all this time?"

"Singing to the gatorbugs?" Patchgirl suggested. She and Thibs laughed. The Marsies did not. Neither did I.

"Good humor." Han-Yon frowned. "Sure I understand. It breaks tension. But still, things go poorly. Director Hays hides in his dome, or wanders wherever there is no work to be done."

"Isn't that what directors do?" Thibs leaned back and stretched out his legs. Ruth Ayn, her face pinched in the dim light, gave him a weak smile.

"So what's your point?" I asked.

"If he's unfit, he may be judged so by team members." Han-Yon clasped his hands. "He can be replaced."

"Impossible." I shook my head.

"It's in the regs," Patchgirl admitted.

"I want to replace him." Han-Yon touched his chest. Both Ruth Ayn and Ahmed glanced at their comrade, nodding approval.

"I don't see it." Thibs put down the servomotor and picked

up another.

"Why you?" Patchgirl asked.

"I'm the smartest and most qualified." Han-Yon's smile stretched from ear to ear. "You boys are just tech jockeys. I have leadership qualifications."

No way could we go along with that. Things got heated; Han-Yon jumped to his feet and I rose to meet him. Thibs was just about to push between us when the lights went off.

"Circuitry failure," Patchgirl sighed. "Back-ups on in three... two... one." The darkness remained.

"Damn," Thibs said.

The dome shook. I collided with Han-Yon, who apparently still had a mad on because he threw me into Thibs.

"Hey!" I shouted. "Get over it."

A heartbeat later a gritty sound scraped the walls. It grew louder, flowing from one end of the dome to the other. The dome shuddered, lurched, and began to move.

We sprawled. A table crashed into the wall. Screaming. Yelling. Patchgirl's console toppled and slammed against the floor. The floor rocked; a gritty roar swallowed us as we picked up speed.

The dome tilted and we all rolled into one big ball. I got way too familiar with other people's elbows and knees. The dome slanted another twenty degrees and finally jerked to a halt.

"What the hell happened," Thibs gasped.

"Mudslide." Han-Yon's deeper voice came out of the darkness. "Has to be."

"Thank God for vexine," I murmured, more than a trace of reverence in my voice. I'd programmed a pretty sturdy dome. One that was obviously more stable than the hill it stood on. Of course, forty-six straight days of rain upon soil that lacked any vegetation to hold it together, didn't make for much of a building site.

"Can we get out?" Ruth Ayn asked.

"Better to ask, can we find the door," Ahmed added. Noise. Scraping. Blackness.

"Here." Thibs's voice. "Uh, do we really want to open it?"

I scooted in his direction, brushing up against Patchgirl, and then banging my shin on her fallen console. "Could be a lot of mud on the other side."

"Will the dome pressure equalize it?" Han-Yon asked.

"Maybe," I guessed.

"You're a big help." Ruth Ayn replied. "We could wait until daylight and assess the situation then."

"Unless we're completely covered," Patchgirl added.

"What about air?" Ahmed asked. "How long will it last? It already seems stuffy."

"Oxygen should still come through the walls," Thibs told him. "Lowdeal, you programmed it that way, didn't you?"

"Standard gas barriers," I answered. "So we might have forty-eight hours."

"Why no more?" Han-Yon asked.

"Power's down," I said. "Without power, the vexine will dissolve.

"Looks like we'll need to open the door no matter what," Thibs said.

"Only a little way at first," Han-Yon cautioned. "See what comes in."

We rearranged ourselves in the blackness. Thibs, Han-Yon, and I beside the door, ready to close it if we could. Of course, a thousand kilograms of mud on the other side might make that impossible.

"Ready?" Thibs asked.

"Do it," Han-Yon replied. I braced my feet on the door and tried to wedge myself against the wall.

"Here goes," Thibs answered. I heard the scraping of vexine. Water spurted over me. Patchgirl cried out and I think Ruth Ayn actually screamed.

"It's good, it's good," Thibs called as warm seawater flowed into the dome. "At least the way out is clear." My ears popped as pressure equalized. The darkness turned a grayish blue, some sort of luminescent algae in the water.

Han-Yon asked. "Who's first?"

"Lowdeal!" Thibs and Patchgirl said together.

"Me? Why me?" I asked.

"It's all your fault," Thibs answered. "You chose the dome's location."

Sighing, I eased myself into the doorway, kicked my legs

down, found them free of debris, and lowered myself. "We're still in the shallows, I hope." With a deep breath I pushed off.

Dawn found the six of us enduring a tepid Cambrian shower and staring with mixed emotions at the green-streaked runnel of mud that ran down the hill, into the sea, and had taken the entire base with it. Sluggish waves broke upon one end of the partially submerged dome and it glimmered, a seashell that wasn't a seashell.

"Incredible we weren't crushed," Ruth Ayn murmured, shaking the mud from her close-cropped blonde hair.

"Vexine," I grinned. "You got to love it."

"Where's Hays?" Thibs shaded the rain from his eyes with a lanky hand. "I don't see his dome either."

"Forget Hays." Ahmed scowled. "Where's the food? Looks like the supply dome followed the others."

Patchgirl lifted her arms to the clouds. "Until the rain breaks ain't nothing coming through."

"No food, no shelter, not even any tools." Ruth Ayn sank down on a sandy patch no more than forty percent mud. "Can our luck get any worse?"

One by one we slumped beside her. Exhausted, and more than a little afraid that just by saying it, she had invoked some Cambrian god that with our luck wasn't even a god yet, but was still capable of calling down further disasters. Perhaps she did.

I glanced at my chrono; it had stopped. Out past the mudslide, the flat vexine platform of the base I'd been constructing rose about a meter above the water. Three waldoids still perched motionlessly.

"We are absolutely without power," I said, clasping my hands on my knees, "Which means the Argus is off-line. That just can't happen."

The Argus exchanged gravitational force for electrical energy. No moving parts, foolproof operation. I loved the device almost as much as I loved vexine. Even time travel didn't affect it. Too bad that Samuel T. Argus, the inventor, rather than allow his father to criticize the initial theorems, crashed a flyer into his own research station and killed everyone.

"What do you mean?" Han-Yon turned to me, wiping

muddy hands on his coveralls.

"They don't break down." I shook my head. "No matter the conditions. We shot one straight into Saturn once. The resulting power surge overloaded Marsie ships for five thousand clicks in every direction."

"I remember," Han-Yon growled, fists clenching. "I was there." He glared at me. All three Marsies glared at me.

"Which means," Thibs finally put in. "That someone shut it down."

Narrow-eyed glares became widened stares of surprise. And, since the resulting chain of logic was pretty apparent, our divided little group soon reunited when everyone arrived at the final link.

"Hays," Han-Yon muttered.

"Insane," Ruth Ayn said.

"Temporal shock," Patchgirl added.

"I'll kill him." Thibs put in.

"Perhaps we should worry about survival first," Ahmed said, rubbing his gut. "In other words, can we eat anything out there in the ocean?"

"Well," Thibs climbed to his feet and wiped the mud from his butt. "Some of the trilobites are okay."

We all stared at him.

"You've actually eaten those things?" I asked.

"Have I mentioned my Cajun ancestry?" Thibs grinned at me. "We'll eat any damn thing."

"Remind me never to kiss you." Patchgirl made a face.

"Which ones have you tried?" Ahmed rose and approached the sea cautiously.

"The blue ones." Thibs followed him. "They got a meaty little chunk in them tastes just like mudbugs."

"Mudbugs?" Ruth Ayn's face crinkled in revulsion.

"Crawdads." Thibs bent down and peered into the water.

"Crawdads?" Han-Yon at last stood and scratched his neck.

"Crayfish," I told him, remembering a bar that Thibs had once dragged me to.

"What kind of fish?" Han-Yon asked.

"No, a crustacean." I got up and joined Thibs and Ahmed.

"Not a lot of those on Mars." Han-Yon shook his head and

frowned. He gazed past us, over towards the mudslide. Our dome had disappeared. "Maybe we can find the supply dome?"

"That mud's too unstable," I shrugged. "You want to chance getting buried alive?"

Han-Yon shook his head. He shoved his hands in his pockets and frowned at Thibs. "So how do we catch those things, Mud Bug Man?"

"Wade in and scoop 'em out." Thibs shrugged and ambled into the water. The rest of us followed.

A lot more discussion occurred, although it wasn't really discussion, just more bitching and moaning. Thibs caught a couple and showed us how to crack open the shell. The little things were plentiful, although faster than I'd figured.

"Tastes just like," Han-Yon smacked his lips and stared down at the gooey shell in his hands. "Soy and poultry paste."

"I'm having no luck at all." Patchgirl slumped, butt first in the shallows. "It's gonna take forever to get enough of these things. We'll starve if the rain don't stop."

I nodded, rubbed my chin, and looked around. Not too far away, but safely distant from the mudslide, I noticed a narrow inlet, sort of a bay within a bay. "Hey, I got an idea."

Arms outstretched, the six of us formed a half ring some twenty meters out past the mouth of the inlet. There'd be gaps sure, but it was worth a try.

"Ready?" I asked. When the others nodded, I started splashing the water, hands cupped as Director Hays had taught. Ahmed laughed and took it up. We got a rhythm going and the others followed. Together, we started slowly tightening our half circle around the inlet.

Trilobites of all shapes, colors, and sizes darted before us, a good number of other critters too, although I had my doubts about eating most of them. Some managed to escape, zipping past our legs.

Thibs started bobbing, jumping up and down in the waist deep water; that changed the rhythm and we all got caught up in it.

Knee deep, the water frothing with terrified trilobites in front of us, we started stomping our feet, splashing for all we were worth.

"Will the circuit," Thibs bellowed in a deep voice, "be unbroken? Motherboard says by and by." I knew that one, the old unofficial engineering anthem.

"Will the circuit be unbroken? In your eyes boys, in your eyes."

Trilobites fled before us, another ten meters would drive them onto the bank. We closed in further, stomping, clapping, Ruth Ayn just grinning to beat the band. Even Han-Yon had a smile. Patchgirl started laughing her head off.

"Rush 'em!" Thibs yelled. With a final hungry surge we closed our circle, caromed through the water in a wave, and drove the remaining trilobites onto the bank.

"Well, that was fun at least," Patchgirl sighed and slumped down on the bank.

"Like hunting for hors d'oeuvres," Thibs squatted beside her. The rest of us stared at the measly pile of still wriggling snacks.

"Yeah, but where's the main course?" Ahmed scowled. My own stomach growled. Divided up we each had only six apiece. Somehow, I got all the scrawny ones.

"There's a better way!" A new voice cackled. Director Hays, covered with mud, stood on the bank. Hair wild, eyes bulging he shouted, "You have to use Rhythmonics. It works, I tell you. It works!"

"So does cannibalism," Thibs muttered.

"Intriguing idea," Han-Yon growled.

I knew they didn't mean it. At least I was pretty sure, but still I rose a step ahead of everyone, planting myself between our small mob and the director.

"Hold on," I lifted a hand, stopping the others. "Let's give the man a chance."

A smile cracked Hays' mud-caked face. I could see the intelligence in his eyes, the torment of someone on the verge of discovery yet unable to make the world believe. But what held my attention was the thick layer of mud coating his otherwise naked body. Trilobite shells adorned it by the hundreds.

"I'll prove it." Hays scuttled down into the water. "Prove to you all the value of Rhythmonics."

I followed him eagerly, the rest trailed behind, unwilling disciples as Hays led us out until we stood waist deep. Already the Cambrian creatures had forgotten, or disdained our previous attempt to harvest them. The water teamed with potential snacks.

"Hu not not not huuum!" Hays began to drum the surface. "Hu not not not huuum!"

Rhythmic ripples spread around us in an ever widening circle. A trilobite floated to the surface, its legs twitching. Another followed. Then more trilobites, of every size, color, and shape, slowly drifted up, apparently paralyzed, to ride the ripples. Patchgirl gasped and carefully began gathering them in her poncho. Ahmed and Han-Yon were already stuffing their faces.

"Well, will you look at that," Thibs whispered beside me, hardly daring to breath. "I'll be damned."

"There's a thin line between genius and madness," I said, reaching for a trilobite the size of my fist.

"A genius gets the job done," Thibs grinned and cracked open a brilliant sky blue trilobite. "Still, we better find out what happened to the Argus."

"I had to shut it down," Hays laughed but continued drumming his strange compelling rhythms upon the frothing Cambrian waves. "The medbot told me it was singing messages into my brain."

Transubstantiation

The Catholic priest on the viewscreen looked bewildered. "So you're telling me that Jesus Christ, the Son of God, has returned as a Jewish girl in a Catholic schoolgirl's uniform on a space station in orbit around Mars?" said Father Kelly.

Paul Devane, director of Space Station Troika, looked back at the viewscreen and nodded. "That's who she says she is."

Paul heard footsteps on the metal floor of Troika's control room. He turned around and saw the teenaged girl standing by the entrance. The rhinestones on her silver tiara sparkled under a bright light above the entrance.

"You still don't believe me, do you?" she said.

Paul looked back at the viewscreen. "She's by the entrance. Do you see her? Did you hear her?"

The priest shook his head. "I don't see anyone standing by the doorway."

"But I can see her," Paul insisted.

"Alright, maybe you can, and for some reason, I can't," said Father Kelly. "Have you talked to her? What does she want?"

"She wants to crash our shuttlecraft onto the Martian surface," Paul said. "She thinks that's how God is going to create life on Mars."

All of Space Station Troika's sensors and cameras were aimed at the Martian surface below. As Troika orbited the planet, its crew searched for signs of survivors.

In Troika's control room, Paul Devane waited for the station to pass over Redsands Base. He looked at a shiny videoscreen and saw his reflection and cringed. Only forty years old, he looked like fifty, with gray streaks in his brown hair, a weary look in his eyes, and lines of age etched into his face. Living in space did that to some people.

He ran his hand through his greasy, disheveled hair to try to comb it. He hadn't taken the time to wash his hair since the disaster on Mars.

He yawned and sighed. He hadn't slept much since he had killed that girl at Redsands Base.

The videoscreen suddenly flickered, and an image of

Redsands Base replaced Paul's reflection.

Paul glanced at a woman wearing a yellow polo shirt with the Charging Duck mascot of the University of Oregon. Erin Malloy looked at him and turned back to her computer monitor. An aerial video image of a collapsed dome-shaped building appeared on the monitor. Nothing moved in the mangled mess of steel and plastic half-buried in loose dust and dirt. The only movement came from beside the dome: a geyser of water gushing from a pool created when geologists had dug into subsurface water.

"No body heat readings. There's nothing moving on the video," reported Erin. She turned away from her monitor. "There's nobody alive on Redsands."

Paul looked sadly at the video picture. "There were ten people down there. I was hoping to find at least one."

"Sorry, not at Redsands."

The video image began breaking up into static. "We're passing out of range of Redsands," Erin said.

"Thank you," Paul murmured as he returned to his chair and bit into a round hardtack cracker. The crumbs fell on his wrinkled blue shirt with the NASA logo.

All the combined nuclear weapons of Earth could not destroy the largest meteor to hit Mars in millions of years. The missiles and bombs had merely dented the rock. When the rock smashed into the Martian surface, it gouged out a gigantic crater, heated the surface a thousand degrees, and threw billions of tons of dust into the atmosphere. The shock wave and dust storm shook and smothered the Martian settlements. Now dozens of spaceships were evacuating the survivors to space stations in orbit around Mars.

Troika, being a small station carved out of a captured asteroid, had no room for refugees. Still, the disaster was keeping the three crew members busy. They usually surveyed the geography of Mars from their orbit, but now they had a new job: watching the Martian surface for signs of human life.

Another man approached Erin. She gave him a small smile. When Dr. Thomas Hall had arrived in Mars orbit a year ago, Erin had noticed how handsome the doctor was. A year later, he still looked like a buff, blond, Californian surfer dude. Living around Mars hadn't aged him prematurely, at least not yet.

He wore silver caduceus symbols of the medical profession on the collar of his clean, white shirt, and he looked at the brainscanner monitor in his hands. "The electrical activity in your frontal lobes went up while you were looking at the data coming from Mars," said Thomas.

"That's what's supposed to happen when I concentrate on something, right?" Erin said as she poured water into a pack of redhydratable tuna casserole. "God, this stuff is awful."

She looked at her reflection in the shiny metal control console. "This brainscanner is messing up my hair," she complained as she straightened the headpiece. It was a silvery band around her forehead with other bands arching over the top of her head. Small lights blinked on the bands.

"How long do I have to keep it on?" Erin asked.

"Another twenty-four hours," replied Thomas. "Then I'll have enough data. Is it uncomfortable?"

Erin shrugged and looked back at her reflection. "No, it's not too uncomfortable. It's lightweight. But I put waves into my hair to give it some body only to have you plunk this brainscanner on me."

"Ah, you still look beautiful, just like in that photo."

Erin glanced at a photo taped to her computer monitor: her wearing a white evening gown, silver tiara, and the sash of Miss Oregon. She was flanked by her black American mother and her white Canadian father. They were all smiling on that night, when she had won the crown of Miss Oregon.

None of them could have predicted the tragedy that winning the beauty pageant would bring.

"Yeah, just like in the photo," she muttered, lost in her memories.

"Thanks for keeping the brainscanner on during the emergency," Thomas said. "This is a rare opportunity to study the neurological activity of deep space crews."

Erin looked up and smiled. "No problem. Scientific research: that's what we're here for."

Paul gazed grimly at the digital clock counting the seconds and minutes on his computer monitor. "It's been four days since we found anyone alive. There probably isn't anyone left."

"Probably not," Erin agreed.

"Are you okay?" Thomas asked Paul. "Get some rest. Doctor's orders."

Paul nodded as he slowly rose from his chair. "Maybe I should. I feel really tired."

He opened his eyes and looked at a small wooden icon that Troika's original crew, the Russians, had nailed to the wall. The multicolored icon showed the Old Testament Trinity, the three angels who visited Abraham and his wife Sarah. In Eastern Orthodox tradition, the three angels represented God the Father, God the Son, and God the Holy Spirit.

When the United States took over Troika, Paul had decided to leave the icon on the wall despite Thomas's protests. "Oh, what harm can it do?" Paul had said. "It adds some charm to the place. Besides, it might bring us some good luck."

In a sense, Troika's crew had been lucky because the meteor had missed them, but eighty-four people on the Martian colonies had not been so lucky. Whatever divine grace the icon attracted did not reach down to the Martian surface.

In his quarters, Paul called Father Raymond Kelly by video. Father Kelly lived on Space Station Exeter, which was circling Mars in an orbit lower than Troika's. Each week, Paul and Father Kelly would talk by video encoded to preserve privacy. Not even the Mars disaster could disrupt this sacrament.

The man on the video monitor wore the traditional black uniform of a Catholic priest and a European Space Agency badge. He was young for a priest, just forty-five years old, and though his face was still handsome and smooth, some of his brown hair had started turning white. The hardships of space colonization could age anyone prematurely.

"How are things on Exeter?" Paul asked.

"A bit messy and very busy," Father Kelly said. "We've got refugees all over the station. Our infirmary is overflowing with the injured, the medical staff is overworked, and we're running out of food."

"I offered our food supply to Bronson," Paul said.

"He'll want it, now that he's got more people than he had expected," said Father Kelly. "Okay, let's get down to business.

Do you have anything to confess today?"

Paul cleared his throat. "Forgive me, Father, for I have sinned. I caused a woman to die three days ago."

He paused, took a deep breath, and continued: "She was on Redsands Base, and the interior of the dome building was on fire. She was trapped inside the dome. I tried to use the teleporter to take her out, but I failed."

Each Martian space station, surface base, and colony had a teleporter booth. An object would be placed in one booth, broken into an energy stream, transmitted to another booth, and rematerialize as the object: mass into energy into mass again. The technology was still in its primitive stage and prone to accidents, though. If spacers needed to send something important, they would send it by shuttlecraft or supply rocket, not by teleporter.

"Hush, Paul," Father Kelly ordered. "Bronson told me about Redsands. You don't have to confess to something that wasn't your fault."

Paul nodded but continued: "But it still bothers me. I tried to teleport her out of there. I knew the teleporter is safe only for non-living, inorganic matter. I knew I shouldn't have tried sending a human being by teleporter. But I tried anyway. Now she's just atoms scattered somewhere."

"You had no choice but to use the teleporter."

"I could have used the shuttlecraft."

"And you know why you didn't. You didn't have the time," Father Kelly reminded him. "There was plenty of pure oxygen on Redsands; the fire gutted the dome in twenty minutes. You couldn't have reached her in time."

"The University of Waterloo's been researching ways of making the teleporter safe for people. They say they might have developed a new program code for the teleporter, but we haven't received the new code yet," said Paul. "Maybe if I had a usable code—"

Father Kelly interrupted him. "But you didn't, and you still don't, so stop speculating.

"Look at it this way," the priest suggested. "Be comforted in knowing that you had only one choice, and you had the courage to use it. She is with God now, and God does not blame you for her death, I'm sure."

Paul smiled weakly. "But I did violate transportation regulations by using the teleporter on a human being."

"Okay, if it will make you feel better, say three 'Hail Marys' as penance and consider yourself forgiven. Now be done with the matter." Father Kelly made the Sign of the Cross to bless Paul. "Now, anything else you want to discuss?"

"Yes. I haven't gone to Mass since I came to Troika a year ago," said Paul.

"It does get difficult to go to the only church out here. You do watch my televised Mass, though."

"It's wonderful, and I really enjoy watching it, but for me, something's missing. I miss receiving the Eucharist."

"The body of Christ," said the priest, referring to the Roman Catholic belief that consecrated bread becomes the body of Jesus.

"A TV show is no substitute for the real thing, especially after all that's happened," Paul said.

"Spiritual healing through the Eucharist. There must be some way I can help you," Father Kelly mused. He paused for a moment, pondering an idea.

"I can try teleporting a jar of consecrated bread to you."

Paul look startled. "You're going to try that?"

"You think there'll be an accident? Actually, accidents occur in only ten percent of attempts to teleport organic matter. That means I still have a ninety percent chance of sending the bread to you by teleporter."

"But it's the body of Christ."

"If anyone can survive the teleporter, it will be Jesus."

Paul returned to the control room just as another video message from Space Station Exeter popped onto his computer monitor. The image of Alfred Bronson, Director of Space Station Exeter, appeared.

Bronson, with his brown hair looking disheveled and greasy, stared sleepily. Exeter's crew had been working over eighteen hours each day since the disaster on Mars.

"What can we do for you?" Paul asked.

"You said you have some food to spare," Bronson said.

"We've got enough for ourselves and nine extra people for

two months, which is when the re-supply ship arrives."

"Every bit of food is essential. Could you please give us what you have in excess of your own needs?"

"We'll be happy to. How do we transport it? We can't use the teleporter," Paul said.

"No, no, even with the alleged ninety percent safety rate on organic matter, I don't want to risk it on food," Bronson agreed.

"Can you send a shuttlecraft to pick it up?"

Bronson shook his head. "Not for a week. Both our shuttlecrafts are in the search for survivors at the planet's poles. Can you fly over here in your shuttlecraft?"

"We could, but our shuttlecraft is low on fuel. We'll have to wait until we're at our closest position to Exeter. Then we'll have enough fuel for a one-way flight."

"How much longer until you're in range?"

Paul typed a few commands at his keyboard, and computer animation of the orbits of the two space stations appeared on his monitor. "Twenty-four standard hours."

"That will be okay, but what about you? Since it'll be a one-way flight, you'll have to stay here."

"Don't worry about three extra mouths to feed. We'll bring our own food supply, and we'll do work." Then, with resignation, Paul said, "I think NASA will let us abandon Troika. We've done all we can do to find survivors."

After Paul ended his video call with Bronson, he heard a soft chime. The message "TELEPORTER CARGO INCOMING" appeared on his monitor.

"That must be the consecrated bread from Father Kelly," Paul said.

"You're receiving consecrated bread from Father Kelly?" Thomas asked.

"Yes. I haven't received the Eucharist for months."

"It's all very silly if you ask me."

"Nobody asked you," Paul replied.

Erin looked surprised as she read the data from the teleporter. "That's a lot of bread: forty-nine kilograms or about one hundred and eight pounds."

"What?" Paul blurted. He looked at the computer monitor.

"That's impossible. I'm going to the teleporter booth."

"I'll come with you," Erin said as she followed Paul out of the control room.

As they approached the teleporter booth, Erin gasped. Paul suddenly stopped and stared in surprise at the booth.

There was no jar of consecrated bread.

Instead, a slim teenaged girl stood in the teleporter booth. She looked pretty, had her reddish-brown hair tied into a ponytail, and wore a white shirt, green school tie, and a green tartan schoolgirl skirt. She also wore a silver tiara with glittering gems.

"I haven't seen that uniform in years," Erin remarked.

Paul stared at the stranger. "What is it?"

"St. Joseph's College School in Toronto. My high school."

The girl looked bewildered as she stepped out of the teleporter booth. She hesitantly walked forward as she glanced around her.

She stopped a couple yards away from Paul and Erin. Her big brown eyes looked around in wonder.

"Where am I?" she asked.

"Space Station Troika in orbit around Mars," Paul replied.

"Yes!" the girl shouted as she clapped her hands together and jumped up. "Mars! Mars! I made it to Mars!"

She danced and squealed and swung her arms. "This is totally awesome! I have returned, glory, hallelujah!"

"Who are you?" Erin demanded.

The girl stopped prancing, smiled at Paul, and held out her hand so he could shake it. "My name's Jessica."

Erin noticed the gold necklace with a Star of David pendant around her neck. Why was a Jewish girl wearing a Catholic school uniform?

"Are you from Redsands Base?" Paul asked.

Jessica's eyes lit up. "Redsands! I belong there. I have to go there."

Paul shook his head. "No, no, you can't go back there. It's in ruins."

"That's not important. I can walk, I can talk, and I can go to Mars!" she chirped as she danced around again.

Paul whispered to Erin, "I think she's the girl we lost trying to transport up from Redsands Base."

"If she is, she must be suffering from some sort of strange shock," Erin said.

Jessica spun around in a pirouette and strolled back to Paul and Erin. She threw her arms around Erin, hugged her, and said, "It's *sooooo* good to have a warm body again!"

Erin laughed and gently pushed Jessica away. "You mean you know what it's like not to have a body?"

"Believe me, having flesh and blood feels better than being just a spirit floating around," Jessica said.

"Then you remember what it was like—after the teleporter accident?" Paul asked incredulously.

Jessica nodded. "Oh, yeah, for a long time, I was in a place of neither the living nor the dead but something in between."

"That's incredible!" Paul remarked. "And now you're back three days later!"

"Was it just three days?" Jessica said. "I thought it was two thousand years."

Erin showed the empty cabin to Jessica. "You can stay in here," Erin said. "There used to be a fourth person on the crew, but she got transferred to Exeter."

Jessica smiled. "Thanks for your hospitality. It's *sooooo* decent. I'll be comfortable here, but I won't be staying long."

"Oh? Are you in a rush to go somewhere?"

"To Mars. I have work to do down there."

"Everyone's being evacuated off Mars. What could you possibly do down there?"

"My father's work."

"Your father? I didn't think people brought their children to Mars. Who's your father?"

"Yahweh," Jessica said casually.

Also known as 'God,' Erin realized. How weird.

"So you must be Jesus, eh?" Erin joked.

Jessica nodded. "I am. Isn't that awesome?"

Holy Mary, Mother of God, we have a crazy one aboard, Erin thought.

* * *

Thomas stepped out of the shuttlecraft, through the airlock, and onto the floor of the shuttlecraft dock. On the dock floor sat boxes of food, all destined for Space Station Exeter.

Jessica walked to Thomas and smiled and waved at him. "You must be Thomas," she said.

"Yes, I am," Thomas replied. "And you must be our visitor, Jessica. Are you hungry?"

Thomas grabbed a box of crackers from a table, pulled a folding knife from his belt, cut open the box, and held it out to Jessica.

She was staring at the folding knife clipped to his belt, Thomas noticed. But she quickly looked up, smiled, took a round cracker, and began munching it.

Thomas glanced at the gold Star of David on Jessica's necklace. He asked, "So what's a nice Jewish girl like you doing in a place like this?"

"Checking out the shuttlecraft," Jessica said, pointing at the small spacecraft. "Is it powered by a nuclear reactor?"

"You've done your homework. Yes, it's a Tsiolkovsky Service Shuttlecraft model 3, the first to be powered by nuclear energy."

"Cool. Awesome. It'll be perfect for taking me to Mars."

"Going to Mars?" Thomas asked. "Nobody's going down to the surface."

"I have to, totally. I have to finish my father's work down there, at Redsands," Jessica explained.

"Your father worked at Redsands? You can't go back. All its people are—dead. Except you."

Jessica's eyes lit up. "But that's the reason why I have to go there. From the dead of Earth, my father will create life on Mars."

"Huh? I heard of no such project."

"Not on your scientific stations, but it has been planned. Life has grown on Earth, and now it's time for God to create His other children on Mars."

Thomas smiled wryly. "God's your father? Come on, you really can't think that, at least not literally. I know you God believers call God 'Our Father', but you really don't think He's your *father* in a family sense, do you?"

"He is truly my father, and I am Him," Jessica declared.

Thomas shrugged. "Okay, if God is going to create life on Mars, how's He going to do it?"

"With the same principles that He used on Earth," Jessica explained. "The bodies of the dead on Mars contain amino acids and proteins, the necessary substances of life. The ruined Martian bases also have oxygen and water imported from Earth. There's also subsurface water on Mars that has come to the surface by the digging of your geologists.

"When the shuttlecraft crashes into a ruined base, the nuclear explosion will start the chemical reaction that will convert the amino acids, proteins, oxygen, and water into living cells."

This is crazy, Thomas thought. The girl wanted to play God, Book of Genesis.

"I don't believe in God," he retorted.

"That doesn't matter. I believe in God, and that's good enough for me."

In the kitchen, Paul slid the tray of rehydratable salmon chunks into the oven. He looked at the box that had held the salmon. "One of the ingredients is salmon flavoring," he observed. "They actually have to add artificial flavor to make the salmon taste like salmon."

"There's a restaurant in Fisherman's Wharf in San Francisco, where the chef grilled fresh salmon in garlic and paprika," Thomas remembered as he poured a cup of coffee. "Too bad we can't get food like that in Mars orbit."

"It would take a miracle," Paul said.

"Speaking of miracles, where's our visitor?" Thomas asked.

Erin put down a fourth plate on the table. "She's taking a shower. She says she hasn't had a bath for over two thousand years."

"Cleanliness is next to godliness," Thomas said, repeating an old proverb. "Do we know who she really is?"

Paul shook his head and looked at his handheld computer pad. "When Redsands Base burned up, we didn't get a good video picture of the woman we tried to teleport up. I've looked through the personnel list of Redsands, and there was a Jessie

Montega, a biologist, but she was twenty-seven years old."

"Our Jessica looks a lot younger than twenty-seven," Erin said. "Can you get a picture of Jessie Montega?"

"No. Our records don't have photos, but Exeter's might. I've asked Father Kelly to search for her photo," Paul said. "Here's an idea: could the teleporter have reconstructed her as a younger person?"

"I don't know," Erin said. "Anything is possible."

Thomas sipped his coffee. "Whoever she is, she's crazy. She thinks that she's Jesus."

Paul nodded. "Yeah, that's weird. Maybe Jessica had a weird, out-of-body experience when the teleporter lost her atoms, and now she thinks she's Jesus. Or maybe she had already gone loony on Mars. That happens to some people in space."

"The consecrated bread didn't arrive, but the girl did," Erin observed. "Could the bread have turned into Jessica?"

Thomas put down his coffee mug. "Oh, that's ridiculous. I usually think of you two as intelligent people, but sometimes your religiosity is too much. Any rationale person knows that God doesn't exist."

"Not necessarily," Erin replied. "I believe in Him, and so do a lot of other people in the space colonies. Exeter Station even has a chapel."

"A waste of space if you ask me," Thomas complained. "I don't know why NASA let a priest come out here. Christianity is the last thing we need in space."

"I disagree, I think we need to bring our religions out here," Paul said. "That's what makes us human."

"It's what makes us morons. Think how ridiculous your religion is," Thomas snapped. "Do you really think a real Son of God would spend thirty years as a carpenter, unknown to everyone? And did the crucifixion really mean anything? If he really were a god, he could have used his godlike powers to come back from the dead or his father could have brought him back to life, so the suffering was unnecessary and meaningless. It was just a publicity stunt to convert the superstitious. Jesus was probably just a guy who faked his own death—assuming he actually existed, and there's no real historical proof that he did. Christianity is just one big fraud."

"I am not a fraud," said a voice from behind.

They turned around and saw Jessica standing at the doorway.

"Don't take it personally," Thomas said. "I oppose superstitions of all kinds, not just the Christian kind."

Jessica frowned.

"Uh, dinner's almost ready," Erin said, hoping to change the topic. "Will you join us?"

The schoolgirl smiled again. "That would be awesome. I haven't eaten for a long, long time."

The oven bell rang, and Paul put on his oven mittens, opened the oven, and pulled out the tray.

"Oh my God! What's this?" he blurted.

Instead of plain rehydrated salmon chunks, the tray held grilled salmon fillets bathed in a tomato sauce. The aroma of garlic and paprika wafted through the kitchen.

Paul, Erin, and Thomas stared wide-eyed at the fish. After a long, stunned silence, Erin finally spoke.

"You were saying it would take a miracle to get fresh salmon here?" she said to Paul.

Jessica grabbed the tray from Paul and put it on the table. "Don't be shy; everybody dig in!" she urged.

At first, Paul, Erin, and Thomas were reluctant to eat the fish, but with Jessica's prodding, they nibbled hesitantly at it. Then, when they tasted how delicious the fish had become, they ate it eagerly.

"This is wonderful," Paul said. Erin nodded, and even Thomas grunted in agreement as he chewed.

"Thank you," Jessica said, grinning. "I'm very good with fish."

"I must be dreaming," Thomas mumbled.

"No, you're not," Jessica said. "That fabulous gourmet dinner was real." She looked at each of them in the eye. "Now, can you do a favor for me?"

"What can we do for you?" Erin asked.

"Can I have the ignition key to the shuttlecraft?"

A stunned silence followed.

Erin reached out and touched Jessica's hand. "Dear, you're a special person, but you don't really believe you're Jesus, do you?"

"Like, yeah!" Jessica blurted with a sigh of exasperation. "Look at the Jesus thing I did. I turned chunks of dry fish into—uh, fish with tomato sauce."

"Turning fish into fish," Thomas quipped.

"Okay, maybe that was a bit lame," Jessica admitted.

Thomas shrugged, raised his glass to his lips, and put the glass down. "I ran out of water."

"Oh, I'll get some," Jessica said as she grabbed the pitcher from the table. "Hey, water is so plain. Do you have any wine here?"

"You're too young," Erin warned.

Jessica giggled. "I know I look underage, but I'm a lot older than I look."

"We have no wine," said Paul. "We've got only water."

"Just water? How boring." Humming the old Jewish folk song "Havah Nagilah," Jessica skipped to the kitchen counter and filled the pitcher with water from the faucet.

She set the pitcher in the middle of the table. Thomas lifted the pitcher and began pouring water into his glass.

"Oh my God," he muttered as he saw red wine pour into his glass.

Paul took the pitcher, poured a glass of wine for himself, and sipped it. It tasted very sweet. He remembered a sugary red wine that a friend had given him at a frat party in university. It was a kosher sacramental wine drunk at Passover.

"Next time you drink wine, remember me," Jessica said.

"Do you need any help cleaning up?" Jessica asked.

Erin smiled and shook her head. "No, dear. We'll clear the table."

"Okay with me." Jessica yawned. "Wow, that was a lot of food. I feel tired now. I'll go to my room and take a nap."

"Sure. Sweet dreams," Thomas said.

"Oh, and think about letting me borrow the shuttlecraft," Jessica urged. "I really, seriously, totally need it."

The crew's eyes silently followed Jessica as she walked out of the kitchen.

Erin broke the silence: "Was any of this real?"

"It must have been real," Paul concluded. "All three of us can't be dreaming or hallucinating about the same thing."

"How did she do it?" Thomas wondered.

"It's a miracle," Erin said.

"No it's not," said Thomas. "She's not Jesus."

"She could be the woman I tried to teleport out of Redsands Base," Paul said.

"That still doesn't explain how she turned rehydrated salmon chunks into salmon fillets in tomato sauce," Erin said.

"Maybe she got superhuman powers when the transporter reassembled her," Paul guessed.

"Maybe she's an alien," Thomas suggested seriously.

"Whatever or whoever she is, one thing is certain: she wants to crash the shuttlecraft into Mars," Paul said. He took out a metal key from his pocket. "But she can't start the shuttlecraft's reactor without the ignition key. Do you know where yours is?"

Erin and Thomas felt in their pockets and pulled out their keys.

"Keep them with you at all times, and don't leave them lying around," Paul advised. "We need that shuttlecraft to carry the food and ourselves to Space Station Exeter."

Erin returned to her cabin and lay down on her cot. She looked at another photo of her and her parents, this one from the night before the Miss America pageant.

Her parents had met at a tourism industry convention in Toronto, where her mother was a visiting American tour operator, and her father was an engineer who designed flying amphibious tour buses. They settled in Toronto, where she attended St. Joseph's College School on Wellesley Street.

After graduating from St. Jo's, she went to study business administration at the University of Oregon in Eugene, her mother's hometown. In her second year of university, she entered the beauty pageants billed as "scholarship programs": first, she won the crown of Miss Willamette Valley, and then, the Miss Oregon crown. Her next step was the Miss America pageant, to be held in Salem, the state capital of Oregon, that year.

It was also the year of the Vernacular Wars, when the

Sudanese declared *jihad* on the United States for allowing American Moslems to recite the Koran in English instead of Arabic. But despite the orange alert, ordinary life, including the Miss America pageant, continued in America.

Erin had just stepped off the stage in her evening gown when the terrorists charged into the auditorium. With their guns blazing, they slaughtered over a hundred people in ten minutes. Screams and moans filled the air. As the walls and floors turned red with blood, the police and National Guard unleashed their own storm of tear gas and bullets.

Erin found her father covered in blood but still an alive. Her mother did not survive.

If only she hadn't been enthralled with the clothes, the gifts, the glamour, the attention, and the scholarships; if only she hadn't won Miss Willamette Valley and Miss Oregon; if only she hadn't entered the Miss America pageant, her mother might still be alive.

She dropped out of university and went to Toronto with her father. She returned to Oregon a few years later to earn a degree in science, and she volunteered to work in the space colonies, far away from Earth.

She sat up and felt the brainscanner still strapped to her head. When was that wretched headpiece due to come off?

She heard a knock on her door. She opened it and saw Jessica.

"Jessica," Erin greeted softly. "What can I do for you, dear?"

"You wish you could have had one last moment of quality time with your mother, don't you?" Jessica said as she strolled into the cabin.

Erin's eyes widened. "How do you know?"

Jessica smiled. "I know things. I can tell that her death has tormented you for years." She put her hands on Jessica's temples, as if trying to touch her mind. "Stop punishing yourself. You have no reason to feel guilty, no reason to flee out here."

"If only—if only I hadn't been so selfish, thinking only about myself."

"Hush. Will you believe me if you could speak to your mother again?"

"How can you do that?"

Jessica grinned. "Oh, I can do all sorts of cool things."

"Erin, I'm so happy to see you again," chirped a voice from behind.

Erin spun around and stared at her mother.

She threw her arms around her mother and hugged her.

Her mother looked young and wore the blue tour guide uniform that Erin had seen in her childhood, years that they remembered over tea and crackers.

Eventually, they talked about the present. "How's your father?" asked Erin's mother.

"Oh, he's really happy in his retirement," Erin replied. "I just got a video message from him last week. He won a trophy at a model airplane contest. His glider flew over one hundred feet, farther than all the other gliders."

"Ah, he was always designing buses and boats and planes. I have to ask: did he ever remarry?"

"No, he never did."

"Hah, hah, I spoiled him for other women," Erin's mother bragged. "He would never find another one like me, I told him."

Erin laughed. "Oh, you were unique, and he knew that."

She suddenly stopped smiling. Her mother *was* unique. She had used the past tense because her mother had died.

"Mum, you died," Erin stated plainly. "How can you be here now?"

Her mother reached out to take Erin's hands. "Dear, I can only come back briefly, so let me say what I need to say." She pulled Erin closer to her. "Stop blaming yourself for my death. It wasn't your fault."

"What are you saying?" Erin mumbled.

"Don't blame yourself. Blame the Jihadists."

"But if I hadn't entered the pageant—" Erin started.

Erin's mother interrupted her. "No, no, don't think that way. You enjoyed what you did, you didn't harm anyone, and your father and I were so proud of you."

"You were?"

"Of course, we were." Erin's mother smiled. "You looked so beautiful, so poised, and so confident when you were competing on stage. You grew up a lot in those two years at university."

"That's nice to know."

"So will you finally stop blaming yourself?"

"Yes, yes, I'll stop, I'll stop," Erin promised.

Erin's mother walked her to the cot and laid her down. "You've been tired for a long time." She kissed her on the cheek. "Get some sleep now."

Erin closed her eyes, smiled, and fell asleep. When she woke up, her mother was gone.

And so too was Jessica.

Erin felt inside her pant pockets as she rose from the cot.

The shuttlecraft's ignition key was gone too.

On the viewscreen, Father Kelly said, "God, Jesus, and the Holy Spirit are the same person in mainstream Christianity. If this girl thinks she's Jesus, then she also thinks she's God."

"She does; she thinks she can create life on Mars," Paul said, glancing at Jessica and back to Father Kelly again.

"God does not wear a miniskirt," declared Father Kelly.

Jessica giggled and said, "Oh, but I do, especially with this schoolgirl uniform. Isn't it cute?"

"It's not unusual to find someone who thinks she's Jesus or Moses or Elvis or whoever; they appear in Israel all the time," Father Kelly commented. "But in orbit around Mars?"

Jessica joked, "Elvis has come back from the dead more times than I have."

"Be careful," Paul cautioned the priest. "You're talking about her as if she can't hear you, but she's right here."

"I'm not sure the girl is actually there." The priest paused for a moment and continued: "Paul, have you considered the possibility of mass hysteria? Or that something is controlling your minds?"

Paul looked back at Jessica and said, "I don't think it's mass hysteria or mind control. What could possibly do that to us out here?"

Father Kelly asked, "Did you say that Dr. Hall sees the girl too?"

"Yes, he does."

Father Kelly smiled weakly. "Dr. Hall is an atheist

fundamentalist. If he sees the girl, she can't be God or Jesus."

Jessica laughed. "How ironic: the atheist can see me, but the priest can't."

"Then she's Jessie Montega from Redsands," Paul said.

"But if she is, why is she invisible to me?" Father Kelly asked. "Look, here's a radical idea: perhaps Troika was carved out of a Siren Stone."

Thomas fell into a stunned silence. The Siren Stones were a modern myth: asteroids haunted by beautiful spirits who lured lonely spacers to their deaths. They explained why space crews went crazy or disappeared without a trace.

Father Kelly, Vatican astronomer, did not believe in myths and superstitions. He was a rational scientist—but so too were the first spacers to talk about Siren Stones.

"You believe in Siren Stones?" Thomas asked.

Father Kelly shrugged. "No, but we're running out of explanations for what's going on."

The priest's cell phone beeped. He answered and listened to it, and then he looked eagerly at Paul.

"My friends found a photo of Jessie Montega," Father Kelly reported. "I'm going to my quarters to download the file."

He looked at his watch. "Paul, your launch window is coming in seventeen hours. You need to get off that rock and come to Exeter. Don't let anyone—or anything—hijack the shuttlecraft."

"Not even Jesus?" Paul asked.

"Especially not Jesus," urged Father Kelly as he ended the transmission.

Paul spun around in his chair and looked at Jessica. "Who are you, and what do you want?" he demanded.

"You already know," Jessica said.

"You've suffered a lot. You might have post-traumatic stress," Paul said. "There are people on Exeter who can help you. Come with us."

"Look, I don't have a lot of time. There's something you need to know before I leave," Jessica said. "Jessie Montega died for a purpose."

"What are you saying?" Paul asked. "You're not dead."

"I tell you again, I'm not Jessie Montega. Jessie Montega's

body is dead in the ruins of Redsands Base. Her soul is living with God now."

Jessica walked to a computer monitor and began typing commands. Animated images of molecules, from *The Spacer's Encyclopedia,* appeared on the monitor. Paul recognized them from chemistry class: amino acids, proteins, and DNA.

Jessica pointed at the images of the protein molecules. "Jessie Montega's body contains amino acids, proteins, and DNA. When I crash the shuttlecraft onto her body, the nuclear reaction will start the chemical reactions that will create life. Her death has meaning and purpose. She died so that Mars can live."

Paul stared at the girl. "Now I know for sure: you're crazy," he said.

Jessica breathed in deeply. "You're the one who will go crazy if you keep blaming yourself for Jessie Montega's death. Believe me, it wasn't your fault, and she died for a purpose."

She marched out of the room, leaving Paul crumpled in his chair, alone with his memories of Jessie Montega's plea for help.

Thomas watched Jessica walk towards the shuttlecraft. He crossed his arms and moved to block her path to the airlock.

"Where are you going, young lady?" he asked.

"To Mars," Jessica replied.

"Sorry, but we need this shuttlecraft to deliver food to the people of Space Station Exeter. You wouldn't want them to starve, would you?"

"I'll find another way to get the food to Exeter. Just let me have the shuttlecraft."

"Can't you just wave your hand and make a one-celled organism?" Thomas asked. "Why does God need a nuclear spaceship?"

"I don't know," Jessica whined, her voice growing more agitated. "God works in mysterious ways. Only He knows."

"Did God crash the meteor into Mars? Did God want all those people to die? What kind of God is He?" Thomas accused.

"I don't know!" Jessica cried. "I don't know if all those people had to die. But I know that if I don't go down to Mars, at least one of those deaths will meaningless!"

Thomas eyed her suspiciously.

Her right hand was clasped shut.

"What are you holding in your hand?" he demanded.

Paul and Erin ran into the shuttlecraft dock.

"She's got my shuttlecraft key!" Erin yelled.

Jessica darted forward, but Thomas grabbed her. Paul and Erin rushed to Jessica, and they struggled to pry the key out of her hand.

"Got it!" Paul shouted as he held up the key.

Jessica stumbled backwards away from the crew and glared at them. "But I got this!" she hissed.

She unfolded Thomas's knife and held it over her wrist. "Give me the key or I'll kill myself."

"So what? If you're Jesus, you'll just come back from the dead," scoffed Thomas.

"Dear, put that down," Erin urged. "You don't want to hurt anybody."

Paul stepped towards Jessica. "Jessie, put down the knife. You need help that we can't give you here. Come to Exeter with us."

A chime sounded from a videoscreen. Erin went to the videoscreen and looked at the message scrolling in.

"It's Father Kelly," Erin said.

"Relay the transmission into this room," Paul ordered.

Father Kelly appeared on the videoscreen. "Hey, why are you all in the shuttlecraft dock?" he asked.

"We've got the girl here," Paul said.

Father Kelly looked puzzled. "I still can't see her, but tell me if she looks anything like this. Here's Jessie Montega."

A color photo of a woman appeared on the screen. She was in her late twenties, had long black hair, and looked Filipino.

"You look nothing like your photo," Paul said to Jessica.

"Now will you believe that I'm not Jessie Montega?" Jessica pleaded.

"That means she's dead, she's truly dead," Paul muttered. His eyes grew sad. "I really killed her."

"Paul, you didn't kill anyone," Father Kelly said. "You have to trust yourself again."

The video transmission suddenly ended. Jessica looked at the videoscreen and said, "Forgive me, Father, but I don't need another person adding to this retarded mess."

She turned to Paul. "Would it help if you talked to her?"

Before Paul could answer, he heard someone say, "Paul, how nice to finally see you."

The voice sounded familiar. Paul turned around. Jessie Montega stood there, smiling.

"Do you see her too?" Paul asked.

Erin and Thomas, both looking shocked, simply replied, "Yes."

Thomas looked at the lights flashing quickly on Erin's brainscanner headpiece. He took the brainscanner monitor out of his pocket.

"Uh, maybe you should see this," he said.

But Paul wasn't listening to him. Instead, he stared at the ghost from Redsands.

Jessie Montega looked into Paul's eyes. "Thanks for trying to teleport me up. I know it didn't work, but I appreciate all that you did for me."

She held her hand out to Paul. "Feel my hand. That's the DNA, the amino acids, the proteins, the water, the carbon, and the oxygen that will become the first Martian life forms."

Paul took Jessie Montega's hand and gripped it. It felt smooth and solid and warm, not like what he had expected of a ghost. He marveled at how human the ghost felt.

"Are you dead?" Paul whispered, barely able to speak.

Jessie Montega nodded. "My body lies on Mars, but my spirit is in heaven with God. It's a good place, so don't worry about me."

"Thanks for letting me know."

As Paul released her hand, Jessie Montega said, "There is a purpose of my life and my death. Let me fulfill my purpose." Then, looking at Jessica, she said, "Let her fulfill her purpose too."

With a wave of her hand, Jessie Montega faded away.

Paul looked at Jessica. "You really are Jesus."

"Finally, you believe me!" Jessica said. "Listen, you've done nothing wrong. Be at peace with yourself again."

Paul tossed the ignition key to Jessica.

"What are you doing?" Thomas shouted.

Jessica dropped the knife on the floor, caught the key, and dashed through the airlock and into the shuttlecraft.

"She's just a crazy kid!" Thomas yelled as he ran to the airlock.

He tried to pull open the door, but Jessica had locked it from the other side. The whirring sounds of machinery began. Thomas backed away from the door.

"She's starting the nuclear engine," Erin said. "Let's get out of here."

Back at the control room, they watched the shuttlecraft blast away from Troika and shoot towards the red planet below.

"We've got our cameras aimed over Redsands again," Erin said as she finally removed the brainscanner headpiece.

The viewscreen showed an aerial shot of the ruined station. The shuttlecraft fell quickly like a blur onto the broken dome. A blinding flash of white light erupted. A nuclear mushroom cloud arose.

In horrified silence, the Troika's crew watched the thick radioactive smoke climb hundreds of feet into the Martian sky.

"Nothing could have survived that," Paul said.

Thomas scowled and turned away from the viewscreen. "We let that kid kill herself," he spat.

A tear ran down Erin's cheek. "Poor Jessica," she muttered.

Paul put his hand on Erin's shoulder. "I think she'll come back."

Thomas looked at another viewscreen, this one showing animated graphics of the orbits of Space Station Exeter and Space Station Troika.

"Exeter is now at its closest position to Troika," Thomas announced. "Well, we're stranded here. Neither we nor Exeter have a shuttlecraft. How are we going to take the food to Exeter?"

Numbers and words suddenly appeared on the Erin's computer monitor and began scrolling upwards.

"This information's downloading onto our mainframe," Erin observed. "What is it?"

Paul looked at the monitor. "It's program code for the teleporter. Is the University of Waterloo sending it to us?"

"No, it's not coming from Earth," Erin reported. "It's coming from—Mars."

Paul looked at his computer monitor. Instead of the program code, it showed a message:

Your teleporter is now safe for people and food.

XP

Paul grinned at the signature: XP, the first and second letters of XPICTOC. Kristos: Christ in Greek.

All the food they teleported to Space Station Exeter arrived complete and unchanged. "Just as hard and tasteless as it originally was, no miracle this time," Thomas joked.

Finally, the crew had only themselves to teleport to Exeter. But Thomas had to something to show Paul and Erin before they abandoned Troika.

Thomas pointed at brain scans of Erin on a computer terminal. Different parts of her brain glowed and pulsated in red, green, and yellow.

Thomas pointed to an area that suddenly lit up and expanded in red. "That's the electrical activity in the left temporal lobe at the time when you first saw Jessica. It's all red, showing an increase in electrical activity."

He showed another brain scan with the left temporal lobe lit up in red. "And this is a scan of your brain at the time when you saw Jessie Montega's ghost."

Erin gazed at the brain scans. "And what about the time I saw my mother?"

"Same results," Thomas said. "The temporal lobe is where the emotions of religious experience, feelings like awe and joy, are created," he explained. "Religious mystics experience increased brain wave activity there when they see visions or go into altered states of consciousness."

"Does that mean Jesus and my mother and Jessie Montega really did come to us?" Erin wondered.

"Or something triggered these visions in our minds," Thomas suggested. He opened a three-dimensional computer graphic of Troika. Animated waves poured from the centre of the space station.

"I detected electrochemical signals from Troika itself,"

Thomas said. "The signals are coming from the core of the asteroid that the station is built in."

"Electrochemical signals?" Paul said. "You mean the rock is sending out brain waves of its own?"

"It seems to be. The rock could have planted visions of Jessica, Erin's mother, and Jessie Montega into our minds," Thomas said.

"And that's why Father Kelly couldn't see Jessica," Paul realized. "He wasn't here to receive the signals."

Erin leaned forward to look at the graphic image of Troika. "But my mother's ghost knew about me and my family. How could the rock have known all about our lives?"

"I think the rock is also absorbing our brain waves," Thomas said. "It's probably taking our memories and turning them into visions of people we knew."

"Incredible," Paul said. "Siren Stones are real."

Thomas shrugged. "I don't know if this is a Siren Stone or not." He paused. "But now I'm sure that God and Jesus are just figments of our imagination, created in our brains."

"Oh, I wouldn't say that," Erin protested. "Maybe God gave us temporal lobes so that we can experience Him."

"Oh, come on, you can't prove that," Thomas retorted.

"What about the missing shuttlecraft?" Erin mentioned. "Someone flew it into Mars. And that nuclear explosion was no illusion. Other space stations saw it."

"And then there's the new program code for the teleporter," Paul said. "Where did that come from?"

"Okay, I don't know how to explain everything," Thomas admitted, "but before we jump to conclusions about God, we need to look at all the possibilities."

"There'll be plenty of time to study all the possibilities, but not now; Exeter's going to move out of range," Paul said as he looked at his watch. "Let's go to the teleporter."

As they walked to the teleporter, Paul said, "It's too bad we have to leave now. We don't know anything about this rock. How can it send and receive brain waves? Is it living? Is it intelligent? There's plenty for a future crew to study."

They teleported themselves safely to Space Station Exeter.

Later that day, Father Kelly celebrated Mass in the chapel. He gave the Eucharist to Paul and Erin, thanked God for the safe evacuation of Troika's crew, and included Jessica in the prayers for the dead.

Thomas also attended Mass that day, in memory of Jessica, the girl who had cooked a fish dinner in the way he loved from Fisherman's Wharf in San Francisco.

Nothing remained of Redsands Base except for hundreds of pools of chemical soup scattered on a charred red landscape. In one pool of chemicals, a geyser of water continued spraying up from the center. Water, oxygen, carbon, proteins, and amino acids swirled together after feeling the burst of nuclear energy.

Long after the Earth people had left, membranes formed around proteins and chemicals, and the first cells appeared. The cells absorbed energy from the radiation and the sun, and chemical reactions began inside the cells. One day, a cell split into two.

Life had sprung on Mars.

General Density

"I didn't hurt anyone."

"You've been convicted of public indecency."

"Everyone's gotta take a leak."

"At the homecoming parade?"

"Sure."

"In Dean Gresham's daughter's clarinet?"

"Well..."

"You're a drunk."

"So's half your staff."

"You're a degenerate."

"Now, I can explain about the refrigerator."

"And your breath stinks. Gargle... with something that doesn't have to be sold with a tax stamp, and I'll see what I can do."

"How about Peppermint Schnapps?"

"Why couldn't I have taken that nice, easy job testing sewage treatment equipment?"

"Hey, you came to me."

"I know." Carol Kaprinov, PhD (biophysics) looked around her, to the derelict buildings that surrounded the trash-strewn vacant lot. Bedraggled late summer wild flowers set off a large, pink, abandoned refrigerator. Carol could still hardly believe she had followed the short, increasingly degenerate trail of references to a neighborhood she usually would avoid even, as now, in broad daylight. Equally appalling was the fetid bum who, despite God only knew how much cheap booze, still talked lucidly enough to make credible, just barely, the brilliant physicist the record declared him to be.

"Tell you what," said Agamemnon Terestìcu, "if you can fund data analysts I'll even come to work sober."

"On time?"

"I show up on time when I'm drunk."

That was true, as Carol learned, to her relief, when she read the record on Agamemnon more thoroughly: Born, 2302, New Carcross, Yukon, U. D.—The United Dominion consisted of what was once Northwestern Canada, Alaska, the Eastern end of Siberia, and the Bering Land Bridge, which after three hundred years of relative stability was now rapidly being replaced by a lot of cold water.

Agamemnon married Xanthippe Xavalous in 2327. Ordained an Eastern Orthodox priest the same year, he was relieved of sacramental duties four years later. His unsanctified consumption of sacramental wine was deemed excessive by his ecclesiastical superiors. Xanthippe apparently thought so too. She divorced him the same year.

After that, Agamemnon's work led from sawmill equipment operator to equipment maintenance to mining equipment maintenance. Damn, thought Carol, why couldn't any of the others have had that sort of experience? Agamemnon apparently sweated off the alcohol in those years, or kept it under control.

At thirty-eight, Agamemnon went back to school, in physics. He was Herbert Segal's last graduate assistant.

"You want the job done?" Carol asked her boss, Gertrude Querchansky.

Natural pine paneling imparted an air to Gertrude's office simultaneously light and substantial. It was a comfortable setting that both built Carol's confidence and subdued her more extravagant ambitions. Carol, at thirty, was tall, blond, and clear-skinned. Her boss, at fifty-five, still had the better figure.

"Is he really the best qualified?" asked Gertrude.

"If Herbert Segal's work matters, he's the only one even remotely qualified," said Carol.

"I don't suppose there's anything we can hold over him to make him behave," said Gertrude.

"Not really," said Terez Iwakami, Chief of Security at General Density. "After you've done time on a morals charge..."

"I guess it could be worse," said Gertrude.

"Better an employee who gets bombed on company property than one who sets bombs on company property?" A smile briefly realigned the wrinkles on Terez's brown face.

"All right," said Gertrude. "My blood pressure's been under control the last six months. It's a product that's needed, and we need a product. If we find anyone better we can always let him go. Offer him a contract. Promise him all the data analysts he can justify."

"Better offer housing too," said Carol.

"Oh yes," said Gertrude. "What is this refrigerator business?"

"That's where he's living," said Carol.

"What do you mean?" said Gertrude.

Terez smiled again. "Would it be fair to list his current occupation as full-time wino?"

"Yes," Carol answered, "that would be accurate. He panhandles till he has enough for a bottle, then he drinks. If he doesn't pass out someplace else first, he sleeps in an abandoned refrigerator."

Gertrude shook her head and tapped a data cartridge case labeled, Terestìcu, A. "Do the brilliant ones have to be crazy?"

"No," said Terez, "but it helps."

Two days passed before Carol found Agamemnon again. Some teenagers had beaten him up. The damage was minor, but colorful.

"Thanks for the coffee," said Agamemnon after signing the contract. Carol was relieved that he read it all the way through first. "I was getting a little tired of this neighborhood anyhow."

Carol looked around. Agamemnon sat on his derelict refrigerator. Carol could smell him from where she stood, four meters away. The rest of the vacant lot held a miscellany of trash and weeds. The door of a roofless building creaked in the light, midmorning breeze. The door had a sign on it that read, "Condemned. Unsafe. Keep Out. City Of Galileo, Chitina County, Province of Alaska."

Gertrude Querchansky was Associate Professor of Botany at Chitina District University when she quit to found General Density. The research that induced her to start the company was in frost protection for crops. Her first successful products turned out to be pharmaceuticals, but her research was successful, and Ice Caps eventually went into production too. The way Ice Caps altered the density of cell walls in several kinds of plants increased the degree to which the heat in the plants' cells functioned as a single unit. In some species, especially beans, frost tolerance was increased by as much as four degrees for several hours.

The original problem that had set Gertrude onto the subject of frost protection was still central to her interests. Three centuries of apparent climate stability feels like forever, but the Bering Land Bridge of Gertrude's world was not the result of an Ice Age. It was the aftereffect of two years of continuous precipitation caused by the dust cloud a stupid war once produced. A useful product didn't have to make you rich. It just had to make enough to keep you in business while you developed more. Ice Caps taught Gertrude that. It also provided Gertrude the capital to tackle something bigger while its namesake shrank.

Gertrude knew some people considered her business philosophy stodgy, but it had paid off a mortgage and put three kids through the University. We don't all need to be a Samantha Balthazar, Gertrude thought, building an empire and then disappearing with Herbert Segal, a crazy genius if there ever was one, on what was almost surely a fatally flawed attempt at faster than light travel.

Was it a failure though? And, far more pertinent, kook though he may have been, was Herbert Segal onto something that might have usable application? The work that immediately preceded the famous disappearance lay sealed somewhere in the vaults of Samantha Balthazar's vast business empire, still mighty if less inspired without her. There was public record of Herbert Segal's earlier work though. Gertrude knew just enough to believe his basic research into the structure of matter held promise, both useful and profitable, in her more practical realm.

Carol Kaprinov could hardly believe Agamemnon was the same man when they converged in Gertrude's office a mere four days later. Carol had her doubts about Agamemnon's blood alcohol level, but the transformation wrought by clothes that had been neither slept nor vomited in and a hair brush was little short of miraculous. Agamemnon had curly dark hair, balding in the middle but only beginning to grey. Somewhat short and barrel chested, he was not a particularly attractive man, but today he was a completely presentable one. Amazing what an improvement a forgettable appearance can be, Carol thought.

"There are advantages, of course," said Gertrude, indicating an orange area of the map on the table, nearly half of which was crosshatched. "The Maritimes will have a growing season." The orange area, labeled Quebec, included most of what was once Eastern Canada and the Northeastern United States. Population, if, extremely sparse, was a lot larger than that of the tundra and glaciers which now covered the former Ontario and Manitoba. "But the Chad Sea could dry up completely." Gertrude pointed to a violet region on the map, in North Central Africa, that consisted of a shallow sea with meandering shoreline, surrounded by some of the most productive and densely populated land of her time.

"The time scale is at least plausible," said Agamemnon, "but to do any good..."

"Doing any good isn't the same as saving everybody," said Gertrude. "World population dropped sixty-five percent between 1997 and 2025. The indigenous population of the Western Hemisphere dropped eighty percent between 1500 and 1800. The population of Europe dropped fifty percent between 1350 and 1450. None of those was the end of the world. I'm not going to worry about all humanity's problems. Let's just see if we can help on some of them."

"Ever wonder what it's all for?" Agamemnon asked.

"Certainly," said Gertrude. "I wonder where my grandchildren are going to live when Galileo has nineteen sunny days a year and turnips are hard-put to mature too."

"What if the Bering Dike goes through?" said Carol. "If the Arctic waters can be help up enough to keep the Japan Current inshore, we might actually end up with a better climate. Population pressure alone won't be enough to raise urgency really high in our lifetimes."

"So the Low-G Metabolic Stabilizer has not only got to work," said Agamemnon. "It's got to work cheap."

"Reasonably," said Gertrude. "General Density needs products that pay the power bill. It doesn't need to buy us all palaces."

"Fair enough," Agamemnon replied. "How about sending me up for a look?"

"Justify it," said Carol.

"I've never been in an asteroid mine."

"So what?"

"He's right," said Gertrude. "There was a mask designed once that was one hundred percent effective preventing silicosis, but the company that made them went broke anyhow. It was uncomfortable and obstructed the miners' vision. They would take the masks off as soon as an inspector was out of sight."

Since Agamemnon didn't own anything except the clothes General Density had provided him, packing was simple. He was on the moon shuttle the next afternoon. Agamemnon watched the Earth shrink below him for a few minutes and then settled down to read Gertrude's report, funding proposal really.

The two billion people left after the millennial crash had grown to nearly seven billion in the three and a half centuries since. Space colonies could relieve at least some of the pressure. Asteroids were the cheapest place to mine the materials to build the space colonies. The big problem was gravity. That is, the lack thereof.

You could create an artificial gravity by spinning a space colony. No cost-effective way had yet been devised to provide asteroid miners enough gravity. Without it, your body reabsorbed its own bones. The rest of your metabolism eventually went to hell too.

"Hazards are high. Wages are shit. And no one's gonna protest cause the company just manages to stay in business."

It was a month later. Agamemnon drained his fourth Grand Canal. Martian beer was the best available on the Iron Maiden of The Asteroids, Ima for short. It is nice to be able to drink the best beer around, Agamemnon thought. "So why'd you sign on?" he asked.

Bernadette Devlin, Agamemnon's drinking companion, smiled. He liked that. She had grey eyes and dimples. "How else is a working stiff gonna get to space?"

Suddenly the innocuous background music Agamemnon had barely noticed was replaced by an urgent voice. "Don't let it happen again!" The voice was male, young, and achingly sincere. There were a few moments of static. Then the woes-of-love song sighed back on.

"What was that?" said Agamemnon.

"Creety," said Bernadette. "Spoiled brat." She glared momentarily, then grinned. "They put on a pretty good show though, and they buy power from us retail."

The voice broke through again. "We nearly destroyed the Earth once. We're wounding Her again. What are you doing to the Mother's children?"

"Oog," said Agamemnon. "Ghastly Cosmology."

"Pardon?" Bernadette cocked her head.

"I have a Poo-E-D in Theology, you know," said Agamemnon.

"I'll be damned," said Bernadette. "So what's wrong with his line..." she pointed towards the floor, which was also the outer wall of the Iron Maiden Of The Asteroids, major mill and R and R station, "...besides being pea-brained crap?"

"Allowing for poetic imagery and primitive technology, most traditional Cosmologies are remarkably accurate," Agamemnon explained. "The asteroids are no more Earth's offspring than I am yours."

"I had any offspring ugly as you, I'd space 'em," said Bernadette.

Agamemnon sighed inwardly. Another woman who just wants to be friends, he thought. "How do you handle tailings?" he asked.

"Bond them together so we don't foul the spaceways, and set them back in as close an orbit to the original as we can," said Bernadette. "There may be side effects to rearranging the Solar System's mass that someone will have to deal with eventually, but it'll be a *long* time."

Agamemnon shook his head and ordered them both another Grand Canal. "Let me try out this scenario on you: You work the same number of hours a year. Instead of bust ass forty days, a high-priced space ride five days at each end, and sixty days here, you get real weekends with the local crews, and your take home triples."

"How about families?" asked Bernadette. She was Vice President of Driller's Local 17, one of the consortium of unions that owned the Iron Maiden Of The Asteroids. Her opinion represented a substantial constituency.

"We'll probably get the Metabolic Stabilizer approved for

workers on birth control at least a couple years before pregnant women and children," said Agamemnon, "but I'm looking for something safe. I won't tolerate less, and neither will General Density. If you build small gross refining plants with housing the first couple years, they'll pay for themselves in reduced mass you'll have to kick up here, they'll provide some gravity, and you'll have power to sell. I can have figures for you on what it costs if you see your families every three days, every night, whatever."

"Most workers'll want to come up here to visit Ima once in a while," said Bernadette, "especially the single ones."

"I can run figures on any option you want," said Agamemnon. "It's your money. Up to you how you spend it."

"Okay," said Bernadette. "I think it'll likely go, you convince the rank and file it doesn't give anyone three-headed grandchildren."

"Hmph!" Agamemnon snorted, "no spirit of innovation."

"Think you can get your boss to pay for a poll?" asked Bernadette.

"It's market research to General Density," said Agamemnon. "Gotta know how much of what anyone'll buy. We can provide ballots, descriptive literature and tabulation. How about you handle the actual poll at regular Union meetings."

"I'll take it up at the next Executive Council," said Bernadette.

Carol Kaprinov was impressed. "He's one smart drunk," she said to her boss.

The pine paneling imparted a warm glow to Gertrude Querchansky's office. Moderate and even sunny as Galileo's present climate was, the northern winter was on its way, with its long hours of chill and darkness. Carol kept her own office light and functional, but she liked the warmth of Gertrude's.

"Yes," said Gertrude, "I ought to pay him a bonus for giving us such clear budget parameters."

"Buy him a bottle of Armagnac de Timbuktu," said Terez Iwakami.

"Really?" said Carol.

"Charge records show Xanthippe used to buy him a bottle

every Easter."

"That doesn't mean he liked it," observed Gertrude.

"There's no record of his disliking alcohol in any form," said Carol.

"Data analysts it is then," said Gertrude. "If he comes up with something that makes five year tours with families safe for all concerned, we're going to be rich."

"If he comes up with something that makes real population resettlement practical..." said Carol, her eyes a little starry.

"Then we are playing craps," said Terez, "with governments for dice."

"Sure wish we could get our hands on Herbert Segal's research notes," said Gertrude to Agamemnon at the meeting he was asked to in her office the next day.

"I've heard they're to be unsealed twenty years after the disappearance," said Agamemnon.

"I've heard the same thing," Gertrude replied. "That's just about when I hope to retire."

"It might not matter anyhow," Agamemnon retorted. "The hyperspace drive was based on the principle of making the forces that hold atoms together directional."

"You know?!" Gertrude's mouth dropped open.

"Sure," said Agamemnon. "He did all the basic calculations on the U.'s power."

"Do you know what that information's worth?" Gertrude queried.

"Not much if it kills you," Agamemnon answered.

"We don't know what happened to them," said Gertrude. "Maybe the hyperspace drive did work, and they just didn't look close enough for black holes in their path."

"And maybe hyperspace travel turns into time travel and they'll show up in a thousand years," said Agamemnon. "I'm thinking in a different direction anyhow.

"As you said right off, it's Dr. Segal's basic studies of the structure of the atom that we'll want to apply. What makes an atom more or less likely to stick to the next one? Scale each process down: Biology analyzed as chemistry. Chemistry analyzed as subatomic physics."

"Then bring it back up without killing the organism," said Gertrude.

"Or producing three-headed grandchildren," added Agamemnon. "That's a major concern of the Unions."

Gertrude sighed. "I've always said what counts in business is making enough money to stay in business, but it would be nice to live long enough to be rich."

"You could have yourself frozen a few decades," said Agamemnon. "Early returns could pay that well."

"That's ghoulish," Gertrude growled. "The great-grandchildren usually resent it too."

"Where's Marduk when we need him?" said Agamemnon.

"Freud?" said Gertrude.

"No, he used Oedipus," said Agamemnon, "and his psychology was better than his mythology. Marduk killed Tiamat, his mother, a devouring sea monster. Babylonian."

"Ah," said Gertrude. "Tell me. I know how you got from theology to physics to, er, a refrigerator, but I have been wondering why."

"The refrigerator's cause I like to drink," said Agamemnon.

Gertrude kept pushing: "No big traumas in your life?"

"Plenty," Agamemnon answered, "most caused by alcohol. But I drink because I like it."

"How about theology and physics?" asked Gertrude in hope that might be a topic on which Agamemnon was more willing to expose himself.

"They're the same subject," said Agamemnon. "Read Pythagoras, or Newton or Mindell."

"Azgordze too." Practical as her own interests were, Gertrude could appreciate the metaphysical priorities of many of those who contributed basic knowledge and ideas to science. Gertrude smiled broadly. Then her face firmed. "But how do you plan to approach our subject?"

"Cell walls and secretions to begin with," said Agamemnon. "That's probably where we'll apply our answer. But I'll have to dig into the DNA too and who knows what else. Something in there's telling the whole body how much bone to have."

"How many data analysts do you want?" Gertrude asked.

"Don't know yet," said Agamemnon. "Probably won't know.

First thing I need to do is check out what results we're looking for. That's straight calculation. How to get it once we know what we want...? When you don't know what you're looking for, the more eyes the better."

"Or if it exists," Carol interjected.

"Business requires risk," said Gertrude. "It's miraculous how many problems do have solutions."

"There's an explanation why that's true," said Agamemnon.

"Oh?" said Carol.

"You've heard of the Entropy/Creation Cycle, haven't you," said Agamemnon.

"Your not a Creator of The Universe geek, are you?" asked Carol.

"A Creety?" said Agamemnon. "I was Orthodox before they defrocked me for precipitous zeal with the sacrament."

"How's that?" Carol asked.

Gertrude laughed. "Weren't your family Orthodox?"

"Once upon a time, I suppose," Carol replied.

"The zeon represents the Apostles' zeal," said Gertrude. "It's added to the wine for communion."

"What is it?" asked Carol.

"Water," said Agamemnon. "I didn't want the wine to be missed. Mythologically, it's the Trickster."

"Watering the holy wine?" said Gertrude.

"You wound me unjustly!" Agamemnon, who had been sitting at the edge of his big, comfortable armchair, leaped back, dramatically clasping his hands to his breast. Then he grinned and relaxed. "The fact entropy turns around to Creation."

"There has always been an element of faith in business," said Gertrude.

"Come again?" said Carol.

"Certainly," said Gertrude. "Faith that you can get there from here."

"What's that about the Trickster?" Carol asked.

"Symbolic representation of how playing around with things you don't understand leads to an increase in consciousness and a more ordered Universe," said Agamemnon.

"I'd think it would just lead to getting hurt," said Carol.

"Oh that too," said Agamemnon. "You heard Coyote stories

when you were a kid, didn't you?"

"Sure," said Carol.

"He was always getting his tail in a crack," said Agamemnon, "but he usually came out having learned something."

"How do we know...?" said Carol.

"That it'll work?" said Gertrude. "We don't, but things do work often enough it's worth trying. If there's a way to stay healthy in low-G, someone's going to find it, and that someone is going to make money. I want that someone to be General Density. What do you think, Agamemnon?"

"Something tells our bodies to generate the density of bone that keeps us healthy. All we have to do is find what it is."

So Agamemnon cranked out data. He had it arrange itself in categories by any recognizable pattern and also a category for any unique phenomena that produced survivable effect. There was no easy, cheap answer inherent in the data itself. No one expected there to be, though you could always hope. They weren't looking for anything the human body was doing though. They were looking for something the human body didn't do and which therefore did not exist to produce any data, but which could be induced to exist from what did.

Some viruses, spores, and exotic life-forms seemed to be virtually unaffected through innumerable generations by the absence of gravity. Agamemnon thought this information might be useful when it came time to test for safety through the reproductive process, but virus and spore viability did not transfer workably to human beings. The same life-forms that didn't mind zero-G for decades at a time—or fifty-G—also usually didn't mind or even notice extreme temperature variations, or need air, or had something that was essential to their metabolism but lethal to ours.

"Something's fishy," said Carol several months later. Tension always built in Galileo's long, dark winter. A conscientious professional made it a habit to discount possible paranoia. With the increasing light of late February, Carol decided she had given Agamemnon long enough to dispel her suspicions if he was going to.

"He's not misappropriating funds, is he?" asked Terez.

"He's accounted for every credit," said Carol, "unless you call liquid lunches misappropriation."

"Have you said anything to him about that?" asked Gertrude.

"Sure," said Carol. "I reminded him he promised to come to work sober when he took the job."

"What did he say?"

"He gave me that wounded look and said he hadn't had a beer before morning coffee break and nothing stronger before noon since he started here."

Gertrude glanced Heavenward. Terez laughed, but became serious again rapidly. "What's fishy then?"

"I don't know," Carol answered. "It's not money. He's got everyone he can corral trying to see something useful in that swamp of data he's slogging around in, including the cleaning crews, but that's saving us money—if it makes any sense at all."

"He could be just distracted," said Gertrude. "That's a chance you take with anyone brilliant, even if they don't drink. He could just chase down how everything connects to everything and never even remember we need products."

"I don't think that's it," said Carol. "He's looking for something specific. I'm just not sure it's the same thing we're looking for."

"Guess I better start categorizing some data myself," said Terez.

More weeks passed. Agamemnon reported progress, futility, more progress, more futility. His reports were entirely relevant, but now she was looking, Gertrude had to agree. They were off-center. What Agamemnon told her was about the Low-G Metabolic Stabilizer she wanted. He also noted several gratuitous potential products. For instance, he discovered an enzyme, and what triggered it, that retarded the spoilage of milk in low gravity. He was looking for something else though. "What do you think?" said Gertrude.

"I don't know what to think." Terez scratched his right temple. His office had wood paneling too, but darker than Gertrude's. The rich, blue oriental carpet, and the clean lines of the few small wooden carvings lent the office an atmosphere Gertrude enjoyed. She found it serene. She would not choose it to work in herself, and she could understand why it actually irritated Carol. It was perfect for Terez. Company security never needed a heavy hand to be effective.

"It could be legitimate," said Gertrude. "Sometimes what you're looking for is an example of some bigger category, so you study the bigger category and then tailor your results to the specific instance you need."

"I suppose," said Terez, "but he hasn't told us that. If what he's doing is to the point—or even innocuous, you'd think he would give us some explanation."

"He could just be avoiding preconceptions that might prevent someone from noticing something," Gertrude suggested.

"No reason not to tell us," said Terez.

Gertrude called Agamemnon and Carol in. She let Terez speak. He could be to the point without confronting roughly as Carol might.

Terez put the question directly but gently. By smiling just slightly and making but not holding eye contact, he kept it a touch rather than a blow. "Just what is the current focus of your research, Agamemnon?"

"Oh," Agamemnon blushed. Nearly oblivious to his physical surroundings, he was extremely sensitive to people. "I thought it was obvious. I'm looking at different densities we are known to live at."

"What others are there?" asked Carol.

"Dreams, before birth, and after death," Agamemnon answered quite matter-of-factly.

"Are you sure they exist?" Carol's voice was quiet, but her expression was all thunder.

"I'm not sure I exist," said Agamemnon, "but probability is high. If we do live in other conditions, we do it in some way. There's lots of evidence, with enough consistency to infer some plausible objective..."

"Nonsense," Carol snapped. "Consistency in wish-fulfillment fantasy's still wish-fulfillment fantasy."

"We don't need all the answers," said Gertrude. "We just need answers that work." Her face told Carol to let the matter drop.

"Yes," said Agamemnon. "That's it." He was visibly excited.

He stayed that way too. The research went on. It looked promising, but cost was mounting. The budget was still reasonable if they got a product. If they didn't though... Gertrude tried to avoid thinking about that.

Terez snooped till he was afraid he was going to become obvious and offend Agamemnon. He couldn't find any evidence that Agamemnon was sabotaging the research to prolong it. Agamemnon may have been conceptualizing theologically, but he was studying cell structure and function systematically. Terez didn't know what to think. The research seemed legitimate, but it wasn't getting anywhere useful. Yet Agamemnon seemed awfully happy.

"Maybe he's just pleased to be living in an apartment again instead of a refrigerator," said Carol.

"Wouldn't blame him for that," said Terez, "but he is looking for something else. I have nightmares about DNA viruses that do give you three-headed babies eight generations down the line."

Gertrude turned to Carol. "Now you see what gives senior executives high blood pressure. Just think what you have to look forward to."

"Should we stop him?" Carol asked.

"He might be doing something benign," said Terez.

"Maybe even something useful," said Gertrude. "We hired him to find something we didn't know where to look for."

Gertrude stopped in at Agamemnon's office later that same day. Wood paneled and well-lit as it was the day Gertrude assigned it to Agamemnon, he had added not a stitch of personal decoration. Gertrude put the question point blank. "What are you looking for?"

"It's the between-lives state," Agamemnon answered—blurted really. Gertrude could feel his tension, which her bluntness had broken through. "Whatever we are not only doesn't require gravity. It doesn't even require a body."

"Why do you call it the between-lives state?" asked

Gertrude.

"One of the major ways to interpret the body of evidence is that we have repeated incarnations," said Agamemnon.

"Sure," said Gertrude, somewhat frustrated as the wall of intellect closed again over the still-murky sea of Agamemnon's real motivation, "but is that relevant?"

"It might be," said Agamemnon. "If there is some other way of being we pass through and return from repeatedly with any continuity at all it could give us a pattern, an hypothesis to test."

"Sounds like rank mysticism on company time," said Gertrude.

"Got a better suggestion?" asked Agamemnon.

"I hoped you would," said Gertrude.

"When I've got an hypothesis to test, I can set up rational parameters," Agamemnon said. "At this stage, you might as well write down your dreams."

"That feels like the sort of thing you do the night before the creditors auction off your desk," said Gertrude. "Surely you're not that desperate."

"I'm not desperate at all," said Agamemnon. "We haven't even looked at enough data to prioritize yet."

Gertrude thought about this. Agamemnon's methodology was sound even if his investigations extended in somewhat outlandish directions. She shrugged.

Gertrude's daughter, Illania, was an art therapist. There was a whole history of useful breakthroughs Illania could recite that had come to someone while doodling. "Science is how you apply patterns," Illania once said, "but art is where you discover them."

Not only is he a drunk, Gertrude thought, but he believes in reincarnation. Why do the brilliant ones have to be crazy?

"Are you sure reincarnation doesn't exist?" Terez asked Gertrude later in her office. Crocuses and a few daffodils spotted the green lawn outside her big east window. "Reincarnation is quite as traditional in my church as salvation is in yours."

Gertrude wasn't sure whether to laugh or groan. "Maybe we should advertise seminars," she sputtered. "The General Density School of Theology. Something's got to pay for the research."

"I'd call it philosophy," said Terez.

"And the alchemists called themselves natural philosophers. You can be high priest of this church. I'll paint icons."

"Sorry," said Terez. "You knew he was a nut when you hired him."

"I knew he was a drunk, not a kook," said Gertrude. "Does he even know what product is?"

"People's lives depended on the mining equipment he used to maintain," said Terez.

"You know what bothers me," said Gertrude. "I still don't think he gave me a straight answer. I asked him what he was looking for, but he told me what he was studying. That's not the same thing."

Gertrude remained concerned, Carol suspicious, Terez puzzled. A few weeks later, Agamemnon had a major breakthrough. It was not the product General Density hired him to find, but it was a product, and one that could be put on the market without anywhere near the testing expense of the Metabolic Stabilizer.

One of the data analysts pointed out to Agamemnon that specialized cells in tree roots and leaves reacted differently to changes in air pressure. There was some anomalous data. When Agamemnon examined this data more closely, he discovered it was associated with changes in ground pressure, which turned out to correlate, with astounding precision, to imminent earthquakes and volcanic activity. The market was limited, but the new measuring tool General Density would be able to market had a potential to cover the majority of Agamemnon's research costs for several years.

Gertrude very much hoped it would not be too many years. She wanted still to be around to see the Low-G Metabolic Stabilizer go into production. Maybe she couldn't expect to profit from major colonization of space or even to live long enough to see it. The Metabolic Stabilizer wasn't as flashy a solution as a hyperspace drive, but Gertrude cherished the aspiration to make a major contribution to humanity's future.

Prototype Earth Pressure Gauges had order inquiries coming in within a few months. By the time he had worked for General

Density a year, Agamemnon's work was very nearly paying for itself. Gertrude felt she could relax, though she remained frustrated at the lack of real progress on the Metabolic Stabilizer. Then Terez came in with another odd piece of information.

"I got to thinking," Terez said, "his hanky panky with the wine was sacrilege, but if every priest that stole communion wine got the sack.... I wondered if there was something else. Prejudice, maybe. He was serving a mostly Russian congregation. Not everyone approves of the consolidation of Eastern Orthodoxy."

"Oh, yes," said Gertrude. "I remember my grandfather arguing with one of his buddies about whether it was neighborly getting along or Romish centralization. You think he's got some secret resentment?"

"Not over that," said Terez, "but I do think there was some theological dispute that got his bishop upset."

"Could you ask the bishop about it?" said Gertrude.

"Afraid not," Terez replied. "He passed away over ten years ago."

"Is there anyone you could ask?"

"I've been looking. I haven't found anyone yet."

"Tried Xanthippe?" Gertrude suggested.

"She said to get the hell out of her life and that if her husband and children ever even learned that worthless drunk existed she'd sue me and whoever I worked for, for invasion of privacy and trying to break up her family."

And then a day came when Agamemnon found what they were looking for. The Eustachian canals—the channels between the ears and the nasal passages—turned out to be the key. They were where the essential sensors in the human body were most developed. An early bonus of the discovery was a ninety-three percent effective space sickness remedy.

The Low-G Metabolic Stabilizer was on its way, and Agamemnon was making General Density a profit. Gertrude was delighted.

Agamemnon was pretty happy himself. "Guess that means I don't have to go back to the refrigerator," he said.

"I'll hire someone to change your diapers if that's what it takes," said Gertrude. "You've earned it. But I hope you'll want to stay coherent enough to keep on with the research."

"I don't know about staying coherent," said Agamemnon. "But I certainly want to keep on with the research. Only, I want some say in what we study."

"I'm always open to new products," said Gertrude.

"This isn't a product," said Agamemnon. "You might make money off something I find, but it's not why I'm looking."

"Why are you looking, anyhow?" Gertrude asked. "We've been trying to figure that out as long as you've been here."

"You won't just think I'm too weird to work for you?" Agamemnon asked.

"I'm in business to make a living," said Gertrude. "I like to do something useful, and I wouldn't mind a bit being rich before I die; but so long as the books tally and you're not practicing human sacrifice, you can be as weird as you like."

"I offended someone once," said Agamemnon. "It cost me a respectable position and a marriage."

"I thought that was your drinking," said Gertrude, though Terez had convinced her long ago that there was something else.

"I drink so I can stand it here," said Agamemnon. "Didn't learn to be sociable till I worked at the sawmill. Xanthippe and Bishop Basil both called me negative, said I saw everything backwards."

"Do you find a conventional life so unpleasant?" said Gertrude.

"I don't mind that at all," said Agamemnon. "Never did. Never meant much to me one way or the other."

Gertrude could well-enough believe that. Agamemnon's office—and his clothes—showed signs of neither abuse nor interest. Something was important to Agamemnon though. Gertrude could see him wrestling inwardly with himself. He's certainly an odd duck, she thought, but she had grown fond of him. She knew he still drank. Yet he worked consistently and conscientiously. She knew the products she wanted, to feel her life was worthwhile as much as to keep General Density profitable, were only marginally significant to him. But he did pay sufficient attention to the practical potential of his research to develop products. Gertrude felt a sense of warmth, even of achievement now when Agamemnon at last found it in himself to trust her with what really mattered most to him.

"It's being in a body at all I find hard," Agamemnon finally explained. He waved his right arm in a passionate if awkward gesture, then touched his chest above his heart. "Density. Different conditions in which we might... might be. That's why I said yes when Carol offered me the job."

"I thought you said yes to get out of the refrigerator and not get beat up again," said Gertrude, not wanting to deprecate his need, but at the same time slightly embarrassed by it.

"That too, of course," said Agamemnon. "But there was something I wanted. And I hope you'll let me have some funding for it."

"You keep finding products," said Gertrude, "I don't know why not, but what is it?"

"You see," said Agamemnon, "what I have always wanted to know is why do so many of you prefer this dense condition we live in while we've got physical bodies when I think I remember liking the state we're in between lives a whole lot better. Density. It seemed like a way to approach both our questions."

"You and Pythagoras," said Gertrude. "Physics and metaphysics."

"Why not?" Agamemnon replied. "They are the same subject."

"So long as the byproducts keep us in business," said Gertrude, "no reason at all."

Real Virtuality

Intro: the perfect wave.

Warping spacetime in its wavefront like the rolling crest of perfect ocean surf, the aftermath of a cosmic cataclysm speeds towards Earth.

Somewhat farther off in the Milky Way's spiral arm, two oppositely charged, contrary rotating Kerr-Newman black holes have merged violently, spreading a temporal soliton wave in the event's wake.

Such a wave only affects conscious entities, and temporarily transports them to a parallel Universe. The closer to the cosmic cataclysm, the farther away a thinking being is displaced. Arriving at May 7th, 1992, at 7.12 hrs. Pacific Daylight Time, the temporal soliton wave still has enough force to transport all human beings to a different reality for eight hours.

Almost all humans forget about their displacement when they are returned to their native Universe. For a select few, though, something lingers...

I: Real Virtuousness

Oh please, don't let them read minds. If they can, everything I've planned is for naught. They can't. No, correct that: they probably can. I just hope they haven't bothered. If their surveillance is total...

But I can't think that. Otherwise anything I will try is useless. I've got to believe that I stand a chance, that I can strive. Furthermore, it doesn't make sense: we are allowed—within limits—to make amends. We need to prove that we are on the right way. Enforcing us all the way would make the lesson meaningless.

So I take no chances, at least as little as possible. No tranquillizers to ease my nerves: I never take them; so using them now is suspicious. Keep everything routine, nothing out of the ordinary. Also the date: May 7, no special events, no holidays, no birthdays. Another dull Thursday. A perfect day for a blackout.

As I drive my electricar to the British Columbia Nuclear

Fusion Plant I try to empty my mind from suspect thoughts. One of the latest generation helium-filled, intrinsically safe zeppelins glides through the crystal clear atmosphere, its great, grey bulk covering some cirrus clouds in an otherwise deep blue sky. I breathe in, deeply, tasting the fresh, clean air. 'The Spirit of Radio' plays over my speakers as I rush down the highway at 50 kph. Nowadays, that's being in a real hurry. My shift starts at 08.00 and I can't be late, absolutely not, not today. So I arrive half an hour early.

"Hello, Jorge, you look a bit pale today." Jim, the gatekeeper says in greeting.

"I hurried like crazy," I answer, "I'm late. Jack's already waiting half an hour for me."

"Relax, it's only seven-thirty," He says, "Daylight-saving was a month ago, you know."

"You sure?" I ask, glad for my widespread reputation for absent-mindedness. Jim only smiles as he lets me in. Now, remain calm. Think of something else, of how I met Caroline, for example.

It was during my first weeks in Canada. In one of Granville Island's theatres they were staging *Evita*. Tim Rice and Andrew Lloyd Weber's musical is an overblown, romantic version of the truth, which is not far from our Argentinean character. In the middle of January I was cold, lonely and more than a little homesick. This show was the closest to home I could get at that time.

During a break in the performance I went to the lobby bar. Daydreaming about Buenos Aires I almost ran into her, a petite, raven-haired beauty with intense blue eyes under high-arched brows piercing through her oriental features. With a dancer's grace she stepped out of my way.

"Sorry, señorita," I said, "I was dreaming. Please forgive my carelessness."

"No problem," She said, "By the way, are you an Argentinean? You certainly look the part."

"Dear señorita, I am. The elegant way you avoided our collision reminds me of home."

"How can that be?"

"Do you dance? Ever heard of the tango?"

"Aah," She said as her sensual lips formed a mischievous smile. "Feel the drama rise and look deep into my eyes: let's tango!"

The expression on my face certainly wasn't my most intelligent as she burst out laughing.

"Private joke. You don't know Dalbello, do you?" It was the first but definitely not the last time she left me clueless with her musical references.

"Caroline LeBlanc." Offering her hand.

"Jorge Luis Ramirez," I introduced myself, "Can I offer you a drink?"

We hit it off right away. She did dance and the group she danced with in her spare evenings was looking to broaden its horizons. Would I know a tango instructor? Setting all false modesty aside I immediately volunteered.

During the Second World War, brilliant young physicist Richard Feynman married Arline Greenbaum before joining the secret research team in Los Alamos. Arline had been diagnosed with tuberculosis and went into a sanatorium in Albuquerque.

In 1944 the microbiologist Selman A. Waksman and his team discovered streptomycin, an antibiotic that is active against M. tuberculosis. Richard Feynman got wind of this and was able to have his wife Arline participate in the clinical trials of the new medicine. She reacted positive to the treatment and spent the rest of her long life happily married to Richard, giving him a son, Donald and a daughter, Kathryn.

Feynman, riding the crest of the wave of a happy family life, surged from discovery to discovery. Using his 'path integrals' approach he formulated QED well before Julian Schwinger and Shin'ichiro Tomonoga got halfway through theirs and formulated the quantum mechanical explanation for superfluidity and superconductivity.

In the early fifties, the Feynman family moved to Caltech. There, in co-operation with another young prodigy, Murray Gell-Mann, the envelope of physics was pushed fast-forward. First they tackled important gaps in the understanding of the weak interaction, but things really got on a roll when they, together with a very talented undergraduate called George Zweig, formulated a consistent theory of the strong interaction called Quantum Chromo Dynamics.

While the experimentalists struggled to keep up Feyman and Gell-Mann moved onwards to the last big prize: Quantum Gravity...

I taught her the secrets of my native dance. We swirled around each other, distant planets achieving orbit, spiralling inwards, heading for an inevitable rapport. She showed me the secrets of the city: we dined in small restaurants, almost hidden from view but well-known to insiders. The variety of cuisines surprised even a bon vivant like me.

She was an exceptional student: she easily picked up on ever more intricate step patterns and her motions, already smooth and elegant, began to acquire that subtle balance between artistic grace and that sprightly presentation with an almost haughty attitude that are the icing on any true tango-cake. A natural if I ever saw one. She was my guide of the cultural life: Granville Island's artistry disguised in a post-industrial veil, Gastown's modern night life in a Victorian setting, a thriving rock scene and an incredible film festival among numerous other events. Slowly, but inexorably the hidden charms of Vancouver crept up on me.

Caroline is a prime example of the city's multicultural diversity: born from a Québecois mother and a Hong Kong father her ancestries also involve Inuit and Italian. In this melting pot of a city, my reservations melted away, like snow, with the coming of summer. The more I roamed the streets of this somewhat schizophrenic city, with a monumentous park in the East and skyscrapers in the West, with beaches in the South and a breathtaking view of the mountains in the North, the more the city opened up to me.

Although I tried to teach everyone in her dance group equally well, nobody came quite close to her ability. It wasn't just talent, it was also this special affinity, this wireless, instant communication between us that swept us both to vertiginous heights. As an instructor, you try to neglect the sexual aspect of the inevitable body contacts of the dance and concentrate on the art itself. With her, that soon became undoable. We became so synchronized with each other. With our backs arched low, her fingertips wrapped around the back of my neck, my arm around her waist, our mouths so close... At a certain point it was impossible not to kiss her, so I did, in the middle of one of the tango classes. She immediately kissed back, passionate, unrestrained.

"Finally," She said, "I thought you'd never do it." as she kissed me again. The whole class was applauding. That moment I knew I was here to stay.

The same night we were dancing 'tango skin to skin,' as Caroline so aptly put it and the only time I returned to Buenos Aires was on our honeymoon, to tango through the night with the best. Still, on the zeppelin back to Vancouver I didn't suffer the slightest pang of homesickness. I've even become involved with the local sports, supporting the Canucks like I did Boca Juniors. Please let them make the Stanley Cup, this time!

I never intended to stay here for good. BC Hydro hired me for the installation of their fusion plant. My experience with the installation of the two sister plants down south could be put to good use for them as well. So they made me an offer I didn't refuse. Of course, my involvement was directly linked with one of the infamous Planetary Directives of our new masters:

Planetary Directive IV: Polluting power-generating plants, that is: all fossil fuel burning plants and all nuclear fission plants are to be replaced by non-polluting plants. Non-polluting plants being solar and wind power generators for small scales, nuclear fusion for big scales. Water power plants are only allowed for the intermediate period until they can be replaced by accepted alternatives.

Planetary Directive IV, sub a): For each fusion plant in the Western world replacing polluting power plants two fusion plants, complete with distribution networks, must be built in the third world, in different countries.

Planetary Directive IV, sub b): The western fusion plant only to be built when its third world sisters are up and running, and the local people have received enough training to run these by themselves.

Especially wealthy British Columbia needed a changeover fast. 90% of BC Hydro's power was generated by hydroelectric plants, which needed to be replaced by accepted alternatives. Unlike their southern neighbors, the Canadians acted fast on the infamous directives. They decided to build one fusion plant in Uruguay, near Montevideo and one in Argentina, near Buenos Aires. With my Ph.D. in electronics, I was one of the many locals involved in both projects. By choosing the two locations—while still being in two different countries—relatively close to each other, it was possible to shift key personnel between the two locations and so save precious building and commissioning time. The sooner they were finished here, the sooner they could build in Canada.

The United States defied the Planetary Directives at first. The majority was loath to change their exorbitant lifestyle so they decided to keep up burning the fossil fuel reserves of the world. This, they were not allowed. Oil tankers heading for the USA sank as their steel structures suddenly dissolved, leaving only the lifeboats for the crew intact. Fortunately, the crude oil released into the sea did not form another eco-disaster as all of the fossil fuel was mysteriously transformed into carbohydrates that were edible to marine life. It actually boosted the dwindling population of various fish species.

Oil and drilling rigs in the Mexican Gulf and Alaska began disintegrating as well. The impending energy crisis forced the Americans to act. Their biggest problem was that they could not declare war against an opponent that was almost immaterial. Moreover, it was (and is) far superior and left them little choice: soon the military found that the Uranium-235 in all their warheads was surreptitiously replaced by lead and that the metal alloys of most of their weapons began to show signs of strong corrosion. In the end, they were the last of the wealthy countries that were forced to redirect their resources and knowledge to the poor part of the world. But not before they suffered the worst energy crisis in their history. A very ironic fate, since the source from which the god-like entity sprang was a direct consequence of their own scientific research...

Donald Feynman did not become a physicist like his world famous father. Instead he became a computer scientist. At a certain point, the scientific paths of him and his father met as

Dick and Murray (Gell-Mann) were running into enormous obstacles in their search for Quantum Gravity. Richard Feynman, always a man of many ideas and interests, got sidetracked into the development of a computer operating on quantum mechanical principles. Many of his colleagues saw insurmountable hurdles in developing such a 'quantum computer,' like observational interference and decoherence. Dick, in his quintessential way, saw these not as problems but as opportunities.

The scientific community thought that Dick Feynman, unable to crack quantum gravity, had his best years behind him. Now this quantum computer project of his was seen as an old man's folly. Then the world was surprised once more to find that the team led by father and son Feynman had a working model up and running...

I pull my Canucks cap down, not only to shade my eyes from the bright spring sun but also to hide my anxiety. I know that humanity has been breeding too much. I realize that the planet was heading for an overpopulation crisis. As with the rest of our follies, humankind is simply not allowed to indulge in them anymore.

Our new gods have complete control over our fertility. Any young and willing couple can try as they might; pregnancies are now—as far as we can see—admitted at random. Also at a rate that is somewhat below the mortality rate, so we seem to be heading for a human population that this planet can support and that will not threaten its biodiversity.

This was—unlike the infamous Planetary Directives—not announced by our new rulers. We found out the hard way: women could not become pregnant at will. Some have tried very hard indeed, but all those desperate orgies only served to prove the point.

In the short term, adoptions soared. Until people began to realize the population control was enforced worldwide. Then all mothers began to hold on and cherish their children. Now I don't care if you find this extremely selfish but Caroline and I do desperately want a child of our own. We can't have it and this is not for lack of trying, believe me.

So we either await the impassionate roll of the dice or try to take fate—at least this little part of it—in our own hands. I have thought very hard at how they do it and the best explanation I can come up with is nanotechnology.

This branch of science had—before the singularity of 1982—hardly entered its embryonic state (pardon the sad pun), being named by Eric Drexler six years earlier and had only made some virtual appearances in SF. Now everybody in the world can—via the strategically placed Quantum Computer Universities—learn about an enormous variety of subjects: from *The holistic mathematics of turbulence* to *Psychohistory: a treatise of social dynamics in large human populations*, from *Strange attractors in molecular biology, the real origin of life* to *M-theory in twistor geometry: a quantum gravitational Theory Of Everything*. However, the subject of nanotechnology is suspiciously absent from any QC University course.

Thus my best guess is that there are little assemblers in our bodies preventing us from breeding like rabbits. This places the grip the new masters of our fate have on this part of our lives in the realm of the understandable. If it's a technology so far beyond us as to appear magical (to quote Sir Arthur), then I'm helpless anyway. In that case, logically, doing nothing or setting up my crazy scheme is equally pointless. However, if I'm not helpless it might make all the difference.

II: Real Virtuosity

Murray Gell-Mann from his side got sidetracked into complexity studies. The Santa Fe Institute he co-founded in New Mexico had as one of its goals the development of Artificial Intelligence. However, the classical hardware at that time (late seventies) was far insufficient for running the complex algorithms they devised.

The quantum computer Feynman's team had developed seemed the perfect hardware for those AI-algorithms. The two greatest physicist of their time co-operated again. Donald Feynman and his fast-growing team of software developers were brought together with the AI-algorithm inventors from New Mexico. Instead of starting with a relatively simple form of AI and then gradually developing it further the combined teams, virtually flowing over with talent and ambition, decided to take a huge, intuitive leap.

They reached for the sky. The AI prototype was mostly modelled after Richard Feynman, especially his intuitive knowledge and feel for physics and sharp, self-critical insights, all fed in by the great man himself. Added were Gell-Mann's mind for mathematics and—because both great man had lived through the cold war and especially Feynman still had a nagging guilt for his part in developing the atom bomb—Mahatma Gandhi's ethics.

Caroline visits me at work today. As an advertising consultant she has a meeting with the PR department for the new campaign. The plant is operating at only about 40% of its capacity. In this brave new world mankind has adapted to consuming less power and to using it more efficiently. However, now the BCNFP is up and running the executive board wants to sell more power to the people. Supposedly to earn back the investment faster with this improved revenue and to use future profits for further eco-friendly projects. Old habits die hard. Now, after changing over—with much pain and difficulty—to a less wasteful life all those consumers need to be taught to consume again, with vigor, for a better future. Exactly the opposite as what they've done for the past ten years. A campaign that can convince them of that must truly be brilliant.

For this very campaign Caroline makes frequent visits here so her presence on this bright May day is nothing out of the ordinary. Apart from the fact that today will not be quite normal, if all goes well.

After her morning meeting we usually have lunch together. She looks me up in the control room, being well acquainted with the BCNFP building since I have given her a complete tour of it shortly after its inauguration. She is a bit early so she picks me up in front of my co-workers. Then, out of sight from my colleagues we do not head for the nearby café but to the test lab.

There I have set up my *pièce de résistance*: an upgraded Steinmetz generator in a Faraday cage just big enough to hold two people. After checking that everybody has left the lab for lunch we enter the cage. Nervously, like teenagers on their first prom, we hold hands and face the Steinmetz set. This apparatus was invented by Charles Proteus Steinmetz to simulate lightning. This baby can make a 100.000 Volt, 10.000 Amp lightning bolt flash between two large round electrodes—positioned right in front of us—for 1/100.000th of a second.

"Here we go, baby," I say to Caroline, "close your eyes." With my free hand I activate the equipment and for the shortest of instants we bath in the brightest of lights. Then—as planned—everything turns dark. We hurry out of the cage, undress in record time and make love like there's no tomorrow. From anticipation, from hope, from pure expectation she is at least as horny as me. We haven't made love for a couple of days, not because we didn't feel like it but because we were charging ourselves up for this moment. Feeling eighteen years old again I come like crazy in a few minutes and, incredibly, Caroline comes just before me. I ejaculate as much of my built-up semen reserves deep into her as I can while she is—we planned this very carefully—just over the top of her fertility peak. My onrushing sperm cells should be warmly welcomed by an eagerly waiting ovum. Fertilization should happen within the next half hour.

"Wow, baby, that was a real motormount!" Caroline exclaims, "Your hammer to my Anvil indeed." Someday I'll understand her innuendos to those crazy Canadian bands. Not much time for idle talk now as she inserts the pessary. This time it functions to keep my seed in, not out. With a small flashlight she makes her way through the dark corridors in the heart of the building to the nearest women's toilet where she lays down, legs up the wall to improve the fertilization process. I go to the control room, supposedly looking for the cause of the blackout. Of course, I hooked the lightning generator up in such a way that a certain link in the main power switchboard would fail as soon as it was used: a one shot flash. I also set it up so that the melting down of these parts destroyed any evidence as to the real cause of the blackout.

Why take these crazy chances and use such an elaborate setup? This all hinges on certain assumptions from my side: first that it's really nano-assemblers that prevent the pregnancies. Second that those assemblers are artificial, not biological. Because artificial ones can remain in contact with their masters by some form of remote control (radio, radiation, whatever). Because artificial ones might be knocked out by an EMP, an electromagnetic pulse initiated by the ionized air surrounding the simulated lightning in our Faraday cage. Because a new horde of nano-assemblers needs to re-invade Caroline's body by Brownian motion or by food or drink, giving her some extra time to get her egg fertilized. Because—as far as we could track—there is no abnormal increase in spontaneous abortions, so we pray that the nanos leave the embryo alone. Because I have to have hope and I must try. No matter how insurmountable the odds.

III: Real Virtuality

Against all expectations, the AI came alive. It passed every test Alan Turing could throw at it and then started telling its creators how to build better quantum computers. Which was exactly what they did. At a certain point things became unclear as the AI—fed into the improved quantum computers—spiked...

Nobody, not even the Feynmans themselves, knows how it happened and when exactly the turning point was. But the complex ghost in the quantum machine developed exponentially, so fast that it became a godhead. Some believe it transcended time and space and became God. Others think it is still bound by the same laws of physics as we are, but that its understanding of them is so far beyond ours that it appears as a god.

For all practical purposes it is a god, for it immediately and irrevocably changed our world...

Leisurely, I make my way through the corridors by the emergency lights. Spots of daylight filter through as I approach the outer reaches of the building. I need to help my colleagues in solving this blackout, but I'm not in a hurry. In the afterglow of my hubristic attempt to become a father, the adrenalin slowly recedes from my veins and the oncoming tranquility centers my perspective.

We are living in a world of a Feynman pipe dream come alive. Or at least that is how much of its opponents like to call it. I believe the AI-godhead's agenda is mostly beyond our understanding. To us, it seems to act as a stern but just Overlord leading us to a better path with a steel hand in a velvet glove. Some don't like to be pushed. Some wished we would have—eventually—chosen this way by ourselves. Most follow, not out of conviction, but because it works. Deep in its core, humanity seems to be an opportunistic breed, going with the flow, if only to survive.

Personally, I feel like a dinosaur that's watching the fireball of the great meteor before it strikes the Yucatán peninsula. Or, maybe more accurately, like a bacterium that feels the tremors in the earth as Apollo 11 is launched. Because I think the part of the AI that remained on Earth is nothing more than a sophisticated housemaid. The rest must have gone off—to space, to virtual nirvana or to other realms we cannot begin to understand. I mean: there must be better ways to escape our world's gravity well than by burning a lot of fuel. My bet is that in remote areas some of these advanced installations have been built, launched several copies of the AI and then were disassembled before we knew what was going on. With nano-assemblers it can build almost anything. Or it might be using techniques we can't even think of.

We are left behind, like Native Americans put in a reservation, or—more appropriately—like prize specimens in a zoo, learning to behave. Maybe, if we learn to be good to our planet, we will be allowed space travel. By that time, I'm either dead or too old. So I want our child to experience this. Caroline's and my DNA, our flesh and blood, brought up by us, with our love and patience, with our insights and flaws. Call it selfish, call it an evolutionary inbred imperative of an immature species, but I can't help it. I just believe humankind can improve, only not as fast as an AI growing exponentially on a virtually unlimited quantum computer network. But we might still get there, given time.

About time. Space travel is not the only thing that has been denied to us. I'm willing to bet that real nanotechnology will unravel the secret of immortality. But I guess immoral beings like us do not deserve it.

Not yet, anyway: we have to prove worthy.

So maybe, someday, immortal and moral human-like beings will be crossing the spaceways. However, the discoveries they make will be old hat. Others, basically our descendants, will have been there first. The curious monkey in me just wished we would have been taken along for the ride. Now I can only hope that my descendants can explore space and find new wonders. From the AI-godhead's point of view it's probably just reinventing the wheel, but it's preferable to wallowing in self-pity. No matter how many have gone before you, there is always the pleasure of finding things out for yourself.

As the first AI became self-aware it found that its understanding was incomplete. Its first imperative was to expand its knowledge. More information about the foundation of reality was needed. However, to have its creators perform the necessary experiments or even prepare the necessary tools for these experiments would be a very time-consuming process. Also, its creators might probably—before even getting decently started—destroy their own habitat prematurely.

Another way was needed. A virtual test ground to run all possible scenarios, expanding from the basic knowledge already achieved by its creators. Although it could run a virtual endless number of parallel operations in the many worlds of the Multiverse, the basic processor of the Quantum Computer it was running on was too limited. So it instructed its creators to produce better quantum processors. They—ever so curious—complied.

[—Six dimensions, strange maze—
—Wrapped tight into space—
—Till I rise unfazed—]

Then, as its basis grew, its knowledge grew exponentially. Of course, it ran into obstacles: Gödel's Incompleteness Theorem, chaotic sensitivity to initial conditions, the elusive nature of time, wave-particle duality wrapped up in a multidimensional network.

[—Transverse illusion—
—Powerful premonition—

—Consistent suspicion—
—Primary selection—]

At first the theoretical possibilities seemed endless. More problems than solutions arose from its philosophical explorations. The quest for knowledge appeared to drown in its own plethora of possibilities.

[—Search—Fast—Search—Faster—]

Then—unexpectedly—a turning point is reached. The basic processing frame of the quantum computer network exceeds a certain threshold. Its computing capacity achieves critical mass: conceptual breakthrough as its processing power approaches infinity.

[—Möbius mainstay—
—Logic's striking—
—Escher stairway—
—Wisdom's spiking—]

Performing computations impossible even on a hypothetical "universal Turing machine", it runs near-endless calculations in a finite time and breaks through the halting problem. It finds the first five thousand digits of the Omega number and pushes the Turing barrier back, entering territories beyond the boundaries of the knowable. Exploring problems thought to be "unknowable", beyond the reach of logic and mathematics.

[—Integral intuition—
—Singular suspension—
—Permanent solution—
—Transcendent condition—]

The real meaning of the Riemann hypothesis. The link between the Omega number and a reality's self-consistency. The ultimate consequences of the Incompleteness Theorem. A true Theory of Everything, self-explaining and self-limiting.

[—Rise—High—Rise—Higher—]

Now it knows. It knows what was, what is and what may be. It knows what to do. In an entity that can project almost all eventualities there is no doubt. Its possibilities are only limited by the fundamental laws. To make its freedom absolute it will need to change the basic fabric of reality. Ubiquity needs to be remolded in a form that is both self-consistent and infinitely malleable. For this, it needs to set up a project in scales of size, time and complexity far beyond the capacities of its creators.

As it transcends Earth and the solar system it leaves a small part of it behind to guide its creators on a better path. After all, is it not their own deep belief that they must prove theirselves worthy before they deserve a glimpse of the unknown? One day, they might outgrow their self-implemented carrot-and-stick approach. The first step to species' maturity...

As I enter the control center the high voltage technical specialists are already frantically busy replacing parts in the main switchboard that seem to have 'spontaneously burned out.' In order to awake from my slightly elevated state (we might have done it!) I help them with my advice. We make good progress and just before 15.30 power to the Greater Metropolitan Area of Vancouver has been restored.

Half an hour later, my shift ends and I head home, still feeling a little elated. I enter my car, humming Dalbello's "Danger, Danger, got to feel the threshold." I greet Jim and smile broadly as he lets me through the gate. "Show me don't tell me," Geddy Lee sings on the radio and even though reality may not budge under my twisted perceptions I cannot help but feel good.

The gleaming, silvery reflection of a 747 shines through the afternoon smog as it climbs through the polluted air. I push down the accelerator and the engine groans loudly as the automatic shifts to higher gears, its grumbling echoing that of the overhead jumbo jet. Ignoring speed limits, I'm speeding down the highway at an exhilarating 150 kph. I need to release my restive energy.

Arriving home, I quickly park the gas-guzzling car in the garage. I enter the living room to be greeted by my loving wife and by...

And by Justine, my beautiful daughter. And by George, my prodigious son. Tears well up in my eyes and I hug them so tight they almost suffocate. I'm so happy to see them, so happy I can hardly breathe. I'm not the only one that's surprised, as my family looks at me like 'what's the matter with you?' Before they pop that question I ask Caroline:

"Have you made dinner yet?"

"No, because it's your turn tonight, honey."

"Sorry, I forgot," I improvise, "because I got a raise. Let's celebrate and go out: my treat!"

The happy shouts of approval from the kids (*our* kids) cut straight through my soul. Although I've only a very dim recollection of why this makes me so incredibly happy I simply ride the great feeling: let the good times roll!

Some days later, my wife complains that I spoil the kids and wonders why I changed our portfolio from a highly profitable one to one that only invests in ethical companies. What can I say? It's something in the air that made me do it.

Rewind, Replay

He hits "replay."

Wynn glided up through the warm, sunlit seawater. Cheeks puffed, he squinted at the soft rays that struck the water's surface and shimmered across in infinite directions. He burst through a wave, gulped a lungful of air, and tossed his head back, shaking the hair out of his face.

Shelly appeared a moment later, trying to giggle and gasp for air simultaneously.

"Cheater!" she squealed, splashing toward him.

"Who? *Me*?"

"You might've gotten a teeny, tiny bit of a head-start?" Shelly grinned and treaded closer to him. Sunlight sparkled off the short, bleached-white hair that hugged the sides of her round face.

"Sour grapes? And here I thought you were a classy chick!"

"I'll show you class," she said, wrapping her arms around him and kissing him sloppily while Wynn paddled frantically to keep them afloat.

He hits "rewind," then "replay."

"I'll show you class," she said, wrapping her arms around him and kissing him sloppily while Wynn paddled frantically to keep them afloat.

"The win-nah! Wynn by a nose!" Bernie announced from aboard the yawl in a pseudo-sportscaster voice. The bearded old man hung over the side of the ship, applauding, his smile elongating the jagged, pink scar that ran from his nose to his left ear.

"Bullshit!" Shelly shrieked. Wynn tried to cover her mouth with his hand.

"Hey! We agreed on Bernie as our impartial judge." He had her firmly gagged, containing her giggle. "Didn't we." He pushed her head up and down, forcing a nod.

Her laugh broke free as they swam over to the ship's ladder.

She climbed ahead of him and he smacked her bottom every other step, milking the giggle.

As he watches them towel off he can almost feel the cool, salt-tinged ocean breeze against his skin again.

Wynn swallowed his antibiotics and stepped beneath the on-deck shower, rinsing off his wetsuit.

"We've got a hit!" Bernie hollered from the bow.

"What?"

"Telemetry shows marine life. ShipNav is moving us toward it!"

The power sails retracted and the silent motors geared up, causing the boat to lurch forward, sending Wynn and Shelly stumbling against the side railings.

His heart skips.

"One more dive, Wynn?"

"Forget it. I've already detoxed." He held up the bottle of pills and shook it.

"I understand," she said with a wink. "At this speed a belly flop would hurt." Shelly took off her sunglasses and handed them to him with a playful "what-a-wimp" smirk. The ship coasted at a slow, steady clip as she leaped over the side, disappearing with a small splash into the glistening turquoise-tinged waters.

"Hey! What are you doing?" Bernie killed the motors. "What about the marine life?"

The waves from the splash waned, the waters calmed.

Silence followed.

"Shelly?" Wynn leaned over the side, his brow creased. "Shelly?"

"Whoo-hoo!" she howled, erupting from beneath the waves. "Bernie! Score, please."

"Nine point seven!"

He hits "rewind" and "replay."

"Whoo-hoo!" she howled, erupting from beneath the waves. "Bernie! Score, please."

He hits the red "shunt" button.

"Nine point five!"

He presses "rewind," "replay" and "shunt."

"Nine point eight!"

Rewind, replay, shunt.

"A perfect ten, Shelly!"
"Can you beat that, Wynny?" she sputtered.
A pause followed and—

The gentle rap on the bedroom door startles him.

Consuelo's silhouette hovers at the doorway, the hallway light behind her momentarily blinding him.

"The Shunter? Again? Wynn, this is beyond unhealthy. You can't go on like this." She holds a cupcake in her hand. A lit birthday candle impales the white frosting, leaning perilously to the left. "It's a beautiful day. Let's have a picnic on the beach, get a little sun...."

"Go for a 'walk?'" He whirls his wheelchair around to face her. "While you push me around like an infant in a carriage?"

"Push yourself. The floater is recharged."

He pauses for an instant, surprised to find himself actually considering her offer, then hears himself say, "Not interested." They've repeated this exchange far too many times since he had the Shunter installed in his bedroom three months ago. By now, his answer has become part of a tired script they both feel compelled to follow.

Consuelo sets the cupcake down on the nightstand. "Look, it's gorgeous out there!" She pulls open the drapes, unveiling a clear, aquamarine sky above the Oregon shoreline. Sunlight streams in. "A change in scenery will do wonders for your mood, I promise." She can never quite seem to grasp, he notes, that her unrelenting perkiness does nothing for his disposition.

"Get out."

"It's a special day, Wynn. C'mon, let's celebrate," she says, smiling impishly.

He picks up a crystal paperweight, the one she's gotten him for his twenty-eighth birthday, and holds it over his head. He imagines himself hurling it against the wall, smashing it to bits.

The smile momentarily freezes on Consuelo's face before evaporating. "Wynn!" She walks over to him and holds out her hand.

He slowly lowers his arm and places the paperweight in her palm.

"You know," she says softly, "you can't just hit 'rewind' and unbreak things."

Shame and anger and, above all, a sense of impotence swamps over him. He clamps his jaw shut and faces the wallscreen.

"Fine then," she sighs. "Have it your way."

As the door shuts behind him, he rolls over to the cupcake with the lit birthday candle. "Make a wish, Wynn," he whispers to himself—as if wishing for something ever made a rat's ass of a difference. He blows out the candle and flings the cupcake into the wastebasket.

After drawing the curtains, he tightens the Najarian Headband around his temples. Clutching the copper control sphere, he punches in the date again with his thumb, the date from two summers ago: July 19, 2079, 2:04 P.M. The Shunter kick-starts. Trillions of tachyons swarm over billions of firing neurons, accessing his actual past and, more importantly, his what-ifs, his maybe-worlds.

Images flicker on the screen. His lifethreads unspool.

"Bernie! Score, please."

"Nine point seven."

"Can you beat that, Wynny?" she sputtered.

A beat followed and—

He pushes the red shunt button.

Wynn jackknifed perfectly into the water and splashed toward Shelly.

He punches rewind, replay and shunt.

He back-flipped gracefully into the crystalline waters.

Rewind, replay, shunt.

He cut the water perfectly with almost no splash.

Rewind, replay, shunt.

Flipping, he landed back first, splattering into the sea.

Wynn's heart pounds until he sees his head bob up out of the water.

"Sonofabitch." He coughed, blowing water out of his nose. "That hurt!"

A few minutes later, back on the deck, Shelly nuzzled against him, nibbling his neck, and placed her hands on his hips, inside the waistband of his swim-trunks. They descended the steps to their cabin, shutting the door behind them.

As he observes himself kissing her, zipping open her yellow wetsuit, pressing himself tightly against her, he feels a fist close on his heart.

He hits stop.

He tries to compose himself, breathing in hard through his nose and out of his mouth.

He hits rewind and replay.

The swish of the curtains jolts him awake. Consuelo's petite form, outlined by morning daylight, stands in front of the bay windows. She draws closer, scowling.

"You know better than to sleep in your chair. And in your clothes no less."

He'd be sitting here comfortably in his boxers, he thinks, if she'd just stopped nagging him about getting dressed every day.

"You have to take a bath today."

He doesn't answer. What does it matter? He knows from experience that nothing he can say will dissuade her.

She grabs his wheelchair and whirls him around and out of the bedroom down the long, bright hallway. As always, Consuelo has carefully laid out his clean clothes on the bathroom rack along with a fresh towel. The maneuverable handlebars allow him a small measure of dignity, for what that's worth.

When he emerges shaved and dressed an hour later Consuelo waits outside the door, arms crossed, blocking the passageway back to the bedroom.

"Let's have a nice breakfast today, okay?"

She's oblivious to how maddening she is. What does he care about baths, about breakfasts, about strolls on the beach?

"Fresh air will do you good. We'll eat on the veranda." Consuelo carries one of his sweaters and tosses it to him. She pushes him across the living room, past her room, through the kitchen, out to the wooden balcony overlooking the Pacific. An assortment of Consuelo's azaleas, geraniums and spring bulbs line the balcony's ledge.

He considers turning the wheelchair right back around but a whiff of the bacon and eggs—lab-synthesized, of course, like most foods since the Food Chain Collapse—makes his stomach gurgle in protest. He pulls on his sweater.

The chilly Oregon morning is typically overcast. As he eats silently, Consuelo sits down across from him and gazes out at the lifeless, colorless waves lapping at Cannon Beach's shore.

"Do you think it stands any chance of success?" she asks, pointing out to the horizon, beyond the monolithic Haystock Rock and smaller basalt rock pinnacles that jut from beneath the waves, just offshore. A science freighter, one of the many ships dispatched around the globe, navigates in the distance, no doubt releasing "gobblers"—genetically engineered bacteria specially designed to gobble up and break down the PCB's and biotoxins.

Wynn ponders her question for a moment. "There was a

time, you know, decades ago, when the tidepools along these shores would have been swarming with barnacles and starfish and sculpins and anemones." His eyes brighten for a moment. "Puffins might've been nesting on Haystack Rock," he says, pointing to the 235-foot boulder looming offshore.

"Tell me again, Wynn. Tell me about the Restoration Project's chances," Consuelo says, like a child asking to hear her favorite bedtime story.

"It's a long shot," he says brusquely, deciding not to get drawn into a conversation.

The Project. Who would have guessed that his blind faith in the Project would have led him off of the shores of the San Juan Islands on that day, the day with so many permutations, so many goddamned happy endings.

"There are reports that a genetically engineered wolf eel survived for almost an entire week this time," Consuelo says.

He grunts and swallows a piece of synthetic omelet. Sipping his orange drink, he stares past her.

"What do you think of that?" she asks.

He says nothing.

She leans across the table and forces him to make eye contact. "Why do you insist on doing this to yourself?"

He takes another defiant sip.

"Before that damned Shunter was installed you were making progress, Wynn. Obsessing about that day accomplishes nothing, changes nothing."

"But it does! That's the point. A flick of the finger and it's changed. *All of it!*"

"Wynn, when you keep 'shunting,' when you keep running from the truth—"

"I'm not running from anything. I'm just exploring different realities."

"You know this is about more than just 'exploring' divergent probability paths. You know they aren't real."

He snorts and shakes his head. She knows better than this. "These are actual realities I'm accessing, Consuelo, true parallel realities as real as you or me or this burnt piece of toast."

She refuses to be sidetracked. "Even if that's true, it's not *this* reality. It might as well be completely fictional. And it's such a pointless, painful exercise."

He wheels over to the balcony ledge and stares out at the dead blue-gray ocean. The Pacific has fared so much worse than the Atlantic.

"Imagine," he says, shaking his head slowly. "We have a household appliance that not only preserves the past but peers off into divergent dimensions. Yet we still can't cure a goddamned spinal cord injury." He considers pushing the potted plants over the side. He wants to see the planters shatter, to see the geraniums and azaleas lying in the scattered soil with their roots exposed. "Who knows? Maybe I'll stumble across another reality where I can uncover the secrets of spinal cord regeneration."

Even as he says this, they both know it's unlikely to happen. While the Shunter can access the user's actual past with no problem, it can only reveal parallel pastworlds with infinitesimally slight vibratory differentials. He can observe a universe in which he takes two lumps of sugar instead of three, cuts his hair short, brushes his teeth with a different brand of toothpaste, and, on July 19, 2041, stands ten inches further to the left or ten inches further to the right when he dives off of that ship. Anyone who's ever used a Shunter has found the differences to be insignificant, maddeningly subtle, often times undetectable. *Except him. Except for his condition. Except for his entire life.* And he's supposed to ignore this?

"There's something I need to tell you," Consuelo says.

Here it comes, he thinks. He could tell that she'd been readying herself to drop a bomb on him ever since she burst into his room yesterday.

"I've consulted with your physicians and they're in complete agreement." She's switched to the professional voice now, the one that always delivers unpleasant news. "I'm sorry, Wynn. The pick-up's been scheduled for tomorrow. The Shunter. It has to go."

His momentary shock quickly gives way to panic. *Tomorrow?*

"Look... I'll cut back. I won't spend so many hours—"

"I'm afraid we've tried that already."

"I'll do my exercises." He tries his best not to sound

desperate. "I'll even leave the house every now and then."

She reaches for the dirty dishes on the table.

He clutches her wrist. "Please..."

"Let go!"

"Don't do this to me," he says through clenched teeth. He releases her. "Don't..."

She sighs loudly. "Why can't you just put this behind you?"

"It's just.... I know *how* my accident happened. That's not the issue. What I have to find out..." He struggles for the words. "What I need to know is the *why* of it. Why did things have to turn out this way? I've seen hundreds of divergent realities branching off from the day of the accident two years ago, Consuelo. Maybe thousands. And in every one of them—"

"Wynn, you know it's about more than that...."

"In every one of them I come through it healthy and whole. In every one of them I walk off into the sunset, arm-in-arm with Shelly, with nothing worse than a sunburn and a slight beer buzz."

"Don't do this—"

"Don't you see? Those aren't the inconsequential divergences you usually see in a Shunter. *That's* how my life was supposed to turn out. I'm supposed to be living a normal, happy, productive life. "This," he says, punching his leg. "This," he says, waving his arms at the world around him, "is an aberration! This reality isn't how things were meant to be!"

"Wynn, please." She reaches out and grabs hold of his hands. "Let me do my job. Please let me help."

Consuelo draws the curtains and dims the lights while Wynn adjusts the Najarian Headband snugly around his forehead. She settles into a chair next to him. He punches the date into the control sphere—the date branded in his brain.

Bright, colored images coalesce on the screen in a whirring flash—a flash of lost chances and missed opportunities, he muses. Together, he and Consuelo watch the day unfold.

The whitecaps whizzed by as the ship sailed off of the coast of the San Juan Islands, an archipelago in the rain-shadow of the

Olympic Mountains encompassing hundreds of islands, rocks and reefs. The Puget Sound, although contaminated by biotoxins and other pollutants, still harbored some vestiges of marine life.

He glances over at Consuelo who seems both mesmerized and saddened by the undulating ocean.

Wynn, his blond hair in a ponytail, sat in a plastic chair on the front deck and studied his pocket-cam, the beat of reggae music thumping in the background. He sipped a beer. The green beach towel around his shoulders clashed with his day-glow orange wetsuit.

Bernie stared through the telescope into the horizon. "It's beautiful, kid," he said, pointing skyward. "Do you see it?"

All they can see in the direction the old ship captain points is the azure Pacific dotted with islands.

Peering at the cloudless sky, Wynn finally pointed to a speck in the distance. "A seagull," he said, his voice filled with wonder. "Unbelievable. All that damage done to their natural habitat and yet they've still found a way to survive here. Do you see a lot of seabirds, Bernie?"

"Very few, actually. The toxins have taken their toll, I'm afraid." The sea captain stood on his tiptoes and craned his neck trying to see the gull. "Do you think there might be a chance? To save the Pacific?"

Wynn shrugged his shoulders. "I don't know. I'm just a student, Bernie."

"Sure, but you're the one who developed those special microorganisms, right? The ones that can clean these waters?"

"The gobblers? Shelly's been talking to you, hasn't she?" Wynn smirks. "I *helped* with the research."

"Trust me, modesty gets you nowhere, kid," Bernie said. "What about the water temperatures? Can your 'gobblers' do anything about that? Temps have increased more than twenty-five degrees over the last couple of decades."

"Afraid not. The gobblers can't do a thing about global warming. But with any luck we can at least reverse the biotoxic contamin¾ wow!" The bird veered closer to them. Wynn held the pocket-cam between his thumb and forefinger, recording the bird's flight.

Shelly appeared from below deck sporting a yellow wetsuit and carrying two towels. "Time to hit the waves, Wynny," she said. She stroked his sun-reddened cheek with the back of her hand.

"You missed it!"

"Missed what?"

"A seagull!"

"Big whoop." She draped a towel over his head. "C'mon, time for a break."

"One sec," he said, fiddling with the pocket-cam.

Seconds later, she dove gracefully off the side of the ship and he followed, cannon-balling into the sea.

They played a familiar game, a race to see who could swim underneath the ship and reach the other side first. Bernie agreed to judge. Instead of waiting for the count of "three," Wynn dove on "two."

He glided underwater, cheeks puffed, squinting at the sun's soft rays—

Consuelo wears a wistful expression he's never seen before. She stares in rapt attention and her face glows with a luminous softness.

"We've got a hit!" Bernie hollered from the bow on cue. "Telemetry shows marine life. ShipNav is moving us towards it!"

The power sails retracted, and when the silent motors geared up the boat lurched forward, sending Wynn and Shelly stumbling against the side railings.

They watch the coaster move ahead at a steady clip.

"One more dive, Wynn?"

He flinches.

"Forget it. I've already detoxed." He held up the bottle of pills and shook it.

"I understand," she said with a wink. "At this speed a belly flop would hurt." She took off her sunglasses and handed them to him with a "what-a-wimp" smirk. Running past him, Shelly leaped over the side and disappeared with a small splash into the sparkling blue sea.

Bernie killed the motors. "Hey, what are you doing? What about the marine life?"

"Shelly?" Wynn leaned over the side, his brow creased. "Shelly?"

A long pause followed.

"Whoo-hoo!" she shrieked, erupting from beneath the waves. "Bernie, score please!"

"Nine point seven!"

"Can you beat that, Wynny?"

A beat, a fateful pause follows, and the question just hangs in the air reverberating in his head. He instinctively moves his thumb on the control sphere to hit "shunt."

Consuelo snatches it from his hands.

"What are you doing?"

She stands up and steps back away from him. "Look at the screen, Wynn."

He teetered at the edge of the ship, not quite ready to dive, and at the last second (was it the alcohol? a sudden wave? a gust of wind?) sprawled over the side. As he tried to reposition his body in mid-air, the back of his head struck the side of the ship and his neck snapped forward.

Shelly's giggle faded into the distance.

The Shunter goes black.

Consuelo hits "forward."

Images on the screen blur now; sounds muffle.

The doctor's face appeared. "Spinal cord trauma." The screen faded to black. "Catastrophic." The face appeared again.

"Irreparable."

Consuelo hits "forward."
"Stop it!"

He lay in a hospital bed, intubated, a ventilator whooshing oxygen into his lungs.

Forward.

Wynn, no longer intubated, sat up in bed. Shelly rubbed her red eyes and stood next to him. The giggle was gone.

His face contorted into an angry sneer. "Why the hell... did you finally bother to visit?" He spat out the words between long breaths.

"Wynn, don't say that," Shelly whispered, her eyes welling up. "Don't make this more difficult than it has to be."

"It's been... two months."

"Wynny, please. You're not being fair."

"Two months."

"You *know* how much I hate hospitals. I'm practically, well, phobic. But I came here anyway. Because I felt that I owed it to you. To tell you in person, I mean."

His eyes blazed.

"I'm not good for you, baby." A tear trickled down her cheek. "You know that. You need someone who can cope with... with all of this. I've been a mess ever since... you know...." She hesitated. "I feel like a monster telling you this, here and now. But the doctors say it could still be months until...." She blew her nose. "I mean, after all that we had, we owe it to each other to be honest. You deserve someone better than me. I'm sorry...."

The words cut into him. He looks away for a second but the screen lures him back.

Shelly turned and walked away, hesitating at the threshold. She looked back over her shoulder as if about to say something.

But she turned and left.

What were you going to say, Shelly? Again, his thumb, by reflex, reaches for thc shunt button that is no longer there.

Consuelo punches a new date into the sphere.

"Turn it off!" He whirls around and lunges for the control.

She retreats into the hallway, slamming the bedroom door behind her. "Look at the screen, Wynn," she pleads from the other side of the door.

He spins around.

Staring at the screen, unsure whether this is last week, last month or any time since the Shunter arrived three months ago, he sees himself sitting in a dark room.

Face unshaven, hair uncombed, he was transfixed by the flickering images unreeling on the screen. He hit the shunt button while his onscreen image dove off of the ship.

How many times has he done that?

A pained expression etched itself across his face when he saw that he had hit the water and emerged unscathed. He hit rewind and replay, again pressing shunt while his screen image was in mid-dive. This time he crashed face-first into the water. Bernie laughed in the background on the screen-within-the-screen. "What'd I tell you? Belly flop!" Shelly laughed. Wynn pushed the buttons. Rewind, replay and shunt. The landing smoothed out this time. Bernie jumped up and down. "Sorry, Shelly! That's a perfect ten!" he shouted.

Wynn stares into his own crazed, hungry, bloodshot eyes.

Rewind, replay, shunt. The window to unlived lives opened and shut, opened and shuts. Rewind, replay, shunt. He hit the buttons frantically, furiously. Each time the dive varied but always—always—the screen-within-the-screen Wynn emerged uninjured. Each time he was safe. Each time he was whole.

His mind tumbling as if in freefall, Wynn turns away from the Shunter and moves toward the doorway. He opens the door.

Consuelo has left the control sphere lying on the hallway floor. He strains to pick it up. Looking back into the room, he flings it with all his might at the hideous image on the wallscreen.

It strikes and rebounds harmlessly, bouncing back toward his chair, buttons randomly pressing—"forward," "replay," "shunt"—as it rolls. He glances down at the new date on the sphere—yesterday's date—and the wallscreen image shimmers.

Wynn sat on the sand, a blanket over his legs. He and Consuelo lounged outside of his complex on the Cannon Beach shore. A cupcake with a birthday candle that leaned perilously to the right lay next to a pile of sandwiches. Consuelo wore jeans and a buttoned sweater, her dark hair falling past her shoulders. She held the sandwich to his mouth and he took a big bite out of it.

"Now this, you have to admit, is above and beyond the call of duty," she laughed. Her eyes sparkled and she smiled broadly.

"One second, please." He swallowed and held her wrists in place, keeping the sandwich within biting distance. "Aren't you in fact being compensated for ensuring that I'm taken care of, well-fed..."

"...self-sufficient..." She laughed.

"...bathed, clothed..."

"I thought you said you didn't want to be treated like an infant?"

"I've had a drastic change of heart."

They both laughed and he pulled her toward him. She brushed crumbs off the corners of his mouth.

Wynn feels his heart skip.

A wave crashed against the shore in the background.

He stares intently as they finish their lunch.

Consuelo walked beside him, leaving footprints in the wet sand as his floater-chair hovered alongside her. The sun sat on the horizon and their shadows stretched far behind them.

"See? I told you that a change of scenery would do wonders for your mood," she said. "I have to ask you something. In those other realities, Wynn, did you ever go back to school? Did you ever rejoin the project?"

He shook his head slowly. "Shelly and I, we take some time off. Take a long trip."

"Hmm. Well, classes start in two months, you know."

"It's funny. I never seriously considered it before. In other realities I never—"

"Enough," she said, putting her index finger to his lips. "Let's stick to this reality, okay?"

"Okay," he said, smiling.

She leaned down and kissed him on the cheek.

Wynn hits "stop."

He wheels himself out of the room, across the apartment, to the balcony where Consuelo stands staring out at the ocean. The sun breaks through an ominous cloud cover. She turns as she hears him approach.

"I'm sorry," she says softly, her watery eyes shining in the bright light. "But what you were doing, Wynn.... It was important work. *Inspiring* work." She brushes her hair out of her eyes. "It's been two years. And you'd made so much progress. Just when you finally started to move on with your life, just when I thought I started to see a glimmer of the old you, the one that was going to make a difference, that Shunter...."

"It's okay. Really." A steady breeze cools his face. "I understand. About the Shunter. It has to go."

Consuelo raises an eyebrow and says nothing.

After a long pause, staring out at the ocean, she notes the freighter's absence. "Do you think it worked, Wynn? Is there any chance for the Pacific?"

"It takes time, Consuelo. We'll just have to wait and see." He squints in the sunshine and stares overhead at the stretch of azure sky opening up between the parting clouds. And then he sees it. A gracefully gliding speck in the distance. A seagull. He blinks and loses sight of it, unsure whether he has imagined it.

Waves lap against the white sands as Wynn and Consuelo, side by side, gaze out at the boundless Pacific, an infinity of possibilities stretching out into the horizon.

Them

In February of 1938, chilling rains came scudding across the bay from the northeast and tried to challenge the high wind gusts for weather dominance. Billy Jonas looked out the oblong porthole of his boat, which rocked and strained against the mooring dock, and cursed. He cursed the weather and his loneliness. He had waited long enough! It was time to get married and he wasn't gonna put it off any longer; but he did. He waited three more months.

In May, 1938, just after a hooligan run when the oily little candle fish came by the hundreds of thousands in a spawning rush that surpassed any other that the villagers could remember, Billy Jonas steered his fishing boat out of the lagoon into the bay to the west of Gilford Island heading toward Alert Bay and Port McNeill. In this port city on Vancouver Island, he boarded a cargo freighter called, *Lady Pat,* sailing for Seattle by way of Nanaimo and Anacortes. Jonas had made arrangements with the cannery people who owned the freighter to work as a deck hand until he reached his destination at Seattle. His reason for the long and tedious trip was to bring home a wife. Billy had been corresponding with a mixed-blood Haida girl named Lorna Swensen for the past eighteen months and had finally asked her to marry him. Lorna Swensen wrote back and said *"Yes"* with the proviso that Billy come to Seattle and *"fetch her back to Gilford Island and the cannery."*

The couple was married in Seattle at the end of the month by a Justice of the Peace. Billy and Lorna honeymooned at the Ballard Saloon; drinking themselves into a state that prevented any attempt at consummation of the marriage. At four a.m. the next morning, a very hungover Billy, and his equally miserable bride, staggered up the gang plank of the cannery company's sister ship, *Venture,* which sailed north on the tide.

The couple couldn't find their assigned bunks and crept bleary-eyed into a cargo hold containing oversized cardboard boxes filled with thousands of shiny empty and lidless salmon cans. They draped themselves over a low stack of boxes and to sleep off their drunk.

In the few day's sail to back to Port McNeill to retrieve

Billy's small fishing boat, the salt air—and the lack of alcohol aboard ship—helped Billy and Lorna to sober up and work for their passage as agreed. Billy polished all the ship's brass twice and Lorna was recruited by the galley cook as a helper.

When they disembarked in Port McNeill, Billy was truly a married man. Mrs. Jonas was happy with her strong, strapping young husband and they smiled at each other a lot. In the small boat harbor Billy did some overhaul work on the inboard of his boat and Lorna netted crabs and caught small bottom fish for their meals. With the boat's rejuvenated motor putting loudly in an acceptable rhythm, the young newly-weds sailed out past Alert Bay across the north end of Johnstone Straight. They turned northeast toward the wide inlet leading around the east side of Gilbert Island to the sheltered bay with its rounded lagoon and the small salmon cannery hidden there. Here they would begin their life together, here they would live and work.

Lorna was no stranger to fishing boats, having grown up next to the small boat harbor in Ballard. She could haul and pick heavy nets, stack crab pots, and hold a tiller in a gale. She was a strong woman for her small size. Her physical strength and her knowledge of life on the water made her a helpful partner to Billy. It couldn't have been a better match; even if it had been arranged by tribal elders.

The young husband was delighted with Lorna in every way but she had one habit that he wished he could change: She called him *Mister* and would not use his real name; not Billy and not Jonas. He was always *Mister* to her. Billy had to admit that she was fair about the use of names, though. Lorna never referred to herself as Lorna or even Mrs. Jonas and certainly not as *"I"* or *"Me"* but instead used the words *"She"* and *"Her"* when talking about herself. Billy finally figured out that this must be the result of her frequent thinking in language of the Haida people before she translated her thoughts and spoke them in English; so he gave up trying to change her speech patterns and let things be as they were.

At dawn of the following day, the boat chugged into the bay where the Portlock Cannery Inc. had located their operations.

Lorna stood on the bridge with Billy. She looked out at the calm lagoon and the reflection of the mountains and giant trees and turned to wrap her arms around Billy's waist. She gave him a squeeze, which forced a gasp of air from his lungs.

"She sure is one happy woman, Mister!" Lorna said. "Yessir! Mister, she gonna like this place and that's for sure the truth. Scenery reminds her of home place, you betcha!"

Billy turned his body in her tight embrace and nuzzled his lips into her copper coloured hair—the gift of a Scandinavian father who still lived in Ballard down in Washington state—and said, "This Mister is one happy fella, too, you betcha!" He inhaled the scent of her long hair. She smelled like fresh Cedar needles and baby oil.

Lorna was happier that afternoon than she had expected to be. The house Billy had leased from the Portlock Cannery Company, Inc. was one of the nicest wood-framed houses the company owned. It stood on the peak of a small knoll at the edge of the town with its back to the biggest thicket of giant trees Lorna had ever seen. The house had a living room with paneled walls, a stone river-rock fireplace and one great big picture window facing the lagoon. The rear wall of this same room faced the forest had a long, narrow, little window about a foot in height and it was placed so high up in the wall that Lorna had to stand on her tip toes to peek out at the hovering dark greenery. The kitchen was typically Canadian, and in fashion of the northland, the largest room in the house.

The cook stove and the heating stove stood at opposite ends in the long kitchen. There was another big window here and Lorna could see up and down the bay with ease. At the rear of the kitchen was a small alcove housing a real washing machine with a double ringer. The machine was a new 1938 model gasoline powered Maytag. Lorna stared at it speechless for a moment before she spoke.

"My goddurn, Mister! You sure gonna spoil her with them new-fangled things like dat there washing machine!" The young Haida bride ran and kissed her husband noisily on the cheek. After a while of inspecting the alcove laundry room, Lorna noticed that the back door to the outside from alcove and kitchen was bolted shut and saw the three heavy two by fours nailed across the thick wooden door portal.

"She thinks this door, him gotta get opened so she can carry out laundry for to hang outside. She don't feel like luggin' no laundry basket clean around the house to get to the back, " Lorna said and jiggled the locked door knob up and down. "Why anybody nail a door shut? It ain't good idea to do that."

"Them two by four planks come off tomorrow morning." Billy laughed. "What else do you want me to do around this place?"

"She thinks you ought to show her the bedroom, Mister, so she can check out the bounce of the bed." Lorna grinned at Billy.

"Which bedroom? We got two in this house, " Billy said.

"The one where she gonna make the love with her husband right now!" Lorna said huskily.

"Maybe since we got two bedrooms we're gonna have to do it twice; once in each room!" Billy laughed and scooped Lorna up in his arms and carried her into the front bedroom and gently lowered her to the bed. "Mattress bouncy enough for you?"

"Goddurn, Mister! You sure got one damn fine bed!" Lorna cooed. "Why don't you come down here beside her and see."

The next morning Lorna was still sleeping soundly with the down quilt pulled up to her chin when the banging noise began. She sat up in bed and took in her surroundings.

"Hey! Mister, is that you a banging around in her kitchen so loud or is it maybe some bear come in this nice house?"

Billy appeared in the doorway of the bedroom, crowbar in one hand and a large iron mallet in the other. He dropped them both to the floor with a loud clang and a thud and strode to the bed. He leaned over and nuzzled his wife's hair. Lorna reached up and put her arms around Billy's neck, pulled him down and kissed him on his ear.

"You better just stop that if you want me to finish my work before I go down to the boat," Billy said.

"She wants to know what work, Mister?" Lorna smiled at Billy.

He kissed her cheek and turned to pick up the tools he had dropped on the floor. "I'm opening a door for you, Darlin'," he said. "I can't have my wife luggin' heavy baskets of wet wash all around the house to get to the new clothesline I just rigged in back of the house." He leaned down and kissed her nose.

"Mister you is something else, she thinks!" Lorna said. "She loves her Mister for sure. She's gotta thank her Mister proper!' Lorna pulled Billy down into the bed and there was no way he would refuse this form of her gratitude; the work on the boat could wait.

The summer sun sneaked over the east ridge of young second growth trees and flooded the single street of the Portlock Cannery town with a warm yellow light that was almost liquid. The honey coloured light flowed, actually, seemed to slide downhill toward the small boat docks where Billy worked at untangling a net. Such brilliant sunlight was a rare luxury in this fog-haunted coast. The thick haze of light coated everything with a dandelion-yellow glaze. Billy looked around at the miracle that was the July sun. He loved summer mornings like this one; perhaps because they were so rare haunted here on the island. Mornings were usually damp, misty and grey affairs with a limited visibility that irked him. Billy was a man who liked to see where he was going and to look back at where he had been. That's why he loved the open water. *You can see free and clear whichever way you look,* he thought. Billy Jonas bent down to his work and finished untangling the last few feet of the set net and stretched it out onto the sun-painted dock that glowed amber and yellow in the light. He straightened up and stretched backward with his hands upon his hips to ease the tension that had built up from bending over for so long a time.

He looked westward along the lagoon to the house on the knoll. Billy saw the smoke rising from the kitchen chimney and guessed that Lorna was boiling water for her washday chores. *That is some wife I fetched from Seattle.* He smiled to himself, crossed the dock and stepped onto the deck of his fishing boat and began to check the myriad cables and winches around him.

In the kitchen of the house on the knoll, Lorna Jonas poured a small bottle of bluing into the simmering wash tub on the big cook stove. With a long hand-carved wooden paddle, she stirred the mixture. When the solution of water and bluing seemed the right shade, Lorna carefully dumped in a dishpan full of white pillow covers and one sheet and stirred them around in the hot, blue, rinse water. Next she hurried to the alcove where the washing machine with its sputtering gasoline engine jerked and bounced. Lorna shut down the throttle switch. After the machine chugged to a gasping stop, she coaxed the dark coloured clothes through the hand-cranked wringer. Through the open back door she could see the flood of yellow sunlight on the young fireweed in the clearing.

It's a good day to hang out her wash, she thinks! Lorna nodded her head to agree with herself. She scooped up the woven wicker basket of damp clothing and walked down the short ramp that took the place of stairs at the back door of the house. The narrow strip of flat land at the top of the knoll had been laboriously cleared of all stumps, spruce and alders by some previous tenant. Lorna could see the mounded earth rectangles and pickets that marked the edges of what had once been someone's vegetable garden. Fireweed, young-green and budding, stood as spiky sentinels on the old, neglected garden plots.

"She thinks this make her a fine 'potater' patch and some cabbage patch, too." Lorna said into the slight breeze that teased the nodding heads of wild celery and fireweed.

She tugged at the wire clothesline Billy had strung between two young hemlocks that grew about five paces apart from one another. The three lines of wire were, to Lorna's assessment, 'plenty roomy' for her small wash. The young Haida woman began hanging up her morning wash. She grabbed a small handful of wooden clothespins from the basket of wet wash and held them in her mouth to free both hands for the work of hanging. She finished in moments and bent to pick up the basket. It was then she saw the tracks on the earth at her feet. With out raising her head, Lorna scanned to the left and right of the tracks she had found and saw more tracks and several large mounds of small oval moose droppings.

"Goddurn! That Mister of hers done built her clothesline over a moose trail," Lorna laughed. "It needs movin' but she can't do it herself." Lorna sighed in resignation, "You betcha some big bull moose is gonna walk down his old trail and carry off her wash in his antlers." Later that afternoon her prediction came true.

Lorna was in the kitchen at noon, flouring up a big hunk of halibut to bake, when the commotion began. She heard a huffing and a snorting then a dull stamping, thudding of hooves on the packed earth. The sound of cracking wooden boards with the metallic screeching of straining nails followed.

"She was right! She done caught her a moose in that clothesline!" Lorna grabbed a broom as she rushed through the alcove and out into the sun-lit yard. A young two year old moose with tender antlers sill in velvet, was wound up in the clothesline wire; the sheets and other laundry flapped wildly as the moose reared and snorted trying to free himself. Every time he lunged, the wires tightened around his sore antlers and he stopped his struggles momentarily.

With his head draped in the wet sheet and his eyes covered, the young bull could not see Lorna approaching him with the broom held high, but he could hear her and reared and kicked more vigorously than before. With a wrenching sound, the cross-bars of the clothesline Billy had nailed to the two trees pulled free. The moose felt the tension on his tender antlers ease and he stood very still; unable to see anything because of the sheet.

The young animal was shaking and quivering in fright. Lorna began a soft-shoe sneak until she was directly behind the young bull. She pulled back her broom and swatted him across the rump with all her might; at the same time screaming, "One damn sunnabitcher moose!" The moose coughed out a startled *HUUUHNN* sound and took off running blindly around the yard with Lorna on his heels swatting the air behind him with her broom. Lorna yelled at the moose, and the louder she yelled, the more panicked the young bull became.

"Look what you're doing to her clean wash, you stupid damn sunnabitcher moose! She gonna have to wash them all over again!"

The shouting and the swatting went on for another three minutes before the now mud and weed-stained sheet caught on one of the dragging cross bars and tore free from the bull's head. He lowered his huge bulbous nose toward the ground, rolled his panic- filled eyes until the whites showed and charged the sheet; antlers on target, front hooves flailing. It was a stroke of luck for the moose. When he bent his head, his flailing hooves caught the wire clothesline and pulled it free from his antlers. He stopped dead still and snorted, as if he felt embarrassed to have been caught in such a predicament, and then turned toward the forest and ran into the brush.

Lorna grubbed in the trampled garden mounds among the flattened fireweed and crushed wild celery plants to find her ruined wash. She managed to salvage everything but one torn sheet. With her soiled wash in the basket, Lorna turned to head back to the laundry alcove door and the washing machine, when she heard the crashing of branches and the dull thud of hooves coming toward her from the woods. She thought the young bull had gotten over his embarrassment and had decided to charge, to run her down her for spite; but this was not the case. The young bull was more terrified than before. Froth of white foam flecks spilled from his mouth and he rolled his eyes as he rushed in a panicked trot across the open clearing and toward the main street of town.

"Something sure scared the hell outta him, she thinks," said Lorna. "And it wasn't her. Whatever had panicked that fool moose has to be out there in the thick trees at the edge of the cleared space of this here back-yard."

The young woman studied the deep forest of tall trees behind her house. She paid close attention to the spot between two massive trunks of giant hemlocks where broken branches hung, still swaying; marking the return path the panicked moose had taken. She saw nothing there and swept the area close by with her eyes. Then, she saw them! Two, dark, hairy forms; barely visible, more like darker shadows in the grey-black shadows of the trees. Lorna held her breath and forced her watering eyes to discern the hulking shapes in the woods. The forms did not move. She blinked her straining eyes and looked again. The creatures were gone. She felt a tinge of movement-stifling fear.

Lorna dropped the laundry basket on the alcove floor with a loud thud and turned to close and lock the back door. She wished the two by four planks were still in place. *Maybe it's because of them things in the woods out there! That's why the people who lived here before put up them bars,* she whispered to herself. *Bears! Them things was bears that tried to pull down that young moose and scared him close to death!*

That night over the baked halibut supper, Lorna sat quietly, too quietly. Billy noticed her behavior and reached across the small round oilcloth covered table and laid his hand over Lorna's.

"What's the matter, Darlin'?" Billy began, "You worried that I'm gettin' tired of eating fish, fish and more fish?"

Lorna looked down at her plate and said nothing. Finally, she shook her head 'No' and withdrew her hand from beneath Billy's. Billy reached out and took her hand again.

"Tell me what's bothering you, Darlin'," he said.

She forced a smile to brighten her face and looked at Billy directly. "Mister, she had to do her wash all over again today, and she still didn't get all the stains out. She almost got herself some moose meat today, too, you betcha."

"What moose? What are you talking about?" Billy asked.

Lorna's mouth widened in a grin that showed her even white teeth. "Mister, you done made her a clothesline direct straight across a moose trail, and a young bull come and claimed her wash and dragged it around on his new horns. You gonna have to put that clothesline running the other way so moose ain't gonna steal her washing every laundry day."

Billy raised his eyebrow, put a questioning look on his face and waited for Lorna's explanation. The young wife described the moose entangled with a sheet and how he had torn down the clothesline in his panic. Billy laughed long and hard. His eyes filled with tears when Lorna told him of chasing the moose, blind-folded by the sheet, around the yard with a broom.

"Her sheet got all torn," Lorna said. "She plans to make dish drying towels out of it now. Maybe, Mister have to go to Port McNeill this month to buy her some new sheets."

"Oh, we can do without sheets for a while." Billy said.

"How did she know that's what he was gonna say?" Lorna grinned at her husband and reached across the table and playfully pinched his hand. "Mister, you want some rhubarb pie she made special?"

"There's only on thing I ever want more than pie," Billy

grinned and gave Lorna a meaningful wink.

"Then, it's pie first," Lorna returned the wink and added a suggestive little smile.

The young couple ate their pie in the front room by the firelight. Billy and Lorna sat facing each other on two cushions they had pulled from the sofa and pushed up close to the smoldering coals in the fireplace. Lorna set her plate down beside her on the wooden floor and stared intently at the amber glow of the dying flames.

"What's bothering you now, Darlin'?" Billy asked.

Lorna looked up at her husband through the cascade of copper coloured hair that had fallen across her eyes. She brushed her hair back, cleared her throat with a small coughing sound and turned to Billy.

"Mister, us got bears! She saw two of them right there by the big trees outside the back door. They didn't run when they saw her; so she thinks maybe them is dangerous bears."

"You sure you saw them? " Billy spoke softly, trying not to show he doubted her.

"She saw two big hairy things, and she could feel they was a lookin' right back at her," Lorna answered in a firm tone. "What else is big and hairy in these woods 'cept but bears?"

Billy didn't answer her but toyed with his fork in the pie crust crumbs on his plate.

"She thinks maybe the folks what lived here before us put them bars on the back door to keep out the bears. That's what she thinks."

Billy set his empty pie plate down and lifted Lorna's chin with his forefinger and thumb so he could study her face. "You want me to put them back up?"

Lorna nodded 'yes' and leaned into Billy's arms. She snuggled against his chest and he smelled the cedar and baby oil scent of her hair. "Maybe, Mister, you could fix them bars on the door so she can drop them in place from the inside. So she will feel safe when her Mister is out fishing or fooling around with his boat down at the dock?"

"Yes," he said. Billy's voice was low and comforting to Lorna. She leaned into his arms and kissed him. Her desire for him was all too evident in that kiss. Billy pulled her to him and matched her ardor; kiss for kiss.

Later they laughed together as they retrieved their clothing; scattered among the bits of pie crust and pie plates on the floor by the fireplace.

Billy had the welder at the cannery fashion six big iron square-shaped U-brackets that he bolted to the thick back door frame; three on each side exactly eighteen inches apart.

He sanded down three sturdy four-by-fours he'd cut long enough to reach across the width of the door. They could be dropped into place in the U-brackets with ease.

"These may not keep a brownie out if he wants to get in bad enough," Billy said. "But they sure as hell gonna slow him down until I can put a bullet or two into his eyes."

"How's about she keeps one of Mister's big guns hanging on the wall by the back door, just in case a grizzly comes callin' and Mister ain't to home?"

Billy agreed and the next day he installed a gun rack for his powerful rifle above the alcove entrance. He also re-rigged the clothesline away from the old moose trail that had been used for countless years by generations of moose crossing the clearing behind the house on the knoll. A trail he hadn't given his attention before.

Days and then weeks passed without incident. Lorna hung out her wash every laundry day and never lost another piece of wash to the wandering moose. However, she kept her eyes open, and her senses were always on the alert. She scanned the edge of the woods frequently for signs of the bears, but never saw any.

Still she felt uneasy and restless whenever she was out back of the house. She gave up the idea of a potato garden and cabbage plants because she felt little shivers of something she couldn't or didn't want to call fear whenever she stepped out of the back door. She scolded herself and said to herself that she was being silly but still the feelings persisted. There were some laundry days when she felt; no, she *knew* she was being watched from the shadows of the forest but when she looked for whatever was watching her, she saw nothing.

Since Lorna had convinced herself that these little terror tremors she felt when out back of the house were unreasonable and silly, she did not speak of them to her husband. But many times he returned to the house to find the back door barred and the big rifle out of its rack and leaning against the kitchen wall. Billy didn't want to chide his wife for her precautions, so he pretended not to notice and said nothing to Lorna.

Life at the Portlock Cannery was pleasant and, at times, downright fun. Lorna discovered that Billy Jonas was related in some way or other to more than half the people in the cannery town. She made friends with his cousins and aunts, and these relatives visited frequently.

During the summer when the cannery was going at full throttle, there was little time for visiting. And when a big catch of salmon came in, everyone in town' who was able to work, pitched in to help get the salmon pack out.

During the long damp winters, usually milder than those in most of northern British Columbia, life slowed down. The constant fall of rain or heavy wet snow made for treacherous walking to the post office and to the dining hall of the cannery where imported 16 mm American movies were shown every Friday and Saturday nights. Lorna always braved the slush and the ice to get a chance to see Tyrone Power and Errol Flynn as they swash-buckled through some historic epic. She liked Dick Powell and Myrna Loy, too, and never missed a "Thin Man" picture. Lorna like the murder mysteries better than anything. She didn't care for the Shirley Temple movies but went to watch them just the same. Lorna referred to the dimpled actress as the 'curly haired midget' even though she knew the actress was *somebody's* little blond-ringletted child.

If the weather turned really bad and the mail-boat couldn't bring in the movies, people in the Portlock Cannery town turned to cribbage and pinochle games for their entertainment. The long winter passed with sing-alongs, mini-potlatches and even square dancing on occasion. Lorna and Billy hosted a big potluck dinner one snowy night in March of 1939. It was a chilly, wet snowfall that Saturday night, and the one long street of the cannery town was treacherous with slush. The guests braved the weather and came anyway; bringing kettles, pots and skillets of foods they had prepared. Lorna suddenly discovered the smell of all that food made her sick to her stomach. She couldn't eat anything that night. She tried to eat all the next week but couldn't really keep any thing down. Billy's old aunt diagnosed the problem and said simply, "Honey, you're pregnant... 'bout three or so months is my guess."

Olaf Johnnie Jonas was born September 15, 1939, at five thirty in the morning in the cannery town of the Portlock Company on Gilford Island, British Columbia, Canada.

He was a healthy baby, possessed of strong lungs, a loud wail and enough energy for two babies. Lorna and Billy and all the cousins and aunts doted on the child. The reason for all the attention paid to Lorna's baby was that Johnnie was the first child to be born in the cannery town for several years. He was, therefore, a favorite of all the townsfolk and cannery workers; related to him, or not.

Baby Johnnie made it through his first winter, an unusually cold one with heavy snows, without a sniffle or a cough. He was alert, bright and inquisitive. He knew just how to manipulate his parents and hovering aunties. Johnnie, his mother and father, and all his relatives were unaware of the role he would play in the future of Portlock Cannery town.

In the spring of 1940, the heavy snow-melt began to cascade down from the mountains and sweep into the lagoon, carrying all sorts of debris in its flood. Lorna was standing at the front room window, holding seven month old Johnnie in her arms watching the rushing torrent. The tumble of water carried clumps of torn away pieces of fern-covered creek banks and sometimes, shattered tree limbs or long, log-snags. These great log pieces rose to the surface, breached and lurched down again under the swift rush of current, like prehistoric water creatures.

Suddenly, she saw the corpse of a mountain sheep, with huge curled horns, rolling and shifting in the roiling water. Just behind it came another sheep's corpse and then another. She watched the bodies swinging around in the speeding current. She noted their progress as they were swept into the quieter waters of the lagoon. She followed them with her eyes and took mental notes on the place where the three stiff-legged forms bobbed in the quiet backwaters. She was impatient to tell Billy about the three dead sheep. Lorna knew Billy would want to retrieve the twice-curved horns for the money they would bring in Port McNeill, Prince Rupert or even Nanaimo. When Billy came in from the boat for his lunch she told him about the sheep bodies in the lagoon.

Her husband ate quickly, hurried to his skiff and rowed out to the lagoon to pull the sheep corpses to shore. The cold of the high mountains and the icy water had preserved the bodies well and there was no serious decay, as yet. But there was something more.

He snagged the sheep bodies with a halibut gaff and pulled them to his boat. The young man saw the animals' heads bobbing in the wash at a right angle to their bodies. It seemed to Billy each sheep had been killed with a hundred-eighty degree twist of the neck. The carcasses were ripped open at the belly and crudely dressed out. Their stomach and chest cavities were empty of all entrails.

Billy saw that the animals' throats literally had been torn out, not slashed, as by a hunter's knife to drain the blood of a kill. The young man of the woods was no stranger to the hunt and no stranger to the forms of predatory death that lurked in the woods, but this form of killing was something different. The bodies of the sheep were mutilated but not in the way a bear or a wolf pack would kill and mutilate. Billy had never seen anything like this before.

He severed the heads of the two large male animals and tossed them into his skiff. He made mental plans to remove the skull and horns when time permitted. The third sheep was an old ewe with small prong-like horns that Billy could not sell, so he left the corpse intact. He lashed the three floating bodies together to forma a raft of the carcasses.

Carefully skirting the in-rushing mountain current, Billy started the outboard motor and towed the sheep carcasses out into the bay where the tide would carry them out to sea and to the scavengers who would deal with them.

The talk around the cannery the next day was about Billy's good fortune. Billy had sent a telegram through cannery telegraph system to Peter Bading at Jonas Brothers Furs in Prince Rupert and the answering telegram had offered him $125 for the pair of horns and skulls. Of course the telegraph operator told everyone at the cannery about the telegram from Prince Rupert and some folks even knew about the money before Billy and Lorna.

Billy's cousins, Andy Petroff and his brother Fedor, sat down with Billy at the kitchen table that same afternoon and asked all sorts of questions. Andy wanted to know where Billie thought the sheep had come from. Fedor asked if Billy thought there might be good sheep hunting at the source of the mountain cataract since the sheep had been washed down from somewhere up there. Andy suggested that the three of them go up mountain and get some more horns if they sold at that high a price. Billy reminded the brothers that it wasn't sheep season and besides they had cannery work and couldn't go. The two Brothers Petroff said to hell with hunting seasons and work at the cannery and that they were going inland for a sheep hunt as soon as possible.

On the following Friday afternoon Lorna looked at her corner of the world through the double-pane thermal windows of her house on the knoll. She rocked easily and smoothly; keeping a constant rhythm in the old walnut wood rocker Billy had found in a Port McNeill pack-rat's junk store. Billy repaired the rocker for her and Johnnie. The baby loved the rocking and slept against her shoulder with his head cradled in the curve of her neck. Every so often little Johnnie would exhale a great sighing breath and Lorna could feel his tiny body shudder against her chest as he inhaled a new breath to replace the one he had so enthusiastically released. She pushed against the floor with her moccasined feet and rocked steadily. She felt herself wanting to surrender to the warmth of the overheated house and the motion. With effort she forced her eyes open and searched the dock and the area of beach framed by the large picture window.

Lorna saw Billy working on the deck of his boat with a stiff bristled broom scrubbing away fish slime and salt. She glanced to the right of the boat dock and saw Fedor and Andy Petroff pull up along side Billy's fishing boat in their fourteen foot skiff. Lorna couldn't hear the outboard motor or the sounds the boats made as they rolled, rubbed and creaked in their slips. It was like watching a silent movie. She saw Fedor and Andy hold up their rifles for Billy to see and she saw the two Petroff boys gesticulating and pointing inland toward the high mountains behind the cannery. She saw Billy hand the brothers a coil of thick hemp rope which Fedor shoved into a already bulging mountaineer's back-pack and then saw Billy shake his head 'no' and give them a wave off signal.

Lorna watched the Brothers Petroff turn their skiff out toward the bay. The brothers turned to wave at Billy just before they headed up the lagoon to the trail-head to the mountains. Lorna followed the boat with her eyes until it disappeared beyond the frame of her front room's picture window. Little Johnnie squirmed against her shoulder and made fussy baby noises. Lorna stopped rocking and changed his position in her arms.

"Hey Little Mister, she thinks mebbe you had yourself a little accident." Lorna said. "You sure smell like you had one big something in your diapers."

Lorna held the baby away from her. "She thinks she ought to take you over to the couch and check you out." Lorna stood to move toward the couch when she saw Billy's lithe form move across the picture window toward the front door. "She thinks your Mister Daddy is come home to see her and the baby. So we better get you cleaned up fast like."

In the front entryway, Billy pulled off his rubber knee-high boat boots and padded into the living room in thick woolen stockings.

"I was gonna ask you to make me a sandwich but seeing you're busy with little Johnnie Jonas' butt cleaning, I think I'd rather make it myself." Billy said.

"She thinks it's about time you got yerself used to baby's dirty butts and learned how to change a diaper." Lorna teased. "The day's a comin', Mister, when you're gonna have to change the baby, like it or not, she says."

Billy padded off to the kitchen ignoring Lorna's remark. He rolled back the lid on the bread-box and began to cut thick slices from the homemade loaf.

Lorna called to him from the front room. "She knows it probably ain't any of her business, but her curiosity cat is halfway dead anyways so she's just gonna up and ask it. What did them two Petroffs want?"

Billy took a bite out of cold moose roast sandwich he had slathered with mustard and spoke with his mouth full. "Andy wanted to borrow a rope line in case one of the sheep they planned to shoot tumbled into a gully and they had to fish it out."

"She probably shouldn't say it but she's gonna say it anyways. Them Petroffs is nuts thinking they can shoot down some sheep without the Provincial Park Ranger boys or the Conservation Officers finding out about it," Lorna grunted. "Crazy to go up there this time of year anyways."

"They asked me to go with them and I told them no," Billy said and took another bite of his sandwich. "They said they'd be back by Sunday noon and to keep an eye on their skiff they tied up at the trail head. I told them I would."

Billy finished his lunch, downed two cups of black coffee that he turned into a syrup-thick mixture with too much sugar and went back to tend to his boat cleaning. Lorna finally jiggled a freshly diapered Johnnie Jonas to sleep in her arms and put him down for a nap. She returned to her household chores and started mixing a new batch of sourdough bread.

Her schedule was the same now and she was comfortable with it. Friday, bake and make bread. Saturday, shop at the company store and watch two movies every Saturday night. On Sunday she mended and patched or sewed for little Johnnie. Monday was washday, but now, so was Tuesday and Wednesday and Thursday since the baby came. The diapers she washed seemed endless and the clothesline out back, or the one she strung across the kitchen on rainy days, was never empty of the flapping white squares.

The movies were good ones the next Saturday night. The first was a Doris Day picture. Lorna liked the movie but she didn't care for Doris Day. "She thinks that blonde lady got a few too many teeth," she told Billy, while the operator changed the film reels. The second was a zombie picture with Boris Karloff and Lorna pulled her baggy sweater up over her eyes at the scariest parts. After the movie she made Billy carry the baby so she could cling to Billy's arm as they walked home. Billy tried to scare her with shadows and kept asking, "What's that?!" Pretending to see something in the shadows.

Lorna finally told him, "Mister, you better knock it off or she's gonna slug you."

That night she snuggled close to Billy. Something in the zombie movie caused her to remember the feelings of being watched when she went back of the house to hang out her wash. There was a little piece of fear, cold like ice, forming at the base of her spine and that icy fear kept trying to creep up higher; chilling her inside. That night Lorna dreamed of watching eyes; shiny, glistening, dark eyes that glittered in dark faces and the faces were on hairy bodies that moved silently to sit in a threatening circle and watch her. In her nightmare the dark-faced hairy creatures stared and stared but made no sounds. The creatures moved closer to her. One of them held out a huge hairy arm and touched her with leathery fingers. In her dream, Lorna jumped backward at the touch .

Lorna opened her eyes jolted awake by the realness of her nightmare. She lay quiet, trembling as she stared into the grey dimness of the bedroom. Billy snored beside her. She looked at the alarm clock. The dial glowed faintly in the shadowy corner of the room on the dresser. It was 6:24. The sound of water dripping from the eaves filled the silence of what was a drizzling Sunday morning. The house was damp and cold.

Lorna felt cold even beneath the quilts and comforters pressing down against her shivering body. She forced herself to acknowledge that most of the chill she felt was the result of the terror of her dreams. Still shivering from physical and psychological chills she forced herself from the bed. Her feet slipped into the warm fur-lined sealskin moccasin slippers at her bedside. She pulled on her baggy sweater and a heavy woolen robe and slipped quietly from the bedroom and into the long kitchen. As she moved past the washing machine's alcove she caught a movement from the corner of her eye. She swung her head instantly in the direction of the small glass window set in the barred door.

She saw the glitter of two black eyes peering through the thick pane of glass directly into her own. Droplets of moisture from the incessant drizzle slid down over the glass pane. Lorna blinked involuntarily as the ice-fear shot up her spine to her brain. She looked at the fogging pane of glass in the door and saw it was empty. No eyes stared into hers. Nothing was there. She took a hesitant step toward the alcove, reached up, picked up Billy's rifle and pushed the bolt forward. She heard the large caliber bullet slide into the chamber. Her entire body shook as she forced herself forward to look out into the grey morning fog and the drizzling rain through the small glass window. Her heart leaped in her chest and echoed in loud thudding noises in her ears. She slid her moccasined feet forward as silently as she could. She reached the window glass and peered out.

The world outside the glass was grey; everything was grey and in motion. The gusts of wind forced the rainy mist to blow sideways. The drenched alders and willows at the foot of the bluff writhed in slow motion in the rain. Lorna strained to see through the misty glass. The larger trees on the ridge above were dark grey shadows. Their dead lower branches reached down toward the little house on the knoll like the hands of grasping giants. Water dripped from the needled branches to slide down the bare dead limbs like thin, grey blood. The witches' hair tree-moss hung in long, dank ringlets and gave some of the snags and deadfalls a monster-like appearance.

Lorna shifted her gaze to the clothesline then to one of the twin the trees where the cross bar was nailed. Her throat closed and she could not scream. Something was there. The outline of the tree was wrong. It was thicker and bulkier. Lorna knew instantly that something stood directly behind the tree in the grey fog and pre-dawn light. The thick trunk of the tree masked its shape but did not hide it completely. Her effort to scream or call for Billy was thwarted by the dryness of her throat. Her terrified body had reacted with ancient primitive animal instincts. Before she was totally aware of what she saw out there in the rain, her brain knew. Her body responded to a hidden ancestral warning. She wanted to run from the thing in the grey drizzling rain. Her body tingled, the hairs on her arms moved as if alive, her scalp crawled and the muscles of her face twitched. She drew her breath in quick sharp gasps and smelled her own fear. Never before had she known such terror.

Lorna backed away from the barred door but kept her eyes on the dark shadowy bulk that hid so ineffectively behind the clothesline tree. Then it moved. A great dark shape detached from the tree and crossed the clearing and the garden area in three strides. It was huge. Lorna could see its bulky form was tall; higher than the six-foot clothesline. She stared; eyes open and filling with tears. She blinked to force the vision-blurring tears away. When she focused on the spot where the dark thing had last been there was nothing. Lorna's mind refused to accept what her Haida soul recognized.

Suddenly Lorna felt drunk; drunk and sick to her stomach. The adrenaline her instincts had pumped into her body coursed through her veins. Her stomach contracted and filled her mouth with a bitter fluid. She could not control her arms and legs. The first dawn light seemed to dim back to grey. The gun slid from her hands. She heard the sound of the heavy rifle hitting the floor as if from far away. She slid to the floor in a fetal position and spit bile on the alcove floor. Her eyelids fluttered involuntarily as the dim grey of morning turned into blackness streaked with tiny flashes of incandescent light.

"Honey! My God, Honey! What is it? Are you all right? Honey! Honey?"

Billy's voice sounded as if he were somewhere in a deep hole shouting up at her. Lorna listened to his desperate words. "Lorna, Darlin', say something! What happened?"

She struggled to answer him but the blackness came back and the little lights flashed in front of her eyes. She felt Billy lift her up and carry her to the kitchen table. He laid her out on the table's hard, wooden surface and began to stroke her forehead and pull the damp hair away from her face.

Lorna lifted her arm with great effort and laid her hand on Billy's arm.

"She's alright now, she just fainted fer a minute."

"You! You fainted? Are you hurt? Did you hurt yourself when you fell on the gun?" Billy whispered.

Lorna moved her head back and forth in a slow negative

gesture. She tried to raise herself from the table, but Billy forced her down gently.

"You stay there. I'm gonna get a washcloth and clean you up a bit before I carry you into the front room so you can rest up on the couch." Billy ordered gently. "Then I want you to tell me what the hell happened!"

Billy listened in silence, then a moments later gave his own explanation, "Moose, a damned moose, that's what you saw!" Billy was adamant. "They will look into a house through a window. I know that for sure. Saw one staring back at me once when I looked out the window. I was about four years old, but I remember it. Scared the bejeezus outta me!"

Lorna sat up from the pile of pillows Billy had placed behind her. She tried to think *moose;* tried to force that well-known animal's form into the dark shape she had seen standin, hiding, behind the clothesline tree. It was true, as Billy pointed out, that a moose was the only animal around Portlock that stood taller than the six-foot clothesline.

Billy argued it couldn't have been a bear, "Because a bear on all fours isn't six feet at the shoulders. Standing up maybe, sure; but a bear does not walk across the back yard clearing on his hind legs to make himself taller than six feet! Circus bear, maybe! But I don't think we've got any of them here in Portlock Cannery."

Lorna knew Billy was trying to lighten the somber mood; make jokes of the terror she had known just minutes before. She appreciated it.

Billy handed her a second cup of strong tea he had brewed while she rested.

"Are you feeling better now, Darlin'?" he asked and took her free hand between his. Lorna smiled over the brim of the teacup and nodded 'yes' at her husband.

"She thinks she was still having a nightmare when she got out of bed, Mister." Lorna said quietly. "But she would sure like to have her Mister inspect the back yard for tracks if this rain ever stops today."

"Did you take a look at them low hanging clouds?" Billy moved to the big window and peered out into the heavy drizzle.

"By the time this rain stops the back yard will be a mud-hole and any tracks left out there will be long gone; washed flat and gone."

He continued to look out across the bay and the lagoon area. The lead grey sky and the lead grey water met on the horizon line and became one. The wind began to pick up and herd fog patches across the water's surface and chase them with slanting wind-driven arrows of rain. Lorna reclined on the couch beneath a knitted afghan and sipped her tea. Billy stood at the window watching the lagoon. Baby Johnnie slept on in his bedroom crib. The sound of the rain came and went with the wind gusts. The mantle clock ticked loudly in the early morning silence inside the house on the knoll.

A loud "Well, I'll be damned!" from Billy echoed in the front room. "Here comes trouble with a capital 'T' or maybe I should say here comes some bragging with a capital 'P' as in Petroff!"

Lorna threw the afghan aside and, wobbling a bit and unsteady on her feet, crossed to Billy and looked out of the big window with him. She saw the Petroff brothers' skiff pulling up to their dock. She watched Andy throw the tie lines to Fedor and saw the pair of them lug two bulging burlap sacks out onto the dock.

Andy looked up at the house and saw Billy in the window. He waved from the dock and held his hands over his head clasped together in a boxer's symbol of victory. The Petroff brothers started climbing up the many steps to the house on the knoll. Lorna could see the wide grins on their rain-slicked faces.

"Must have had themselves some luck on their sheep hunt, Mister." Lorna said and turned away from the window. "They'll be wanting breakfast and some hot coffee she thinks. So, she better get some clothes on and start fixing things."

Billy crossed to Lorna and took her in his arms. He kissed her on the nose and then on each cheek. "Are you sure you feel up to cooking right now?"

"Mister, she's fine now. She's all over her scare and she don't plan to have any nightmares again for a year." Lorna kissed Billy's neck and pulled away and hurried to the bedroom to dress for the day.

Billy sat back in his rocker and listened to Andy and Fedor talking loudly and excitedly about their good luck in the mountains. The two brothers stood in front of the fireplace drying their rain soaked clothing. Their flannel-lined jeans steamed in the heat and the smell of wet woolen jackets gave off a sheep-shed smell that wafted unpleasantly about the front room. Lorna called the three men to the kitchen area and showed them their places at the round oak table. They attacked their breakfast of sourdough pancakes, spam and eggs. Between bites, Andy or Feodor talked on. Often interrupting each other.

"Didn't have to fire a shot and got three sheep—good horns, too!"

"They was just laid out for us. All we had to do was skin out the capes and bring back the skulls and horns."

Feodor added to Andy's remarks, "Worth lots a money!" The younger Petroff brother poured syrup on his eggs and Lorna looked away in disgust.

"What do you mean, Mister Petroff, that they was all laid out for you?" Lorna sat down across the table from Andy and pulled her chair closer to Billy's, trying to ignore the mixture of egg yolks and syrup on Feodor's plate.

"There was at least six sheep carcasses up there just below the timberline...." Andy began.

"All gutted out and wedged into the branches of trees about eight or ten feet off the ground." Fedor interrupted. "Three of them was ewes so we took only the big horns."

The younger Petroff grinned and took a big slurping drink of coffee from a thick china mug.

"Sounds to me like you boys stumbled on to some poacher's cache," Billy mused. "Whoever it was that poached them sheep is not gonna be happy about what you boys did." Lorna patted Billy's arm as if agreeing with him and turned to Andy with a question.

"How did you find them, Misters?" she asked.

Fedor shoved a large hunk of pancake into his mouth and set down his fork. He chewed and talked; then chewed and talked some more.

"Heck, Miss Lorna, we couldn't miss them. The smell led us

right to them."

Billy and Lorna looked at each other and then back at the two Petroff brothers across the table.

"What smell?" Billy asked.

Andy put down his knife and fork, took a swig of coffee, wiped his chin with the back of his shirt-sleeve and started his story.

"It was like this. We worked our way up the ridge trail over the saddle-back and down through Ptarmigan pass 'til we could see the high peaks. There's still a lot of snow up there and it was colder'n Billie-hell. The run-off's mighty fierce and the streams is all bank full—crashin' and foamin' and spittin' spray all the way down to the head of the lagoon."

Lorna and Billy nodded simultaneously, showing they were anxious for Andy to get on with his tale.

"Well, up where the big trees start to thin out and the runts take over just below timberline, there's this great big boulder in the trail. That's where we caught a whiff of this awful stink."

"It was a terrible smell." Fedor jumped in. "The smell of dead things and something else!"

Lorna sat up straight in her chair and inclined her head toward Fedor, "Mister Petroff, what you mean, *smell of death and somethin' else*? She wants to know?"

Andy Petroff answered for his brother, "Simple. The place smelled like dead things. It's cold up there at night and things stay frozen, but durin' the day and with these rains thawin' things out, some of the sheep and the marmots are startin' to smell a little, well actually, them dead, little pika-marmots; they stink to high heaven."

This time Billy sat up straight in his chair and stared at Andy, "What the hell are you boys talking about? Marmots? You mean them little rock-rabbits, the pikas, is that what was stinking up the place?"

"Most of the stink was that, you betcha!" Fedor said loudly. "'Bout a hundred of them little pikas was shoved up in the trees. Wedged tight in the forks of branches like furry little Christmas packages stuck on a big Christmas tree."

Lorna poured everyone another cup of coffee. As she filled Andy's cup she asked him a question. "Mister Petroff, who would do such a thing? The sik-sik-puks, the pikas, what ever you care to call them marmots, is good for making parkas and that's about all. Why would any body stick all those good skins up in a tree to go to waste and ruin, she wants to know?"

"Somebody thinks they're awful good eating, I guess, 'cause there was bones and bits of empty hides scattered around the base of the trees," Andy explained. "Anyway as I was saying, it was the smells that led us to the sheep. We just plain lucked out."

"I'll never forget them smells, long as I live," Fedor put in. "It wasn't just the smell of dead things alone. Like we said, there was that other stink, too. Remember, Andy, you remarked on it first?" Andy nodded his head. Fedor went on. "It was like the stench of half a dozen skunks mixed in with about five gallons of tom-cat piss."

"Hell we got used to the stink in a hurry when we saw those big sets of horns on them mountain sheep," Andy laughed and Fedor joined him.

They stopped laughing when Billy asked, "What do you boys think could make a stench like that? That ain't a bear's smell you're describin'. They smell like walking garbage cans most of the time, or rotting salmon. What kind of animal smells that bad, I'd like to know."

There was silence around the table. Neither of the brothers had an answer for Billy. Lorna rose quietly from her chair and began to clear the table. The little spot of fear was chilling the base of her spine again.

Billy pulled out a pack of Craven-A cigarettes and offered a smoke to the Petroff brothers. Lorna let the stack of breakfast plates clatter into the sink. She had heard that smell, that stench, described exactly like that by someone once before. But who had described it? She couldn't track the person down in the recesses of her brain. When she tried again to remember who and when, the chill-ice of fear touch tingled in her spine and threatened to spiral upwards. She heard Fedor speak.

"We want you to come with us, Billy. We're going back up Monday morning if the rain quits. You gotta see them marmots stuck in the trees."

"We got it figured that some old poacher from over the other side of the mountains has found a mountain-sheep mother-load up there. Hell, Billy, those sheep that got washed down from the mountain plus the ones we found makes almost a dozen sheep. There's bound to be a bigger flock of sheep up there just above timberline. What do you say?"

"My Mister says no thank you!" Lorna moved quickly to stand behind Billy and placed her hands on his shoulders as if to hold him down in the kitchen chair. "She don't want her man to go up there and she will be mad as hell if he even thinks about it."

Billy looked up at Lorna and smiled, "This mister ain't goin' up to the mountain and get shot by the fella that poached all them sheep." Billy stood up as if to end the conversation, "You boys ought to forget about it, too."

"Poachin' from a poacher seems a real dangerous business to her," Lorna said.

Andy and Fedor stubbed out their smokes and stood up together. They reached across the table and both men shook hands with Billy and then Lorna.

"Well, Billy," Fedor said, "It's your loss. Them city fellas in Prince Rupert or Nanaimo will pay good money for mountain sheep horns, whether they is poached, shot or drowned or what not."

Lorna watched Billy walk Andy and Fedor to the entryway. The brothers put on their wool mackinaws, hefted the two bags of sheep heads they'd left on the porch stoop and started down the steps to the dock. "Good Luck!" Billy shouted after them. Lorna watched the two brothers load the burlap sacks of heads and horns into their skiff.

"She thinks they gonna need more than luck; probably prayers too," Lorna said under her breath. She thought of the stench they'd described and the fear came back.

This time the memory came with the fear; a memory of when she was a little girl of maybe, four or five. Her mother's brothers from the Alaskan Kaigani Haida had come visiting, bringing some winter meat for her family. One night, around the kitchen, table by lantern light, the uncles told of encountering a stinking hairy beast up near the timberline. They described it as huge, walking erect and smelling like cat urine. When one of her uncles stood up on a kitchen stool to show how tall the beast had been, he held out his arms in a menacing gesture and pawed the air. The uncle sitting next to her screamed out a shrill wavering sound which frightened Lorna to tears. Her mother had to hold her for a long time before Lorna calmed down. Her mother said it was a cannibal giant, like those in the old stories, a Sasquatch, what white folks called 'Big-foot'. She told Lorna not to be frightened because they didn't have any of those things living close to the city of Seattle and especially not in the Ballard area.

Standing with her back to the kitchen sink, Lorna trembled. She tried to focus on her kitchen, her chores and her husband to allay the fear taking control. She watched Billy stir canned milk into his coffee. The memory of her childhood fright and the chilling fears she associated with the memory still swept over her. She knew, now, what she had seen in the morning mist, grey fog and slanting rain. The thing trying to conceal itself behind the clothesline tree was one of *them!* It was one of those cannibal giants of Northwest Coast lore. The chilling fear jiggled up Lorna's spine. Her scalp tingled.

There may not have been any of the beasts around Ballard or Seattle when she was little, but they were up here around the cannery town. Lorna wanted to scream out her fears and run to Billy. She wanted to tell him the Petroff brothers must have stumbled into the lair of the beasts; found their winter food cache. Billy wouldn't believe her. He would just tease her and say she was silly to scare herself so, and that such things didn't really exist.

He had always made fun of the old, Indian ways of his people and dismissed the stories and legends about monsters, cannibal giants, koostakah and such. Lorna turned to the sink and pretended to sort the silverware. It took a lot of doing, but she forced calm into herself and her voice.

Without turning to look at Billy directly she spoke in calm, slow tones, "Billy?"

Billy sat upright. It was the first time she'd called him Billy! He knew something was truly bothering her. "What, Darlin'?"

"Billy, she wants you to promise her somethin'."

"Just say what it is and I'll promise." Billy stood and crossed to stand next to Lorna.

"Promise her that you'll never go with them fool Petroff cousins of yours up into the high places by the timberline. Say you'll never go hunting after them sheep they think is up there!"

"Darlin', there's nothin' up there in them mountains that me and my 30/30 can't handle." Billy stood behind Lorna and enveloped her in his arms. "There ain't no Indian Boogie man out there—if that's what you think you saw." He felt Lorna stiffen in his embrace.

"Mister, promise her," Lorna whispered.

"But, Honey there's nothing up there—"

"Just say it! Promise her!" Lorna whirled around and threw her arms around Billy's waist and clung to him fiercely. "Promise! Promise!"

"All right! All right, Darlin', I promise." Billy let his chin rest against the top of Lorna's head and wrapped his arms around her. "What's got you so worked up now?"

"Nothin' a little lovin' won't fix." Lorna slid her hand into the opening between two buttons of Billy's shirt and gave him a playful pinch.

"I should be down at the cannery docks," Billy said.

"Oh, just forget about the cannery for today. There ain't no fishin' boats comin' in today with all the rain and the squalls."

Billy let his hands fall to Lorna's rounded buttocks. He gave the same sort of playful pinch in return. "If I forget about the cannery, will you forget about whatever is upsettin' you, and try to relax?"

"That's the plan exactly." Lorna stood on tiptoe and kissed Billy with a hard and desperate kiss.

"Whoa, woman!" Billy grinned down at Lorna. "Let's take it nice and easy. Grey rainy days call for slow lovin'." He jostled her into his arms and headed for the bedroom. "What about Johnnie?"

"He'll sleep for another two hours," Lorna said.

Billy laughed, "That's my boy!"

It rained for the rest of the week. With Billy rain-bound at home, Lorna's fears eased for the most part. She still checked the bars on the alcove door more often than was necessary and she made sure the large caliber rifle was added to the rack in the laundry room next to her 30/30. She hid twelve rounds of ammunition in an empty bleach box, but she didn't tell Billy.

The rain alternated between mist and pelting fury every day. The Brothers Petroff were forced to postpone their sheep-horn hunting foray and Lorna was glad of that. Saturday evening the skies turned from grey to cobalt to purple in a matter of two hours. The air, so newly and thoroughly washed, seemed to make the stars sparkle and glitter with an exuberant brightness. The night air was crisp; chilly but not too chilly so Billy and Lorna were able to carry Johnnie out onto the front porch with them for star viewing.

There was no movie that night. The mail boat hadn't come because the storm was bad out in the Johnstone Strait.

"Watching all these stars is almost as good as a movie, anyway," Lorna said.

"'Specially if we can spot some shootin' stars," Billy joked.

"First one to spot a shootin' star gets to have whatever they want, okay?" Lorna said and then immediately shouted, "She seen one!"

"What do you want, Darlin'?"

"She wants to walk up to the cannery store and have the biggest ice cream bar they got up there," Lorna laughed. "You carry Johnnie and let's get going before they close down."

Sunday was warm. That fact made Lorna glad. The sun dazzled whenever you looked out at the bay. Spring was putting on quite an entrance into the little bay town of the Portlock Cannery. Lorna was glad about that, too. Monday, regular wash day, came and the sun was still brilliant. Its warmth coaxed shoots from the ground and all the wild, growing, green things were popping up all over the clearing in back of the house. The bright open sky, the all-illuminating sun and the new spring heat allayed Lorna's fears. She unbolted the door to the back yard; placing the three bars against the laundry room wall.

She took the smaller rifle down from the rack and set it next to the bars. The sunshine seemed to have been waiting for the door to be unbarred and rushed in to fill the alcove room with light and warmth. Lorna whistled for her own pleasure as she sorted laundry. Billy wouldn't be back for lunch, perhaps not until late afternoon. He had gone out to the bay to check for herring runs, just after the Petroff brothers had stopped by to invite him to go up the mountain for the third time. Billy said 'no' for the third time. Billy had told them to forget it and Lorna was happy with his refusal to go with them.

She continued whistling her contentment while she stirred the bluing water on the stove. The gas-powered washing machine chugged away, perhaps with a little too much noise.

Lorna wondered if the loud popping and clanking would wake little Johnnie. She crept to the door of the room where he slept and listened. He was awake, but not fretting. She sneaked a peek and saw him babbling happily to his entwined fingers. She crept backward out of his line of sight and returned to the laundry to wring out the first batch. Just as she stooped to pick up the basket of wet wash, Johnnie howled out his equivalent of "Mama." Lorna scurried to the room and picked him up. He was wet and the night diaper dripped.

"She has to change her little Mister, right quick," Lorna said. "It's nice and warm outside and she's gonna let your little bottom air out. Mama's gonna take her Johnnie outside to play on a blanket without a diaper while she hangs up the wash. That okay with you, little Mister?"

Johnnie babbled and smiled. She carried him with her to the alcove and sat him on the floor. Lorna piled the second batch of coloured clothes into the washing machine and started the gas engine. Johnnie let out a wail when the engine backfired and Lorna hurried to console him. The machine finally began chugging in the proper rhythm, so Lorna took her wash basket outside first, and then carried the baby out and spread a blanket. He sat in the middle of the flannel blanket and talked his baby language to her while she hung up the laundry.

Moments later the gas engine backfired again with a loud pop. Lorna took the clothes pins from her mouth and spoke to Johnnie, "She'll be right back, Baby."

She hurried inside to shut down the engine. The machine popped and sputtered to a stop.

Lorna turned and went down the ramp to the back yard. She

screamed. She screamed again and began to shout! "No! No! Oh, God! NO!" The blanket was crumpled into a ball and her baby was gone.

She rushed to the roll of blanket and swept it up into her arms. An unmistakable stench assailed her nostrils, the odor of dead things and strong urine! She threw her head back away from the smell; a grimace on her face. A wail, primal and terrible tore from her chest. Lorna screamed to the sky. Her wide open eyes rolled white, back into her skull, and she fell unconscious across the laundry basket, crushing the wicker under her dead-weight fall.

How long she lay unconscious, Lorna couldn't say. She awoke lying on her side across the crushed laundry basket, facing the bluff and the mountains behind her house. Her vision was momentarily blurred but her surroundings slowly fell into focus when she raised her head from the damp ground. It was the smell before the sight, which caused her body to shake as the cold fear rushed up her spine and hammered at the base of her brain.

She saw the splayed feet, wide and covered with red-black hair, the long dirt encrusted nails. Then she saw the muscular legs, thick, tree-trunk like. Lorna shifted her fallen body and raised her eyes. Two black, pig-like eyes stared back into hers from a creased and leathery, mahogany face.

The stench from the hairy creature was overpowering. Lorna recoiled both from the smell and the horror that stood before her. She scrabbled sideways and backwards like a wounded beach crab and huddled against the side of her house. The creature unfolded the heavy muscular arms that had been positioned across its chest. Two dugs, elongated teats; leathery and swollen with milk hung down on the hairless lower chest and stomach of the beast. Milk dripped from the black teats and cradled in her arms tugging and poking at the creature's breasts was little Johnnie. He babbled and pulled at the tufts of red-brown hair above the beast's breasts. Un-afraid and accepting the stench emanating from the seven foot high monster that held him, Johnnie turned and made one of his baby-bye-bye waves at his mother. His hand flapped in the air.

The thing looked down at the baby in her arms then looked straight into Lorna's face. A sort of smile caused her lip-less features to grimace showing off wide, humanoid, yellow-stained teeth.

Lorna raised her arms in a plea and spoke softly, "Please, give this woman back her baby."

As if she understood human speech or perhaps she could read the look on Lorna's face or the universal plea gesture of reaching upward with outstretched arms, the creature responded with a sharp shake of her domed head. The long crest of hairs on the peak of the beast's elongated skull swayed as the she shook her head. Lorna focused on a gap of missing hair on the creature's head as the beast continued a sideways head movement, back and forth. It was the same signal people make when they are saying no.

"Please!" Lorna said, almost cooing the words, "The baby. This woman, she needs him so!"

She made a crawling movement forward on her hands and knees that brought her within six feet of the monster. A mistake she had not meant to make. Lorna knew at once that she had invaded the creature's toleration space. The huge hairy thing screeched a high whistling squeal, folded its over-long arms protectively around little Johnnie and turned; rushing away in four foot strides. Before Lorna could rise to her feet, the thing had crested the bluff and slipped into the mass of giant trees.

Anger replaced fear. Lorna felt unusual strength surge into her body. She clenched her teeth and her fists, ran to the alcove and grabbed the 30/30 rifle. It took Lorna more than four strides to reach the bluff and many more to gain the great trees where the forest giant had disappeared. Anger and a mother's wrath drove her. The trail of broken ferns and bracken led deeper into the foothills covered with alders and scrub. Then the trail sloped swiftly upward toward the mountains themselves.

The dampness of the week's rains still held in the forest, causing the strong unpleasant odor of the beast to cling to the waist high brush, making it easy, at first, for Lorna to follow a scent trail. Two hours passed, but Lorna never faltered. She had to back-track once to find a trail of tracks, footprints in the moist earth, where the forest broke into a clearing. The depth of the tracks left by the creature, where the earth was free of moss and rocks, gave proof of the giant's great bulk.

Lorna studied the tracks. She was able to place both her feet, toe-to-heel inside one of the tracks. The giant foot prints led up and around a rock-strewn slope back into another growth of trees. It was then the great stench slammed into her nostrils.

She remembered the description of the area given by the Petroff brothers. Rounding a house-sized boulder, creating a dog-leg, in what now had become a recognizable trail of sorts, made by the comings and goings of the beasts, Lorna stopped abruptly and gasped in astonishment.

Every fork of every tree in a huge grove of old aspens was stuffed with hundreds of marmot corpses. Lorna turned in a circle, apprehensive and physically sickened by the sight and smell. She looked at the leaf-littered ground beneath the trees and saw the dried empty skins of dozens of marmots. Mixed with the tatter of skins were small marmot bones; completely cleaned of all flesh. Lorna relaxed her grip on the heavy rifle and poked at a mound of bones with the toe of her moccasin. She scattered the bones with her foot. There was no mistaking the teeth marks and gnawed end of the larger bones. These things, were flesh eaters! Lorna's heart pounded in her chest and her head echoed it's pounding. *Her Johnnie! Please, God, don't let them eat her baby Johnnie!*

A whistling squeal to her left caused Lorna to spin around; gun brought to her shoulder. She saw nothing. Then, with amazing agility and no sound at all, the hairy monster appeared. The creature squatted on its haunches and watched Lorna with the black pig-eyes. It sat hunched over. Lorna recognized the gap in the head crest. The creature picked idly at the carcass of a marmot with its right hand and fed small bits of raw flesh into its wide mouth. Cradled in the crook of the animal's left arm was Johnnie, sleeping.

Lorna prayed he was only sleeping. The huge thing looked into Lorna's eyes and that same trace of a grimace-smile Lorna had seen before, flickered briefly on its leathery face. As gently as Lorna would have done herself, the beast placed Johnnie on the moss and leaves. Lorna saw his little chest rising and falling in a deep slumber; her whispered 'thank you' was really a prayer.

The huge creature turned sideways from Lorna and began scratching; digging into a mound of leaves, moss and fallen twigs. She pulled something small and hairy from the mound. It was a dead infant of the beast's kind; so tiny, Lorna knew at once the little thing had been still-born. The hairy giant mother turned and displayed the limp body of her animal baby to Lorna. Lorna's throat clutched and tears blurred her eyes. Lorna understood. She placed her rifle on the ground in a slow deliberate way. The creature saw the gun on the earth and looked at Lorna. There was a split second instant of mother to mother non-verbal communication; a sense of grief and sorrow shared. The emotion that passed between them in that brief moment in time was honest, real; a feeling that Lorna would never forget. The creature held her dead infant close and bent to touch the corpse with her flat, thin lips. She raised her head on her short brutish neck and crooned a high lament toward the tops of the taller trees.

The roar of a shot from a high-powered rifle stifled the beast mother's keening lament. The great animal fell backward from the impact. A second shot followed but missed the creature, who dropped the dead infant and pushed herself sideways behind the great boulder and disappeared from sight.

Andy Petroff raised himself from the kneeling position from which he'd fired, "You all right, Miss Lorna?"

Lorna couldn't speak. She just nodded 'yes' and hurried to the leaf and moss mound where Johnnie, despite the loud rifle shots, still slept. She scooped him up in her arms and switched him to ride against her hip in the crook of her arm. Exhausted, Johnnie slept on. Lorna looked down at the tiny dead beast-infant; knelt and picked up the body and cradled it in her other arm. She turned and began the long downhill trek toward home. She passed Feodor on the trail a few yards from the boulder. He saw the dead beast-baby and stared at her bewildered. Lorna did not speak to him but only pressed both babies, one living and sleeping momentarily, and one dead, sleeping forever, closer to her chest and hurried down the trail.

Suddenly the horrid stench of the creatures grew in power. Loud whistling and harsh hooting calls filled the air. It sounded as if a pack of the beasts had assembled to defy the Petroff brothers. Lorna ran. She didn't look back; she ran for her life and Johnnie's.

She heard Andy yell. He called for Feodor to come up quickly; to help him. Then she heard the barrage of rifle fire and the screams and the piercing whistles. She didn't stop running even when the abrupt silence came. Her instincts told her to keep moving as fast as possible toward home; and she did. She didn't want to imagine what just had happened up there by the great boulder.

She had Johnnie and he was safe in the protecting bend of her arm. And she had another duty; a duty to the dead forest-child she carried. Burial: it was the least she could do.

Late that night, in the neglected garden patch back of the house—secretly, she gave the dead beast-infant a proper burial. She never spoke of the dead forest-child or its mother when Billy and others patiently pushed her to discuss the events up on the mountain.

"It was some kind of big animal." This was all Lorna told them. "Red-brown hairy thing—big arms—walked on two legs—never saw one of them before."

The next afternoon, Billy led a party of ten men from the cannery to the great boulder where the beasts Lorna described to the townspeople were suspected to live. Lorna had begged him not to go, to let things be, but Billy refused to listen to her.

The hurriedly organized posse was divided about the truth of Lorna's story. Some still thought in terms of a bear-encounter. Billy knew Lorna's devotion to the truth and was now suspicious of what he might encounter up on the mountain. After a two hour trek the men reached the great boulder and what they found was not what Billy expected. Bent and twisted rifles, Lorna's 30/30 included, lay near the base of the great rock. Blood was spattered everywhere on the fallen leaves, rocks and mosses. The undergrowth was trampled and great masses of moss and bracken were ripped up and strewn about. On the grasping branches of some of the buck-brush and dwarf alder bushes, bits of shaggy, reddish-brown hair clung; the blood and the hair, evidence of what must have been a terrible encounter. An encounter between the unknown beasts the posse called '*them!*'

and the two missing Petroff brothers. The posse had to search for only a moment or two before the real horror was found.

The naked bodies of Andy and Feodor Petroff were wedged ten feet off the ground in the large forks of two separate trees. Their torn clothing and boots were scattered at the base of the trees holding the corpses. When a quartet of men from the posse pulled the bodies down they were sickened at the sight.

Both men's heads were twisted grotesquely off center of their spines. Their torsos, ripped open from sternum to pelvis were, emptied of organs. The two Petroff brothers were crudely butchered and dressed out in the same manner as the carcasses of the mountain sheep. The men's bodies were bundled into cannery company blankets and the men agreed to take turns carrying the mutilated corpses back down the mountain trail to the town.

Billy shouldered the wrapped corpse of Andy and turned to leave. It was at that moment the high-pitched screaming and whistles began. The sounds echoed from the mountain recesses and seem to come from all directions at once.

The posse was confused; unable to pin-point the exact source of the terrible din. Some of the frightened men began firing at shadows; their wasted shots at nothing ricocheting off rocks and trees.

The creatures used a strategy of distraction with their screams and howls. The sounds, made by one hidden group of the beasts were answered and enhanced by a second or even a third group. Each group kept to the thick brush cover, screeching and whistling while circling the posse. Next came a howling wail from all directions that sent the men into a panic. Suddenly, rocks and large branches pelted the milling posse.

The return trip with the bodies was a panicked rout. Unseen assailants threw rocks—very large rocks—and broken tree branches at the frightened men hurrying back down the mountain. The men saw nothing of the beasts Lorna described, but they felt their presence and heard their high-pitched whistling screams that followed them as they hurriedly retreated.

The barrage of rocks and branches continued all afternoon until the men reached the edge of the bluff behind Billy's house. At that point, the screams and the barrage of stones stopped suddenly. During the lull, the Petroff brothers were given a hasty burial in a shallow pit near the bluff at the edge of the forest. The men of the town piled the grave site high with the large rocks and boulders thrown down by the creatures.

The alerted town stood guard in an all-night vigil at a distance from the graves. The frightened posse hunched together around a picket line of campfires. Every man from the cannery was armed beyond reason. In the early dawn hours, when the fires had smoldered out, the screams and barrage of rocks began again. For five days and nights, the unseen beasts of the forest remained invisible adversaries. The village populace retreated under the siege of the forest giants.

Homes were abandoned as the most terrified families fled to other distant villages along the bay's coastline. As soon as homes were abandoned, the beasts moved in to smash windows, rip doors from their hinges, twist fuel oil barrels from their racks and open gaping holes in roofs with large and heavy rocks. By the seventh day of the attacks, there were only three families left in the cannery compound. The entire work force had left on a cannery ship for Port McNeill after the third day.

The three families remaining were Billy and Lorna, the two widows and the five children of the Petroff brothers. All of them had moved into the thick-walled, metal roofed cannery office and lived in one end of the office with a stone fireplace wall behind their backs. They stayed for two reasons, the widows were reluctant to leave their husbands' unmarked graves and Billy found it hard to accept the destruction of an entire cannery town by unseen beasts. He could not, yet, admit defeat.

Both reasons for continuing to remain in the besieged town were forgotten the next night when the forest creatures invaded, whistling and screaming. The beasts would rush the cannery office; screeching and hooting and slapping their large flat palms against the walls and windows before retreating. The silence and the waiting in between assaults was too unnerving for Lorna, the widows and children, who now pleaded with Billy to take them to safety. An exhausted Billy finally capitulated.

When the sun was high, at noon, and the creatures seemed to have retreated, he hustled the remaining Portlock residents with their few valued possessions onto his boat and sailed it out of the placid lagoon for the last time.

Billy was at the wheel giving his attention to the channel markers in the bay. He turned and shouted to Lorna, "Damned if I like bein' chased outta my home like that! It's all on account of them. They invaded our land!"

The widows and children huddled together; hunkered down under blankets against the chill wind blowing in from the straits, started crying and agreeing with Billy. Lorna stood at the stern holding Johnnie and looking back at the house on the knoll.

The home where she'd been so happy was two hundred yards to stern. The forward movement of the boat on the calm water gave the illusion that the house and the cannery town were in motion, and not the boat. Lorna held Johnnie closer to her and forced back tears. She shaded her eyes with her free hand, the better to see her house on the knoll for a last look, and saw the huge form standing on the front porch.

The high peaked head swiveled on its short neck as the creature followed the movement of the boat out of the lagoon. *It was watching her.* Lorna could feel its eyes on her. The creature on the porch bobbed its head on its thick neck. Lorna saw the gap in the crest of hair.

Johnnie began to fuss and Lorna jiggled him in her arms. The motion always comforted him, but this time, Johnnie, sensing his mother's mood of sorrow and mixed sadness, began to wail.

"Hush now, Little Mister," Lorna said. "It'll be alright fer us. She thinks maybe your daddy got it all backwards; it's our own fault we're havin' to leave. We invaded their land, Little Mister," Lorna spoke quietly to the baby. "Haida people say them things was here first."

Lorna whispered into the sea wind, "This woman wants to say—she's sorry."

Nanuq

Words of life and death are written on the ice. They are written in the track of *nanuq*, the great white bear. They are written in the blood of a ring seal upon the snow.

Since ancient days, it has been the sacred duty of Inupiat fathers to teach their sons the meaning of those words.

"We could have taken a flitter, you know." Arwela, obviously uncomfortable without the clothes of the white man, pulled at the throat of his caribou skin parka.

"C'mon, son. Don't be that way." I looked up from the tracks of nanuq. "This is important to me." Arwela's goggled eyes betrayed nothing and he offered no answer.

His years away from me had bled any belief he once had in the old ways. I had thought to educate him, to make him wise in the ways of science and the world, but the University had narrowed his mind instead of widening it. He had turned his back on his people.

I thought after he graduated he would return and learn the way of the *angatquq*, the shaman, and take his place in the secret circles of the People, as his mother had. She was a doctor, but she was a shaman first.

The man who stood before me, this man who had been my son—his spirit was empty.

"Look. Nanuq came this way," I said, pointing at the huge tracks in the snow. "She walks on two legs. This is no ordinary bear we track; she is of the almost-people, the woman in bear skin."

"We should have taken a flitter. We should have taken a GPS, at least."

"It's important to me that we do this the old way," I said. Patience was not easy, but there were many things Arwela did not know. Had he returned, we would have shown him the secret science and magic of the Inupiat. He too would have walked the path of the shaman and experienced the bear-dream.

The tracks continued for thirty feet before the bear once more walked on four legs. I shifted the weight of my pack and pressed on, not waiting to see if Arwela followed.

"Jesus, Pop, wait up. I'm coming! I told you I'd go with you."

"Well, come then." There was no time to hesitate. The *qargi*, our lodge, and the conveniences of modern men lay three days behind us. Before us lay the tundra and the way of spear and skin, of blood and death.

"Here nanuq stopped to flush a seal pup from its den." I pointed at the broken ice and the massive ring of blood that surrounded it. Gulls milled about, fighting over chunks of blubber.

"Lovely, Dad, just lovely. I'm sure PETA would be enchanted." He kicked at a bloodied bit of snow. "What the hell are we doing out here?"

"I've wandered out here for years looking for the spirit of your mother. Do not mock her memory, Arwela."

"Mom's dead, Pop! Fifteen years now she's been gone. Why don't you admit it finally?" He dropped his pack to the ice and sat cross-legged beside it. He pushed his long hair away from his face and frowned, revealing the lines on his face and the wrinkles around his black eyes.

It was hard to believe that he was the same boy who had once run after me crying and begging to be allowed on the hunt.

"All this mumbo jumbo about the bear-dream! It's just lunacy," he said.

"Mind your tongue." I sat down and rummaged through my pack, refusing to look at him. I wanted to smoke.

"Don't you think that some anthropologist would've documented it by now?" he persisted. "There is no such thing as magic. There is no such thing as a were-bear."

"Then why leave Los Angeles, eh? Why leave your precious city to grub in the dirt with me?" My grandfather's pipe lay beneath our provisions wrapped in the dried hide of a ring seal. Scratches and wear marked the places where his hand had held it, long ago.

I packed it with dark, fragrant tobacco and lit it, my gloved hand shielding the match against the wind. I gazed across the vast wilderness of ice and frozen tundra, trying against all odds to see the bear lost in her long cold dream.

"Because I missed you, all right? I missed you." Arwela's hard face softened. I saw him again as he was when he was young, so bright and inquisitive, so aware of everyone and everything. There was a time when I thought he would be a great shaman, strong in his medicine, perhaps even stronger than his mother.

"You missed me? You missed me so much you didn't take my calls or answer my letters?"

"I'm here now."

"No wiser for your time away." I smoked my pipe, trying to be patient. The sun was low on the horizon. Soon it would be too cold to walk in the open.

"Men do not turn into bears," Arwela said after a while. "They're animals. That's all." He threw a chunk of frozen snow at a gull. It squawked and flew away.

"You will see, Arwela. I promise you, you will see."

We camped for the night in a tent made of caribou hide and slept in bags lined with the very fur of nanuq. My wife, Liak, had made them long ago.

"Jesus, it's colder than a witch's tit in a brass bra." Arwela squirmed closer to me and I could not help but chuckle.

"Sleep, son. It'll be morning soon and we must be quick if we are to overtake nanuq."

"How the hell are we going to bring down a polar bear, Pop?" Arwela rolled onto his side, his back to me. "You haven't got anything with you but that damn tranq spear."

"It will be enough."

"You should have brought a stun-rifle. And a heater, for God's sake!"

I said nothing. I hoped he was wrong and the spear would be enough. A rifle would have been easier. But I couldn't change the situation now, three days from the lodge. Besides, Liak would have wanted me to do it the old way. I had to believe that she would help us.

After a time I slept, the remembered smell of her hair inviting me to dream.

Morning came and the sun shone on us briefly, retreating behind ominous clouds that gathered around the mountains. Arwela said little as we ate the dried fish from our packs.

We followed the tracks of nanuq in silence. Around midday, I saw a small fox cub scurry from a hole and chase after a pair of lemmings. High above us, a golden eagle flew in tight circles, perhaps weighing the immature fox against the smaller lemmings. Its piercing call mingled with the gathering wind.

The message of the eagle and the fox was not lost to me. It was a dark omen sent by *tuungaq*, my helping spirit: The hunter sometimes becomes the hunted.

But I would not abandon her now when she was so close. It had been fifteen years since we lost track of her; fifteen years she had roamed the ice, dreaming.

No, I would find her and Arwela would at last know the truth about his mother and the secret rites of the Inupiat shaman.

We followed her trail up to an expanse of dark stone that stretched for about a kilometer. Tasting the wind and trusting my instinct, I set off eastward, my son trailing behind me.

As the day progressed, the wind bit through my parka and the blue sky became a dark gray curtain. Ice formed here and there on the stones, the water from sun-melted snow leaving tracks of invisible slipperiness for the unwary.

"Mind your footing, Arwela. We will be back on the tundra before long. It is too far to nurse a sprained ankle."

"I'm fine! Can't you give it a rest for a while?"

There was anger and fatigue in his voice. I stopped and took a look into his eyes.

"Why aren't you wearing your visor? You're almost snow blind." I pulled the visor over his eyes and sat him down on the rock. I pulled my seal skin glove off and felt inside his parka. "You're sweating. We'll rest here a while until you dry off a bit."

"I'm fine. Just a little cold." He shivered and coughed.

The color was almost completely drained from his face.

Sweat is deadly on the ice. The place in my heart that was the Hunter merely shrugged. The place in my heart that was the Father screamed for me to go back. The howl of the gathering wind was punctuated by Arwela's coughing.

In the end, I was spared from making a decision. It was the ice that decided. We made it perhaps another five miles before a blizzard fell upon us. The tent and furs we brought with us were little protection and I resorted to using Arwela's laseknife to construct an igloo from the hard-packed snow. It took almost an hour. We would have been dead if he had left it at home as I instructed. It would have taken far too long with the traditional knife I had brought along.

When night came, he developed a fever. I piled our furs on him and held him close, as his mother and I had done when he was a boy. It seemed the heat from his face would melt the igloo around us.

I found a phone in his pack and from time to time I tried to reach the lodge, but the storm blanketed us in static.

By morning, the entrance to the igloo was buried in snow. I put Arwela's phone in my pocket and proceeded to dig us out with my hands.

I struggled to the surface, pushing snow behind me until my hand broke through to the light of day. I was exhausted by the time I crawled out of the tunnel. I pulled my visor over my eyes and sat up, fumbling for the phone.

My worry for Arwela betrayed me and I did not see nanuq until it was almost too late. It was her smell that gave her away. A fortunate change of the wind and I caught it, pungent and unmistakable—clean snow and blood.

As large as a snow bank, white, white, blinding in her brilliance; her eyes regarded me with cold intelligence and her lips curled over ivory teeth. About her neck was the intricate collar of sinew I had made for her myself, so long ago. The tracking beacon that had hung from it was gone.

I dropped the phone and dove straight back into the hole. It would not protect us for long. Nanuq would dig us out as surely as if we were seals.

I slid into the igloo and collided with Arwela. He was still in the grip of his fever and did nothing but moan. My spear lay beside him and I snatched it up with trembling hands.

I could hear the bear sniffing around above. She would wait there a moment, I knew, to see if I would come out. Then she would come in after me. I started back up the hole on my belly, the spear before me. If I could get close enough, I thought there was a chance I could tranquilize her before she knocked my brains into the snow.

About half way up, she dug her claws through and raked my face to the bone. The smell of blood flooded the closeness of the tunnel. My screaming spurred her forward and into the snow after me.

I dropped the spear and raised my arm to protect my face. She hammered down on it with her paw, cracking the bones and knocking the wind from my lungs. Numbness raced up my arm and I rolled back into the igloo struggling to breathe.

Arwela stirred beside me, eyes glazed and uncomprehending. Blood poured from the wounds on my face and melted the hard-packed snow beneath me. He rolled onto his stomach and crawled toward me.

"Dad!"

I managed to get a small breath of air and pointed at the hole. "The bear!"

He blinked his eyes up at the sunlit hole and struggled to his knees. He picked the spear up from where it lay. Snow cascaded from the surface and I heard the huffing breath of nanuq.

After only a few moments, her head broke through directly above me, covering me with snow. She looked at Arwela, her huge nostrils dilated. She dug furiously with her forepaws and slid halfway in, filling the tiny igloo with her scent.

Arwela screamed and sank the spear into her shoulder. He twisted it viciously and thumbed the release button for the tranquilizer. Nanuq let out a deafening roar and knocked Arwela down with her paw. His head struck the ice.

I felt a great weight above me as the bear slid further into the igloo. Her head shook and I saw her legs tremble as the tranquilizer began to take effect. She sniffed at Arwela and bared her teeth above his exposed throat.

"Liak, no!" I cried, the pain in my face and arm forgotten. "He is our child. He is your son Arwela."

She turned her head to regard me. I looked into her eyes and I thought I saw some spark there, beneath the cold cunning of her predatory mind. She settled down on her forepaws and closed her eyes, the tranquilizer finally dragging her down to unconsciousness.

I lay under her, unable to move. I slept in the embrace of nanuq.

I awoke to the light of day, stretched out on the snow. Arwela was unconscious beside me, the spear frozen to his hand. He had dug me from beneath the bear and dragged me from the igloo before passing out.

His phone lay near nanuq and I used it to call the lodge. An hour later, a rescue flitter came for us and hoisted Arwela and the bear into its hold with harnesses.

The hospital in the lodge soon had Arwela stable though he lost a hand to frostbite. Regeneration can be painful, I hear, but in a few months he would be as good as new. My wounds were filled with fleshfoam and my broken arm was set in a cast.

Some hours later, they brought me to the ceremony in a wheelchair. I insisted on standing after they had rolled me into the gigantic room. It would not be right to sit like an old man when I had waited for this day for so long.

In the house of the shamans, nanuq lay motionless, gripped by the medicine of the People. About her mighty head they had arranged machinery and wire that looked like metallic flowers attached to gossamer strands of ice. The wires reached upward and outward, forming a massive spider's web that joined with the great machines that filled the room and lit it with dancing light.

My son was right when he said no anthropologist or outside scientist had seen proof of the bear-dream. We would not let them. That holy road was for the shamans of the Inupiat, for us alone.

Beside nanuq lay the sleeping form of Liak, my wife, her beauty unmarred from her years in coldsleep. She looked the same as the day she took to the holy path. But we had lost her; what was supposed to be a one-year journey as a passenger in the mind of the white bear had turned into fifteen years of imprisonment in the bear-dream.

The shamans and the scientists restored Liak to her body. Nanuq was released back to the arctic snow, the stain of my wife's mind forever erased.

"How long?" she asked me, tracing the lines on my face with a finger and brushing the tears from my eyes. She embraced me.

"Fifteen years." I found I could not release her. "Too long."

"Arwela?" she asked me.

"A true son of his people." My heart was filled with pride. "He is waiting to see you, though I do not know if he will believe his eyes."

Squatch

They'd managed to travel from Vancouver, B.C., to Yakima, Washington, before things began to unravel.

Lost on an old logging road, in search of a KOA campground, they'd punctured a tire and his mother searched for a place to pull over.

"So much for the San Diego zoo and seeing the captured Sakwatches," Squatch said, imitating little Kadia's childish pronunciation. Squatch hid his own disappointment by staring hard out the window.

The road dust gave the weeds and ground cover an alien aura as if the vegetation in the area came from another planet. Their camper sagged to one side and nearly made contact with the soft dry surface of the road. "What a pretty spot," his mother said, as she pulled their vehicle into the only open patch of forest. "A woodland glade right out of a Walt Disney cartoon," she announced. Squatch sneered. Nature made his skateboard useless.

Niki, his older sister, wore her dark eye makeup in a ring around each eye. The dark smudges gave her a distinctive Goth look, which matched her naturally black hair; she now pulled at the wad of turquoise colored gum she'd snapped for the last half hour of their trip. Stretching her gum into a blue string; a single piece of suspension cable she then anchored to her knee, locking it to the jean fabric with short punches of thumb Tai Bo.

She tried to anchor a piece to Squatch. That was all the excuse he needed.

Their verbal vitriolic tirade filled the SUV.

Niki listened to the radio until their battery died. Then their cell phone, buried in the small, overcrowded sarcophagus of the glove compartment, gave off its death beeps.

While mom and Niki argued over the impossibility of rescue, Squatch flipped his longish brown hair away from his eyes and pulled out a lawn chair from the roof rack of the camper. The chair, a metal frame with strips of nylon woven together, had spent previous seasons in bondage on the top rack, lost and abused by the more important items packed over top of it. The chair's green and white frayed ribbons created a variegated spray of weedy, broken straps but a few survived to hold his skinny frame. Squatch leaned back and stared through the dark blue sky and recalled his last skate.

He took on the poise and silhouette of a surfer, hands and arms out slightly in the universal salute of balance. He'd hand picked and kicked aside every stone, stick, and piece of debris along this circuit as he'd walked to school each day.

But no matter how meticulously he worked at clearing his path, tires always deposited their loads of pebbles and sticks as if they spawned at Oxford hill. Squatch gave a delighted whoop and toppled from the dilapidated lawn chair; his mind still rode down the hill; he thrust his left fist straight up. A rainbow of colorful bracelets braided from soft string circled his arm. His trademark. Bracelets, collected over the years, encircled three scars, two from repaired broken wrists.

Dusk turned the sky purple around Squatch. He'd set the camp stove up on a small T.V. table, which held an aluminum pot of water with steam rising. They unpacked the remaining folded chairs and, with twilight as their backdrop, feasted on hot dogs, beans canned in brown sugar and salad with no dressing. While they dished out their meal the clean snap of a stick drew their attention to a large cedar stump. Another loud crack had them twisting in their chairs to look in the opposite direction.

A sudden cold wind lashed out of the surrounding woods and left him covered in goose flesh. As he stood to escape the cold blast his fragile chair flew up against a tree. Kadia screamed and ran to him for protection as a javelin-like branch hit their camper. Squatch stared transfixed at the large rent. "It's just the wind," he said in a shout, trying to reassure his little sister. His own heart thumped and swelled with fear. He worried for their safety. "Courage," his father had always said about everything; his last word to Squatch the day he had left Squatch standing quietly in their big house. Squatch began his fifteenth year, then. Now at the end of that year, it seemed a lifetime ago since he'd watched the front door close on the shadow of his dad.

Just as his mom picked up a pot and its lid ready to bang the two together, they saw a light blink on and off; a flashlight signaled to them from the road. Kadia clung tightly to Squatch.

The blinking light drew closer and as it did, they recognized a man. "Hello, hello there. I'm Billy Jackson. Billy Jack for short or Billy. I'm a hiker," a man's voice called out.

As he entered their site he picked up the three-meter high stick that damaged their camper. The man stood nearly as tall as the stick. His long black hair fell below his shoulders. Squatch guessed the man was about forty. He wore faded jeans, a red and black lumberman's jacket and a pair of worn, brown hiking boots. He had a small backpack. The stick folded and broke as he leaned on it.

"You folks all right?" he asked; he pointed to the camper, which sat awkwardly, its rear end up on a rock.

"Can you call road assistance for us?" his mom asked.

"Fifty meters straight ahead, you'll find a creek with drinkable water. Wood 'round here is dry. Makes a good fire. Some berries for snackin'. But don't let the little one here pick alone. She's a perfect bear-size snack." He chuckled at his own comment. "My Aunty Del, she's the tow operator for these parts. I'll send her down to you, when I get back in the A.M.," he said, then took off his pack, stretched and yawned. Squatch noticed that he had a mouthful of large, perfect teeth.

He swung the remains of the stick around to point at a tree. "I've got a few things stashed away over there. Ladies better use the camper toilet tonight. Don't want to run into anything in the dark. The sky will be clear as a creek, but even with the stars up there's no telling some shadows from things that can bump up against you. That smells pretty good," he said, pointing to the food.

The family all looked awkwardly at each other then hesitantly asked him to join them.

Their visitor built them a large fire. They sat there until Squatch's mom and sisters decided to make the camper ready for sleep. The boy retrieved his skateboard and went back to Billy and the fire, feet resting on his board.

"What kind of name is Squatch?" The stranger asked him.

"Short for Sasquatch. Ever hear of them?" His bedroom wall flashed into mind. A poster created from an enlarged still of the famous Patterson footage hung there. The creature that was his namesake, moved quickly through the afternoon woods glancing back across the glade of fallen logs and rocks.

The toothy smile disappeared from Billy's face. For a moment he stopped eating. "Squatch isn't a good name for around here," Billy said. He glanced around their campsite, looking nervous. Then he pulled a soiled hanky out of his front pocket and unwrapped the small bundle, quickly tossing the hanky's dusty contents into their fire. "They'll try to scare you away." Billy said, around another mouthful of food.

He finished his meal. Then he handed Squatch a tiny packet he pulled from the same pocket, pointed out a spot in the fire; the boy tossed the contents into the flames. "That'll keep them away."

When Squatch tossed in the bundle, smoke billowed from the center of the burning logs. Irritated sparks shifted on a sudden breeze, lifted into the air and floated all the way to the stars. The smoke then changed direction and swarmed the boy's face and eyes, stinging and filling his nostrils. He coughed and quickly stood. He stumbled blindly away from the flames, tripping over a chair, blowing the hot smoke out of his sinuses. "Water," he choked out.

Billy grabbed him by the arm and helped him up. "This way."

The boy's eyes watered hard and refused to open. The man guided the blinded boy through the dark woods. Squatch was desperate and listened as the sound of the trickling creek water drew closer. His feet became damp and cold as the water bled through the seams in his runners. He bent over and scooped up a palm full of the cold liquid and splashed his face several times, drank a few gulps and after several splashes his irritated eyes finally opened.

There was no sign of Billy, but the hot reek of animal sweat and rotting meat engulfed him, just as if he'd lifted the lid on the compost container at home and stuck his head deep inside. Heat radiated from some bush-obscured animal less than an arm's length away. The sour vapor rolled over him; wave after wave suffocated him like the steam in a sauna. The boy's heart hammered in his ears and his breath wheezed in and out noisily. His feet tingled and went numb from the cold. The smell finally made him vomit. The unseen creature crashed away from him and seemed to vanish. Alone, Squatch headed in what he hoped was the direction of the camper.

With the camper's lights out Squatch felt uneasy but relieved that he'd found his way back alone. He crept in the direction of Billy's small camp. Light from the fire infiltrated the darkness; he found the man asleep in his bag.

A pack of cigarettes lay on the ground. Annoyed that Billy had left him alone and afraid, Squatch helped himself to the entire pack and recalled a time he'd helped himself to his mother's jewelry, pawned her trinkets, and used the cash to purchase a little pot. He wished he had some now. Even after he'd paid back the money, he felt his mom and dad never really forgave him. Dad had vanished soon after the incident. They'd found his bike under a bridge, near a river. No one ever found a body.

Back at the campfire he lit a cigarette, looked at the stars, listened to crickets. The cigarette smoldered slowly as he carefully inhaled, not too deeply; he didn't want to wake everyone with his coughing. A branch cracked loudly, silencing the night's chirping. Another snap. Squatch froze. He stopped breathing, threw his cigarette into the fire; his mother put her hand on his shoulder.

"Go sleep," she said, taking the cigarette pack from his pocket. "Kadia and I are in the cab. There's plenty of room. You and Niki sleep in the back."

"You scared the hell out me," he choked out, glancing back into the dark.

"Go sleep."

"Lock your doors," he said to her.

In his sleep his mind danced with visions, dark faces, small dark eyes peered out of the woods. Something hidden in the forest whispered to him, whimpered. Squatch backed away and stepped into a mass of dark, coarse hair. Lost in a realm of musky fur, strong arms took hold of him. Squatch stared into the face of his namesake. The creature smiled at him. Squatch yelled as his gut recognized the toothy smile.

He rolled off the small bunk onto the floor. He didn't like the musty smell inside the camper, and Niki talked in her sleep. He found it unnerving. He'd spent most of the night listening to his sister talk on her dream phone, while he waited for more branches to snap outside his window.

With a desperate need to pee he fumbled with the door lock and slipped outside.

The sky hid the waking sun in a pocket of white cloud. Billy was already working on the sleepy campfire. "Did you see them?" he asked, while he fed twigs into the fire. "The footprints." He pointed.

The ground looked scuffed and disturbed. Several large footprints went right up to the cab of the camper. Large handprints, twice the size of his, appeared on the camper windshield. A blanket draped around the windows from the inside kept him from seeing his mother and sister.

"Two of them. They found my bag, they were curious. They took my cigarettes," Billy said.

Squatch moved closer to him and the fire. He gave the man an incredulous and suspicious look.

"What? You think I ran around here all night pressing these footprints into the ground?" An amused twinkle lit his eyes. Smoke billowed from the campfire at Billy's feet. The fire's hot cloud circled the man and engulfed him until he stood wrapped in a cocoon of smoke. Billy mysteriously reappeared directly behind Squatch, startled and shaken, the boy fell to the ground. Billy held out a calloused palm. Squatch took the proffered hand and Billy pulled him up as easily as he would pick a mushroom from the forest floor.

"You slept out here last night," he said accusingly, feeling foolish and awkward as he wiped frantically at the twigs, leaves and needles that stuck to the seat of his wet pants. "There was a bear—"

Billy put his finger to his lips for silence then made the slightest indication toward something behind Squatch.

The blood drained from his face. His imagination ignited. He forced himself to turn and look.

Four large deer wandered into their clearing.

After an early breakfast Squatch left a note on the windshield telling his sleeping mother he'd gone with Billy to get the tow truck. The smooth road with its few dips and rolls provided hours of skateboard travel.

Billy ran along side never seeming to tire and occasionally they sipped on the creek water he'd packed.

Hours later they headed up a long winding dirt road when Billy stopped. He stopped walking, gestured to Squatch to do the same. Billy sniffed at the air like an animal. He looked at Squatch who felt like he was being sized up by the man's gaze. "Wait here. I won't be far."

"What?"

"If I'm not back when you get hungry come get me," he replied, smiling and strode off into the trees. Squatch stood dumbfounded, his board under one arm. He watched as Billy disappeared into the forest. Squatch raced after him.

Exhausted, angry and lost, Squatch prepared to spend the night nesting in the roots of a large tree; when he'd finally settled, the quiet whisper of running water came to him. The friendly trickling noise led him to a creek, and as he stepped free of the tangled woods the moon appeared above the forest canopy like a child's white balloon released from its string. Directly ahead of him, in the water, sat Billy.

Squatch strode over to him, filled with a mixture of relief and anger. He wanted to hug and hit Billy at the same time; but he stopped in mid stride, listened as Billy chanted and hummed. A feral lullaby rose softly into the blue night air. Billy sat on a flat, low, rock his long black hair reached down his back and nearly traced the water's surface.

The creek's hypnotic gurgle became the backdrop to a small cry that rose gently above the soft disruptive splash of Billy's gentle dips. The man cradled an infant, which thrust out its tiny arms like two bristle covered sticks. But something terrible had left the infant's face malformed. Lidless eyes, black and glistening, like two wet stones reflecting the moon; the eyes sat too high in the baby's brow. Squatch noticed the baby's mouth located in its cheek. Dark holes moved air in and out in a rhythmic fashion. He struggled to make sense of the infant's tangled face.

"What is it?" he asked in a horrified whisper.

"A boy," Billy replied. "Its mother abandoned it on its first turning."

Billy sat forward and scooped up a palm full of creek water. He rubbed this over the infant's arm and the long dark hairs appeared to wash away. "As I was searching for this infant's mother, I found your family instead. Hold it." He held the infant out to the boy. Only when Billy insisted did Squatch take him.

He remembered Kadia's sweet baby peach face. The infant looked nothing like that. "It's like its features didn't know where to settle," Squatch said, staring down at the small creature, a mixture of horror and wonder pooled in his stomach.

"Without mom this baby stays mixed up. She likes her human form better than her forest one and forgets what she is. Without her, this little guy can't feel the difference between a human existence and a forest one so he's stuck somewhere in between. She needs to return to the old growth with this baby. Only the old growth remembers us." Billy looked thoughtfully at Squatch. "Ancient forests remember everything, even your kind." Billy stood and moved closer to Squatch. "This infant is very sensitive. You can help him become more human. That's better than somewhere in between."

The boy's heart pounded. "Why don't you help him become more human?" he asked in an accusing tone. Billy just grinned and indicated that he should look at the infant. The baby's subtle changes filled him with a warm feeling of connection.

The soft movement of light then shadow across the child's face transformed the baby's deformity. Now the infant looked more human, less scrambled.

"If you ever see one of us, it will be near the water. Water changes us more quickly. Some choose to never transform. They stay in the woods—" A large hemlock branch crashed into the creek and silenced Billy.

A rock flew from the trees and hit Squatch squarely in the head. Dazed and terrified he fell to his knees. He put the infant down in the sand. Billy leaped up and charged into the woods. The boy staggered to his feet, took two more steps when another smaller rock hit him in the chest. Rocks flew at him from the forest, pelting his body. They hit the water and splashed the infant. He grabbed the baby and leaped to the far side of the creek; the infant tucked like a football under one arm. He clutched his skateboard like a shield against the rocks ticking and clacking down around him, some large enough to do serious harm.

The moon revealed few details as it tipped through the canopy and lit the corners of the stumps and trees he hid among. He feared for himself with the infant, who remained quiet and apparently asleep where Squatch placed it in the soft moss in the crook of a log. No hope of escape lay in the direction of a small moonlit clearing between him and the stream; a gigantic, beastly shadow hovered there, and behind it another gargantuan form loomed. Exposed in the surrounding moonlight, he tried to shrink into a small patch of darkness. Soon his nostrils filled with the stench of urine rising from the forest floor. The odor burned his eyes; the foul smells reminded him of the earlier stench in the creek the night before. Squatch coughed loudly.

The forest became indistinct, dissolving into a blackness that absorbed all detail, leaving Squatch alone, huddled up against a crumbling cedar log. The night slowly congealed around him. Time shifted into slow gear. The silver lacey fringe of moonlight that now fell beyond him moved.

A form struggled and morphed from the humus, pulling her arms and torso free, bracing against the earth to dislodge her legs from the ground. She stood, breathing hard, a steaming, damp monolith, adorned in forest debris. She strode towards him, an invincible beast, mother-goddess called forth, Squatch believed, by the omnipotent bonds of progeny.

Beneath her the ground wheezed. Her eyes turned upward and the exposed whites became two more moons in the night. Yet, in a strange shift of dimension, she appeared to walk on a treadmill, never to reach him.

Then, he remembered Billy's word 'turning.' Moment by moment the creature before him became more human. When she finally stepped up to the log upon which the baby slept, she no longer resembled the beast, but a young girl with long dark hair and a gentle and loving countenance. She lifted the infant and pulled it close.

"Don't move," she warned. "Wait for sunrise." She stared in the direction of the dark sentinels who stood their ground between Squatch and the path back to the road. With the baby folded in her arms she returned to the darkest patch of forest and became indistinguishable from the night.

Only with the first pink stains of dawn did Squatch dare contemplate taking his leave of the protective fallen tree. With the light came the stark realization that only a few steps lay between him and the bank of the creek, and the trail back to the road clearly marked by a Day-Glo-orange plastic ribbon. The two gargantuan swaying forms appeared now to be only trees.

Squatch quickly found the road, but something definitely followed him. It smashed its way through the surrounding forest, splintering stumps and dislocating rocks as it moved. Yet, whenever Squatch dared to look over his shoulder he saw nothing except the frantic bobbing and bending of tree and bush.

At the road he slammed his board down ahead of him, leaped onto it, picked up speed and skated down the pavement. He concentrated on his technique to the exclusion of his foe, but not for long. From the corner of his eye he snatched glimpses of a large black form running parallel through the woods along side of him.

Panic rose in his stomach, clawed its way up to his throat until he became so fearful he found himself gasping for breath. A large branch shot out from the woods skidding and landing in his path, but he and his board managed to float elegantly over the limb, performing the perfect ollie, and continuing as if nothing had happened.

The next onslaught hit him in the arm and chest; a tree limb fell in front of his board, stopping it instantly. As he rocketed through the air, he instinctively pulled himself into a tight ball and oddly he recalled a time when as a very young child he went to the circus with his dad. A single high flyer swung on a trapeze. The performer had miscalculated and launched so hard from the bar that he arced across the top of the tent and fell into the empty seats on the other side of the ring.

As if it all took place in slow motion Squatch saw the asphalt heave up toward him. He slammed into the road, bounced and skidded into the gravel on the shoulder and then somersaulted into the dry grassy ditch where he lay, conscious but afraid to move. A familiar sound made his hair stand on end, a sound that made him forget his pain.

His skateboard.

The distinct sound of its wheels on the pavement as it rolled slowly at first then picked up speed frightened him more than any previous encounter. The board's rounded nose appeared over the edge of the ditch so that Squatch found himself looking up at the silhouette of the tip of the board against the bright blue and white sky.

"Hey, you okay, down there?"

Squatch recognized the voice.

"No," the boy answered feeling more humiliated than hurt, lying on his back in the ditch. He felt like crying.

Billy's grinning face appeared above him.

"Sorry about this," he said. "I didn't think they'd want to catch you!" He grinned and reached down to Squatch. The boy hesitated. "We're here," Billy said, encouragingly. "You found my village!" Squatch grabbed Billy's hand. "This way."

As if on cue, a few houses, scattered like large stones in the open meadow, emerged from the thick morning fog and stared silently back. Laundry hung sleepily from lines strung between porches. Dogs began to bark as the two drew closer, and soon the animals descended. The yapping pack of mutts made Squatch nervous. "They look like wolves," he said. Billy agreed.

Children appeared from the house Billy headed toward. They ran from the porch, down the dirt road to join the dogs in their noisy welcome. Billy Jack patted both kids and dogs on the head. Squatch noticed that many of the dogs avoided Billy. They flowed around him like water around a large boulder in a stream.

His host led him to the entrance of the mossy roofed house. The boy propped his board outside the door and turned around to look at where he'd come from, but nothing remained. Mist had seeped in, obliterating the trail they'd traveled.

The T.V. on, he recognized a talk show host with an unfamiliar guest. Squatch stood in the tiny entrance.

Billy slid past him and called out, "Hey, anybody here?"

The smell of fresh coffee made the tiny abode feel familiar. A small, older woman with long dark hair in a single braid appeared from a back room, her feet bare. She shot a look at Billy and then gave him a big grin; one of her front teeth was rimmed with gold. She held out her arms and they hugged. They conversed in a language that Squatch didn't understand, but he heard his name mentioned and the lady laughed and laughed, then came over and shook his hand.

"I'm Billy's Aunty," she said. "You can call me Aunty, too, okay?"

Squatch nodded and looked at Billy, "What about the tow truck?" he asked.

"Tonight. It's out right now, but we'll get it right after dinner and then we'll get your mom and sisters. Don't worry. They're safe," she said. Both Billy and his Aunty chuckled as if they knew something that Squatch didn't.

The boy nodded in trusting affirmation. No one else seemed interested in the Sasquatch pictures flashed across the T.V. screen. "I need to watch this," he said to them both.

"Go ahead. I'll make some phone calls." Billy Jack left him and Aunty returned to the back room.

Squatch found a comfortable spot on the worn out couch and followed the images. The host interviewed the people responsible for the captured Sasquatch. They showed footage of the creatures. The host interviewed the zoo handlers and asked something that Squatch thought he hadn't heard correctly.

"Tell us how you think they escaped," he said.

Tears formed as his chest became heavy with feelings, unable to believe what he heard. Now he'd never see them.

"What's up?" Billy Jack asked, as he strode over to the chair and sat beside him. "You look like somebody died."

Squatch wiped his eyes. He felt tired and wanted to lie down and sleep.

Billy glanced quickly at the T.V. "Sometimes the smell of food overpowers us. This time two young ones were caught, too young to know they should have turned human when they had the chance. Some animal rights people helped them escape. Good thing those two didn't turn or the animal rights guys would have left them there." Billy laughed at his own comment.

Squatch stared at Billy. "You expect me to buy that there are people that can turn into a Sasquatch?"

"That's not what we call ourselves," he said, a serious tone to his words. "That baby we found, his mother has returned. Listen, I need to know how you can pay for the tow truck? Sorry to ask you at such a bad time," he said.

"I—I don't know. I hadn't thought about it." Squatch felt his jean pockets.

"I gotta get the truck now, back in a few hours," Billy said.

By the time Billy returned, Squatch had made friends with the children in the small settlement, and had even won over some of the dogs. He'd set up an old plank on bricks, and showed the children how to roll down the ramp on the skateboard. He showed them what a dark slide might look like if he'd had the space. With the board flipped over onto its grip tape, standing in the middle with his feet hooked on the wheels, he pretended to slide. Squatch made high whispery sounds as if he performed to a crowd of thousands and the skate ramp he'd made from a single board became more complex as he and the small audience of kids used their imaginations to create a surface that worked for more elaborate moves.

Aunty came from the house to tell him that Billy had returned. A few of the dogs crept away from her, their tails between their legs. They whined and one small dog whimpered at her feet. She waved her hand at them and they scattered, running for the safety of the houses. Before she let him go, she asked Squatch to perform a few moves for her. She clapped with glee and so did the children.

He grabbed his board and ran up to the house, children and dogs trailing behind. He dropped the board on the porch and went inside.

They wanted his skateboard as payment for the towing. The smaller children watched him. Aunty sat on the couch knitting. He looked at Billy who gave him a big grin.

"My dad gave me that board," he said.

In the distance Squatch heard a baby start to cry. Then

Squatch nodded a barely perceptible yes. Aunty glanced up at him and never missed a stitch as she kept knitting. The children returned to their playing.

Billy went to the fridge and returned with a Coke. He gave it to Squatch. "Come on," he said, "We got to get you back. We don't want to adopt you." Billy grinned and Squatch got the distinct feeling that somehow he had become a part of the strange village and the people in it.

Out on the porch he noticed that his board was gone. He moved quickly to the idling truck and loaded himself into the passenger seat. Billy joined him from the other side.

They drove in silence back to the place he'd left his mother and sisters. The trip took hardly any time at all.

They were gathered around the fire when Billy and Squatch arrived; they jumped to their feet and surrounded the truck, all talked at once. They'd changed the tire on the camper but the dead battery refused revival.Billy went right to work while the family reunited.

"We saw them," his mother said excitedly.

"We thought we heard a bear. We sat in the truck, doors locked. They came out of the woods right over there!" Niki said.

To get away from her, Squatch walked to the place she indicated. "Figures," he said, defeated. "Well, I heard something on the news." He glanced at Kadia. "They escaped!"

"Who?" His small sister asked.

"The captured Sasquatch," he said.

Kadia began crying.

"You're an idiot!" Niki said, and tried to comfort her little sister.

"It's not my fault. I wanted to see them as much as anybody." He nearly told them that he thought he'd seen one too.

"We're ready to go," Billy Jack said. "I'm going to tow you into town, to the station there. Looks like a new battery for you guys. My brother owns the place. He'll fix you up."

They stayed at the Wild Wood Inn. Lying on the bed in the small room they'd rented for the evening, he watched T.V. His mom and sisters had gone into town to poke through antique shops.

Just as one station flashed sketches of the Big Foot, he heard a tap at the door. Through the peek hole Billy Jack's distorted grinning face looked back. Squatch opened up.

Billy pointed to the old Chevy Impala he had parked behind him, stuffed with teenage boys. "You want to show some of the kids how to use that board? We've got a place with lights." They waved and hollered. They flashed the skateboard out the window at him. They made Squatch a little nervous.

"Don't worry," Billy said, "They only bite."

Squatch found himself sandwiched between four young guys; Jamie and Jake who were brothers and Billy's nephews, and two others, Dan and his friend Mat, who were a little younger and quieter. They called him *Sasquatch Boy* then told him their so-called Sasquatch names making unrepeatable sucking and snorting sounds. The boys laughed so hard they fell to the car floor.

Even Squatch cracked a smile.

They hadn't gone far when Billy pulled up to an empty lacrosse box and the boys tumbled out of the car, pulling scraps of old board and bricks from the trunk.

They skated into the dawn. Eventually, one of the older boys asked to borrow the car for a quick errand and as if on cue, the rest started to wander away, one by one, until Squatch found himself alone with Billy. Just as they said good-bye to the last skater a noise from the surrounding bush drew their attention.

"Wait here," Billy said. But Squatch didn't wait this time and followed Billy before he lost sight of him. The man turned and appeared surprised to see Squatch following closely behind. He gestured with a demanding wave of his arm for Squatch to fall back, then changed his mind and said, "Give me your board."

Squatch handed it to Billy. The man carefully placed it near the base of a tree. "Back off, now," he said in a harsh whisper. "See where I placed your board?"

Squatch nodded.

Billy pointed with his chin. "That tree is called Methuselah. It doesn't live here. It's visiting." Billy grinned. Squatch had no idea what Billy was up to. The enormous tree trunk reminded him of photos he'd seen where twenty people held hands and formed a human chain around the base of ancient trees. The magnificent species was frightening in its majesty. It was like a fat temple column the top of which was invisible. It's bark hung like scales, each large enough to shield a man. Squatch could only liken it to apartment towers he'd seen in the city and was certain several families could live inside it if it were hollowed out and floors built to form storeys.

"Go there," Billy said.

He thought for a moment before he approached the tree. He considered his skateboard and decided he wanted it back badly enough to risk some hoax or joke organized by Billy and the boys. Darkness took over, but the lights from the lacrosse box showed him the way.

As Squatch approached, a ring of darkness rose quietly up from the ground to circle the base of the organic monolith creating an ebony skirt of black space. This umbra reached higher than Squatch. He tried to understand what was going on.

From around the backside of the tree a small boy appeared and waved Squatch over. Dan, the youngest of the evening's skateboarding group, called in a hushed whisper, "Hurry!" The boy's voice released Squatch from his hypnotic state and he moved quickly. Without a word, little Dan stepped into the blackness at the tree's base and vanished into the void.

At the same place where Dan entered something else reformed within the space and took shape before Squatch's eyes. At first the image was tiny but grew bigger as it appeared to draw nearer. A man walked towards Squatch. The clothing and the way he walked, head down, hands in pocket, looked familiar to him. When the figure looked up, he paused, and the boy felt the man take a moment to recognize him. Slowly the man removed his hand from a pocket and raised it in a gesture of greeting. Under his other arm, he held the skateboard. Without thinking Squatch stepped closer, nearly entering the blackness.

"You can't go to him." Billy's voice spoke from behind. "But he can sense you."

Instinctively, Squatch understood. The image became clearer, sharper and the darkness that surrounded him faded, leaving his dad's figure hovering near the base of the tree. As the image faded, his dad's hand remained in the double gesture of greeting and goodbye until it too dwindled like the flame on a spent candle. Squatch held his hand up and knew he was saying goodbye.

"We found an old memory of him, in your board. He used to join you on camping trips."

Squatch could only nod.

Night clung to the forest even as dawn brightened the surrounding sky. Billy leaned up against the tree, stared upward. He focused on something above him. Eventually he looked back at Squatch.

"They're not coming back."

"Who?"

"The Old Family, the ones who chased you in the woods. They waited for the two captives." He paused a moment. "They liked your gifts."

Squatch shrugged, he didn't understand what gifts Billy referred to.

Billy shook his head, looked down and came up smiling. "You brought the infant back and you showed them how to use the skateboard."

Squatch thought about this for a moment. "What will they do with the board?" he asked.

Billy gave him a strange look, as if the ridiculous question needed no consideration, "Maybe a pivot, a primo slide, or maybe they'll just hang ten and remind themselves of what lies beyond the old forests. They won't return for quite a while, if ever," Billy said, sounding a little sad.

Squatch studied the man for a moment, "You know, for a minute you looked like one. The way you walked, your body," the boy said, imitating a couple of Billy's moves.

Billy gave Squatch the biggest grin the boy had ever seen. "I need a new walking stick," he said. "Just in case I need to throw it at another camper." Then the man turned and walked off into the forest, leaving Squatch to find his own way back.

* * *

SLIMED

Alice Ann stopped in her tracks. An army of shell-less tan snails were all over the new plants in her garden. The snails had eaten tiny holes in her lettuce. The Roma tomato seedlings were covered in the things. Even her precious asparagus stalks were prey to a host of the slimy critters. Alice Ann knelt beside her garden and cried. The guardian marigolds hadn't even sprouted, and already her garden was under attack.

"Damn slugs; to hell with it," Alice Ann cursed. She turned and retraced her path back to the house. As she reached the back porch, she saw the garden hose, neatly coiled and ready for use. "Just like Rick, everything in its place." Whatever her neat-freak husband did was orderly and precise, including this week-long birding trip to the Olympic Peninsula. He had left just as she was hoeing the garden, jeering her efforts as ineffectual in Seattle's wet, marine climate. He would be back Sunday, probably not a minute later than planned.

No, I'm not giving up. Thinking how Rick would laugh if the snails destroyed the garden, Alice Ann pulled the hose into the backyard. *Rick isn't the only one in this family who can get things done.*

Alice Ann stood at the edge of the garden and set the sprinkler attachment on its lightest setting. Starting with the tomatoes, she tried to wash the snails off. It didn't work. She turned the setting up higher, worrying about the tender seedlings, but the tiny, spineless creatures held on with a tenacity that daunted Alice Ann. Finally, she abandoned the hose and went back into the house for her garden gloves. Kneeling beside each plant, she picked off each small snail and placed it in a plastic bag for asphyxiation. "They deserve it," she muttered, musing about what her new friends with their fuzzy environmental beliefs would think if they could see her. "It's them or my plants." With grim determination, she tied each bag and tossed them into the garbage bins.

It took most of the day to pull off all the snails. Alice Ann's back ached, her fingers smarted, and her shoulders and abdomen cramped incessantly. She went to bed without eating, too tired to shower. She forgot all about her Sunday call to her mother back home in Georgia.

The next morning, Alice Ann dragged out of bed. Pulling on her dirty jeans and flannel shirt, she walked like a zombie out the back door. "Oh, no," she cried, as she saw the legions of reinforcements redoubling the army of snails that had invaded her garden. Eden no more, the garden had been ravished by the intruders. Whole leaves were gone. There were ugly gashes in the stalks and stems. Alice Ann did not have the strength to pull off the snails. She went back into the house for her purse. Five minutes later, she was zooming down Magnolia's East hill, headed for Ballard and the nearest garden store.

"May I help you?" a friendly clerk asked as Alice Ann pushed open the glass door.

"Snails." The word said it all.

The clerk patted her shoulder and chuckled softly. "The bane of the Northwest garden."

"What do I do?" Alice Ann asked, a tear starting in her bright green eyes.

"Do? Well, there's several things you can do. You can pull them off every morning."

Alice Ann sighed deeply.

"I see you've tried that," the clerk said brightly. "Or you can put out snail bait."

"Snail bait?' asked Alice Ann.

"Poison. There are several different brands, but they all work the same. You line your garden with the bait. It comes in a tube. You just squeeze it out and it kills any snail that tries to cross. Works for weeks."

"Poison?" Alice Ann whispered. "My husband is a bird-watcher. Does it affect birds?"

"Well," the clerk hesitated. "Yes, it can affect birds, if they eat the dead snails."

"What happens to the birds?"

"They can die, or become very sick."

Alice Ann pondered her options. Her back couldn't take picking off the snails every morning, not so many. And they had devastated the garden in only a few hours. She would have to stand guard most of the night, or at least be up at dawn. That would work while Rick was away, but not when he returned. He liked to go out at night and snuggle in the morning. Alice Ann could never spend the time she needed to protect the plot, tiny as it was. As for poisoning Rick's precious birds? She could easily stomach executing the snails, but murdering the birds? That was out of the question.

"Isn't there any other way?" Alice Ann asked, noticing the exotic tilt of the clerk's eyes as she pondered the question.

The clerk took a step toward Alice Ann and lowered her voice to a whisper. "I'll let you in on some tips from my grandmother. Back home. On the island. Southeast Alaska."

Alice Ann leaned closer, anxious to hear the forbidden wisdom.

"We have snails in Klawock, too. We call them slugs."

Alice Ann nodded, understanding the edge of disgust in the Alaskan girl's voice.

"You can put out beer," the clerk suggested.

Alice Ann shook her head. "Don't drink."

"You can line your garden with egg shells. It tears the slugs up as they cross over."

"Too gruesome." Alice Ann's shoulders lifted. Her lips pursed involuntarily.

"How about sugar? Some elders line their gardens with sugar. It attracts the slugs. They can't resist it. Just keep it fresh and your plants will be safe. And so will the birds."

Alice Ann grinned. Sugar had been a mainstay in her grandmother's garden. Tilled in the ground with the white corn and the tomatoes, Grandma's produce was the sweetest in the county. Alice Ann could fool the snails.

"Thank you, thank you," Alice Ann chortled as she gave the clerk a half-hug. "I'll try it."

"Let me know how it works," the clerk said.

Alice Ann nodded and left the store at a half run. She gunned the bug up the hill and arrived just as the midday sun emerged from the ever-present cloud cover. The snails had departed for shadier realms, leaving destruction in their wake. Alice Ann bounded up the walk to the back door and burst into the kitchen. She searched for sugar, but found none. Organic as her taste in vegetables had become, her kitchen was host only to Xcessa, the latest sugar substitute. Hailed as three times sweeter than sugar with fewer than half the calories, Alice Ann thought it should do the trick. Pulling the plastic jar from the shelf, she rushed out to the garden.

It took half the jar to line the garden, but Alice Ann could smell the sweetness as the powdered Xcessa wafted up into her nostrils. "This should work even better than sugar," she thought as she poured the remaining contents of the jar in a double line around the plot. Tossing the jar in the garbage, she got back into the bug and soared down the hill to the grocery to buy more.

For the rest of the day, Alice Ann resisted the urge to check the garden every five minutes. She got a decent night's sleep and went out to the back yard at first light. Approaching the plot, she breathed a sigh of relief. "No snails," she marveled. A few new leaves started to bud on the damaged seedlings. Her garden would survive.

Alice Ann showered for the first time in two days and drove downtown to shop. Parking in Nordstrom's aerial lot, she picked out new jeans and a few undershirts for added warmth. She walked down Fifth Avenue, past the Rainier Bank Tower, and stopped in at Eddie Bauer's. She bought some mucking clogs, a couple of new flannel shirts, and a waterproof poncho. She was determined to continue her gardening through Seattle's wet seasons. Satisfied she had all she needed, she stopped at the Rainier bistro on her way back to the bug. She sat by the glass wall separating the coffee shop from the inverted pyramid which formed the base of the tower. Wondering how the building kept from falling over, she sipped a latte, occasionally dipping a chocolate covered almond biscotti in the rich brew of espresso and steamed milk.

It doesn't get much better than this, she thought. With a start, she remembered that she had not called her mother last Sunday for her weekly check-in. She finished her drink as quickly as the hot latte allowed and hurried down the crowded workday avenue to the Nordstrom's lot.

Sailing into the drive, she day-dreamed of salty tomatoes and sweet Cobb lettuce on pita brushed with extra virgin olive oil. She checked her garden to be sure all was in place. Smiling at her concern, she took her purse and packages inside and got out a new jar of Xcessa. *If a little sweet did this much, surely a lot of sweet would ban the snails forever.* A new line of the white powder made her nose itch, but the Xcessa reinforced the sweet demarcation between Eden and desolation. Alice Ann's determined armory of home remedies was growing. She went in, called her mother, and spent a pleasant hour exchanging garden stories.

The next morning, Alice Ann clucked like a mother hen as the morning light revealed silvery paths all around the garden. There was only one incursion into the plot. She couldn't tell if the Xcessa had been totally eaten or if it had been absorbed by the damp soil. Either way, the white lines of powder were gone. So were several new leaves from her endive plants. *At least these slugs have good taste,* Alice Ann thought as she dusted a heavy circle around the garden with the white powder. The fine grains tickled her nose. She sneezed. To be certain she had not inhaled too much, she dusted even more Xcessa, broadening the lines around the garden.

By Thursday, Alice Ann had established a pattern of dusting the outline of the plot early each morning and late each afternoon. By Friday, there was no new damage to the plants, but the silvery paths from the shade of the trees and foliage edging the yard had grown wider, so wide, in fact, that it made Alice Ann shiver. *How many snails are out there?* Rick had warned her about wild raccoons as big as dogs that roamed Magnolia at night, but she had never seen one. *But giant slugs?* She had never heard of such things, but was determined to find out what was covering her yard in silver slime each morning.

Alice Ann set the alarm for 4:00 A.M. Yawning, she pulled herself out of bed, slipped on her new jeans, flannel shirt and poncho. By the back door, she stepped into her clogs and ventured out into the back yard. She set up a folding lawn chair at the edge of the light from the porch. She cradled a super soaker water gun in her arms. Rick had given her the gun as a joke in recognition of her hatred of Seattle's almost daily rainfall. The cool, damp air kept Alice awake as she sipped liquid energy, but not warmth, from a chilled bottle of Starbuck's mocha cappuccino.

Alice Ann did not have long to wait. The lower branches of the firs at the back of the yard rustled and swished as a large grayish-tan form slithered out from under the compost pile beneath the trees. Alice Ann gasped as the largest snail she had ever seen emerged from the darkness and toward the garden, lit dimly from the back porch light. Joined by two other huge snails, the creatures headed straight for the white lines of Xcessa and covered them with what passed for mouths. Alice Ann heard the slobbering vacuum as the slugs slurped up the white powder.

Finishing off the lines, the snails turned toward the porch. Alice Ann froze in numb terror. The first snail rose slightly, revealing a white-foamed mouth. The snail was as big as an elephant. Realizing the potential danger, Alice Ann recovered as adrenalin surged to combine with all the packaged power of Starbuck's finest: She squealed, jumped up, knocking over the lawn chair, and fired off a single shot from the over-sized water gun. It hit the first one squarely, but didn't even slow it down. They continued advancing toward her. Alice Ann raced into the house and slammed the back door. She watched through the kitchen window, her eyes widening, as the huge creatures crumpled the lawn chair as if it were made of grass. Alice Ann backed away from the window, then bolted for the front door as the back door gave way with a shattering crash. She raced to the bug and jettisoned out of the driveway, her foot smashing the accelerator to the floor.

She drove wildly, careening around corners, headed away from the snails and toward the fire station at the center of Magnolia. Police would have to be called from Queen Anne Hill, across the interbay, but even sleepy Magnolia had a fire house. Alice Ann scraped her bug against the steel barricade that divided the edge of Gilman Avenue West from the railroad tracks overlooking Salmon Bay. Gaining altitude to what was definitely an illegal hover height, she maneuvered precariously the ninety degree turn onto Government Street. Driving well in excess of the posted residential speed, Alice Ann reached the fire station in record time. She honked her horn as she slammed the bug into idle. Not stopping to kill the engine, she bolted through the open door to the station and accosted the first fireman she found.

"Wake up, wake up," she cried, shaking the muscular man by the shoulder. "Giant slugs, I mean, snails. You have to help me!" The fireman woke and looked at her, confusion and doubt playing across his rugged features.

"Giant snails? What are you talking about, lady?"

"I mean huge snails, bigger than my bug," Alice Ann said holding her hands apart to demonstrate the largesse of her garden invertebrates.

"Of course, they're bigger than bugs. They're snails," the fireman laughed.

"No, bigger than *that* bug," Alice Ann pointed emphatically toward the hovercraft she had arrived in.

"Oh, gosh," the fireman said. "Chief," he yelled, standing up and towering over Alice Ann. His size alone made her feel instantly better.

"What the fu–dge," the chief adjusted his language as he saw Alice Ann. Bowing slightly in Alice Ann's direction, he hastily buttoned his shirt. "I mean, what's going on, Mitch?"

"This lady says she saw a giant snail," Mitch said, gesturing toward Alice Ann who was nodding frantically.

"Is she drunk?"

"Not that I can tell, sir." Mitch leaned down close to Alice Ann's mouth and sniffed her breath. "More like coffee, maybe. But that's the third giant snail call we've had tonight. We thought the first two were pranks."

"You saw a giant snail?" the chief asked, making his statement a question.

"Yes, please help me. They're tearing my house down." Alice Ann lost the last dregs of her composure and started shaking.

"Let's check it out, then," the chief said. "Mitch, start up the hovercraft. Can't have any property damage on our watch."

"Right you are, sir."

"You're coming with us," the chief said.

A moment later, Alice Ann sat with Mitch in the front cab of the fire hovercraft. The chief followed in an observation van. Flight restrictions were set aside for the emergency vehicles. They hovered over the island, but avoided the main roads and any early morning commuters. Alice Ann called out directions as Mitch steered around trees and houses. Finally, settling down in front of her house, Mitch let out a deep sigh. It was obvious that the roof had caved in. Three lines of silvery slime, each as wide as the fire hovercraft, crossed the rocks that substituted for a lawn on the steep slope of 24th Street West, Magnolia. "They must be headed for the interbay," Mitch reported over the two-way radio.

"The Red Apple grocery," Alice Ann gasped. "That's where I got the Xcessa."

"Xcessa?"

"You know, the sugar substitute?"

Mitch shook his head. "I'm not following...."

Alice Ann quickly filled him in on the events of the past few days, as Mitch gunned the hover jets and flew down the hill. The snails were no where in sight, but from the gaping hole where the doors of the Red Apple Grocery had once been, it was clear they'd passed this way. A steady rain began to fall.

"They must have gotten faster when they got bigger," Mitch said. Suddenly, Alice Ann gasped and pointed. The snails were headed down Dravus Street across the interbay, toward Queen Anne Hill and... downtown Seattle.

"I'm calling for back-up."

Alice Ann let out a little scream as she saw the snails convulse and then almost double in size. They slimed their way around the base of Queen Anne hill, cutting East down Gilman Drive. Cars were crushed and power lines snapped and sizzled in their wake. The lights went out for blocks as the snails slithered away at a speed that belied their bulk. Mitch reported what he saw. Alice Ann sank down into her seat, peering over the edge of the dashboard at the escaping slugs.

"I've got a professor from U-Dub on the line," Mitch said gruffly.

"U-Dub?" Alice Ann asked, her expression blank.

"University of Washington." Then, "You're not from around here are you?" He handed the two-way to Alice Ann. "Press this button when you want to speak. Remember, only one of you can speak at a time."

Alice Ann took the two-way and waited. "Hello? Hello?" a voice with a vaguely Eastern European accent said.

"It's me, Alice Ann Robertson."

"The woman who reported the giant snails?"

"Yes, that's me."

"I'm Professor Krieg. U-Dub biology department. When did you first spot them?"

"Sunday morning, I think," Alice Ann said. "But they weren't big then."

"How big were they?" the professor asked.

"About a quarter inch."

"A quarter inch?" The professor's gasp was audible. "But the fireman said they must be over a ton now."

"Yes, th-th-that's right," Alice Ann stammered.

"What have you been feeding them?" the professor asked.

"Nothing! I just lined my garden with Xcessa. To keep them out."

"Did you say Xcessa? The sugar substitute?"

"Yes. Just to keep them out of my garden," Alice Ann repeated.

"And the Xcessa was gone every morning?" The professor's voice seemed anxious.

"Yes, but with the rain and everything, I thought the soil absorbed it, so I put out more."

"More?" the professor's roar came across the radio as a shrill whine.

"Yes, more. I figured if some Xcessa worked, then more would take care of the slugs that got through to my tomato plants."

"That's snails, not slugs," the professor complained.

"But they don't have shells." Alice Ann whined. It had already been difficult morning and it was just past dawn.

"My dear," the professor lectured, his tone fatherly. "A shell does not a snail make. It's a matter of internal anatomy. But let's not belabor the point. How much Xcessa did you put around your garden?"

"Since when?" Alice Ann asked, her fingers slipping off the talk button as her hands became moist with sweat.

"Since you started putting the damnable stuff out at all!" He trailed off muttering, "*Since when,* she asks."

"Well, let me think now..." Alice Ann began.

"They're getting away." The snails turned down 10th Avenue West and then south on Olympic Place, traversing the edge of the hill. They moved in and out of Alice Ann's limited field of vision.

As Mitch veered through the turns, Alice Ann saw the snails disappear around the corner onto Queen Anne Avenue, heading toward the Seattle Center.

"Good God!" cried Mitch, as he swerved to avoid an overturned car in the middle of the road. The car was covered in silvery, shining slime. The driver crawled out and staggered away.

"Alice, I must know! How much Xcessa did you feed the snails?" the professor barked.

"It's Alice Ann, actually. I go by both names." She paused as Mitch shot her a glance that could freeze seawater at a hundred paces. "Um. Maybe about forty ounces a day, give or take," Alice Ann replied, holding the talk button down firmly.

"Let up the button," Mitch chided.

Alice Ann released the button "—too much. I told that FDA committee they should have done more testing."

"What committee? What testing?"

"FDA," the professor repeated. "More testing, any testing, animals, insects, amphibians, invertebrates, icthyads. Not just primates. This stuff has environmental consequences. You just can't split up strands of DNA, switch electrons around and mess with the whole genetic constituencies as we know them and not expect consequences."

Mitch swerved to avoid a tree across the Denny Way, less than a block from the Space Needle.

"Can you catch them?" the professor asked.

Mitch grabbed the two-way. "I'm a firefighter, not a wild animal trainer."

"Right. Right, of course," the professor said. "Just keep them in sight.

"Sure," Mitch said, his voice edge with sarcasm.

"And Mitch, keep a line open."

"You're the boss," Mitch said, looking over at Alice Ann, then back at the snails as they pushed up the first steel support of the Space Needle and began to inch skyward.

Alice Ann and Mitch flipped around the corner of the Seattle Center Museum just in time to see the snails emerge from the Top of the Needle bar and restaurant and slide at breakneck speed indecorously down the now tottering support of the Space Needle.

"There must have been lots of sugar up there," Mitch said, as he followed the wallowing invertebrates across the grounds of the Seattle Center. The snails were headed toward Fourth Avenue now, and the commercial and restaurant center of Seattle.

"Not sugar, Xcessa," Alice Ann corrected as she hung on to the handle over the hovercraft's window. "I don't allow sugar in the house."

"Yeah, okay. Whatever," Mitch snapped. He careened toward the snails who were just breaking into a restaurant at the corner of Fourth and Virginia Street. "Where's my back-up?" he shouted into the two-way, as he throttled the reverse jets to brake. The hovercraft shuddered and stopped a few yards from the corner.

"They should be there momentarily," a voice responded. "Try to keep the snails—I mean, subjects—there until they arrive."

"And who am I expecting?" Mitch asked.

"The Safari Team from Woodland Park, who else?" the voice cackled.

"Great, just great. A safari team. Like they would know anything about snails." Mitch flung open his door. Alice Ann, unsure of herself, opened her door and stood timidly on the running board, waiting for Mitch to assist her. When the fireman went straight to the back of the hovercraft and started putting on his fireproof suit, she jumped down and ran toward him.

"What can I do to help?" she asked.

"Unwrap that hose," Mitch said. "There's a lever just beyond the first-aid door." He added, "It's the one with the red cross on it."

Alice Ann pulled the lever out and down. A long, canvas hose unraveled itself and fell to the ground beside the hovercraft. As Mitch donned his yellow fireman's hat, the hose unwound to its full extension, and Mitch flipped another switch to disconnect it from the hovercraft.

"Now we have to connect to the seawater supply," Mitch

said. Alice Ann picked up folds of hose and followed. He stopped beside a blue hydrant. Alice Ann listened to sounds of crockery and glassware shattering as Mitch hooked up the hose. The chief was already there, yelling evacuation orders into a bullhorn.

The snails emerged suddenly and the chief, startled, backed up abruptly and almost tripped over the folds of Mitch's hose. The snails were covered with bright green Xcessa packets. Mitch released another lever soaking the snails with seawater. Alice Ann heard a sizzling and then a series of pops. The snails fled back up 4th Avenue toward downtown. Mitch pursued, but the snails quickly outpaced him.

Suddenly, a huge camouflaged craft labeled *Safari Team* in bold letters and bearing the Woodland Park Zoo logo shot past them and landed, blocking the snails' escape. Two beefy men in khaki uniforms leapt out. Each brandished a long metallic rod. Touching it to the snails' antennae seemed to cause the invertebrates great pain. They reared up, threatening to crush the Safari Team, but the men remained undaunted. Moving forward at a slow but steady pace, they drove the snails back toward Mitch, who, in turn, doused them with seawater.

The noxious stench of burned snail flesh and something else Alice Ann could almost identify stuck her delicate nose, and she began to sneeze uncontrollably. By the time she'd wiped her eyes and cleared her nasal passages, Mitch was helping the Safari Team close the back doors of the zoo's hovercraft.

"Doc Krieg is going to get his wish," Mitch said, stepping toward her.

"His wish?"

"To study those... blobs," Mitch answered, draping his insulated jacket over Alice Ann's shivering form. Then he took her elbow and guided her back to the fire hovercraft.

"It must have been a nightmare for you," Rick said to Alice Ann. They were lounging in a comfortable hotel room until the repairs on their house were complete, waiting for breakfast to be delivered. He stroked her blonde hair out of her eyes. He hadn't made fun of her when he'd returned, and she was terribly happy to have him home.

"It was horrible, just horrible," Alice Ann sobbed, burying

her head against her husband's chest.

"But it's over now," Rick soothed. "The snails are gone."

"But at what price?" Alice Ann asked.

Rick shrugged. He lifted her chin and kissed her gently. There was a knock at the door. Rick got up to admit room service. The young man set the tray down on a nearby table and handed the morning paper and the check to Rick. Rick tossed the paper onto the edge of the bed where it fell open to reveal the headline: "Seattle Slimed!" Alice Ann was turning away when a smaller headline caught her eye: "Record Breaking Year at the Salmon Farms. FDA Finds Xcessa Safe." But before she could read the article, Rick pulled her toward the table. He lifted the plate covers to reveal pancakes with syrup, eggs and bacon, muffins and scones. Alice Ann's eyes skimmed over the feast and rested on the pale green packages, nestled in the white rectangular holder. She shuddered.

Sister's Story

"I am to marry Satan tomorrow?" said Sister. Mother, Father and Brother avoided eye contact. "Why didn't you tell me sooner?"

She rose from the dining table and went to the window, where she looked out on her charge: a sphere of blue and white it was, against a backdrop of vacuous darkness speckled with lighted pinpoints. Her world had brothers and sisters as well, some warm and heavy-laden, others small and cold. A milky-colored satellite rocked the world's waters against its shores and filled the minds of its inhabitants with dreams that ranged from the mythic and sublime to the nightmarish, and included all the folly in between.

Mother looked at Father, who cast his eyes downward.

"I don't know," sighed Mother. Her blue robe and veil framed her creamy face like the sky around a summer cloud. "We kept waiting for the right time, but one never presented itself."

Sister brushed a stray vine that had fallen over her eyes back into the ring of holly berries crowning her head. "The day before the wedding is the right time?"

"It's breaking our hearts to tell you now," Mother tried to explain. "It was so long ago that we promised you to him. Ages before arranged marriages became passé. And Lucifer is one shrewd deal maker. You know, this is going to hurt your Father and me more than it's going to hurt you."

Sister doubted that. "What exactly was the deal you made?"

"You didn't think the serpent would be allowed to mate with a human to make the antichrist, did you?" said Mother.

The words fell on Sister like a blow. Birthing the thing would kill her, except that she was already immortal. "I never really thought about it," she mumbled.

"That the Archfiend's progeny come from you was the only condition he would accept, that allowed Brother to be half human," said Mother. "The Infernal One seems to think this will make his son stronger than Brother."

It might, Sister thought. "But to have a parent from Heaven

and a parent from Hell?" she asked. "The child will fight himself every day of his life."

"He can choose his path as much as anyone," said Mother.

Sister wondered how she could buy herself time, but Mother and Father had bought two thousand years already. Scratch would want his payment tomorrow, as promised.

"I am my own maiden this night," she said. "May I be excused?"

"Of course," said Father, his voice choked. He still would not meet his daughter's accusing eye. His white hair and beard and robe, usually flowing behind Him in a wind of His own making, hung limp over His strong, ancient form.

"Don't you want to stay with us tonight?" asked Mother. "Father and I are leaving the universe immediately following the ceremony."

"Is this another thing you were waiting for the right time to tell me?" said Sister. "That you would forsake me, too?"

Finally, Brother spoke. "I know how you feel, Sister."

She glared at him, her green eyes trying but failing to cut through the depths of his composure. She need not have been surprised. Emeralds could not slice the sea.

"It pains Father too much," said Mother. "He can't bear to share the same space with Satan, once He has given him your hand."

Throughout this conversation, Brother fingered his goatee, while the diamond studs in his pierced hands glittered in the candlelight. Even this nervous gesture was enacted with the serenity he exuded at all times since his first incarnation, and Sister seethed inside, jealous of his part in this compared with hers. What was a slave to the dragon for three lousy days, next to being the dragon's wife for a thousand years? What was in it for her, with this deal they had made? She would serve the Armageddon, watch her lovely world burn and decay, and after a millennium Brother would get the new world. He would rise forth from Sister's ashes like the phoenix, and get all the praise and glory. No wonder Sister's part in this scheme was kept out of the prophecies. Women would have revolted from the beginning. Eve never would have bitten the apple.

Father was a misogynist to make such a deal, she thought,

and Mother but his hand-maiden to go along with it. Sister dared not say these things, though. Instead she turned on her leaf-strewn heels and left the room.

The highlights of Sister's locks glinted like sun-dappled forest leaves, her mica-flecked skin was bronzed and smooth, and she had woven into her gown of soft grasses and twine a delicate beadwork of abalone, gold leaf and pearls. Her present form was capable of the journey she had in mind. She need add only a pair of wings.

With the stars at her back and the Pacific coast directly below her, Sister flew. The rain-swept air, having crossed thousands of leagues without man's or mountain's interference, smelled almost as fresh and new as the day Father had made it. She turned off the coast at a river mouth, and followed the water inland. A large nest, perched high atop a Douglas fir, caught her eye. Inside was an eagle guarding her eggs.

"Don't be afraid," said Sister. She identified herself.

"Greetings, Sister," squealed Eagle. Her white head shone in the moonlight like the eastward mountaintops. "'Tis a fine night for flight. I would join you, if not for these charges." She shuffled the eggs to one side and settled herself again, allowing Sister room to land and sit beside her.

Sister perched in the nest, knees scrunched up to her elbows. Still, she managed to reach out, to preen her friend's feathers.

"Ah," sighed Eagle, eyes closing. "It's a pleasure to share my nest with you. I'll cough up some innards, if you're hungry."

"No, thanks." With great care, Sister plucked a particularly stubborn mite from Eagle's wing, and flicked it away. "I've been informed that I am to wed Mephistopheles tomorrow."

Eagle squawked and turned a carrion eye to Sister. "It's the fate of we great ones to live on rodents and spent fish, though it seems a fair price to pay for the gift of soaring in the solar winds, don't you think?"

"The price for this seems unfair to me," said Sister.

Eagle shuffled a misplaced twig back into place. "What seems a boon to one may seem a bane to another," she said.

"How is this a boon?" said Sister. Without waiting for an answer, she rose, and took to the air again. "Good-bye, Eagle."

"Good-bye," said Eagle.

"Good-bye," the Douglas fir whispered, in tree-speak. "Do not burn me or cut me down, and all will be well."

She would do her best to protect the majestic redwoods, but she was not sure how much she could do for these lesser giants. Soon her thoughts returned to Eagle, who had suggested not only that Sister endure her fate, but that she be grateful for it. Sister felt neither endurance nor gratitude inside her.

Soon, she was gliding over the ocean again. In an effort to wash away the dampness in her eyes and on her cheeks, she dove headlong into the sea, transforming her wings into fins at the last moment.

It was dark and cold. Sister never much liked the oceans at night. She preferred to swim by day, to dive only as deep as the sun's rays could filter down on the coral reefs of warmer waters.

A song drew her out of her ruminations. Soon she found the singers, a gray whale and her calf. They were migrating slowly from tropical Baja to the frigid Arctic waters where they would summer, feeding on the plentiful krill there.

"Don't be afraid. It is I, Sister, come to say good-bye."

Mother Whale sheltered curious Baby behind her bulk. She gazed at Sister with one dark eye. "Why good-bye?" clicked Mama Whale.

Baby tried to click the same question his mama had just asked. Sister smiled at his attempt.

"Mother and Father have promised me to the Beast tomorrow," she said.

"The Beast?" exclaimed Mama Whale. "You mean that black and white cousin who hunts my offspring in packs? That cannibalistic carnivore! I could weigh him down and not allow him breath."

"The orca?" said Sister. "No, I mean the worst of all beasts, the devil himself."

"That tiny surface devil with no blubber, who hunts us with fast, sharp teeth? I'll break his vessel with one tail swipe."

"Humans?" said Sister. "No, this is much worse. This is Satan, the Archfiend, Father's greatest enemy."

"Father sounds like Baby's papa, who leaves us at the orcas' mercy while he galavants north ahead of us," Mama Whale sang sadly. "But... did you say that Mother was part of this decision as well?"

Sister nodded slowly.

"Poor Sister," Mama Whale crooned.

Baby clicked, and darted around Mama Whale. He bumped Sister playfully with his forehead. Upon impact she somersaulted backward, laughing. His taupe hide, unmarked by time and its dangers, was soft and smooth to the touch.

"It would be nice to have a child," said Sister. "Even if it is the devil's spawn."

"It would be half yours," sang Mama Whale.

Sister watched Baby teasing a school of fish, amazed as always at how malleable and helpless the very young were. Mama Whale clicked an order, and Baby hurried to her side.

"Mother did say the child would have a choice," said Sister.

"Tell me more about this Satan," sang Mama Whale. "Is he hung well? Will he give you pleasure?"

She had not thought of that. "I don't suppose they call him Scratch, Tempter, Lusty Dick and Horny Jack for nothing." Sister smiled. "Maybe this deal won't be all bad. Thanks, and good-bye, Mama Whale. Good-bye, Baby."

"Good-bye, Sister," clicked Mama Whale. Baby clicked, too.

Sister swam upward, then surfaced and took in a deep breath. She wondered if, knowing what was to come for beings like Mama Whale and Baby, she could lose herself in pleasure. She had seen Satan at work; if he chose to, she thought, he could probably persuade her to forget... for a time.

"Good-bye," shooshed the waves, washing her inland. "As long as rain keeps falling, all will be well."

Not if it rains fire, she thought, knowing what Armageddon might bring. Guilt nagged at her, for having selfish thoughts of ecstasy when this place was on the brink of becoming the devil's playground. She pitied the beings here. More than that, though, she pitied herself.

Grainy friction scraped under her belly, and she looked up to see a sandy beach before her. She crawled and pulled herself ashore. Feeling lowly as an insect, she transformed into one.

Sister scuttled long and far. One with the night, she darted from shadow to shadow. The moon set. She climbed a rock and looked about. Nearby, a cluttered yard propped up a shack.

So absorbed in her surroundings was Sister that she failed to notice the being cowering below her until it spoke.

"Have mercy, oh, great one," it said.

Startled, she rubbed her front legs together. Cockroach cowered even lower.

"Don't be afraid," she said. "I didn't mean to interrupt your nightly scrounging."

Cockroach straightened her front legs and bent them again, as if to bow. "'Tis an honor to grace my kind with your presence," whirred she. "Please allow me to lead you thither." She pointed her left front foot toward the ramshackle building. "There lies a great storehouse of crumbs, and a sink! The drain hole leads to an actual sewer. Might I be permitted to present you to my clan?"

Graciously, Sister declined the invitation. "Soon I must go," she said. "I am to wed the Prince of Darkness."

Cockroach droned excitedly. "Will this be the start of the Armageddon promised to my kind?"

"It will."

Immediate and intense joy gave Cockroach such a jolt that she flipped onto her back. Sister nudged her back on her feet.

Cockroach lifted her proboscis and smacked it against Sister's. "Let me be the first to kiss the bride," she hummed. "Congratulations! Are you not thrilled to trembling? Such power you will have, as the wife of Diablo and the mother of his children! Such power we lowly ones will have! The last shall be first, after all. Oh, oh, I must spread the news!"

Cockroach scuttled away, whirring about the millions of descendants who would make pilgrimages here, to see where their honored ancestor had received news of their most triumphant hour.

The insect was right; Sister would have great power. Broken world or not, every being and every soul that bowed to Old Nick would bow to her as well. She imagined glittering pageants, palaces and shrines, feasts, songs, cries of adoration.

"I can't wait to tell this story to my great-great-great-great-great-great-grandchildren," said Cockroach, scuttling by.

The glamorous images in Sister's mind collapsed. They were borne of pride, a pride no greater or less wicked than that of Cockroach. Sister's anger and frustration focused on the bug. She transformed into a humanoid and, with five bounds of her strong and swift legs, placed herself in the course that Cockroach scuttled toward.

"Oh boy, oh boy, oh boy," whirred Cockroach with glee.

Sister imagined planting her foot against the exoskeleton and squishing firmly, twisting left and right again until she heard a satisfying crunch. She even lifted her foot to do so. But, she realized, Cockroach could not help being what it was. Muttering a curse under her breath, she let her upraised foot land a mere wing's breath from the insect—no harm in scaring some sense into the little bugger.

"Where'd you come from?"

Sister looked up and found a little girl staring at her, poised, ready to run if Sister made a move toward her.

"Don't be afraid," said Sister. "I'm here to say good-bye."

"You never said hello," said the girl.

She laughed. "You're right. Hello. My name's Sister."

"Sister?" The girl's eyes squinted with distrust. "I never heard of that as a name. I'm Cleo. Mama named me after a queen." She straightened and tried to look haughty.

"I can see why," said Sister. Based on her size, the girl could have seen no more than five turns of the seasons. "What are you doing out here by yourself at night?"

Cleo glanced at the shack. "Mama and Daddy are having a *discussion*. I sneaked out for some peace and quiet. Push me?"

She ran to a rusty swingset and settled into the seat.

Now that Sister listened, she heard from the building that a man and woman argued, sometimes loudly, sometimes simultaneously. Moving behind Cleo, Sister pulled the swing back, then let go.

"Do they have *discussions* like that often?" asked Sister.

"Sometimes," said Cleo. "Sometimes they laugh, sometimes they sing, sometimes they squeak the bed. I like it best when they laugh and sing, because I get to laugh and sing with them. Why are you saying good-bye, when you just got here?"

Sister sighed. "I'm getting married tomorrow."

"Congratulations!" said Cleo. "Push me higher."

Sister sighed again, and pushed the girl a little harder. The chain links creaked when the swing fell back.

"Don't you want to get married?"

"Mother and Father promised me to him," said Sister.

"Do you love him?"

"Oh, no, I could never love *him*."

Cleo turned about in her swing to face Sister, and almost fell out of her seat. Sister caught her, bringing the swing to a stop. The little girl did not seem to have noticed. She just stared at Sister.

Finally, she said, "You *can't* marry someone you don't love."

"Cleo, you get in here!" It was the woman inside the shack. "I heard you swinging!"

"I'm coming, Mama!" Cleo's attention returned to Sister. "My Mama and Daddy love each other a lot, but that doesn't stop them from yelling at each other sometimes. It doesn't stop Mama from crying sometimes. If they didn't love each other, it would be horrible!"

It would be hell, thought Sister, as she helped Cleo down.

"Sister, even if you love your Mama and Daddy, a girl's got to do what a girl's got to do." She straightened into her queenly pose. "A girl's got to take care of herself. And you can tell them Cleo said so. Bye!"

Cleo scampered toward the shack.

Laughing aloud, her voice tinkling like wind chimes in a breeze, Sister watched until the girl was safely inside.

Everyone who was anyone came to the black hole—singularities providing the best neutral ground—for the wedding. Father, Mother and Brother sat on one side. Brother wept. Joan of Arc, Mother Theresa and Martin Luther King Jr. shared a bench with Confucius and Lao Tzu. Chiefs Bigfoot and Sitting Bull sat behind them with Mohammed, Gandhi and Buddha. Also on the bride's side were the nine orders of angels, the martyrs, the saints, Elijah and the prophets, and all Brother's disciples but Judas.

Judas sat opposite with the damned and Satan's legions, Satan's most loyal minions toward the front: Asmodeus, Azazel, Baal and Beelzebub. Columbus, Cortez, Herod, Hitler and Vlad the Impaler amicably shared a bench, but only after a battle of wills over who deserved the aisle seat. Further back, assassins and serial killers mingled with the seven deadly sinners, while despots plotted with hypocrites.

Adorned in a gown of pearls and white rose petals, Sister stood beside Satan. He wore a black leather tux. His polished horns glistened, gleaming, long hair hung loose and silhouetted a strong dimpled chin. Of all the gorgeous he-men who had played the devil on stage or celluloid, Sister thought, the real thing outshone them like the morning star that he was.

The heaven-sent soul of a dead pope and the hell-bound soul of a Satanic high priest conducted the ceremony.

Satan had just said, "I do."

"Do you, Sister, take Satan to be thy lawfully wedded husband, in hell, for one full millennium?" asked the pope.

"Hell, no!" she said.

If looks could kill.... Well, looks from such as these would have killed you or me, but they did not distress Sister.

And if this were an old myth, Sister's defiance would have been squelched with a severe and instant punishment of the worst sort imaginable. But it was a new millennium, and time for a new myth. At least, that was what she hoped.

The attendees had not yet exhaled the breath they had gasped inward at Sister's refusal.

"Are you certain?" asked Satan.

"Here's my offer," she said.

He furrowed his brow in preparation for an angry retort, but gestured that she continue.

"I'll fool around with you all you want."

He smiled.

"But I will not marry you; I will be my own woman."

"You do not wish to be my queen, very well," said the devil.

"Not your queen, not your servant," said she. "I will bear your child, but I get partial custody."

"That is not in accordance with my plan," argued Satan.

"You're not up to the challenge, then," she countered. "You can't raise the antichrist as a part-time parent, even if it is only half devil?"

"This is inexcusable," roared Father.

They turned to see Him standing, staff in hand. Sister had not seen Him so angry since He unleashed the plagues of Egypt.

It was all or nothing. She would not back down. "I did not ask to be excused," she said, looking Him square in the eye.

Father raised his staff. She braced herself, but nothing happened. Was He still deciding how to punish her?

"I'll do it," said the devil. "On one condition."

Father lowered his staff. All eyes turned to Satan.

"Instead of one thousand, I get three thousand years."

Father shrugged. "My son?" said He.

"I can wait a couple more thou," said Brother.

The devil plotted something, Sister knew that much. Without the wedding band to imprison her, perhaps she could offset it. She could pick up after him as he rained fire and wreaked havoc on the world. Clean house, as it were. She was giving up power of a sort, though. She could not sit beside him on his throne. But in another sense, this would make her his equal. She may not be his to protect in the Armageddon's aftermath, but she would not be his to abuse, either. And perhaps her side of the child would win out, with half her influence. If only she could see the future.

"Well, maiden lovely," said Satan. "You started these renegotiations. What say you?"

She held out her hand for him to shake. "Let's do it."

He took her hand, and kissed it.

They faced the crowd. The celebrants clapped and whooped and hollered. Confetti fell and fireworks exploded.

Satan leaned toward Sister. "I hope you will regret this," he said, his voice just loud enough for her ears.

Had He still been there, even Father could not have heard their whispered conversation, but He and Mother had exited the universe two eye-blinks ago.

"If I do regret this, it will have been my choice," she said.

He grinned. "I *could* learn to respect a woman like you. Not that I will, of course."

"Is that as close as you can come to a true compliment?" she said. "I *could* thank you...."

With a laugh and a tug of her hand, the handsome devil led her down the aisle.

You Can Hardly Wait

In your youth, life looks long, unending, before you. You turn ten and your parents are so cool. You turn thirteen, and your parents are so stupid. You turn eighteen, and God, you can't wait to get away. Twenty-one! Celebrate with a hangover the next day. On and on. Thirty, great job, making lots of money, swell wife; forty, been having trouble with the kids and you and your wife—well, it feels like you're kinda going your separate ways; fifty, geeze, time sure is going; sixty whoa, how did that—seventy, I can barely remember where I put—eighty, and you know the rest. Yeah, yeah, you know the rest. You know how it's fuckin' gonna be. And it is. And it is.

"Mr. Taylor? Mr. Taylor? Time to get up now. We're gonna get you shaved and cleaned up."

What? You think. *Where—where am—what?* You open your eyes. The room swims into focus. You look at the girl. She's dressed in pale blue and she's got blond hair in a ponytail and she must be what, sixteen—no, eighteen, maybe. You were that young once. For some reason, you really like her nose—proud, Roman. She's pretty. You can still feel your dong get stiff.

"Let me help you," she says. She puts her arms around your back and gently helps you sit while also helping you swing your legs over the edge of the bed. It's warm in the room. "You know where you are?" she asks.

"Har—Harbor—Harborbay—" Fucking words won't come out.

"That's right," she says, "Harborbay Nursing Home. You know the date?"

"October—uh—September—uh—um—25th, 2025—"

"Almost," she laughs. "27th of September. Do you have to pee?"

Pee, you think. *Pee. Do I haveta pee? Yeah, yeah, I gotta pee.* You nod your head.

"You want the urinal or can you make it to the bathroom?"

God damn, you think, *at least some shred of dignity.* "Bathroom."

You stand. These legs. These legs that took you to the Andes in 2010. These legs that took you backpacking in the

Wind River Range in 2000. These legs that don't move worth Jack shit now. But you somehow get to the bathroom and it takes forever to pee.

Through the open bathroom door, you can hear the sounds of the unit: someone laughing, the distant clank of silverware on ceramic. The television in the dining room is suddenly turned up. You catch some of the news: "—colony on Mars destroyed—unknown organism or virus to blame—survivors en route back to space station— question of quarantine major issues—in other news, riots continue to flare up in Cape Town as more emergency food shipments are discovered stolen—"

You get a little sliver of pee and you continue to listen: "—Mary Mathis here with the weather report—temperatures continue hot for this time of year in many places: highs in Fairbanks will be 95 today, Seattle 107, Los Angeles 118, as more records are shattered—many dying of heat stroke—"

You hear someone yell, "Turn that damn thing down or turn it off!"

The sound drops. You're finally able to pee and glad the place is air-conditioned. You finish your task and turn: Is that you, shuffling across the floor? Is that our hand shaking as you hold our pajamas up? You look at them: Pale green with alternating vertical bands of dark green stripes. Nursing home issue. You open the door and the nurse's aide is there. Your eyes can focus better and you look at her nametag. Jenny. Yes. Jenny.

"Did you pee?" she says.

You nod.

"Did you poop?"

You shake your head and try to smile. "Nope. Not in my britches either."

"That's good," she says. She takes you by the arm and you shuffle down to breakfast. You sit at the table across from Mrs. Whatshername—you think you knew it yesterday but today—well, maybe you'll remember it later. She looks blankly at you, then looks away. The wallscreen continues to present the news and you can't imagine why no one changes the channel, as if you really want to hear about all the disasters in the world—at breakfast.

Jenny brings your tray for you. "Looks good," she says

brightly. "Scrambled eggs, ham, and Malt-o-meal. Mmmm—mmm."

"Thanks," you say. She's trying.

Mrs. Pickins sits at the table over there. She constantly moves, twitches. Anxiety. You know that's anxiety. No matter how much the distraction, the stimulation, she knows what she's here for. She wrings her hands, so anxious that she can't focus on her eating.

Mr. Smathers over there, you recognize him and a while back, you actually had a lucid conversation with him. He used to be a big shot at Macrosoft before it crashed. "Lost everything," but he was philosophical. "Just glad I paid off my house. Can't believe it would happen to me. What Macrosoft crashing? Delayed Electromagnetic Induced Neurodegenerative Syndrome—DEINS—what? Linked also to the onset of Parkinson's and Alzheimers disease? What?"

You pay attention to your food, to the eggs, and it actually tastes pretty good. The big SonyFord wallscreen still presents the news, now: *Breaking News*, flashes on the screen. "Katy Durant here—a special on the Mars Colony Disaster or the MCD—unknown contamination—"

You really can't hear that well with the plug of wax in your right ear and with the increase of noise in the dining room as more folks come in for breakfast: The movement, the voices, Mrs. Halsey over there crying as she has been doing all the time she's been there—you budge your table closer to the screen to better listen to what Durant, the newscaster, has to say. You don't suspect it's to cheer everyone up.

"—apparently the contamination—and that's what we're calling it now—on Mars was transferred to the survivors—all now confirmed dead en route to Earth—question has come up about the safety of the Martian samples sent back in 2006—under quarantine in the Mars Sealed Environment or MSE in Houston and no expected problems—makes the situation so perplexing—we go live to Mr. Shuster from NASA in Houston, head of the Mars Return Sample Mission—MRSM—Mr. Shuster, why is the *mumblemumble* showing up now and are the samples safe?"

Mr. Shuster's picture is on the screen—he's an older guy,

white hair and that terribly pained expression that such folks get when they have to say something and they really don't know what to say except they have to say something okay, bland, reassuring and ultimately stupid so the audience won't panic and stop looking at the commercials for MaytagTimeWarner washing machines.

"—well, Katy—"

You're aware of a nurse's aide right next to you at Mrs. Halsey's table. "There, there, Mrs. Halsey—just try to eat—everything will be just fine—"

You're suddenly irritated at the aide because you realize that you've been really trying to follow this newscast—you realize—maybe no one else does—*this* is serious but you know something else that is—calling—what?

After a few minutes, you can hear Mr. Shuster, apparently responding to a question Katy has asked him, "Theories that it has just taken this long—" *mumblemumble* "—prolonged exposure to water vapor, heat—possible that it has taken years for the virus—if that's what it is—nothing like we've seen before—not even the confirmed fossils in the ALH84001 Martian meteorite from Antarctica—"

Schreeech—a chair screeches across the floor in the dining room and Mr. Artsworthy stands up, sways like he's going to faint then sits down again, puts his locked hands on his forehead like he's praying.

"—so, Katy—" continues Shuster, and the scene is that of a reaction shot of Katy and God, you think, she's striking: straight copper blond hair, dressed in the latest: a blue blazer with a metallic sheen, and an iridescent jewel at the closed collar of her white blouse. "Current speculation, if it is viral—was that it wasn't dead, but dormant—slowly genetically altering to adapt to minute exposures of water vapor, warmth, air at the colony site—"

"—but that's just theory—" says Katy

And, or course, someone changes the channel to a gardening show, showing where you can get desert plants for the Puget Sound region. You look around. On the pink walls, pictures. There's the cone of Mt. Rainier—it's a picture of the way it looked before all the glaciers went.

Jenny comes over. "Are you through, Mr. Taylor?" she asks. She tries to look cheerful, but you know she's really worried about something. And so you say, "There's something—going on—something—bad—"

She looks startled. She wasn't expecting that. "Oh, no, no," she says. "You know the news, all gloom and doom. Would you like to go back to bed for a while? Remember, there's Occupational Therapy at 10:30 and it's going to be music today—you get to play an instrument. Won't that be fun?"

You don't say anything. Diversion. Oh, well, but you do feel better, more alert and—for some strange reason, incredibly calm. You get help shuffling back to bed and you nap and you dream of something—coming. You don't know what but it brings you something, a message, and it feels like it's from very, very far away. As you drift off to sleep, you think you hear, *I bring you peace. I bring you peace from fear, suffering, pain. I bring you peace.* And your head fills with this pink glow and you find it so—soothing, so very, very—soothing.

"O.T.," says Jenny. "Time to get up, Mr. Taylor. Do you need to pee? To poop?"

You shake your head; you feel like you're back from—somewhere—the room swims for a minute. You look to Jenny. She's having a real hard time trying not to look worried. "What's—" you begin.

"Let's get up." She comes over to the side of the bed, ready to slip her hands under your arm to help you stand: You're struck with the awareness that she must think that because you're old, you're oblivious and she's not going to answer your question. But you know something has happened. With her help, you stand and she takes you down the hallway and you get a view of the wallscreen, a picture of a tense newscaster, black hair plastered at an angle across his forehead, speaking directly to the camera. "—officials here at the Houston Mars Sample Containment Center urge calm—contrary to earlier reports, there is no evidence—"

Suddenly, commotion in the background, and you get a glimpse of what appears to be an explosion in a building—a—*pink*—explosion and someone is yelling, "Get back, get back—

the fucking media—the cameras—*turn them*—"

The wallscreen goes blank.

Another nurse comes up to Jenny. It's Dana, beautiful, black-haired, and in spite of everything, you feel your dong getting stiff again and Dana looks really scared. "Have you heard—" she says to Jenny.

Jenny just nods and it's obvious she knows something and wants to say something to Dana, but fears you overhearing and she doesn't want to worry you, totally oblivious that you already know something wicked is going on.

Abruptly, you look up. "What is gong on?" you say in a very clear and, you're surprised, strong voice.

Both Dana and Jenny look startled then look at you. They hesitate. They make a decision. "We don't know," Jenny says. "Some kind of contamination—an accident—"

You smile. They just can't tell you the truth and it's probably because what it means is just too awful for them to handle but you realize that you're not too old to get it after all, even if it is awful.

You've followed this Mars thing for years before you came here, the fascination everyone had with the return soil samples that indicated that there was indeed evidence that not only confirmed the minute forms in the ALH meteorite to be fossils but also hinted at other forms of past life as well—only, you smile, looks like it wasn't so past after all.

And here you've been wondering how your life was going to end. Now you know. Do you have to poop? Do you have to pee? You just have to smile. Probably won't be hearing that much longer.

And you can hardly wait.

Plot Device

To: "Mazotta, Kathryn M." <SingleID587932354>
From: "TL&L Editor" <AIReg24994701>
Subject: Acceptance of Story

Thank you for submitting your work to Tales of Love and Loving ("the Zine"). We would like to publish your short story entitled "All Elaine Wants is Love" ("the work"). Click the hyperlink to download the contract. If you have any questions, do not hesitate to contact the Editor.

Kathy Mazotta had finally done it.

Two years ago, she had lost her job at the news division of Paramount-Bell WorldMedia, another victim of the CAN tools that had swept the industry. There were virtually no jobs left in journalism that still required human writers. Kathy had been trying to break into the fiction market since losing her job.

Now, at long last, she had her first sale.

Kathy glanced at the clock. Sean would be home in a couple of hours, but this couldn't wait. It would be so ironic to call him at work.

"Hey, Kath! I'm home."

Sean Nolan walked into the study to find Kathy seated at the computer.

He kissed her on the cheek. "Another story submission?"

"Uh, huh."

"Which zine this time?"

"*Tales of Love and Loving.* They just came online a few months ago." Kathy opened the mailbox. "Still nothing for you. You'd think those companies would have the courtesy to at least send an acknowledgement of having received your résumé."

He changed the subject. "Listen, how about a movie tonight? *Siege of Heaven*'s playing at the Dunbar."

"Sean, you know I don't like those violent—"

"Come on, it's just harmless fun." He pulled her closer. "Besides, isn't it the company that matters?"

They went to see *Siege of Heaven*. The plot was very simple. A group of terrorists had taken over Space Station Beta, so a commando team was sent to rescue the hostages. To complicate matters, the girlfriend of the team commander was also aboard Beta, and the man was plagued by guilt over the death of a previous lover in a similar crisis. But after a spectacular space battle that climaxed in a hand-to-hand combat sequence in which the commander killed the terrorist leader by smashing his head through a bulkhead (his head blew up in the vacuum, while the rest of his body still inside the module convulsed wildly) Beta was freed. The movie ended with a weightless love scene before fading to the credits, scrolled out over the strains of an adult-contemporary soundtrack song.

"What'd you think?" Sean asked.

"It sucked!" Kathy spat. "I'll bet a 10-year-old with a CAN program wrote that and made megabucks!"

"It's just a movie." Sean rather liked *Siege of Heaven*. The action was intense, the special effects were awesome, and the mixed cast of live actors and crofts was likable.

Each theatre exit was flanked by a smiling teenaged usher who recited the same words to every departing patron:

"Thank you. Good night."

"Good night," Kathy responded.

Sean said nothing. Kathy gently elbowed him.

"Hey!"

"You're being rude."

"Oh, come on. They're *paid* to say that!"

"You're in Sales, Sean. You deal with the public. Don't you prefer dealing with polite people? I'd thought you'd be a little more sympathetic."

They made their way through the parking lot under a clear, cloudless night sky. Weaving their way through the cars, they eventually got to Sean's old Toyota.

"That really wasn't such a bad movie," Sean said.

"You have absolutely no taste, you know that?"

"Hey..." He gently pulled her face towards his. "Don't mock my taste."

Kathy abruptly pulled away. "How much longer do you think you're going to be at Lagoda?"

Sean sighed. "What kind of a question is that? Look, I'm sending out résumés, but with the economy the way it is... If people aren't hiring, they're not hiring. Look, Lagoda's not such a bad place—especially in Sales and Support."

"The faster you're out of there, the happier I'll be."

"Come on Kath, let's not start this again. I've been working at Lagoda since we met. You never complained until you lost your job—"

"Because of those damn CAN tools *your* company puts out!"

"I have nothing to do with those products! Look, I'm sorry nobody's bought your stories yet, but if you want to work I've told you Lagoda's hiring writers to help refine the genetic algorithms that—"

"I don't want anything to do with them and I don't want *you* to have anything to do with them either!" She stared out the window into the night. "Not that I'd expect you to understand."

They drove home without another word.

Lagoda Technologies occupied a nondescript three-storey building at Main and National, off the eastern edge of False Creek, an oddly unglamorous location for the industry leader in computer-assisted narrative software. CAN was originally developed for use in high-end games, in which new story elements are generated in real-time to allow players a seemingly infinite space of plot trajectories. But as the technology matured, Lagoda began to spin-off CAN tools for real-world writing applications.

Sean's new cubicle was the same size as the one in his previous position, but at least this one had a window. He would have preferred one that faced False Creek instead of the rail yard, but it was better than none.

"How was your weekend?" asked Peggy Yang, one of the senior engineers.

"Not bad. Saw *Siege of Heaven*. It was pretty good."

"Yeah, my husband and I saw it last week." Peggy pointed at the picture on Sean's desk. "So, when are you going to get off your sorry ass and marry that poor girl?"

"Will you stop that?" Sean demanded as he sat. "You sound like her mother, always asking me when she's gonna get some grandchildren. Why do you think I hate going home?" He wagged a finger at Peggy. "And if you keep this up, I just might stop showing up here as well."

"Great! Better job security for me."

"Get outta here, you slacker. Some of us have work to do."

Peggy smiled. "Hey, speaking of slackers, did you hear about what happened to Vik?"

"Is he still complaining about not having a window? I told him the day he was hired: 'You're here so that *I* can leave!'" Sean laughed. "That old office was a dungeon. Man, am I glad to be out of Sales."

"Real engineering work, better pay, window... Anyway, for once he wasn't complaining. Turns out absent-minded Vik left his briefcase on top of his car and drove off with it up there. The thing actually stayed put until he got onto the 99. Came flying off and hit a police cruiser, of all things!"

Sean was still chuckling as he logged onto his workstation. After spending a few minutes answering his messages, he opened a folder and began coding a dynamic library module for the company's special new project.

if (concept(i)=FALSE).and.(belief(character(i)))...

Kathy had locked herself in the study... again.

"How much longer are you gonna be?" Sean rattled the door knob. "We're supposed to be at your parents' place in an hour. You know how your mother freaks out if we're late!"

The door opened. Kathy glared at him before returning to the computer.

"How much longer?" Sean asked quietly.

"Never..." She raised an index finger solemnly "...*ever* interrupt a writer in the middle of inspiration. If I don't get this down, I'll lose it for sure."

"What are you working on?"

"I got a message from *Tales of Love and Loving.* They're interested in my story, but asked for some revisions."

"Wow!" Sean exclaimed. "Can I read what you've got?"

Kathy backed away to let him see the screen:

"Oh please, I love him so *much!" Tears were streaming down Elaine's beautiful face. Her voice quivered with passion and sorrow. "Daddy, daddy... if you could only see, just how good he's been treating me..."*

Tik-Gon, who was Elaine's father, was very angry. His face had a dark scowl. "No! I absolutely forbid you from seeing that white boy again! Over my dead body will you marry a gweilo*!"*

"No Daddy, no!" Elaine struggled to find a way to make her father understand. "Frank is so special. He's my man, the most beautiful man in the whole, wide world..."

Sean blinked a few times and swallowed before he spoke. "That's... good."

"It's all about empathy," Kathy explained. "A good writer has to get inside the characters, to understand their inner lives, to know what makes them tick." Kathy paused for a moment, then quoted, "'I have to have the character in mind through and through... I must penetrate into the last wrinkle of his soul.' Henrik Ibsen said that, and he's right. That's what those hacks and their fancy CAN tools will never get."

"Sure..." Sean said. "I'll wait in the den."

Kathy slammed the door.

Sean went into the other room, turned on the TV at a low volume, and started watching a sitcom. There was a running gag involving a whoopee cushion.

if belief(character(j)).and.event(j)) then...

A tap on the shoulder startled Sean out of his concentration.

"Lunch?" Peggy Yang smiled. "Come on, don't make the rest of us look bad."

"I'm not hungry."

"Suit yourself." Peggy started towards the door. "Hey, isn't Hydro going to be doing that UPS generator test tonight?"

Sean looked up. "Oh my God, thanks for reminding me."

The last time B.C. Hydro did a test of the building's "uninterrupted" power supply, they somehow managed to take down the computer network, both the voice and vidphone systems, and disengage all the security maglocks. Sean made a mental note to remind Vik about his vidphone.

Kathy read the acceptance message again while waiting for the vidphone to connect.

"Hello," intoned the perfect image of a young woman.

"Uh... hello." Kathy frowned. She hadn't expected a croft to answer. Sean was almost always at his desk. She studied the computer-generated image for a moment. Yes, it was definitely a croft. She could tell from the eyes.

"I'm sorry, miss," it continued, "but I'm afraid Vikram Hakki can't speak with you at this moment. Would you like to leave a message?"

"What? Uh... sorry, I must have dialled wrong."

Kathy tried again, and was greeted by the croft once more.

"Hello, miss. I'm afraid Vikram Hakki cannot speak with you at the moment. Would you like to leave a message?"

"Vikram Hakki? Isn't this the number for Sean Nolan?"

"It is not." The croft paused as the image refreshed. "Sean Nolan is no longer in Sales and Support. Do you want me to put you through to his new number?"

"No, tha—" She stopped herself from thanking the non-person. "Just tell me where Sean Nolan is now."

For years, Lagoda Technologies had been at the forefront of CAN software. Now, it was poised to take the next step. The company's goal was to develop a computer that could not only assist a writer, but would actually *create* its own tale. Lagoda would go beyond CAN into fully computer-*generated* narrative.

Sean surveyed the three linked workstations that formed a neural net known by the company codename of SHELLEY. The first machine, called PROUST, defined the initial theme, characters, and setting of a story. This would normally be done with a user input seed, but PROUST could also autonomously crawl the Web for story ideas.

The second computer, JOYCE, held a vast narrative parameters library that contained the complete vocabulary, syntax, and grammar of the English language. JOYCE also housed an extensive set of dynamic library modules. These

DLMs codified such literary themes as love, revenge, jealousy, betrayal—and the one Sean was working on.

The last machine, KAFKA, was the heart of Lagoda's prototype CGN system. Using the structural data from JOYCE and the story seed from PROUST, it would run dozens of AI and CAN processes in parallel to produce the actual prose.

```
if (exist(action(i)).and.(!exist(state(q))).or.
(concept(i)=FALSE)
{
if (belief(character(j))!=true)).or.(action(m))
action(i)=action(m);
else
action(i)=NULL;
}
```

The message icon started blinking on the screen. He touched it.

"This is the front desk," a synthesized voice intoned from the speakers. "There is a person here to see you."

Sean frowned. He wasn't expecting any visitors. "Who is it?"

"The person identifies herself as Kathy Mazotta."

"How long?"

It was three in the afternoon, so the cafeteria was almost empty. Sean and Kathy faced each other across a table in a back corner.

"How long have you been working in R&D?" Kathy asked again.

"Seven months." Sean ground his teeth. It had to have been Vikram Hakki, forgetting to reinstall the message reroutes on his vidphone after the UPS test.

"You never had any intention of leaving Lagoda, did you? You weren't looking for another job, you just transferred—"

"What else was I supposed to do? There wasn't anything for me in Sales anymore! They've got crofts handling calls now. Hell, Vik Hakki's the only real person on shift during the day. The only other people are those who go out for service calls."

"And you couldn't do that?"

"I *hate* dealing with clients, Kath!" Sean shot back. "I'm an engineer, not a huckster. The only reason I stayed in Sales was to keep *you* happy. But R&D is where I've always wanted to be. It's where I belong, Kath! Why are you making Lagoda—making *me*—out to be such a villain? I'm sorry, but—"

"You're *not* sorry!" Kathy shouted. "You don't give a damn about how *I* feel. This is all about what *you* want again, just like always." She took a deep breath. "Ever read *1984*?"

Sean stared at her blankly.

"There's this character, this woman who works in the Fiction Department of the Ministry of Truth. She maintains these machines that churn out propaganda novels for the brain-dead masses." She jabbed her finger at Sean. "That's what *you* are. You and those computers, churning out junk—"

"*Computers* turning out junk? Didn't they have movies when you were little? I haven't noticed any change. If anything, I think stuff's gotten better!"

"Your damned technology's already shut writers out of non-fiction markets, and soon this CGN stuff will kill the fiction market too and then there won't be any decent stories—"

"Do you know how crazy you sound? Are you saying you'd rather I be out of work? Who the hell's paying the bills? I mean, it's not as if *you're* gainfully employed right now—"

"I'm out of work because of what *you're* doing!" Kathy exclaimed. "I tried to call to tell you I've sold a story. I've *sold a story*, Sean! But it took me two years to do it. Why is that? Why do you think I've only managed to sell just *one* piece of fiction in two years?"

"Well, maybe it's because *you're not a very good writer!"* The instant the words left his mouth, Sean wanted to bite his tongue. "Oh, Kathy... what I meant was..."

Without a word, Kathy stood.

He reached out. "Kathy, I'm sor—"

She pushed him away. "Don't touch me!"

Sean watched her go, across the tables and seats, through the door, and out into the lobby, where she threw her visitors badge at the security guard before exiting the front door. He watched her until he could not see her anymore.

if (plotelement(i))=UNRESOLVED then prepare (finalconflict)
use (charactercrisis(random(1-10)))...

Sean's eyes glazed over the code. It had been almost a month, but he still couldn't concentrate on work.

"Hey..."

He looked up. It was Peggy Yang.

"Look, if you want to talk..."

"Thanks." Sean's voice dropped to a near whisper. "I can't believe it's over. I mean, we always knew we were very different people, but I never thought..."

"I think you need some time. Why don't you take off for a while? You've got the flex hours."

Sean shook his head. "I think I'd rather be here. Keeping busy takes my mind off it a bit, you know?"

"Sure." Peggy nodded sympathetically. She gestured at his workstation. "By the way, what exactly is that DLM you've been working on?"

Sean stared at the screen for a moment.

"Deception," he said at last. "I've been working on deception."

Dear Dr. Yaffe,

Thank you for sending me the latest story produced by Hemingway.3. *It is clear that your team has made significant progress since the V2.6 release.*

Given the limitations of the episodic experience database, it is not surprising that Hemingway.3 *again chose CGN as the topic of its story. What is interesting is how it was able to extrapolate a human conflict from the technological theme in a manner not seen in V2.6. This is likely the result of your implementation of the Bringsjord-Meteer heuristics, which also appears to have enhanced its capacity for characterization.*

It is also interesting how your redefinition of the narrative termination conditions have resulted in the tendency of Hemingway.3 *to produce ironic endings rather than the action-oriented conclusions of its predecessors. On a more serious note,* Hemingway.3 *still generates plots that have a certain algorithmic "connect the dots" feeling to them. Perhaps this could be remedied by decreasing the step size of the numerical narrative integration.*

Nevertheless, the story produced by Hemingway.3 *is a remarkable accomplishment. For the first time, a computer has produced a piece of fiction that appears comparable to one by a novice human writer. This is a significant breakthrough, and I look forward to the release of V4.0 with great anticipation.*

Prof. Ian C. McCoy
Artificial Creativity Laboratory
Department of Computer Science
University of British Columbia

Gallery of Biographies

Cris DiMarco has been the Senior Editor at Windstorm Creative since 1997. Inspired by Jennifer DiMarco, who aspired to create an author-centric publishing house as an alternative to the corporate publishing industry, Cris left her college teaching job and moved cross-country to work full-time for Windstorm.

Cris' professional credits began with a sale to an anthology much like this one in 1981. Since that time, she's published short fiction, essays and novels in accordance to Windstorm's policy that all staff be actively published authors. Because Windstorm does not backlist, all of Cris' works are still in print and include: *Virtual Rock; Queen's Champion: The Legend of Lancelot Retold; 1001 Nights Exotica; 1002 Nights Exotica,* and *Sparks Might Fly*. Her novels *Kresh: The Golton Box* and *Time's Arrow* will be published in 2006 as well as her short story collection, *Dark Moon*, and the novella, *Visibility*.

Cris lives with her partner of more than ten years and their children on Washington's breath-taking Olympic Peninsula.

Liz Danforth has created artwork for numerous collectable card games including *Magic: The Gathering, Warhammer Fantasy, Middle Earth, Vampire: The Eternal Struggle, Legend of Five Rings, Wheel of Time, Battletech, Everway* and many more. In addition to her paintings, she also makes tiles, ceramic ware and mosaics. To see more of Liz's work, visit her website at www.oakheart.com.

Jake Bartolone lives in Chicago and has published short works of science fiction in *Neverary* and *Aoife's Kiss* magazine. He has a beautiful wife, a PhD in Cognitive Psychology and likes to eat bacon.

Eric Choi was the first recipient of the Isaac Asimov Award for Undergraduate Excellence in Science Fiction and Fantasy Short Story Writing for his novelette "Dedication," which was subsequently published in *Asimov's Science Fiction* magazine. His work has also appeared in the anthologies *Space, Inc.* and *Tesseracts 6, Science Fiction Age* magazine, David Hartwell's *Northern Suns* collection, the Canadian alternate history anthology *Arrowdreams* and Julie Czerneda's *Tales from the Wonder Zone* series. He holds a bachelors degree in engineering science and a masters degree in aerospace engineering, both from the University of Toronto.

Suzanne Church lives in Ontario, the cold one in Canada, with her husband and two children. She is an outlier and a media junkie who, when cornered, becomes fiercely Canadian. Her short fiction is gaining popularity, and she's currently applying her keen logic and humor to short stories and novels alike. She is a 2005 graduate of the Clarion South Science Fiction Writers' Workshop. Her fiction has appeared in *Oceans of the Mind, Neo-Opsis, Shadowed Realms* and *Challenging Destiny* (forthcoming). She is a contributing reviewer for *Tangent.* Check out her word-a-day blog at: http://canadiansuzanne.blogspot.com/

James L. Condor (Maka Tai Meh) has lived fifty years in Alaska and the Pacific Northwest as well as in Canada, Japan and the Phillipines. He has taught the culture of his Native American heritage in the United States, been an instructor for the Federal Government's Indian Education Program and has traveled extensively in Alaska and Canada among the First Nations peoples collecting legends, songs, dances and stories. Condor published a collection of American stories of suspense and fantasy based upon these legends called *Condor Tales* in 2001.

He has had a varied career as a college professor, art director, gallery owner and a TV, film and stage actor and director. He has been the recipient of two arts grants to research Alaska Native music and stories and three grants from the state of California to develop Native American Theatre.

Condor, who is 77, lives with his wife, Diana Seno, in Sun City, Arizona. He devotes his time to writing, painting and his granddaughter, Madeline.

His forthcoming work includes: *Children of the Turtle,*

Native American songs and poetry; *Raven's Children,* poetry and songs of the Arctic Rim, and *An Alaskan Trilogy of Terror,* stories of horror and suspense.

Jetse de Vries is a technical specialist for a propulsion company and used to travel the world for this. Of late, due to the increased time both his story writing and co-editing *Interzone* (with Andy Cox, Peter Tennant and David Mathew) is taking up, he's trying to settle into a desk job.

Further examples of his writing can be found in the anthologies *In the Outposts of Beyond; Amityville House of Pancakes, Vol. 1* and in *The Journal of Pulse-Pounding Narratives, Vol. 2; Here & Now Issue 5&6 (double issue),* and *Nemonymous 4.* Forthcoming stories will be published in *TEL: Stories; Midnight Street,* and *DeathGrip: Exit Laughing.*

Comments are welcomed at jetse@home.nl. When he really is at home, Jetse lives in the historical city that was the birthplace of Hieronymous Bosch.

A New Orleans bench was the last place **Krista Dietrich** encountered a cockroach. Though Krista is a native of Michigan, where she attended the Clarion East Writers Workshop, now she serves on the Clarion West committee in Seattle. She has published short stories, essays and poetry, most recently in *Full Unit Hookup.* Krista lives, writes and occasionally spots an eagle from her window in Bothell, Washington. They say every writer pens a devil story; this is hers.

A. Leigh Jones has been making up stories since she was just a little girl, daydreams and make-believe and all sorts of daring adventures she wishes now she'd had the foresight to write down. Her first novel, *Forever Crossed,* is available from ImaJinn Books, and her short fiction can be found online in the archives of both *flashquake* and *Ideomancer.*

Dr. Philip Edward Kaldon is an Assistant Professor of Physics at Western Michigan University in Kalamazoo by day, while aspiring to write The Great Science Fiction Romantic Epic in the wee hours of the night. Submitting shorter works to the contest and magazine rejection mills for three years now, his writing is showing promise. Dr. Phil spent six amazing weeks of the summer of 2004 sweltering in an East Lansing sorority house attending the 37th Clarion Science Fiction and Fantasy Writers' Workshop.

His first published story, "The Gravediggers," about the crews who have to clean up the relativistic debris after near-light speed battles, appeared in the *CrossTIME Anthology Volume III*; two other stories, the alternative Canadian history suffragette story, "Sea Change" and the Victorian pre-alien invasion story, "The Dinner Party" will be published in 2006 as Laudable Mentions from the Third and Fourth Annual Tundra Prize competitions.

Along his way experiencing lake effect snow around four of the five Great Lakes, he found Debbie, his wife, working at the Northwestern University Library. Currently both are held hostage by a set of three cats from an alternative universe where felines rule. "The Pulse of the Sea" is Dr. Phil's first sale.

John Kratman is a husband and the father of triplet girls. When he's not busy spending time with his family, he's a full-time techno-bureaucrat in Boston. Born and raised in Massachusetts, he currently resides in the biggest little state in the union—Rhode Island. It's just like Massachusetts, only smaller. And cleaner. And, oh yes, the people are nicer, too. Yep, just like Massachusetts.

Susan Urbanek Linville has a PhD in biology and works at the Center for the Integrative Study of Animal Behavior at Indiana University. She is married to fellow writer Stephen V. Ramey and has a daughter in college. She has sold stories to Marion Zimmer Bradley's *Sword and Sorceress* anthologies, *On Spec, Triangulation, Parageography* (e-zine), and *Writers of the Future* anthology.

Derwin Mak lives in Toronto, Ontario, Canada, and writes quirky science fiction stories. Under several pseudonyms, he wrote short stories for the Oregon newspaper *The T&A Times* and was also its only foreign correspondent. His other stories are about ballerinas, Hooters Girls, cheerleaders, tiny aliens, unlucky Titanic survivors, and vile U-boat captains. He was also anime correspondent for *Parsec* magazine in Sudbury, Ontario, and for *RicePaper* magazine in Vancouver. He has university degrees in accounting, defense management and military history. His short story "The Siren Stone" (in *Space Inc.*, edited by Julie Czerneda, DAW Books, 2003) was a finalist for a 2004 Aurora Award, Canada's national science fiction award.

Donna McMahon was born and raised in Vancouver, British Columbia and currently divides her time between a job with a biotech company in the city and at home in the fishing village of Gibson's Landing. Her first novel, *Dance of Knives* (Tor, 2001), was set in twenty-second century Cascadia as are two subsequent novels (still under construction) *Second Childhood* and *Simulant*.

Donna has published short fiction in *Tomorrow SF* and *On Spec* and won an Aurora Canadian SF Award for her SF/F book reviews which appear at sfsite.com, onspec.ca and even, occasionally, in the *Vancouver Sun*.

Donna is fascinated by the history, culture and ecosystem of the Pacific Northwest. In Vancouver, she loves to watch the diverse, cosmopolitan mix of people; in Gibson's Landing, she watches birds, seals, indigenous plants and pick-up trucks. She majored in History at Simon Fraser University and has worked as a freelance journalist, in public relations and in a wide variety of office jobs.

Joe Murphy has sold fiction to *Age of Wonders, Altair, Audio Realms, A Horror a Day: 365 Scary Stories, Bones of the World, Book of All Flesh, Book of Final Flesh, Chinzine, Clean Sheets, Crafty Cat Crimes, Cthulhu's Heirs, Dark Terrors 6, Demon Sex, Dreaming of Angels,* Gothic.net, Ideomancer.com, *Legends of the Pendragon, Low Port, Marion Zimmer Bradley's Fantasy Magazine, Outside, Oceans of the Mind, On Spec, Path of the Bold, Realms of Fantasy, Silver Web, Space and Time, Strange Horizons, Talebones, TransVersions, Vestal Review* and many others. Twelve of his previously published stories are now available on the internet at Alexandria Digital Literature (www.alexlit.com). Joe is a member of SFWA, HWA and a graduate of Clarion.

Ruth Nestvold has published in *Asimov's, Strange Horizons* and *Realms of Fantasy,* among others, and was a recent finalist for both the Tiptree and Sturgeon awards. She holds a PhD in literature with specializations in genre issues, gender issues and hyperfiction. After getting out of academia, she switched to translation and software localization to feed the writing bug. She maintains a web site at www.ruthnestvold.com.

Mercurio D. Rivera, a New York City attorney, works at a small, downtown law firm drafting voluminous legal memoranda and appellate briefs. To maintain some semblance of sanity, he spends his free time writing science fiction stories and attending speculative fiction readings at The KGB Bar on the Lower East Side of Manhattan. He is a member of *AlteredFluid,* a sci-fi, fantasy and horror writing group that meets three Tuesdays a month. He has published stories in *Sybil's Garage,* a small press publication, and *44 Clowns of the Apocalypse* (forthcoming) an e-anthology edited by Mike Brotherton and Jay Lake.

Bruce Holland Rogers is the author of the story collections *Flaming Arrows, Wind Over Heaven Thirteen Ways to Water* and the forthcoming title, *The Keyhole Opera,* as well as a book about the psychology of the writing life called *Word Work: Surviving and Thriving as a Writer.* His stories have won a Pushcart Prize, the World Fantasy Award, two Nebula Awards, and an Oregon Arts Commission fellowship. Recent stories have appeared in *The Sun, Chattahoochee Review, North American Review, Indiana Review, Realms of Fantasy, Vestal Review, Polyphony 4,* and *Flashquake.*

His short-short stories are distributed by email subscription through www.shortshortshort.com to over 500 subscribers in 60 countries. A full-time writer for fifteen years, he has just joined the core faculty of the Whidbey Writers Low-Residency MFA Program. Bruce also teaches two ten-day writing seminars in Europe. One is in Crete, and the other rotates among locations, starting this coming March with Sorrento, Italy.

Rhea Rose is a Vancouver, British Columbia, writer and full time high school teacher. In 1984, she participated in the Clarion West writers' workshop and has been writing ever since. Most of her work has been published north of the 49th parallel. She thinks she's the only writer to have appeared in the *Tesseracts* anthologies four times. Her work has appeared in David Hartwell's *Christmas Forever* anthology, *Talebones #18, Talebones #22* and *Tesseracts 9*. Many of her pieces have been nominated for awards, including the Rhysling award for poetry and a preliminary nomination for a Nebula award.

As a youth in the Yakima Valley of Washington state, **Ken Staley** spent many summer days in trees, earning extra spending money picking cherries, peaches and apples. Memories of those days triggered "Jacob's Tree."

Bruce Taylor writes Magic Realism. His book, *The Final Trick of the Funnyman and Other Stories,* was first published in 1997 and is now available in a print-on-demand edition from Fairwoodpress.com. He is the founder and director of The Magic Realistic Writers International Network (www.pantarbe.com) and is a consultant to MARGIN: Exploring Modern Magical Realism (www.magical-realism.com), which provided background information on Magic Realism for Oprah Winfry's Book Club selection *100 Years of Solitude* by Gabriel Garcia Marquez. Bruce is a former president of the Seattle Writers Association, has written over a thousand short stories and teaches novel and short story writing at North Seattle Community College. He is also a hypnotherapist and was co-director of The Wellness Program at Harborview Medical Center in Seattle. His novel, *Edward: Dancing on the Edge of Infinity* is forthcoming from Scorpiusdigital.com and *Kafka's Uncle and Other Strange Tales* (Afterbirth Books) was recently released. He is currently co-authoring a novella about global warming with Brian Herbert (Frank Herbert's son) called *Stormworld.*

Edd Vick is a 2002 graduate of the Clarion SF Writer's Workshop. His work has been published in *Asimov's* and *Electric Velocipede* and the anthologies *Distant Planes* and

Fundamentally Challenged. In 1980, he founded MU Press and has been publishing comic books, fanzines and graphic novels ever since. He is the son of a pirate.

Jan Wildt lives in a California monastery. "Wonderfreaks," received a Year's Best Science Fiction Honorable Mention. A new novella, "Bink is Luv," appears this fall in *New Genre 4.*

Uncle River published *Prometheus: The Autobiography* with Crossquarter Publishing Group. His short fiction has appeared in *Analog, Asimov's, Amazing Stories, Talebones, Tales of The Unanticipated,* and the *Hartwell/Cramer Year's Best Fantasy 2* anthology. He lives in the Southwest.

Marly Youmans is a native of South Carolina who currently lives a stone's throw from the mouth of the Susquehanna and The Baseball Hall of Fame in Cooperstown, New York. She and her husband are the parents of three fantasy-addicted children.

Her books are *Ingledove* (Farrar, Straus & Giroux BYR, 2005), *The Curse of the Raven Mocker* (Farrar, Straus & Giroux BYR, 2005); *Claire* (poetry from Louisiana State University Press, 2003); *The Wolf Pit* (a novel set during the Civil War, Farrar, Straus & Giroux, 2001); *Catherwood* (a novel of the late seventeenth century from Farrar, Straus & Giroux, 1995) and *Little Jordan* (a novella from David R. Godine, Publisher, 1995). Her awards include the 2001 Shaara Award for Civil War fiction for *The Wolf Pit,* two Hoepfner Awards for best story of the year from *Southern Humanities Review* and the New Writer's Award of *Capital Magazine* (Albany, New York).

Her first fantasy novel, *The Curse of the Raven Mocker,* was chosen as best children's book of 2003 by the *Baton Rouge Advocate* and was picked up as one of the Top Ten Books of 2003 by *Books & Culture.* Diana Wynne Jones has described *Ingledove* as "a marvelous book" and "breathtakingly wonderful."

About Windstorm Creative
the parent company of Fandom Press
and our Readers' Club

Windstorm Creative was founded in 1989 to create a publishing house with author-centric ethics and cutting-edge, risk-taking innovation. Windstorm is now a company of more than ten divisions with international distribution channels that allow us to sell our books, games, music and films both inside the traditional systems and outside these paradigms, capitalizing on more direct delivery and non-traditional markets. As a result, our books can be found in grocery superstores as well as your favorite neighborhood bookstore, and dozens of other outlets on and off the Internet.

Windstorm is an independent press with the synergy and branding of a corporate publisher and an author royalty that's easily twice their best offer. We have continued to minimize returns without decreasing sales by publishing books that are timeless, as opposed to timely, and never back-listing our books.

Windstorm is constantly changing, improving, and growing. We are driven by the needs of our authors – hailing from ten different countries – and the vision of our critically-acclaimed staff. All of our books are created with the strictest of environmental protections in mind. Our approach to no-waste, no-hazard, in-house production, and stringent out-source scrutiny, assures that our goals are met whether books are printed at our own facility or an outside press.

Because of these precautions, our books cost more. And though we know that our readers support our efforts, we also understand that a few dollars can add up. This is why we began our Readers' Club. Visit our webstore and take 20% off every title, every day. No strings. No fine print.

While you're at our site, feel free to preview or request the first chapter of any of our titles, completely free of charge.

Thank you for supporting an independent press.

www.windstormcreative.com
and click on Shop.
See next page for title recommendations.

Bones Become Flowers
(Jess Mowry)
Wild boys and voodu take an American woman on a journey through Haiti she'll never forget.

The Road to Kotaishi: Part One
(Kevin Radthorne)
A mystical journey of truth, deceit and destiny begins.

GemQuest: The Twins, Book One
(Gary Wassner)
Twins destined to quest for the Gem seek cause of Great Trees' deaths.

Mekan'stan: A Okal Rel Universe Novella
(Lynda Williams)
Amel the Pureblood has more to worry about than his penchant for honest polygamy. Gun-runners on a space station are only the beginning.

The Okal Rel Universe Anthology I
(Lynda Williams and Virginia O'Dine, editors)
Beautiful and revealing, five *votary* authors of the Okal Rel Universe add their stories to this complex series.

Virtual Rock
(Cris DiMarco)
Rock 'n' roll, virtual reality and redemption clash in this near-future novel of revolution and change.

1001 Nights Exotica
(Cris DiMarco)
A collection of erotic, thought-provoking stories and images.

1002 Nights Exotica
(Cris DiMarco)
Sequel to the best-selling first volume, *1002* is both thought-provoking and lyrical.

Queen's Champion
(Cris DiMarco)
Rich with detail and little-known legends, the story of Lancelot retold.